Before he left, Liam turned around and gave her a hard look that sent a little shiver down her spine. She chose to blame it on the cool night air, instead of the chill in his eyes.

"Remember what I said about staying away from Peter Callahan and his assistant. I don't care what you suspect them of—I am the law here and you are a professor who is very far away from home. Make no mistake; I like you, but that won't keep me from tossing your ass into jail if I have to." He turned his back on her and left, slamming the door behind him to emphasize his point.

Baba scowled at the place where he'd been and fingered the perfectly applied bandage on her elbow. It had been a long time since anyone had bothered to take care of her— she couldn't tell if she liked it or not.

Berkley Sensation titles by Deborah Blake

WICKEDLY DANGEROUS
WICKEDLY WONDERFUL

Specials

WICKEDLY MAGICAL

Wickedly Dangerous

DEBORAH BLAKE

BERKLEY SENSATION, NEW YORK

BERKLEY SENSATION

An imprint of Penguin Random House LLC
375 Hudson Street, New York, New York 10014

WICKEDLY DANGEROUS

A Berkley Sensation Book / published by arrangement with the author

ISBN: 978-0-425-27292-3

PUBLISHING history
Berkley Sensation mass-market edition / September 2014

PRINTED IN THE UNITED STATES OF AMERICA

10 9 8 7 6 5 4 3 2

Cover art by Tony Mauro.
Cover design by Sarah Oberrender.
Interior text design by Kelly Lipovich.

Penguin
Random
House

ACKNOWLEDGMENTS

This is my first published novel, and it was a long time coming, so I have a lot of people to thank. I promise the acknowledgments in the second book will be much shorter . . . (And if I leave out someone important, it is from exhaustion, not intent.)

Big, huge thanks go to my agent, the amazing Elaine Spencer of the Knight Agency. I couldn't ask for a better advocate for my books, and I am grateful beyond words to be working with someone so savvy and enthusiastic. Thank you for your faith in me . . . and for all those revision notes that made my writing better. (Really, I take back the cursing. Mostly.) And to Lucienne Diver, who kindly helped to hook us up, and who has done more than her fair share of cheerleading along the way. Knight Agency peeps rock.

I feel equally fortunate to have an editor who is such a joy to work with. Thanks to Leis Pederson for taking the chance on this debut author, and for all those revision notes that made my writing better. (Really, hardly any cursing at all.)

Humongous gratitude goes out to all my First Readers, who suffered through the first draft of this book, and in most cases, many others. Lisa DiDio is the best critique partner anyone could ever hope for, and not just because she threatens to kick me with her Uggs if I don't get off my butt and WBW. You're next, babe. Judith Levine has read every book I ever wrote, and is single-handedly responsible for the fact that Leis didn't have to take out an extra 2,625 commas. She also happens to be my mother and a pretty fabulous writer too. Alex Bledsoe is an inspiration in everything he does, and I'm honored to have him on my team and in my life. Mindy Klasky is a writer and editor extraordinaire, and her input has always made my books better.

I spent the years prior to getting published in fiction in two ways: first in writing seven nonfiction books for Llewellyn Worldwide, where my amazing editor Elysia Gallo put up with all my newbie-author shenanigans and generally taught me everything I needed to know about how to be a professional, and second in establishing lasting relationships and—when I was lucky—true friendships with many talented authors, editors, and agents.

These folks cheered every success and commiserated at every setback and taught me more than I can say. Many, many thanks to the remarkable Candace Havens, the best mentor a beginning writer could want, and in no particular order: Nancy Holzner, Heather Long, Tanya Huff, C. E. Murphy, Lisa Shearin, Jim C. Hines, Jeri Smith-Ready, Patience Bloom, Marlene Stringer, Maria V. Snyder, Jennifer Crusie, Lani Diane Rich, C. S. MacCath, Yasmine Galenorn, Annette Blair, Linda Wisdom, Dakota Cassidy, Donna Andrews, Julie Butcher, Tamora Pierce, Louisa Edwards, Katie Fforde, Trisha Ashley, and Carol Berg.

Thank you to my family, for encouraging me to be as weird as I wanted (which is pretty weird) and for cheering on all my endeavors. Big love especially to my kid, Jennifer Holling-Blake, for being such an inspiration with her own creative undertakings, and for bragging about me to everyone she meets. (Silly girl. The check is in the mail.) And to my friends, who are among the best people in the world. Ellen Dwyer, who keeps the cats fed when I travel; Blue Moon Circle, who keep my spirit fed; and especially Robin Wright, who was there at the very beginning of it all, writing and reading and making notes on printed-out reams of manuscript in the bathroom, since that was the only place she got five minutes of peace from her kids.

A big huzzah to the Betties (you know who you are), many of whom are also talented writers, and especially to Skye and Sierra for their never-ending support and *Castle*-watching. You two rock. And to my gang at the Creativity Cauldron, who took my online writing classes and insisted on sticking around afterward.

And last, but not least, to @HarriedWizard—because witches and wizards have to stick together.

You have probably heard of Baba Yaga—the wicked witch of Russian tales who lived in a log hut that walked about on chicken legs, rode through the forests in a giant mortar steered with a pestle, and ate small children if they didn't behave. According to legend, Baba Yaga usually appeared as an ugly old crone, although she also wore other faces, and sometimes gave aid to a worthy seeker, if such a one could pass her tests.

You probably think you know who Baba Yaga is. But you'd be wrong. Because I am Baba Yaga, and this is my story.

NE

THE CRACKLE OF the two-way radio barely impinged on Liam McClellan's consciousness as he scanned the bushes on either side of his squad car for any sign of a missing seven-year-old girl. He'd been down this same narrow country road yesterday at dusk, but like the other searchers, he'd had to give up when darkness fell. Like the rest—volunteers from the nearby community and every cop who could be spared, whether on duty or off—he'd come back at dawn to pick up where he left off. Even though there was little hope of success, after six long days.

His stomach clenched with a combination of too much coffee, too little sleep, and the acid taste of failure. Liam McClellan took his job as sheriff very seriously. Clearwater might be a tiny county in the middle of nowhere, its population scattered between a few small towns and a rural countryside made up mostly of struggling farmers, overgrown wilderness, and white-tailed deer, but it was *his* tiny county, and the people in it were his to protect. Lately, it didn't seem like he'd been doing a very good job.

Mary Elizabeth Shields had disappeared out of her own

backyard. Her mother had turned her back for a moment, drawn by the flutter of a bright-hued bird. When she turned around, the girl had vanished. Such a thing would be alarming enough on its own, but Mary Elizabeth was the third child to go missing in the last four months. To a lawman, that meant only one thing: a human predator was stalking the children of Clearwater County.

There had been no trace of any of the missing children. No tire marks, no unexplained fingerprints, no lurking strangers seen at any of the places from which the children had disappeared. No clues at all for a tired and frustrated sheriff to follow. And this time it was personal; Mary Elizabeth's mother was one of his deputies. A single mother who adored her only child, Belinda Shields was beside herself with grief and terror, making Liam even more discouraged over his inability to make any headway in the case.

A rabbit bounded out of a tangle of sumac, and Liam slowed to avoid hitting it, his tires sending up a spray of dusty gravel. In his rearview mirror, he thought he caught a glimpse of an old woman walking by the side of the road with a basket of herbs over one gnarled, skinny arm. But when he looked again, no one was there.

The gauzy fog of an early summer morning gave the deserted back road a surreal quality, which only heightened as he came around the bend to his destination to find a totally unexpected sight.

When he was out here last night, the wide curve of road that ended in a patch of meadow overlooking the Clearwater River had been empty. This morning, there was a shiny silver Airstream trailer parked in the middle of the crabgrass and wildflowers of the meadow, along with the large silver Chevy truck that had no doubt hauled it there. Liam blinked in surprise as he eased his squad car to a halt a few yards away. He didn't know anyone in the area who had such a fancy, expensive rig, and he couldn't imagine a stranger being able to navigate his way into the back-of-beyond corner on a bumpy tertiary road in the dark.

But clearly, someone had.

Swinging his long legs out of the driver's-side door, Liam thumbed the radio on and checked in with Nina in dispatch, hoping fervently she would tell him the girl had turned up, safe and sound.

No such luck.

"Do you know of anyone around here who owns an Airstream?" he asked her. "Any of the gang down at Bertie's mention seeing one come through town?" Bertie's was the local bakery/diner/gossip central. Nina considered it part of her job to swing by there on the way to work every morning and pick up muffins and chitchat to share with the rest of the sheriff's department.

"A what?" Nina asked. He could hear her typing on her keyboard in the background. The woman was seventy years old and could still multitask with the best of them. The county board kept pressuring him to make her retire, but that was never going to happen. At least, not as long as he still had a job.

"It's a big fancy silver RV trailer," he explained. "I found one sitting right smack-dab in the middle of Miller's Meadow when I got here just now."

"Really?" She sounded dubious. "In Miller's Meadow? How the heck did it get there?"

"Your guess is as good as mine," Liam said, scratching his head. He made a mental note to get his hair cut; it kept flopping into his eyes and annoying him. It seemed like a trim was never enough of a priority to make it to the top of his overburdened to-do list. "Drove here, I guess, although I wouldn't want to haul a big vehicle down this road if I didn't have to."

He told her to hang on for a minute, then walked around and checked the license plate on the truck. Returning to the car, he read off the numbers. "California plates, so someone is a long way from home. Hard for me to imagine anyone driving all that distance to upstate New York in order to park out here at the ass end of nowhere, but I suppose we've had tourists do stranger things."

"Huh," was Nina's only response. Clearwater County

didn't get much in the way of tourism. A few folks staying at the bed and breakfast in West Dunville, which had both a tiny winery and an antiques shop, as well as an old mill that housed a surprisingly good restaurant. Campers during the summer who used the small state park outside of Dunville proper. Other than that, the only strange faces you saw were those of people driving through on their way to someplace more interesting.

More tapping as Nina typed in the information he'd given her. "Huh," she said again. "There's nothing there, Sheriff."

"No wants and warrants, you mean?" He hadn't really expected any; not with an Airstream. But it would have been nice if the gods of law enforcement suddenly decided to smile on him and just hand over a suspect. Preferably one who still had all the children alive and well and eating cookies inside a conveniently located trailer. He sighed. There was no way he was going to be that lucky.

"No anything," Nina said slowly. "There's nothing in the system for that plate number at all. And I can't find any record of a permit being issued for someone to use the spot. That's county property, so there should be one if our visitor went through proper channels and didn't simply park there because he got tired."

Liam felt his pulse pick up. "Probably a computer error. Why don't you go ahead and check it again. I'll get the inspection number off the windshield for you too; that should turn up something." He grabbed his high-brimmed hat from the passenger seat, setting his face into "official business" lines. "I think it's time to wake up the owner and get some answers."

The radio crackled back at him, static cutting off Nina's reply. Any day now, the county was going to get him updated equipment that worked better. As soon as the economy picked up. Clearwater County had never been prosperous at the best of times, but it had been hit harder than most by the recent fiscal downturn, since most people had already barely been getting by before the economy slid into free fall.

Plopping his hat on over his dark-blond hair, Liam strode

up to the door of the Airstream—or at least, where he could have sworn the door was a couple of minutes ago. Now there was just a blank wall. He pushed the hair out of his eyes again and walked around to the other side. Shiny silver metal, but no door. So he walked back around to where he started, and there was the entrance, right where it belonged.

"I need to get more sleep," he muttered to himself. He would almost have said the Airstream was laughing at him, but that was impossible. "More sleep and more coffee."

He knocked. Waited a minute, and knocked again, louder. Checked his watch. It was six a.m.; hard to believe that whoever the trailer belonged to was already out and about, but it was always possible. An avid fisherman, maybe, eager to get the first trout of the day. Cautiously, Liam put one hand on the door handle and almost jumped out of his boots when it emitted a loud, ferocious blast of noise.

He snatched his hand away, then laughed at himself as he saw a large, blunt snout pressed against the nearest window. For a second there, he'd almost thought the trailer itself was barking. Man, did he need more coffee.

At the sound of an engine, Liam turned and walked back toward his car. A motorcycle came into view, its rider masked by head-to-toe black leather, a black helmet, and mirrored sunglasses that matched the ones Liam himself wore. The bike itself was a beautiful royal blue classic BMW that made Liam want to drool. And get a better-paying job. The melodic throb of its motor cut through the morning silence until it purred to a stop about a foot away from him. The rider swung a leg over the top of the cycle and dismounted gracefully.

"Nice bike," Liam said in a conversational tone. "Is that a sixty-eight?"

"Sixty-nine," the rider replied. Gloved hands reached up and removed the helmet, and a cloud of long black hair came pouring out, tumbling waves of ebony silk. The faint aroma of orange blossoms drifted across the meadow, although none grew there.

A tenor voice, sounding slightly amused, said, "Is there a problem, Officer?"

Liam started, aware that he'd been staring rudely. He told himself it was just the surprise of her gender, not the startling Amazonian beauty of the woman herself, all angles and curves and leather.

"Sheriff," he corrected out of habit. "Sheriff Liam McClellan." He held out one hand, then dropped it back to his side when the woman ignored it. "And you are?"

"Not looking for trouble," she said, a slight accent of unidentifiable origin coloring her words. Her eyes were still hidden behind the dark glasses, so he couldn't quite make out if she was joking or not. "My name is Barbara Yager. People call me Baba." One corner of her mouth edged up so briefly, he almost missed it.

"Welcome to Clearwater County," Liam said. "Would you like to tell me what you're doing parked out here?" He waved one hand at the Airstream. "I assume this belongs to you?"

She nodded, expressionless. "It does. Or I belong to it. Hard to tell which, sometimes."

Liam smiled gamely, wondering if his caffeine deficit was making her sound odder than she really was. "Sure. I feel that way about my mortgage sometimes. So, you were going to tell me what you're doing here."

"Was I? Somehow I doubt it." Again, that tiny smile, barely more than a twitch of the lips. "I'm a botanist with a specialty in herbalism; I'm on sabbatical from UC Davis. You have some unusual botanical varieties growing in this area, so I'm here to collect samples for my research."

Liam's cop instincts told him that her answer sounded too pat, almost rehearsed. Something about her story was a lie, he was sure of it. But why bother to lie about something he could so easily check?

"Do you have some kind of ID?" he asked. "Your vehicle didn't turn up in the database, and my dispatcher couldn't find any record of a permit for you to be here. This is county property, you know." He put on his best "stern cop" expression. The woman with the cloud of hair didn't seem at all fazed.

"Perhaps you should check again," she said, handing over a California driver's license with a ridiculously good picture, "I'm sure you'll find that everything is in order."

The radio in his car suddenly squawked back to life again, and Nina's gravelly voice said, "Sheriff? You there?"

"Excuse me," Liam said, and walked over to pick up the handset, one wary eye still on the stranger. "I'm here, Nina. What do you have for me?"

"That license plate you gave me? It just came back. Belongs to a Barbara Yager, out of Davis, California. And the county office found an application and approval for her to camp in the meadow. Apparently the clerk had misfiled it, which is why they didn't have it when we asked the first time." Her indignant snort echoed across the static. "Misfiled. Nice way to say those gals down there don't know the alphabet. So, anything else you need, Sheriff?"

He thumbed the mike. "Nope, that will do it for now," he said. "Thanks, Nina." Liam put the radio back in its cradle and walked back over to where his not-so-mystery woman waited patiently by her motorcycle, its engine pinging as it cooled.

"Looks like you were right," he said, handing her license back. "Everything seems to be in order."

"That's the way I like it," she said.

"Me too," Liam agreed, "Of course, it kind of comes with the job description. One half of 'law and order,' as it were." He tipped the brim of his hat at her. "Sorry for disturbing you, ma'am."

She blinked a little at the polite title and turned to go.

"I'm going to leave my squad car here for a bit," Liam said. "I'm continuing a search down the riverside. Unless you were planning on pulling the Airstream out in the next couple of hours, the car shouldn't be in your way."

Stillness seemed to settle onto her leather-clad shoulders,

and she paused for a second before swiveling around on the heel of one clunky motorcycle boot. "I wasn't expecting to leave anytime soon." Another pause, and she added in a casual tone, that mysterious hint of an accent making her words musical, "What are you searching for, if you don't mind my asking?"

The wind lifted her hair off her neck, revealing a glimpse of color peeking out from underneath the edge of her black tee shirt.

Liam wondered what kind of a tattoo a BMW-riding herb researcher might have. A tiny rose, maybe? Although in Barbara Yager's case, the rose would probably have thorns. Well, not likely he'd ever find out.

"I'm looking for a little girl," he answered her, dragging his mind back to the task at hand. "A seven-year-old named Mary Elizabeth who disappeared six days ago. I don't suppose you've seen her?"

Barbara shook her head, a small groove appearing between the dark arches of her brows. "Six days. That's not good, is it?"

She pulled off her sunglasses to reveal startling clear amber eyes surrounded by long, dusky lashes. For a moment, staring into them, Liam felt like he was falling. Up into the sky, or down into a bottomless pool of water, he couldn't tell which. Then she blinked, and was just another woman with beautiful eyes in an oval face with sharp cheekbones and a slightly hawkish nose.

Liam shook himself and thought longingly of coffee again. He didn't know what the hell was wrong with him this morning. Stress, he figured. And too little sleep.

"No, it's not," he said. "Neither is the fact that she is the third child to go missing in recent months." The muscles in his jaw clenched, hating to say it out loud. It was bad enough to have the numbers racing around in his head all day, and haunting him all night. Three kids, four months, six days, seven years old. It was like a demented counting book used to scare disobedient children. Or incompetent sheriffs.

Barbara gave him an odd look; some indecipherable mix

of anger, concern, and resignation. He had no idea what it meant, other than that she clearly didn't like the idea of little girls disappearing any more than he did.

"Well," she said shortly. "We can't have that, can we?"

No, he thought, *we really can't.*

WO

BABA SCOWLED AT the Airstream until the door decided to stop playing games and settle into place, then slammed it shut behind her, dropping her full saddlebags onto the floor with a thud. Green matter spilled out in a puddle of curly-edged ferns and frothy Queen Anne's lace, its pungent odor warring with the sharp scent of her anger.

"Problems with the law?" Chudo-Yudo asked, jerking his muzzle in the direction of the sheriff's retreating form. "I could eat him if you like."

Baba rolled her eyes. Her traveling companion may currently look like a large white pit bull with a black nose and soft brown eyes, but his instincts were still all dragon. His dog form was a lot easier to fit into the trailer, though, since in his true form his wingspan was over ten feet.

"Not at the moment," she said, kicking her boots off and strolling over to the half-sized refrigerator to mull her limited breakfast possibilities. "The sheriff seems harmless enough. But I think I may have found out what called us here. He told me they've had three children go missing." She scowled at the scant inch of orange juice hiding behind the bottle labeled *Water of Life and Death.* "Remind me to get orange juice the next time I go into town, will you?"

She gave up on the fridge and grabbed a granola bar out of a cupboard overhead, munching on it as she fiddled with the coffee machine. Nothing in the Airstream ever worked exactly as expected, and she really wanted coffee, not hot chocolate, tea, or, gods forbid, liquid gold. That one had been hell to clean up.

"Orange juice. Right." Chudo-Yudo pulled a huge bone out from under the couch, ignoring the fact that the space was taken up by a large drawer. The laws of physics didn't work all that well in the Airstream either.

"So, do you think someone invoked you to find one of the children? Usually they're blaming you for disappearances, not asking you to solve them."

Baba snorted. "That was in days gone by, old friend. No one even remembers the Baba Yaga anymore; certainly no one who realizes it is a job title, not the name of a single person. If we were in Russia, maybe, but who here would know to call on me for a favor?"

She sniffed the coffee, which only smelled a little like the blue roses that made up its essence, and settled down with boneless grace onto the couch. She scratched Chudo-Yudo's head absently, hearing her nails *scritch* on nonexistent scales. A puff of contented smoke escaped from his canine snout as he lay his massive head down on her bare feet.

"So how are you going to find out if you were called to this benighted backwater to search for missing children or for some other reason?" Chudo-Yudo asked, his words distorted by the bone hanging half in and half out of his mouth.

Baba snapped her fingers, and a local newspaper appeared out of the herb-scented air. "I expect someone will come tell me, alas." She sighed. She was a lot more comfortable with dragons than she was with human beings, for all that she had been born one. Many, many years ago. Before she met the preceding Baba, who had rescued her from a barren Russian orphanage and set her on the path that had led her to a flower-filled meadow, an attractive sheriff in desperate need of a haircut, and a mystery with her name written all over it.

LIAM SLAPPED AT another whining mosquito and took off his hat to wipe his forehead with an already sodden hand-kerchief. He'd searched for over three hours along the river's muddy banks, and the only things he'd found were empty beer bottles, a snapping turtle in a bad mood, and an old red ball that had clearly been there for years. He'd made a note of the ball anyway, just in case, but he finally had to admit that he wasn't getting anywhere. It was time for him to head back into the office; those piles of paperwork weren't going to fill themselves out. And Nina got snippy when he didn't check in every couple of hours. As if he were likely to run into something more dangerous that an irate turtle out here.

Still, he made all his officers follow a regular check-in schedule, and as Nina liked to remind him, part of Liam's job was to lead by example. Never mind that he had more than ten years' experience on most of them. And that he hated having to conform to anyone's rules, even his own.

As Liam came into the clearing where he'd parked, Bar-bara Yager opened her door and stepped out to raise a hand in greeting. Like the first time, her appearance seemed to cause his mind to stutter and spin, and his heart to beat out of sequence. Then she took a step forward, and the world fell back into place.

He coughed, trying to catch his breath. Too much time out in the hot July sun. Or low blood sugar, maybe. He'd skipped breakfast, as usual, in his eagerness to get to the search.

"Are you okay, Sheriff?" the dark-haired woman asked. She seemed more curious than concerned. "Would you like a glass of water?"

"That would be very nice, thank you," Liam said with gratitude. Water, that's what he needed. He'd forgotten to take any out with him. He followed her into the Airstream when she beckoned, and looked around with interest. It was compact and surprisingly luxurious; the furniture was covered with rich jewel-toned brocades, velvet, and what he thought was some kind of nubby raw silk. Not standard issue, even for a top-of-the-line model. It was a strange contrast with the black leather. The woman was a puzzle. Liam didn't much like puzzles. He preferred things to be simple and straightforward. Like that ever happened.

"I've never been inside one of these before," he said, accepting the crystal goblet she handed him and draining it in one long swallow. "It's pretty impressive."

"Thank you," she said, refilling the glass. "All the comforts of home without the pesky land taxes."

Liam pulled his sunglasses off and stared at her. "You live in it year-round? I thought you taught college in California. There was a Davis address on your driver's license." *Lie number two*, he thought.

Baba shrugged. "I teach on and off. More off than on, these days."

Movement caught Liam's eye, and he took an involuntary step backward as a huge white dog crawled out from underneath the dinette and spat an equally huge bone at his feet. Its black tongue lolled, as if it was laughing at him.

"Holy crap!" he said. "That's a big dog."

"Yes," said Baba. "But a small dragon." She shook one slender, grass-stained finger at the animal. "Behave, Chudo-Yudo. He's a guest."

The dog gave a conciliatory woof and sat back on its haunches, brown eyes watching Liam's every move.

"Chudo-Yudo? That's an unusual name." Liam liked dogs, almost all dogs, but he wasn't going to make the mistake of trying to pet this one. No wonder she called it a dragon; it looked as fierce as one.

"It's Russian," she said.

"Ah, that explains the accent!" Liam said, pleased to have solved at least one mystery. "I couldn't quite pin it down."

Baba narrowed her eyes and folded her arms over her chest, the motion causing another glimpse of color at the bottom of both tee shirt sleeves where they cut across her biceps. *Interesting*, Liam thought.

"I don't have an accent," Baba said, speaking slowly and clearly. The foreign lilt clung to her words like honey, regardless. "I got rid of it years ago."

Liam shook his head, pushing the resulting flow of hair out of his eyes with an impatient hand. "It's not very strong, but it is there. You shouldn't try to get rid of it, though. It's beautiful." He caught himself, feeling the tips of his ears flush hot with embarrassment. "I mean, it's nice. It doesn't sound like everyone else." He stuttered to a halt before he could shove his foot any further into his mouth.

The white dog snorted and coughed, rolling on the floor. *Great. At least I've amused her dog.* He was fine with belligerent drunks, completely capable of dealing with thieves, drug dealers, and even the occasional murderer. But apparently one woman who smelled like flowers was enough to turn him into a babbling idiot. It had to be the heat.

He put the goblet down in the sink and started wandering around the trailer; as much to end the awkward conversation as to take advantage of the fact that his newest—and only—suspect had conveniently invited him inside her home. Besides, it was seriously cool.

"Do these dinette benches fold out to be beds?" he asked. "My parents had an RV for a while, although not one nearly as nice as this, and it seemed like every other piece of furniture was actually a sleeping area in disguise." He looked inside a cupboard, impressed by the clever way everything was kept from moving around when the Airstream was on the road.

"That's what it said on the brochure," Baba said. She watched him poke around, her only response a raised eyebrow. "I rarely have guests."

Liam stopped in front of what looked like a closet and tugged on the handle. It didn't move. His lawman's instincts went into high gear. Locks meant secrets. And people rarely hid things for no reason. A frisson of disappointment made his hand feel like it was vibrating.

The cloud-haired woman was at his side before he even realized she'd moved, the pit bull at her feet. "That door has kind of a tricky latch; it's meant to keep it from opening when the vehicle is in motion." She put one lightly callused hand over his, making the vibration slide up his wrist and into his arm. A tiny click made the handle buzz against his palm, and then the door swung open to reveal a mundane wardrobe full of black leather pants and patchwork peasant skirts. A silky red minidress winked at him enticingly from one corner before Baba closed it up again.

"Seen enough, *Sheriff*?" she asked, a little acerbic. Apparently he hadn't been as subtle as he'd thought. "Or would you like the grand tour of the entire trailer, so you can make sure there are no small children tucked into the storage bins?"

Liam smiled, trying to take the sting out of his words. "Sure, if you're willing to give me one."

Baba heaved a sigh and rolled her eyes, but proceeded to show him every inch of the Airstream, from the bedroom closets at the far end of the trailer, to the tiny shelf in the corner of the shower, which he was interested to see was across the hall from the toilet. She showed him that too, although it was so small, he wasn't sure how anything could have been hidden in there. There were herbs everywhere; hanging from the ceiling, confined to jars, tucked into corners. Other than that, there was nothing unusual. Still, the back of his neck itched with the feeling of *something wrong*.

All he knew when they were done was that there were definitely no children tucked away, or any sign that there had ever been any. But then, he hadn't really expected there to be. If this odd lady was collecting other people's kids for some reason, she was clearly too smart to keep them in the place she lived.

"Satisfied?" she asked, leaning against the dinette table, one slightly dirty foot swinging idly. "Or did you want to check my pots and pans, in case I cooked and ate them?"

Ouch. "No, of course not," he said. "I apologize if I offended you. Besides, that kind of thing only happens in fairy tales and on *CSI*."

"CS what?" Baba said, as if she'd never heard of it.

"*CSI.*" He looked at her expression to see if she was kidding, then looked again. It was still blank and baffled. "You know—the TV show? There are a whole bunch of them. *CSI: New York*, *CSI: Miami.* For all I know, there's a *CSI: Alaska* by now."

"Oh, TV," Baba said dismissively. "I don't watch TV."

Liam glanced around the Airstream and realized what he'd missed on his first pass through. No television. Just a bare spot on the wall where one would usually be, opposite the dinette, where you could see it from the couch in the lounge area beyond.

"You're kidding," he said. "You don't watch TV at all?"

She wrinkled her nose. "I read."

"Huh." Liam tried to imagine life with no television, ever. It wasn't as though he had much time to spend in front of one, but a cold beer and a baseball game on a Sunday afternoon could make a bad week a lot better. "I get that there's not much worth watching on TV these days, but don't you at least miss watching movies?"

Another odd expression flitted across her face. He was usually good at telling what people were thinking; it was part of his job. But Barbara Yager was impossible to read.

"I don't watch movies either."

"What, *never*?" Liam had never met anyone who didn't like movies.

"My foster mother, the woman who raised me, didn't believe in them." Baba gave a tiny shrug. "She thought they were newfangled nonsense, designed to distract the ignorant masses from real-life problems, so they wouldn't make a fuss. I suppose I never bothered to find out if she was wrong, after she was gone."

"Your foster mother must have been an interesting woman," Liam said, thinking that sounded better than saying *nuttier than a fruitcake.*

Baba's lips twitched. "Oh, that she definitely was."

Liam had a sudden thought. "Wait—do you mean you've never actually seen a movie? Not one?"

"Nope."

The concept floored him. "You never saw *Star Wars*? *Ghostbusters*? *Casablanca*? You never saw *The Princess Bride*?" Good grief. That should be against the law. He should arrest her, just on general principle.

Baba rolled her eyes. "Princesses. Highly overrated, most of them. But no, I have never seen a movie."

"You know, if you're going to be in the area for a while, there is a theater in town that shows classic movies for a couple of bucks on Tuesday nights," he said. "You should go sometime."

One feathery eyebrow floated upward again as she gazed at him. "Are you asking me out, Sheriff?" Humor lurked in the depths of her clear amber eyes.

"Am I—what? No, uh, I mean, no, of course not. I just meant, uh, that you should go. By yourself. Or not." Liam seriously considered taking his gun out of his holster and shooting himself. The woman was a suspect, for god's sake. Or suspicious anyway. And besides, he didn't date. Had he actually accidentally asked her out? Surely not.

As if things couldn't get any more mortifying, his stomach chose that moment to rumble loudly. Baba bit her lip, clearly trying not to laugh.

"Sorry," he said. "I skipped breakfast. I guess this is my body's way of telling me to get back into town. Thank you for the water. Enjoy your visit to Clearwater County." He tipped his hat at her, shoved his sunglasses back onto his face, and strode out the door with what was left of his dignity.

On the bright side, after this, those piles of paperwork were going to be a positive relief.

THREE

BABA WATCHED THE tall lawman walk away, his back rigid and broad shoulders squared—standing at the window long past the time when the dust from the squad car's tires was just a memory. Outside, a small bird twittered until her glare sent it winging away to friendlier skies. Distant thunder growled over the hills.

"I think he likes you," Chudo-Yudo said, laughter rumbling in his deep, white chest. He crunched on the bone again, slobbering a little because he knew it irritated her. It was boring guarding the Water of Life and Death day in and day out for centuries. It might be the stuff that gave the Babas their longevity and a boost to their magical abilities, but the rest of the time, it just sat there. A dragon had to find amusement somewhere.

"Don't be ridiculous," Baba said, finally pulling herself away from the empty view. "He just thinks I'm hiding something, so he's poking around." She twitched a finger and the bone turned into a butterfly and flew away. Chudo-Yudo's jaws snapped shut on nothingness and he let out an indignant *whuff*.

"Well, you *are* hiding something," the dog pointed out. "Just not what he thinks you are hiding." He scratched at an ear with his hind leg. "I'm pretty sure I'm going to have to eat him, before this is all done."

"Maybe."

"So, are you going to go see a movie?" Chudo-Yudo asked. "With the handsome sheriff, before I eat him?"

"He didn't ask me," Baba said, feeling grumpy for no obvious reason. "And even if he had, he's too young for me."

Chudo-Yudo snorted, sounding more dragon than dog for a moment. "You're eighty-two, Baba. Everyone is too young for you."

"Not Koshei," she argued.

"Koshei is a dragon. Even when he looks like a Human, he's still a dragon," the dog said. "Wouldn't you like to spend time with one of your own kind occasionally?"

"Humans are hardly my own kind," Baba said, flopping down on the couch. "Not anymore. Not since I came to live with the Baba Yaga, and grew up to be one. Besides, Koshei and I get along fine. He shows up, we have sex, he goes away. Why would I want anything more than that?"

Chudo-Yudo stared at her. "If you don't know, I suspect that answers the question."

She jumped back up, skin too tight around her bones and the walls closing in like a narrowing tunnel under the earth. Or maybe the damned dragon-dog was just getting on her nerves.

"I'm going for a walk," she said, thumping in her bare feet over to the wardrobe. A graceful woman, she could make an impressive amount of noise when she was in the mood. "Try not to break anything while I'm gone."

She jiggled the wonky handle and pulled the door open. Glared at the clothes inside and shut it again. Slammed it with the palm of her hand, jiggled the handle again, and opened the door to see the Otherworld passageway. "Fucking door," she muttered, and walked through, slamming it behind her. Crockery rattled in the kitchenette cupboards.

"Well, that was interesting," Chudo-Yudo said to himself,

hauling another bone out from underneath a couch that had no underneath. "Change is in the air. Babas hate change. This is going to be fun." He settled down to take a nap, humming a little Russian lullaby he'd learned back in the Old Country long ago from a peasant woman. He couldn't remember if he'd eaten her or not, but he liked the song anyway.

AS LIAM HIT town, emerging from scrubby fields back into an area with cell reception, his phone beeped insistently at him to let him know he had voicemail. A quick glance showed him three messages from Clive Matthews, president of the county board, and all-around pain in his ass.

Liam contemplated throwing the phone through the window and running it over with the squad car. He settled for shoving it back into its holder on his belt. He knew what the messages would be without listening to them anyway: *Why haven't you solved these crimes yet? Why don't you have any leads? Maybe we should consider replacing you with someone more competent. Call me when you have something to report. And you'd damned well better have some-thing to report soon.* The man had had it in for Liam since he beat out Clive's son in-law for the sheriff position. Clive had already made it quite clear that if Liam couldn't solve these crimes, or god forbid, another child went miss-ing, he could kiss his job good-bye.

Liam pulled up to a spot in front of Bertie's, got out, and plunked some change into the meter. A tattered pink poster with a gap-toothed youngster on it fluttered at him from a telephone pole, asking *Have you seen this girl?* Suzy Townsend, the first child to go missing, almost five months ago now. That had been late February, bitter cold and snowy with a wind that gnawed at the bones. Suzy had been visiting a friend's house; the two small children bundled into snow-suits, making angels in the front yard. And then her friend's mother went into the house to answer the phone, and sud-denly, there was only one.

Suzy's poster had company now, a multicolored patchwork of proof that he was failing at his job. A woman he knew from the Methodist church's potluck dinners, passing him on the street, averted her eyes and scowled as she went by.

The bell over the door dinged as he entered, barely audible over the hum of voices and the clatter of dishes. As he stood, waiting for his eyes to adjust to the dimmer light inside, he cast his glance over the room, scoping out the vicinity more out of habit than any expectation of trouble.

At a few minutes after noon on a Friday, the small restaurant was almost full. There was no décor to speak of, unless you counted Bertie's collection of license plates from all the states she'd lived in before she settled on upstate New York, and a lopsided bulletin board layered with announcements for the next library book sale, a yoga class for seniors, and the usual collection of kittens in need of a good home. Some of the fliers were so old, those kittens probably already had kittens of their own.

The mismatched tables were covered with cheerfully worn red-and-white gingham-checked plastic tablecloths, and the napkins were paper. But the customers usually sounded happy, and the place smelled like fresh apple pie and hot coffee.

Liam used to think Bertie's was heaven. Now the conversations were muted, and people shot sideways glances at their neighbors when they thought no one was looking. There were barely any children in evidence, despite it being the midst of summer vacation. Folks were keeping their kids close to home these days. Inside, behind locked doors. All the children who'd disappeared had been outside when they vanished; that knowledge turned the playgrounds into ghost towns of abandoned swings and vacant monkey bars, and emptied the swimming pools of their laughing, cannonball-jumping, Marco Polo–playing youthful summer crowds. Clive Matthews had a few choice words to say about that too.

A waitress came up to Liam, menu clenched in white-knuckled hands. "Any news?" she asked. Her son went to school with the missing boy, number two. Liam just shook his head.

Then he caught sight of Belinda Shields across the room, sitting with her elderly parents at a table full of barely eaten food, and he had the cowardly impulse to back out the door, get into the car, and go pick up something at the pizza place down the street. It was already too late, though, as their eyes met over the heads of the other diners, and she waved a hand for him to join them.

Damn.

Liam nodded at the people he knew—which was most of them—as he crossed the black-and-white squares of the old linoleum floor, avoiding the missing tile by table number six out of mindless habit.

"Hey, Belinda," he said. "Hey, Mr. and Mrs. Ivanov. How are you all doing?" He knew how they were doing, of course. Belinda's parents looked liked they'd aged twenty years in the last six days. They doted on their late-in-life daughter, and even more on their only grandchild, especially after her drunken fool of a father took off and never looked back. Mrs. Ivanov's gentle face was pale and bewildered, her wrinkles falling in on themselves as though they'd given up trying to hold on to any expression other than sorrow.

Belinda was in her uniform; she'd insisting on working, but when she wasn't actually on the search, she spent most of her time giving out tickets to people who stepped the tiniest bit over the line. Masses of tickets were accumulating on his desk for people parking an inch into a crosswalk, jaywalking when there was no traffic, or walking their dogs without leashes. Hardly anyone complained. The locals all brought the tickets to him to deal with, and the few tourists just shrugged and paid the insignificant fines, figuring that's what they got for not knowing the rules. He didn't know what else to do, so he let her keep working. If that's what she needed to stay sane, who was he to take that away from her?

Of course, the county board didn't see it that way; four different members had called to question his judgment in the matter, although he could hear Clive's voice behind them all. He didn't care. Either they trusted him to do his job or they didn't. Unfortunately, it was starting to look like they didn't.

"Is there news?" Mariska Ivanov asked eagerly. Her hands knotted together under the tabletop as if weaving arcane symbols of hope.

"No, I'm sorry, nothing," he said. "We've had a number of calls to the 800 number, but none of them have panned out so far." He patted her on the shoulder. "I'm sure something will turn up soon." He wished he felt as confident as he sounded. The truth was, there was such an absence of evidence, even the state police, who had shown up after the second disappearance, reluctantly concluded that there were no leads to follow up on. They showed up periodically, looking over his shoulder and criticizing his lack of progress, but didn't have the men to spare for a case with no suspects and nothing to definitively tie the three disappearances together.

"Sure, sure. Soon," Mariska's husband said, not believing it any more than Liam did. "You sit with us, yes? Eat some lunch. I hear you were out searching all morning, you must be hungry." Belinda's parents had Russian accents too, much stronger than the slight lilt he'd detected in the herbalist's voice. They'd defected during the cold war; scientists, both of them, although from what he'd gathered, they'd given up their life's work, rather than hand it over to any government, and taken up farming instead. After all they'd survived, he knew they would survive this too. But he wasn't sure they'd want to.

"I was out by Miller's Meadow, checking the river," Liam said, pulling out a faded blue wobbly-legged chair and sitting down reluctantly. "I know it is really too far from the house; five miles or more, but kids love that stretch of water, so I thought I'd have a look. Anything to avoid the paperwork on my desk, you know." He smiled at them and they all smiled back, none of them very convincingly.

"Did you find anything?" Belinda asked. She looked like

she always did, mouse-brown hair in a short, tidy French braid, pale pink lipstick, tiny gold studs in her ears. Only her red and swollen eyes gave her away, and the dark circles underneath them. "At the river?"

Liam shook his head. "No, nothing. Sorry."

Lucy, a comfortably middle-aged waitress whose plump form was a walking advertisement for Bertie's food, appeared at his shoulder to offer him the choice between meatloaf and fried chicken, and save him from apologizing again. Not that any amount of *I'm sorry*s could make up for his not finding Belinda's child. Or anyone's child.

"Any news, Sheriff?" Lucy asked, chewing on the end of her ballpoint pen. She drew a picture of a chicken on her pad, her idea of shorthand, and stuck the pen into her fluffy blond tornado of hair. "You know, I can't believe that a local would have anything to do with these disappearances. It must be one of them tourists. You just can't trust those people. They never shoulda opened that bed-and-breakfast in West Dunville."

Behind her, a balding man in a Yankees tee shirt turned bright red, grabbed his female companion's hand, and left his table without a tip. Liam sighed.

Desperate to change the subject, he said, "Hey, you'll never guess what I found down at Miller's Meadow. One of those fancy silver Airstream trailers. Belongs to a woman from California, some herbalist professor type name Barbara Yager." He added cheerfully, "She even has a bit of a Russian accent. Maybe she's a long-lost relative. She says people call her Baba."

Belinda's mother dropped her coffee cup, spilling milky brown liquid everywhere. Her face turned two shades paler than it had been, and Lucy clucked at her as she mopped at the table with an already sticky cloth.

Mariska insisted she was fine, but Liam could see her hands shake as she asked him, "This herbalist, was she an old woman? Ugly, with a long nose and bad teeth?"

He blinked. "No. Not at all. Her license said she was thirty-two, although she didn't look nearly that old to me.

Her nose might have been a little long, but her teeth were fine."

Belinda laughed, a rusty sound. "You're hardly an expert on women. I'm surprised you even noticed she had teeth."

"Hey," he said, pretending to be wounded. "I'm a professional lawman. I notice everything. And I know plenty about women."

Belinda's father came to Liam's defense in his usual well-meaning but clumsy fashion. "Sure he does, honey. He was married, you know."

An uncomfortable silence flattened the air around the table. Lucy cleared her throat and said, "I'll go get that chicken for you, Sheriff," and scuttled for the kitchen. Nobody mentioned Liam's wife. Ex-wife. Whatever she was.

Melissa had left town two years ago, after spending the year before that trashing what was left of their marriage and her reputation. Shared tragedy should have brought them closer together. Instead, it had torn them to shreds and left nothing behind but dust and tears and a few pieces of stale popcorn from the circus she'd run away with.

Into the echoing chasm of their conversation, Mariska said hesitantly, "Are you sure the woman said her name was Baba?"

"Yes, pretty sure," Liam answered, grateful. "It's an odd nickname, isn't it?"

"Yes, yes it is." Mariska stood up, tugging on her husband's arm. "We should get going, Ivan. Those cows aren't going to milk themselves, and we should let Belinda get back to work." Her face had gone from pale to flushed, and she had a strange look about her; Liam hoped that the stress of the situation wasn't making her ill. He stood up as the women rose from the table.

"Belinda, why don't you walk us out to our car, dear?" Mariska said, still pulling at her baffled husband. "Sheriff, it was nice to see you."

Ivan pushed away his hardly touched plate of meatloaf and stood up. "Are you going to be at the anti-fracking meeting later?" he asked Liam. "I know I should stay home, under the circumstances, but the issue is so important, I hate to miss it. If the land goes, what do we have left?"

"I don't know, Mr. Ivanov," Liam said. Hydrofracking was a hot-button issue in Clearwater County, with about half the folks believing the drilling process would destroy the environment and contaminate the water table, and the other half insisting that leasing land to the natural gas companies was the only thing that would bring in much-needed money during the recession.

Liam tried to stay out of anything even vaguely political, although he sure as hell wouldn't want them drilling on his land. "I'll make it if I can. I'm supposed to be off duty, but the last few meetings have been a little . . . unsettled . . . so I might come just to keep an eye on the hotheads and make sure no one gets too worked up." At least this might be one instance where he could actually do the job he got paid for.

The old man held out one gnarled, arthritic hand for Liam to shake, making *I'm coming, I'm coming* noises at his wife. "Well, we really appreciate everything you are doing to try to find our *malenkaya devotshka*. You're a good man."

The three of them left, and Liam sat back down with a thud. Lucy put his lunch in front of him and he took a bite, but it tasted like sawdust mixed with bitter desperation.

How could Ivan thank him? He wasn't doing *anything*. Nothing at all, except spinning his wheels and wasting the taxpayers' money. What was worse, he knew in his gut that if he didn't find any answers soon, another child would go missing. And there didn't seem to be a damned thing he could do to stop it.

OUR

BABA TURNED SIDEWAYS past blue-tinged trees covered with hanging chartreuse ivy and slipped back through the door to the mundane plane. Stepping out of the minuscule wardrobe, she banged her head on the low doorframe and muttered a few rude words; it seemed like both worlds were against her today.

She had hoped for a pleasant stroll; something to wash away the vague feelings of unease she couldn't explain. A trip to the Otherworld should have been a calming retreat. But none of the paths she was used to seemed to be there, and her friends on the other side were either hiding or having fun without her. Something was clearly off-kilter, but she wasn't in the mood to figure out what. It was her job to watch over the doorway between the Otherworld and the mortal lands, but it wasn't her job to police either. And she had enough problems on this side of the door. There was something "off" about the local environment; she just couldn't figure out what it was. If she stuck around long enough, she'd have to look into it.

As she slammed the closet shut behind her, Chudo-Yudo

lifted his massive head from where it was resting on what looked like the remains of one of her favorite spike-heeled boots and said, "About time you got back. We've got company."

Baba's heart did a little dance to music only it could hear. "Oh?" she said in a casual tone. "Anyone we know?"

The dog snorted. "It's not that yummy sheriff, if that's what you were hoping. It's a woman. She's wearing a uniform like his, but she fills hers out a lot better." His tongue lolled in a leer.

"Has she been here long?" Baba asked, walking over to look out the front window. Chudo-Yudo padded over to stand next to her and gave a canine version of a shrug.

"You know I'm not good with time. If it's not a century, it's not long. But I can tell you that she spent a while walking around this thing trying to find a door, before she gave up and went to sit on her car and wait."

"Oh for the love of all that's sacred!" Baba smacked the wall with one curled fist. Hard. "House! Make a damned door and leave it there." There was a brief pause, and then the front entrance reappeared, shimmering for a moment before settling into place with a disgruntled thump.

Baba glared at it. "How am I supposed to blend in with the Humans if you keep playing these silly games? I have half a mind to go back to living in a hut with chicken legs." The Airstream seemed to shiver. "Right, then. Let's see who our unexpected guest is."

She opened the door and stuck her head outside, taking a minute to check out her visitor before the woman noticed her. Uniform aside, the woman didn't seem like anything unusual; pretty in an unexciting sort of way, if you disregarded the droop to her shoulders and the sadness on her face. Baba didn't, of course. Those things meant something in her line of work.

"Hello," she called. "Were you looking for me?"

Her visitor jumped up, startled. "How . . . I couldn't find, I mean . . ." her voice dwindled away as she took a few steps toward the trailer. She walked slowly, her feet dragging as if unsure they wanted to take her in this direction, but eventually ended up at the front door. The difference between the deputy's five foot two and Baba's five foot ten was noticeable; the woman had to tilt her head to look directly into Baba's amber eyes.

"Are you Barbara Yager?" she asked, finally meeting Baba's gaze.

"I am." Baba didn't smile. Those who sought her out always had to pass certain tests. Getting through the door wasn't supposed to be easy. If it were, then everyone would want to do it.

"Uh," the woman squirmed a little, but didn't look away. "Are you also the Baba Yaga?"

"I am. And you are?"

"Belinda Shields," she said. And then added. "My daughter is the one Sheriff McClellan was looking for."

"Ah." That explained part of it. "So, are you the one who called me here, then?" Baba scowled, but the woman stood her ground.

"No, that was my mother, Mariska Ivanov. She'd heard stories in the Old Country about how the Baba Yaga sometimes helped those in need. I mean, she told me the stories too, when I was growing up, but I thought they were just fairy tales and—"

"And she believed," Baba said, cutting to the marrow of the matter. "And so she summoned me, and now you're here."

"Yes." Belinda squared her shoulders and looked Baba in the face. "Can you prove you are who you say you are?"

Baba suppressed a sigh. Things used to be a lot simpler, back in the old days. "You're not supposed to need proof, you know."

The smaller woman stared at her through red-rimmed eyes. "I'm a cop. Humor me."

Tiny swirls of energy flowed from Baba into the ground. "Fine. How's that for proof?" She gestured at Belinda's feet, which were now firmly attached to the earth by the thorny vines of a wild rose entwining mockingly around her boots, poking tiny holes in the thick brown leather.

"Oh." Belinda looked down, blinking in mixed shock and relief. "You *are* the Baba Yaga. Will you help me find my daughter, please?"

"It is not that simple," Baba said. "If your mother told you the stories, then you know that there is always a price. Are you willing to pay it?"

"Anything," Belinda said, her eyes shining with unshed tears. "She's my child. I would trade my life for hers, if that's what it takes."

Baba felt the universe shift; reality changing in some minute way to accommodate the bargain offered and accepted. No turning back now. She was well and truly involved.

She sighed, snapped her fingers to make the vines slither grudgingly back into the soil, and gestured toward the Airstream. "Let's hope it doesn't come to that, shall we? You'd better come inside. We have a lot to talk about."

BABA PUT A kettle on the stove for tea and started pulling assorted herbs out of jars to toss into the teapot. After a minute, she realized that her guest was still standing awkwardly by the door, and waved her toward a seat at the dinette table. Too many years living with the old Baba and minimal contact with normal humans meant her manners were less than smooth. She did much better with tree sprites and talking dogs.

Chamomile for calming, she thought, crumpling a few white-and-yellow flowers between her fingers and releasing their pungent odor into the small space. *Rosemary for remembrance and honesty. Lemon balm for healing.* Without turning around, she said, "So, tell me about your daughter."

Belinda made a sound that caught halfway between a sigh and a sob. "She's seven; just celebrated her birthday two weeks before she disappeared. Small for her age, with long blond hair and blue eyes. She takes after her father, not me," she added, as though answering a question that most people asked. "She's beautiful."

"Of course she is," Baba said impatiently, pouring hot water over the herbs to steep. She realized with a start that she'd never turned the stove on. The water still got hot, because she wanted it to, but she'd have to be more careful if she was going to have wayward guests and snooping sheriffs around. "But I want you to tell me about *her*. What is her essence? What makes her unique? I can't find her if I don't have any sense for who she is."

She turned around, leaning back against the counter, and gazed calmly at the distraught mother, waiting for her to say something vaguely useful.

"Oh," Belinda took a moment to think. "Well, she's smart. She already knows her alphabet, and how to write her own name, the whole long thing: Mary Elizabeth Shields. She loves the color yellow, hates Brussels sprouts, and she wants a dog in the worst way. She's been bugging me for a puppy for years, especially since her father left." She sniffed. "If she comes home, the first thing I'm going to do is get her a damned puppy. I don't care if I end up walking it every single time."

Chudo-Yudo chose that moment to appear from the back of the Airstream and let out the short, growly bark that was his version of "hello." It gave most people a sudden inexplicable desire to be elsewhere, but Belinda just smiled and held out a hand to be sniffed.

"What a handsome dog!" she said, which got her the honor of a wet black nose pressed against her knee. She took the hint and scratched him behind the ears, and Chudo-Yudo's eyes drooped closed in doggy bliss. "Is he a pit bull? What's his name?"

"Chudo-Yudo," Baba said and waited to see how extensive the tale telling had been.

"Chudo-Yudo; wasn't that the name of the dragon who guarded the Water of Life and Death?" Belinda asked. "Is he named after that Chudo-Yudo? How cute."

Cute. Baba shook her head. "He *is* that Chudo-Yudo. And don't call him cute. It will just give him a swelled head. And look at the size of the one he's already got."

Belinda's eyes got big. "He's a dragon? But, but, he looks just like a dog."

"Looks can be deceiving," Baba said, a warning hum behind her words. "Often."

Belinda started, probably feeling the menace of something she couldn't quite put her finger on, but knew alarmed her. Baba had that effect on people. Often. Sometimes even on purpose.

Baba changed the subject, pouring tea into two pottery mugs carved with ancient magical symbols and decorative chickens, placing one in front of her visitor. "So, your daughter is the third child to be taken. Do the children who vanished all have something in common, that you know of?"

Tired brown eyes gazed back at her. "Not that we've been able to find. And believe me, Sheriff McClellan has been looking for a connection. Not to mention the state police, who searched every database they had for any disappearances remotely like these. There are two girls and one boy, between the ages of two and eight, from different areas of the county. They don't all go to the same school; their parents aren't members of the same organizations. Nothing."

"Interesting," Baba said. "And no evidence of any kind left behind at the scene?"

"None." Belinda nibbled on an already ragged nail. "You'd think they vanished into thin air." A single tear tracked down her face, as if she'd cried so much already and it was the only one left. "I swear, I turned my back for less than a minute. I heard her giggle, like she'd seen something funny, and when I turned back around, she was just *gone*. The state police didn't find anything more than we did."

Chudo-Yudo raised the corner of one pink-edged lip to reveal sharp and shining teeth. Baba nodded back in agreement. There was something very wrong here. More wrong than three missing children. *Otherworld involvement* wrong, maybe. That would explain a lot.

"Huh," Baba said, for lack of anything more helpful. "So, tell me about your child's father. Is there any chance he was involved? Anything . . . unusual . . . about him?"

Sometimes if one parent came from the lands beyond, they eventually returned home, taking the child with them. Not that many there had children anymore, even on the rare occasions when they dallied with the mortal kind. These days, an Otherworld child was a rare and precious thing, a treasure to be prized above all else.

Belinda gave a sharp, harsh laugh, like a bullfrog as the night came down. "Not likely. Eddie didn't want anything to do with Mary Elizabeth, not once the thrill of proving his manhood was gone. He was my "bad boy" walk on the wild side. When I got pregnant, I made the mistake of marrying him. Spent the next five and a half years putting up with his drinking and his lowlife friends." She shook her head, as if in wonderment at her own stupidity. "I stuck with him for far too long, even after he started beating me, but when he drove drunk with Mary Elizabeth in the truck, I finally came to my senses and kicked him out. As far as I know, he's not even in the area anymore."

Well, that was a boring old Human story. But at least it sounds like the father wasn't part of the problem. That wouldn't have explained the other children anyway.

Baba plucked at the sleeve of Belinda's uniform, trying not to make a face at the slick artificial feel of the tan poly-cotton blend. If it were hers, she'd work a little magic to turn it into something more comfortable and flattering. "I'm surprised he had the nerve to beat on a cop; you folks usually stick together, don't you?"

Belinda gave another laugh, this one filled with genuine humor; her smile made Baba revise her original estimate of "just pretty" up to "almost beautiful, when her life hasn't been ripped apart."

"Oh, no," Belinda answered. "I wasn't with the department when I was married to Eddie. I got the job afterward."

"So you'd be safe if he came back?"

"So I could shoot his ass and get away with it."

It was Baba's turn to laugh. Not because she didn't believe Belinda, but because she did. Damned if she didn't like the woman.

At their feet, Chudo-Yudo's furry white sides shook with amusement too, and they exchanged glances.

"Very well," Baba said." I will help you."

Belinda looked like she couldn't decide if that was a good thing or not. "Because I said I would shoot my ex-husband?" Clearly, she thought that was a strange factor to consider in her favor.

"Because you're willing to stand up for yourself and your child," Baba clarified. "You're no damned princess waiting for someone to come and rescue you. Although the shooting thing helped, I won't lie."

"That's great," Belinda said. "But what can you do that the entire sheriff's department and the state police couldn't?"

Baba shrugged. "We'll just have to see. Something will come to me. It always does." Her face grew even sterner than usual. "Now, about that price." She tapped one finger against her full lips as she thought. "I think we'll go with the traditional three impossible tasks. I find that usually separates the men from the boys. Or girls, in this case."

Belinda's eyes widened. "You mean you won't even try to find Mary Elizabeth until I do three *impossible* things? That's . . . that's . . ."

Baba shrugged again. "You came to me. That's the way this works. Even the Baba Yaga has to play by certain rules." She didn't mention that her favorite hobby was bending those rules until they resembled origami done by a drunken blind man.

Since some of a Baba's power came from her connection to the Otherworld, there were certain conventions that had to be followed. Of course she'd start looking into the matter right away, but Belinda didn't need to know that. And as long as the woman accomplished three tasks eventually, the principle would be considered fulfilled.

"Fine, then," Belinda braced her narrow shoulders. "What is my first task?"

Baba put on her best portentous voice. This was the official bit. "You must discover for me what is causing the disruption of nature's balance in this region. I can hear the land and water and air cry out in anguish. Tell me what is as the root of their pain, and I will help you."

Part of her job as the Baba Yaga was to maintain the balance of the natural world, but even with control over the elements, it was an impossible task in this day and age. There were too few Babas and too many humans bent on destroying the planet. But since she was here anyway, she might as well figure out what was disturbing the local equilibrium and set it right. By setting her new client to find the problem, she could kill two birds with one uniform-clad stone.

To her surprise, the woman laughed. "I thought this was supposed to be an impossible task. I can answer that question right now."

Baba took a slow breath. *Well, that was unexpected.* It was rare for anything—or anyone—to catch her by surprise. Interesting. Perhaps she wasn't dealing with two separate issues after all. The mystery deepened.

"Is that so?" she said, expression bland and unimpressed. "Tell me, then."

"It's the hydrofracking," Belinda said, as if everyone knew about it.

"The *what*? Is that some kind of curse word?"

Belinda's mouth twisted. "It should be. Hydraulic fracturing is a way of forcing water, mixed with chemicals and sand and other things, sometimes including radioactive trackers, down deep into the earth under extreme pressure. It can contaminate the water table for miles around, it causes water and air pollution, and the waste water it generates is highly poisonous."

Baba felt her jaw drop open. "Why would anyone do such a thing?" Humans were even more insane than she'd already thought.

"Money," Belinda replied, her tone so bitter that the herbs on the shelf above her head shriveled inside their jar. "Hydrofracking is used to access natural gas deposits. The gas companies pay a lot of money to lease land so that they can use it for drilling. And a lot of people around here are desperate; the small farmers can't compete with the big agribusinesses, and plenty of folks in this area never had any money to start with."

Baba shook her head. "Still, how can they not see that destroying the water and the land will make things worse for them?" Chudo-Yudo growled, and she reached down to pet him in a rare gesture of solidarity.

"Damned if I know," Belinda said. "But some of it is greed and some of it is ignorance, I guess. And the gas company hands out lies like they were Halloween candy." She got a slightly wicked glint in her eye and stared at Baba thoughtfully. "There's a meeting tonight in town. You should come. It's supposed to be for the anti-fracking folks, but usually the pro-fracking folks come too, including the local head of the gas company, Peter Callahan, who's the biggest douchebag I ever saw. I'd kinda like to see what happens if you meet him."

"You *really* don't like this man, do you?" Baba raised an eyebrow. It wasn't as if she had any big plans for the evening. "Is the sheriff going to be there?" *Not that she cared.*

"I expect so," Belinda said. "We've had some fights nearly break out at the last couple of meetings, so he'll probably have a few us there in uniform just to keep things civil. Why, did you want to ask him some more questions about the kids?"

Chudo-Yudo made a choking noise, and Baba kicked him with one bare foot. It was like kicking a brick wall. You'd think she'd learn.

"Yes, of course," Baba said. "Fights, eh? I like fighting." She cracked her knuckles and Belinda jumped, possibly realizing a little too late that maybe this hadn't been her best idea. "Suddenly this place is looking like a lot more fun. Fighting. *Excellent.*"

BABA RESTED HER shoulders against a cement-block wall at the back of the ugliest meeting hall she'd ever seen. Why an otherwise lovely town full of quaint old buildings would choose to hold its important gatherings in a modern beige-on-taupe-on-tan brick eyesore was beyond her. Rows of dinged gray metal folding chairs were filled with muttering people; the rank odor of their sweat and resentment offended her sensitive nose, and their churning emotions made her wish she'd stayed home where there was only a fire-breathing dragon to deal with.

Still, she was there, so she may as well make the best of it. Maybe she'd learn something. Or get to hit someone. Either one would be good. Both would be splendid.

From where she leaned, she could see most of the room. A row of dignitaries sat up front at a long, lopsided table with a matchbook shoved under one wobbly leg. Off to the left, Liam held up a wall in much the same position as she did, and watched the area with a wary eye. He'd raised one eyebrow as she'd entered, and for a moment it had looked as though he was going to come over and greet her, but he'd been waylaid by a middle-aged matron wearing a too-tight flowered dress, and in the end, he'd stayed where he was, a strained expression on his rugged face. Her heart had done a weird pitter-pat when she'd seen him, like she had one too many cups of coffee. Or stayed up all night dancing in a fairy circle. Except she hadn't done either. Recently.

From within a cluster of sympathetic neighbors, Belinda held a whispered consultation with an elderly woman whose eyes widened at the sight of Baba. The woman bowed her head respectfully in Baba's direction, clutched her equally elderly husband's hand tightly, and then turned resolutely to face forward, as if not wanting to draw attention to any connection between her and the stranger.

Baba didn't blame her. People were already giving Baba curious, vaguely uncomfortable glances when they spotted her, like a pack of coyotes sniffing at a wolf who had somehow wandered onto their territory by mistake. Maybe she should have changed out of the black leather pants, black tee shirt, and motorcycle boots. Oh well, it wasn't as though she would have blended in, no matter what she wore.

"They're not being unfriendly," Belinda said, coming to stand next to her against the back wall. "They're just on edge because of the missing children, and of course, the hydro-fracking. As far as they know, any unfamiliar person means trouble."

Baba snorted. They had no damned idea.

Up front, a microphone let out an unearthly squeal that sounded like a mermaid with laryngitis, and a plump, jowly man with a receding hairline and an expensive suit cleared his throat and said, "I'm Clive Matthews, president of the county board, as most of you know. Let's get things started, shall we? I'm sure we all have places we'd rather be than this lovely meeting hall, eh?" He gave a practiced chuckle, and Baba thought, *Politician.*

Ten minutes later, when Matthews had rattled on about how important the issue was without in any way saying anything substantive, or, in fact, actually getting the meeting started, she added to that observation: *Pompous windbag with delusions of grandeur not accompanied by any particular wealth of personality, looks, or charisma.* And seriously considered turning him into the toad he so strongly resembled. Only the fact that his audience might possibly notice the difference kept her twitching fingers at her side.

"Let's keep in mind that both sides are entitled to their opinions," he was saying as she pulled her attention away from daydreams of a cold beer, "and that we're gathered here to discover facts, not to argue. The county will be holding a vote soon to decide whether or not to enact a moratorium on drilling."

He scowled out over the crowd, his double chin aquiver with dignified self-righteousness. "I am against the moratorium, of course. The county needs the money that drilling will bring with it, along with the new job opportunities, improvements to our roads, and many other benefits." He turned to gesture toward one of the men sitting at the long table behind him, the only other one wearing a suit, instead of casual everyday clothing.

"Here to tell us all about how safe the hydraulic fracturing process really is, and what we can expect when his company expands their holdings into our area, is Peter Callahan, of the East Shoreham Oil and Gas Company." Clive clapped his meaty hands together as the other man approached the mike; about a third of the folks in the room followed suit, while the others sat in stony silence, their lack of enthusiasm as palpable as the full moon's tidal pull.

Next to Baba, Belinda crossed her arms in front of her chest and glared at the handsome man in his well-tailored suit, her grief forgotten for the moment as she listened with obvious skepticism to his smooth explanations of foolproof safety records and guaranteed profitability. An undercurrent of something foreign and malicious eddied through the room, prickling at Baba's senses like briars in a hedge.

She swung her head to and fro, sniffing at the air surreptitiously, looking for the source of the odor of *wrongness* that clung to the atmosphere, causing the people around her to stir into restless agitation. Toward the front of the room, one burly man stood up and started yelling obscenities at the speaker, and Liam pushed off the wall he'd been holding up to move decisively in that direction.

Baba let her eyes unfocus as she scanned the hall, lighting finally on a figure in the front row that blurred and sparkled with that aura that indicated someone or something wearing a glamour. Glamours meant magic. And someone with something to hide. Which in turn meant a whole host of other things, none of them good, since there shouldn't have been anyone using magic with such a distinctly Otherworld feel to it.

She cursed quietly under her breath in Russian, the sound blending in unnoticed amid the rising murmur of tense voices, as the woman swiveled her head and caught Baba's eyes with a steely-eyed gaze. Something malignant stirred behind those gray orbs, sending a shiver up Baba's spine.

"Who is that woman?" she asked Belinda, using one sharp elbow to get the deputy's attention. "The one down there with the platinum blond hair in a chignon, wearing a yellow dress?"

Belinda looked surprised, although whether it was because she hadn't expected the question or because she was amazed Baba knew the term *chignon*, it was impossible to say.

"That's Peter Callahan's assistant," Belinda said, peering

across the room to be sure they were talking about the same person. "Maya something or other. Although, if you ask me, she might actually be a bodyguard. Apparently he started getting death threats about six months ago; she showed up not long after that, and since then, I haven't seen him without her by his side." She shrugged. "I don't know why the company didn't hire some big muscle-bound guy. Maybe they didn't want to be obvious about it."

Baba pressed her lips together, not wanting to let what popped into her mind slip out of her mouth. Not to Belinda anyway. *Six months ago. Right before children started disappearing. A coincidence? Possibly. Or . . . possibly not.* But something in that glance said she was trouble. It just remained to be seen what kind.

The prickliness under her skin intensified almost to the point of pain, and Baba straightened, giving Belinda a shove in the direction of her parents. "Get your parents out of this room. Now." Belinda gave her a startled look out of wide eyes but didn't argue, setting off toward where the old couple sat. Around the space, arguments were erupting into raised voices, like a hornet's nest disturbed by a thrown rock. Baba headed toward Liam, whose attention was divided between the profanity-spouting farmer and two of the men at the front table who were screaming at each other, dueling charts in upraised hands.

He spared her a frustrated glance as she appeared at his shoulder; the two-inch heels on her boots made them almost the same height, but the irate citizen he was confronting dwarfed them both.

"I don't know what the hell is wrong with these people tonight," Liam said, shaking his head. "It's like they've all lost their minds." He glared at the large fat man in overalls, who finally slumped back into his seat. Baba could sense the anger and frustration coming off him in waves.

"I think they had some help," Baba said, stomping on one particularly loud argument with her heavy boots. The people involved stopped yelling at each other and clutched their feet instead. "This isn't normal." She had to raise her voice to be heard over the increased volume surrounding them; clearly things were heading rapidly from Not Good to Worse Than Not Good.

Liam separated a couple who were shoving at each other in the middle of the aisle and said, only a little disbelief in his voice, "You mean you think someone put something in the coffee?" He glanced around at the spreading mayhem. "Or the ventilation system? But why would anyone do such a thing? What would they have to gain?"

Sure. Or cast a spell that ramped up everyone's preexisting anger. Baba decided it would be better to just nod. "Maybe someone doesn't want rational discussion about the issue," she said. And then added, "Duck."

He ducked, and a chair came whistling through the air where his head had been. Baba vaulted over his crouched form and threw a roundhouse punch into the face of the man who had thrown it, dropping him like a stone. She grinned. *This was more like it.*

But Liam spoiled her fun by saying, "Damn it, someone is going to get hurt. I've got to figure out some way to calm these people down." He cast a slightly desperate look at Clive Matthews, whose eyes were narrowed as he searched for someone to hold responsible for the chaos, and said through clenched teeth, "The county board has been looking for an excuse to replace me. This ought to just about do it."

Baba sighed and looked around in resignation for a solution that didn't involve cracking heads together while cackling gleefully. The sight of a sprinkler system set into the dingy ceiling gave her an idea, and she wiggled two fingers behind her back. Water sprayed down over the crowd, instantly soaking everyone in the room. People squealed and ran for the exits, most of them looking equal parts baffled and annoyed as they returned to their senses.

She nodded at Belinda where she stood next to the control panel, elderly parents nowhere in sight. Liam gusted out a sigh of relief, spotting his deputy at the same time.

"That was quick thinking. Cooled everyone down anyway. Although no doubt the board will have something to say about the mess and the expensive water damage." His face looked grim under its wet coating.

Also, running water short-circuits magic, Baba thought. She said out loud instead, "Oh, I think you'll find that the sprinklers went off by themselves. Some kind of malfunction, no doubt. From the look of the rust on that panel, it hasn't been opened in years." She gave Liam a bracing thump on the shoulder. "And I'm sure there won't be any lasting damage." Another finger flick turned the water back off. The woman called Maya had disappeared, making her exit with the rest of the crowd. Too bad—Baba had a sudden urge to have a chat with the mysterious blonde.

"Huh." Liam looked up at the sprinklers and over toward Belinda, who was being berated by a decidedly damp Clive Matthews, his thinning hair dripping messily down over the blood vessel pulsing in his forehead. "I guess I'd better go rescue my deputy before she's forced to shoot the president of the board in self-defense."

"In that case, wouldn't you be rescuing him?" Baba said with a hint of a smile. Then, more seriously, "I need to talk to you." *And not just because you look incredibly hot, standing there with your soaking-wet shirt clinging to those broad shoulders and muscular chest.*

Liam's eyes narrowed. "About who might have done this? Or about the missing children?" All his attention was suddenly focused in her direction, a constricted beam of penetrating light.

"Maybe neither. Maybe both." Baba wiped water off her face and wrung out her mass of dark hair. "I have a possibility, but no proof." And no idea what the hell a human sheriff could do against a supernatural-wielding opponent. But he still had the right to know. As he'd said when they met, these people were his responsibility. Besides, she'd promised Belinda that she'd help—and a Baba's promise was both rare and unbending. Much like the Babas themselves.

"I see." He didn't look convinced. "Well, I have to deal with this, and we both need to change into dry clothes." He looked admiringly at Baba's own dripping form, trying to hide a smile. "How about you give me an hour and meet me at The Roadhouse? It's a bar on the way out of town. You would have passed it on your way in from where the Airstream is parked."

She nodded. "It's a date," she said. There was no need for her to return to the trailer for new clothes, of course; she could dry herself with a thought. But she had something else she wanted to set into motion before she and the sheriff had their little talk.

There was something going on here she didn't understand, but she trusted her instincts after all these years, and her gut was telling her that the three missing children and Maya's magical riot act were connected somehow . . . and that things were going to get worse before they got better.

It was time to call in some assistance—and she had just the men for the job.

FIVE

THE ALLEY WHERE Baba had left the BMW was dark and smelled like things best not looked at closely, but it was also deserted and likely to stay that way, which suited her purposes just fine. She could ignore the smell; this wouldn't take long.

She brushed away a drop of water that rolled down her neck and tried to pull her clammy tee shirt off over her head. The damp cloth clung to her curves, thwarting her, and she finally just growled and snapped her fingers. The shirt vanished with a faint "pop," leaving her clad in dry leather pants, a black lace bra, and three elaborate tattoos.

A white dragon with green eyes coiled around her right bicep, a red dragon with slanted golden eyes curled around her left bicep, and a black dragon with long whiskers lay across her upper back and shoulders. She stroked them like the old friends they were, and recited a summoning chant in Russian that brought back memories of the old Baba standing in front of a smoky fireplace, stirring something that smelled worse than this alley. The memory made her smile, and helped her ignore the tiny shuddering sting each tattoo let off as it shivered and squirmed, eyes glowing momentarily in the dark night.

"There," she said to herself in a satisfied tone. "That ought to put the cat among the pigeons."

She hummed a little as she glanced down at the black leather pants, and shook her head. With another snap, she pulled more suitable clothing out of the closet in the Airstream, using her magic to transport it through the ether. Although if there was any outfit perfect for hanging out at the local tavern and telling an attractive but clueless shaggy-haired sheriff that his town may have been infested by creatures he didn't believe in . . . she didn't know what it was.

HE'D DONE IT again, Liam realized, as his gut tightened and his pulse beat a tango against the side of his throat. He'd possibly maybe appeared to ask Barbara Yager out. How did he keep doing that? He hadn't asked anyone out in years, either accidentally or on purpose, and never said yes to any of the women who'd asked him. He put all that energy into his job instead. And yet somehow, he'd arranged for her to meet him at a bar. She'd said, "It's a date." But she didn't really think it was a date, did she?

No, of course she didn't. She'd said she had something to tell him about the case, and he'd merely suggested a place they could meet up to have that conversation. That's all it was. Business. Sheriff business, nothing more. The concern died down, to be replaced by a certain disappointment that he shrugged off with practiced ease. Life wasn't a fairy tale. You did what you had to do and got on with it, that's all. And tried not to get trampled as the people around you got on with theirs.

For tonight, that meant listening to whatever Barbara Yager thought she knew—although since she'd just arrived in town, he doubted there was anything she could tell him that would help. Unless she was going to confess, of course. Still, he desperately needed to get a lead on this case and couldn't afford to dismiss anyone. And perversely, he enjoyed her company. Although he couldn't figure out why, since she was odd, mysterious, and infuriating.

Not his top three traits in a woman, for sure. It had been so long since Melissa . . . left . . . he didn't really remember what those three were. But not odd and mysterious and infuriating. He much preferred his life predictable and calm. That's why he was sheriff in a little corner of nowhere, instead of someplace noisy and crowded.

Although The Roadhouse was certainly both.

Liam eased the squad car into one of the few open spaces of the gravel parking lot in front of the long, mustard-colored wooden building. It didn't look like much from the outside. Which was probably just as well, since it didn't look like much on the inside either. Truth in advertising, you might say.

Nonetheless, The Roadhouse was a favorite with the locals, a no-frills country bar with live music on most nights and all the fried food you could eat, including the best chicken wings in the county, if you didn't mind having the skin on the inside of your mouth incinerated.

He left his gun locked in the glove box, since he was technically off duty, and strolled in through the entrance, wearing the same thing most of the others inside were wearing: blue jeans and a tee shirt. A few of the women were wearing tight skirts and dancing to the band playing bluegrass-funk with more enthusiasm than talent on the platform to the right of the bar. Round wooden tables sat four to eight people each, with just enough space between them for the overburdened servers to slide through with trays of drinks and artery-clogging delicacies. The air was redolent with the scent of old beer, new cologne, and the occasional whiff of pot smoke from a dim corner, which Liam determinedly ignored.

The place was packed—except for the area around Baba, who perched on a stool surrounded by empty space, as if she had an invisible Do Not Approach sign over her head. People were staring at her but trying to pretend they weren't. He didn't blame them. She looked damned good.

Better than good, really, in a skinny black halter top that revealed lots of creamy white cleavage and bared her flat midriff and toned arms, and some kind of short, hippie-looking multicolored skirt. Spike-heeled sandals rested on the brass rail that ran along the bottom of the bar, and her dark mass of hair swirled around her shoulders and flowed down over her back. A half-empty beer bottle sat in front of her, some fancy foreign brand Liam would have sworn The Roadhouse never carried.

Mouth suddenly dry, Liam walked up to her and noticed something remarkable. More remarkable than the smell of orange blossoms in the midst of a dusty country bar.

"Those are some tattoos," he blurted out. "Very unusual." He slid onto the stool next to her and gestured to Tyler, the bartender, to bring him his usual Samuel Adams, wishing he'd thought before he'd spoken. *Nice opening line, McClellan. Smooth.* What was it about this woman that turned him from a tough rural lawman into a babbling idiot?

Baba's teeth gleamed in the dim light as she gave him the hint of a smile. "Thanks," she said. "I'm quite fond of dragons."

Liam had the feeling she was teasing him, but couldn't figure out how. Then Tyler put Liam's beer down with a foamy thud, and Liam decided he didn't care.

Cool and slightly bitter, the first sip tasted like heaven and the second like wherever people in heaven went on vacation. "Ah," he said with a sigh, "that's better."

"A good beer is one of the great blessings of the universe," Baba agreed, taking another swallow of her own.

"You've got that right," Liam said, making the "two more" gesture at Tyler when he could catch the bartender's eye. The tall, skinny man with fading red hair moved so fast, pouring drinks and uncapping beer bottles, his hands were a blur of syncopated motion.

The tip jar in front of him held a mountain of change, and he smiled cheerfully all night long, no matter how rude or drunk anyone got. If they hadn't attended the same grief support group for a couple of months, Liam would never have guessed that old sorrow wormed its way through Tyler's bones like bindweed in a field of corn. Losing a child would do that to you. Liam knew that better than anyone.

"Here ya go, Sheriff," Tyler said, full bottles dangling from one large, big-knuckled hand. He winked at Baba. "Nice to see you finally hanging around with a better class of people."

Baba bit her lip, clearly amused.

Liam just rolled his eyes. "I'm a policeman. I usually spend my time with either criminals or lawyers. Hard not to improve on that company."

The bartender grinned, working some sort of alchemical magic with orange juice, vodka, and about six other ingredients. "I heard there was a commotion over at the fracking meeting. Did somebody finally take a shot at Peter Callahan?" His freckled face looked mildly hopeful.

"Not this time," Liam said. "Just high tempers getting the better of folks. No big deal."

Tyler nodded and moved off, taking his potent elixir with him.

"You know that wasn't just high tempers, right?" Baba asked, a serious look replacing her amusement at Tyler's good-natured ribbing.

Liam sighed, draining the rest of his first beer and plunking the bottle back down on the bar. On the other side of the room, the band surged enthusiastically into an Elvis medley.

"We're not going to be able to hear ourselves think in here," he said. "I don't suppose you play pool?"

One corner of Baba's mouth edged up, and she put her own empty bottle down decisively next to his. "I have been known to knock a few balls around, from time to time," she said. An evil glint flitted into her eyes and then vanished before he could be sure he'd actually seen it. "I find it mildly entertaining."

They picked up their full beers and made their way through to the back room, where the repetitive clicking of hard-plastic balls could be heard over the blessedly muted noise from the front of the bar.

Liam grabbed a pool cue off the wall and racked the balls while Baba chose her stick. He pondered the many questions he'd like answers to, trying to figure out which one to start with—and whether there was any point in asking any of them, since his companion seemed as disinclined to give him straight answers as the wind was to blow on command.

He jiggled the rack a little until the balls were all sitting the way he liked them, then removed the white triangle and hung it back in its place on the wall. Across the table from him, Baba looked as cool and implacable as always.

"So," Liam said, his tone studiously casual as he chalked the end of his cue. "How about some stakes to make things interesting?"

One dark eyebrow rose. "Gambling, Sheriff? I'm surprised at you." She applied the blue cube of chalk to her cue, blowing the excess off with a gentle puff of breath that did risky things to the neckline of her top. "I'm afraid I'm not in the habit of carrying much cash."

He shrugged. "I was thinking of something less tangible, actually, but more valuable to me. How about for every ball I sink, you give me an honest answer to whatever question I ask?"

The second brow rose to join the first. A slight rounding of her cheeks hinted at unexpressed mirth. "How very traditional of you. Questions. I truly dislike answering questions. Couldn't we just play strip pool instead?" She eyed him pensively. "No? Too bad."

The base of her stick tapped the floor as she thought briefly. "Very well. For every ball you sink, I will give you an honest answer. But in return, for every game *I* win, you will grant me one day of grace out at the meadow; no harassment, no poking around. Peace and quiet to do my work."

He pondered that for a moment. It seemed like a pretty good bargain; he only had to sink individual balls to get his reward, she had to win entire games to reap hers. "Done," he said, and gestured toward the table. "Ladies first?"

Baba shrugged. "All right," she said. "Although I'm no

lady." She assumed the classic stance, with her left hand forming a bridge to support the cue while her right supplied power to the stick. Liam was mesmerized by the sight of her bottom swaying as she bent over the table, but the resounding crash of balls colliding and ricocheting around the felt tabletop focused his attention back where it belonged. The innocent-looking cue ball spun slowly to a stop as three colored rounds plopped into the nets, one after another.

"That's solids," Baba said brightly, and proceeded to run the table, sinking all of her balls with effortless ease, one after another. The steady *thunk* of her stick against the cue ball sounded like a clock tolling midnight. Liam just stood there, mouth open, as he lost the game without ever getting the chance to make a move.

"I think I've been hustled," he finally said, as the eight ball slid neatly into the corner pocket.

The dark-haired woman shrugged again, eyes twinkling. "Hey, the stakes were your idea, not mine, Sheriff." She took a long swallow of beer, then started racking the balls again. "But I expect you to hold up your end of the deal and give me the day I won."

"Fair's fair," Liam said. "As long as you don't do anything illegal."

"Who me?" Baba gave him her best attempt at an innocent look. A man two tables over tripped on his own cue and fell into the guy next to him, almost starting a fistfight. Liam snorted, not impressed.

"My break," he said. He'd been playing pool in this bar since he was in high school, sneaking down the big elm tree outside his bedroom window to come hang out with his friends. If he couldn't manage to sink a ball when it was his turn, he'd turn in his badge and take up spot welding.

He blocked out the chatter from the neighboring tables and the music from the front room. The elusive ribbon of scent that teased him from Baba's direction was harder to ignore, but he bent over the smooth green felt and inhaled the odor of chalk dust and spilled beer instead. The cue ball shot off the tip of his stick with a solid, meaty thud and turned the geometric precision of the amassed balls into spiraling chaos. The number three ball raced away from its fellows and slid into the corner pocket with a satisfying whoosh, like a rabbit diving into shelter with a coyote hot on its heels.

Liam felt a slightly predatory rush himself as he straightened up, cocking his head at his opponent. "Stripes," he said. "And my first question is this: who did you think was responsible for causing all those people to get so out of control at the meeting, and why?"

He bent down to take his next shot, gesturing with the stick toward the side pocket. "Five ball," he said. "Well?"

Baba shrugged. "A waste of a perfectly good question, Sheriff, since I was going to tell you that anyway. But I should make it clear from the start that I don't have any evidence; just a very strong suspicion."

"Considering I've got nothing," Liam admitted with chagrin, "that still puts you at an advantage over me."

Baba muttered something that sounded distinctly like, "You have no idea," then added more to the point, "I think it was the woman who works for Peter Callahan. Belinda said her name is Maya something and that she got here right before children started disappearing."

Liam was so started by this pronouncement, he muffed the shot, sending the ball skidding into one of Baba's and nudging it into a better alignment for her next turn. Profanity made it as far as the inside of his lips and hung there, largely unspoken.

Baba stalked around the table, eying all the possible angles. Liam just eyed her.

"What makes you think Maya Freeman has anything to do with this?" he asked. "She may have shown up around the right time, but I've looked into her background and everything checks out."

One solid-colored ball zoomed past him into a corner pocket, rapidly followed by another two in a blur of rainbow colors. "Appearances can be deceiving," Baba said coolly. "And that woman is not what—who—she appears to be. All

I can tell you is that I saw her do something suspicious at the meeting. Maybe it had nothing to do with the ensuing upheaval, but I wouldn't want to bet your town's safety on that, would you?" The eight ball followed all its fellows in as if to punctuate her statement.

Liam sighed, as much in anticipation of more futile phone calls as at the loss of the game. "I'll delve a little deeper, see if I can turn anything up." He started racking the balls again, trying not to be distracted by his opponent's amber gaze. "I have to admit, there is something about the woman that makes the back of my neck itch."

Baba's shoulders relaxed microscopically as she realized he wasn't dismissing her suggestion out of hand, and he didn't have the heart to tell her he still found her a heck of a lot more suspicious than Peter Callahan's fancy assistant.

"That's two days you owe me now," she said in a satisfied tone. "Are you sure you don't want to quit while you're ahead?" A tiny smile played at the corner of her full lips.

He shook his head and leaned into the break, pushing his frustration into the forward movement of the stick. A yellow ball raced across the green surface, hung for a moment on the edge of oblivion, and then fell over with a swish. Liam grinned at Baba as he knocked a second solid ball in right after it.

"No thanks, I'm good," he said. "And you owe me two more answers."

Six

LIAM PONDERED HIS next two questions, not wanting to waste either one—since there was a distinct possibility he wouldn't get another chance. The woman played pool like she did everything else, with an almost scary competence and cool grace.

Baba's sly half smile didn't help his concentration any. He didn't understand what it was about her that shook his usual self-possession. Yes, she was beautiful—in the same way a bolt of lightning is beautiful when it shatters the night sky, or a lioness is beautiful as it races across the veldt. This was not a safe or gentle woman, no damsel in distress in need of rescuing. Any knight in shining armor who dared such a thing would probably find himself picking bits of his own sword out of his teeth.

Not that he was any kind of knight. Or interested in having any woman in his life, much less this prickly, mystifying, cloud-haired stranger with her secrets and her lies. That all ended long ago, when the world fell out from underneath him, changing in an instant from a place of warmth and joy to a dark and cruel mockery, empty and cold.

He'd tried to stay strong for Melissa, because that is what you do when you love someone. But she couldn't be strong for him. Or even for herself, more's the pity. And then she was gone, swallowed up in an ocean of secrets and lies, and he vowed never again. Never again. And meant it.

As much as he missed sex, nothing was worth putting himself through that kind of pain and betrayal again. And being a sheriff in a small town meant he couldn't exactly get away with temporary, meaningless liaisons, even if that were his style, which it wasn't.

So why did his fingers itch to run themselves through the silken length of that dark hair every time he saw it? Why did he catch himself staring at her lips, her eyes, the sway of her hips? It's like that feeling you get when you stand at the top edge of a tall, tall building . . . that momentary urge to step into the abyss, and see what it would be like to fall, and keep on falling. And to hell with the crash that would hit you at the bottom.

"Sheriff?" An amused-sounding voice cut into his reverie.

God, he had to get more sleep.

"Right. First question," he said after a brief pause. "Have you lied to me?" Liam felt as though the world was holding its breath as he waited for the answer; although why he thought she would tell him the truth now if she hadn't before, he wasn't sure. Even so, for whatever reason, he believed she would stick to their bargain.

Baba gazed at him steadily, amber eyes clear and guileless. "Not nearly as much as you think I have, and not about anything important."

A weedy teenager approached the table with a quarter in his outstretched hand, ready to put it in the slot that would reserve the next game for him. A frown and a minute shake of the head from Liam sent him scuttling toward one of the other tables. Liam turned the look on Baba, who wasn't nearly as easy to intimidate, unfortunately. Apparently that was all the answer he was going to get from her on that subject.

Fine.

He walked around the table, ostensibly gauging his next shot, and ended up standing close enough to feel the heat of her skin. The room held six tables, and maybe twenty people, but for a moment, it seemed as though they were alone, held in isolation by a bubble of reality in which only the two of them existed.

His voice was low and serious. "Second question: what are you *really* doing in this area?"

She took a long swallow of beer before saying in a matter-of-fact tone, "I came because Mariska Ivanov called me for help in finding her granddaughter." A tiny smile flickered on and off like a lightbulb in an electrical storm. "But there *are* some very interesting plants growing in Clearwater County, so I didn't lie when I said that was why I was here. I just didn't tell you the entire truth."

Huh. Liam rocked back on his heels; whatever he'd been expecting, that hadn't been it. "I didn't realize you knew the Ivanovs," he said, trying to figure out if he believed this any more than he did her previous story.

"I don't," Baba said in a calm tone. "But I like Belinda, and I want to help."

Liam was confused. "Are you some kind of private detective?"

"Not at all," she said, gesturing at the table and the cue he was holding. "I'm a professor and an herbalist. Were you going to take another shot anytime soon?"

He drew in a deep breath through his nose, trying to curb the impulse to strangle her with her own flowing locks. *Odd, mysterious, and infuriating.* The woman was going to drive him insane. Even when she was telling the truth, he couldn't get a straight answer out of her.

He bent over the table, and said without looking at her, "You need to stay out of police business, *Professor* Yager. Stick to your herbs. I'll take care of Belinda and her family."

"Really?" Baba drew out the word in a voice that lowered the temperature of the room about twenty degrees. "Because it seems to me that you can use all the help you can get.

Since, as you yourself said, you have *nothing*." The last word was squeezed through gritted teeth, and the sharp edges of it caused his fingers to slip on the cue, sending the cue ball bouncing uselessly off empty air.

Baba stared at him for a moment and then took her shot—and all the ones that came after, dropping striped balls into the pockets with the precision of a surgeon.

"Three days," she said, emptying her beer bottle and setting it down on the side wall ledge with a decisive click. "Had enough yet?"

Liam shook his head and plucked the white plastic triangle off its hook, arranging the balls in silence. He fought back fury at her implication that he couldn't protect his own people. More because it felt true at the moment than because it wasn't. Around them, laughter and petty quarrels echoed from the other tables where people played for fun and not in a battle for . . . whatever it was they were battling for. He wasn't sure either of them knew.

A bright green ball slid into dingy white netting. Dozens of questions vied to be next, but what came out of his mouth was, "Are you married?" He could feel the tips of his ears burn. For once he was thankful he still hadn't had time to get his hair trimmed.

Baba's eyes widened in surprise. That was some consolation.

"I mean, do you have a significant other? You know, someone I should contact in case you get into trouble with the law?" Something he was almost completely certain would happen sooner or later.

She opened her mouth to answer, but whatever she was going to say was drowned out by the sound of roaring as a bevy of motorcycles glided by the window, shaking the brick walls so hard, Baba's empty bottle fell over and rolled onto the floor.

Over by the back door, kept propped open for air and so the smokers could run outside for a quick puff between games, a waitress named Ellie peeked her head out cautiously and withdrew it, looking for all the world like a startled turtle.

"Oh my god!" she squeaked, almost dropping the tray of glasses she carried. "We've been invaded by a motorcycle gang!"

Liam walked over and looked out the door himself, Baba and most of the others in the room peering over his shoulder. He saw three bikes gleaming in the light from the solitary street lamp: a luminous white Yamaha, a hulking black Harley, and between them, looking like a thoroughbred between a show pony and a Clydesdale, a low-slung red Ducati. There was no sign of their riders, who had undoubtedly walked around to enter through the front of the bar.

Liam rolled his eyes and suppressed a sigh. "Three motorcycles is hardly a 'gang,' Ellie," he said. "There are more bikes than that parked in the front lot; I'm pretty sure I saw the Kirk brothers come in on theirs, and plenty of folks around here ride." He gave the crowd his professional "move along, nothing to see here" smile.

Ellie scowled at him, her thirtysomething face already looking middle-aged after a decade of dealing with rowdy drunks and too many late nights.

"I've never seen those motorcycles before, Sheriff. And three may not be a gang, but it sure as hell can be trouble." She sniffed, empty bottles and abandoned glasses clinking together on her tray as she slammed them down on her way out of the room.

"I guess I'd better go see what the cat dragged in," Liam said, leaning his cue against the wall in resignation. "I'll be back in a minute."

Baba trailed out behind him, the beginnings of a smile starting to form on her lips. "I'll come with you. I have a feeling I know who your visitors are." At his questioning look, the smile grew a fraction wider, but she didn't say anything else.

They got into the main room just in time to see three men enter the bar and take a few steps inside, looking around as if searching for someone. The first man was tall, slim, and elegant in the slightly too-handsome manner of a movie star or a Tolkien elf. He wore his blond hair long and loose, touching his broad shoulders, and his white jeans and white linen shirt were so spotless, they shone like the sun on water. Women all around the room suddenly found a reason to touch up their lipstick.

The man next to him was shorter, with long black hair pulled back in a tail, and the dark slanted eyes, flat cheekbones, and Fu Manchu mustache of the Mongolian desert. He moved with the loose gait of a man who knows many martial arts and has mastered them all, and the red leather jumpsuit he wore fit him like a second skin.

Their companion made them both look almost ordinary; a massive giant of a man with coarse brown hair and a braided beard, wearing a black leather jacket that jangled with silver chains, worn black jeans, and dusty boots that Liam could have fit both of his feet into with room left over to spare.

They all looked attractive, confident . . . and dangerous. Liam could feel his muscles tighten in response, like an alpha dog whose territory has suddenly been invaded. When they crossed the room to stand in front of Baba, it was all he could do not to growl.

The blond man swept down in a graceful bow. "Baba Yaga, how lovely to see you. You are looking as glorious as always." The Asian man snorted, but both he and the walking mountain standing next to him inclined their heads briefly.

"Yager," Baba corrected. "Barbara Yager. No nicknames here." But Liam was disconcerted to see her wearing the first broad smile he'd ever seen on her face. "You are very prompt. I wasn't expecting you for a few days. Tomorrow at the earliest."

The big man grimaced. "We were sitting around with nothing to do in Kansas City. Believe me, we were happy for a reason to leave." Unlike Baba, he spoke with a very strong accent. *Were* sounded like *vere*. Liam suddenly felt like an extra in the movie *The Russians Are Coming, the*

Russians Are Coming. He looked around to see if anyone else had noticed, but the room was so loud, the three could have been speaking in pig Latin and no one would have heard it.

Liam cleared his throat. "Friends of yours?" he asked.

"More like employees. They work for me, on and off." Baba patted the blond man on one shoulder, and Liam spotted what looked like a tattoo of a white dragon curled around his collarbone with its face peeking slyly from underneath the elegant linen shirt.

He raised one eyebrow. "Really? And what does an herbalist college professor need with a three-man private army? What do they do for you, go into the woods and pick pretty flowers?"

The huge man scowled and bared his teeth, but Baba just laughed. "If I ask them to." She waved one languid hand from left to right, blond to black to brown.

"Meet my Bright Dawn, my Red Sun, and my Dark Midnight. This handsome fellow is Mikhail Day." The blond man bowed to Liam, who only narrowly restrained himself from bowing back, and no doubt looking like a fool in the process.

"Gregori Sun," she said, and the Asian man put his palms together over his heart and tilted his head. "And this large person is Alexei Knight." The big man, who must have been at least six foot eight, and as wide as the other two put together, just stared at Liam, his eyes narrowed as if he was trying to calculate the force it would require to snap the smaller man in half.

Baba either didn't notice his attitude, or didn't care. "Boys," she said, "meet Sheriff Liam McClellan. He's the law here, and a good man. Try not to piss him off."

Liam was torn between ridiculous pleasure at being named a "good man" and irritation at what were clearly more secrets and lies from Baba. Whose last name might or might not be Yager.

The balance slid heavily in the direction of displeasure when she added, "Sorry about our game, Sheriff. We'll have to play again some other time," then walked off without a backward glance. She hummed as she went, and the few folks who had been staring at them suddenly seemed to lose all interest in the visitors, turning back to their beers and their conversations.

As the odd quartet made their way across the bar and out the front door, Liam realized two things that made his already dismal mood turn dark and stormy: inexplicably, he was actually feeling a little bit jealous. And Baba had never answered his last question.

BABA SCRATCHED CHUDO-YUDO idly behind the ears as she explained the situation to the White Rider, the Red Rider, and the Black Rider. Pledged to the service of the Baba Yagas, even Baba herself didn't know exactly what kind of creatures they were behind their human masks. All she knew for certain was that they were immortal, powerful, and on her side. At the moment, that was more than enough.

"So," Mikhail drawled, leaning forward to look at the laptop on the table in front of them. He and Gregori were tucked into the banquette seats with Baba. Alexei, whose bulk would never have fit in the limited space, had propped himself against the counter across the way. Baba thought she heard the trailer groan slightly as it adjusted to his weight.

Mikhail went on, recapping what Baba had just spent twenty minutes telling them in one brutal sentence. "You're saying we have three children who have mysteriously disappeared with no explanation, a disturbance in the balance of the natural world that may or may not be related to Human gas drilling, and some woman wearing a glamour who you *think* may have used magic to disrupt a town meeting."

He gestured at the pictures of the children on the screen in front of him with one manicured finger. "I can see why you called us in. This is a mess." The accent that sometimes sounded harsh coming from the other two turned to music when it came from his well-formed mouth, but didn't make his words any less painful.

Baba breathed in and out through her long nose, striving for an equanimity she didn't feel. She always had a hard time maintaining her emotional distance—part of a Baba's job description—when children were involved.

She tapped the photo of Mary Elizabeth Shields, clearly visible in the article posted by the local newspaper. Sometimes Baba thought the Internet was more amazing than magic; or at least more mystifying. As much as she disliked and distrusted modern technology, computers had proven to be more enticement than she could resist. The ability to do research wherever she was had won her over, although the rest of the time the laptop lived in a cabinet with some old books and Chudo-Yudo's spare water bowl.

"This child is the one we are specifically looking for. Her grandmother is from the Old Country and knew enough to call me in. And her mother asked nicely and agreed to my terms; the bargain is made with her. But if you see any of the other missing children in your travels, I want to know immediately." Her full lips drew together in a thin line.

Gregori shrugged. "I suspect that if we find them at all, it will be together. It would be too much of a coincidence for three children to disappear at the same time. Unless the first one gave someone else ideas, I suppose."

"Yes, but that person may have split the kids up and sent them elsewhere," Alexei disagreed, his voice a low rumble that made the windows rattle. "Or disposed of their bodies, I suppose."

Under her hand, Chudo-Yudo stiffened, and Baba patted his head with tense fingers. "That is, of course, a possibility. But for now, I am assuming they are still alive and in need of rescue. I want you three to go out into the local area—and as far afield as you think reasonable—and look for them."

"If the children are anywhere to be found, we will find them," Gregori said with finality. "This Maya woman is using enchantments of some kind; are you assuming she is somehow connected to the Otherworld? Or could she just be a local witch who is using them for dark rituals? Such people do exist, after all."

Baba's stomach clenched, the stone that had taken up residence within growing larger by the minute. "I'm going to have a little talk with her," she said through gritted teeth. "We'll see what she has to say about all of this. But the magic felt like ours, not something Human, as much as I could tell across the room. And she felt like . . . more, somehow."

"If she's using them to fuel evil, the process might change them beyond recognition, if they even survive at all," Alexei added, his gray eyes fixed meaningfully on Baba. He'd been around when she was growing up; he'd watched the old Baba raise her, and seen her move further and further from her human roots as the magic she learned changed and twisted her body and spirit in ways that were no less powerful for being invisible.

Baba shook herself like Chudo-Yudo after a bath, throwing off the gathering gloom that threatened to cloak her in despair. "Well, we can only do what we can do. You boys go have a look and see if you can spot anything the sheriff missed. I'll tackle pretty Miss Maya tomorrow. Check in if you find anything."

"I might keep an eye on our mysterious lady myself," Gregori said, quiet menace emanating from his slender form. "See if I can spot her doing something incriminating."

Baba nodded, but said, "Keep out of sight, Gregori. You were all seen with me at the tavern, unfortunately, so she'll know who you are. And keep away from the locals—I've already had people down at the local diner ask me if I was related to the Ivanovs, because we all have Russian accents." She frowned at this, since she'd been certain hers was so faint as to be nearly undetectable. Apparently not. "The last thing we need is a bunch of people wondering why the place has suddenly been overrun with foreigners."

He blinked at her, unspoken reproach in the tiny movement.

"Right, sorry. What was I thinking?" She grinned. "If you don't want her to see you, she won't."

"And I have no desire to mingle with the peasants," Gregori said. "We leave such things to you, dearest Baba."

"About that sheriff," Mikhail winked at her as he got up from the table. "You know he likes you, right?"

She would have said she didn't remember how to blush. She would have been wrong. Heat flooded her cheeks as she shook her head. "Don't be absurd. I'm his biggest suspect."

Laughter rumbled its way out of Alexei's huge chest. "Doesn't mean he doesn't like you, Baba." He chucked her under the chin like he used to when she was only as tall as his knees. "You grew up to be a beautiful woman. Men are attracted to you all the time; you just don't notice."

"She noticed this time," Mikhail teased, and Chudo-Yudo let out a barking laugh.

"Oh, get out of here," Baba said with asperity. "Go do your jobs and stop trying to provoke me. Just because you're immortal doesn't mean I can't turn you into toads and lock you in a golden cage for a decade or two."

"You only did that once," Gregori pointed out. "And the guy *was* trying to kill you at the time."

"So maybe I need more practice," Baba snapped. "Who wants to go first?"

The three Riders all left in a hurry, the sound of their engines lingering in the air like a symphony of metal, magic, and mayhem waiting to happen.

SEVEN

BABA CHANGED INTO a short red silk chemise and settled into a tapestry-covered chair, trying to calm her frazzled nerves with a good book and a glass of merlot from a winery in the Napa Valley whose vineyards she'd saved from a pixy infestation. The owners, a pair of old hippies whose years of acid use allowed them to see things most people didn't, gratefully sent her a few of their best bottles every year.

She sipped it from an old silver chalice, a gift from another grateful client, enjoying the velvet texture and hints of rich oak backed by notes of plum and cherry. With her bare feet resting on Chudo-Yudo's broad back and the mellow buzz of the wine floating through her veins, she finally began to relax for the first time that day.

Naturally, someone chose that moment to knock on the door.

"Gah," she said, sliding her feet to the floor with a thump. "You have *got* to be kidding me." Chudo-Yudo snorted a laugh as she got up and stomped over to the front door. "If that's some local yokel wanting a cure for his warts, I swear I'll kill him and bury him in the backyard!"

"You only did that once," Chudo-Yudo said, his muzzle gaping open in a doggy grin. "And that guy was trying to kill you too."

"Oh, shut up," Baba muttered. Nobody gave her enough credit for being bloodthirsty. She yanked open the door and said in an unwelcoming tone, "What?" But the space in front of the Airstream was empty.

"Huh," she said, and closed the door. "That's odd."

She went back over and sat down again, but as soon as she picked up her goblet, the sound of rapping echoed through the trailer. Baba scowled and got up again, bare feet padding across the antique Oriental carpet. She'd reached her hand out to turn the knob, when Chudo-Yudo said, "Uh, Baba? Wrong door."

She looked at him. "You could have told me that the first time."

He wandered over to stand in front of the closet that led to the Otherworld. "What fun would that have been?"

Baba rolled her eyes, nudging him with her toe to get him to move out of her way. Irritation made sparks fly into the night air when she rattled the tricky handle and yanked the door open. But her bad mood fled like a startled rabbit when she saw who was on the other side.

"I don't believe it!" she exclaimed, and threw her arms around the last person she expected to see—and the one she needed the most, right at that very minute.

KOSHEI HUGGED HER back, grinning from ear to ear and looking as devilishly handsome as always. His short, dark hair curled endearingly over his forehead, accenting his light blue eyes and high cheekbones. The close-cropped, neatly trimmed beard and mustache gave him the look of a Roman Centurion who'd wandered out of a storybook into a time not his own; fitting, of course, for the long-lived dragon, who had undoubtedly meandered in and out of many a legend before winding up in the middle of hers.

"My darling Baba," he said, nibbling lightly on her neck

before releasing her and standing back to have a good look at her. "I've missed you too." Mischief flashed in his dark irises as he took in her attire.

Baba rolled her eyes, moving away to a marginally safer distance. Not that any distance was safe when Koshei was around. She thought it was unlikely that he'd actually missed her—or noticed how long it had been since they'd seen each other, for that matter. But it was nice of him to say so.

Koshei had been the companion of the Baba before her; for all she knew, he'd been the companion of all the Babas in their line back down through history. After all, dragons could live for a very long time, even without magical assistance. Humans might think the arrangement was strange, but the Babas existed in a different world that went by very different rules. And in that world, which was often a harsh and unforgiving place, you took your pleasure where you could find it.

Koshei glanced around the Airstream, taking in the empty beer bottles and grease-stained pizza boxes the Riders had left behind. "I'm hurt," he said, without any evidence to demonstrate his claim. "You had a party and didn't invite me." Chudo-Yudo snorted with amusement and strolled over to open the fridge with his large teeth, miraculously fetching their visitor a beer without breaking it into sharp-edged shards.

"Good dog," Koshei said with a straight face, giving Chudo-Yudo the treat he'd had tucked in the pocket of his tailored charcoal-hued pants. "Nice to see you, old friend."

"Oh, don't encourage him," Baba scolded. "You know perfectly well he can only pull that off about a third of the time. The rest of the time I'm left cleaning up a big mess."

Koshei wrapped one muscular arm around her and smiled cheerfully. "What are you complaining about? You can use magic to clear the place up in a split second. Besides, it's not like I'm trusting him to carry the Water of Life and Death." He looked at her meaningfully.

"Fine," she said, sliding out of his embrace long enough to find two miniscule glasses and get the Water of Life and Death out of the fridge. At Chudo-Yudo's indignant *whoof*, she added a small bowl to her treasure trove and returned to sit on the couch next to Koshei. "Just a tiny bit for each of us—the queen doesn't hand this stuff out like a party favor, you know."

Golden fire shimmered in effervescent droplets as she poured a precious measure of the liquid from its enchanted flask into each of their cups. The aroma of a perfect spring day filled the trailer, smelling like meadows and seashores and youthful ardor. Baba let one heavenly sip lie on her tongue; it tasted of sunshine and flowers, with a slight aftertaste of dust and decay. Her eyes closed as the power of it overwhelmed her senses for one long, timeless moment, suspending her between the worlds of forever and perhaps.

Koshei made a sound like a boulder crashing down a hillside. "Gods, that's good." He leaned his head back, pale cheeks flushed with the aftermath of drinking an elixir that both extended life and aroused it. When he looked at Baba again, myriad gold flecks were mirrored in his eyes. A playful smile tugged at sensual lips in a way that made Baba remember all over again why she had been so glad to see him walking through the wardrobe door.

"So, do you want to tell me what is going on that required you to call in the Riders?" he asked, flicking an empty cardboard box with one long finger. "Is there anything I can help with?" He moved his hand to slide up over her thigh, playing with the edge of the silk that lay there. "Things have been way too quiet lately. I'm bored."

Baba touched her tongue to her lower lip, trying to catch one last hint of sublime sweetness before returning to harsh reality. The eternal energy of the Water pulsed hotly in her veins, distracting her from the current crisis and making her think of dark caves and passionate lovemaking in the long nights of the Otherworld.

She took a deep breath to try to focus and explained the situation with the missing children to Koshei as succinctly as she could while still listening to infinity echoing at the back of her mind.

"If you want to help," she said finally, gazing up at him and finding the expression she expected—patient, listening, and a little bit amused at her concern for the mayfly lives of humans, "you could have a look around the Otherworld when you go back. See if you can find out who my mysterious woman might be. I'm guessing she's a local witch with unusual power, but she had a touch of the Otherworld about her, so maybe someone from the other side has had some dealings with her."

One broad shoulder lifted in a shrug as calloused fingers moved to cup her bottom and lift her onto his lap. "I'm happy to do it," he said, scorching her with his glance. "But it is going to be a little difficult to track her down if you've never seen her without her glamour. For all you know, she isn't even a she." He muffled a short laugh into the skin over her collarbone, licking a line of fire across her body.

Baba's breath caught on a sigh. From under closed lids, she teased him by saying, "So, you don't think you can find out who she is? Pity. I should have asked one of the Riders to find out."

Koshei snorted, lifting his mouth from her tender skin just in time to keep the flames from singeing her. "Foolish girl. Of course I will find her. In the morning. For now, I have better things to do." He smiled his devilish smile and caught her mouth in a deep, passionate kiss that made her want to dance naked under the moonlight on a distant shore, while drums beat and torches flared.

And then, for some inexplicable reason, Liam's face rose up in her mind, like water thrown on a bonfire; cool and dousing, reminding her that she was supposed to be doing a job. She pulled back from the kiss abruptly, blinking as if drawn back from a dim cavern into bright daylight.

Koshei roared with laughter at the confusion on her face. "You've met someone," he said, an unholy glee lighting up his already bright eyes. "Someone who has taken root in that impenetrable heart of yours. It's about time."

Baba shook her head, trying to settle her thoughts back into their comfortable patterns. "No. Well, maybe. He's a Human."

The dragon tilted her chin with one gentle hand. "You're Human too, darling Baba, for all that you try to deny it. If you like him, have a fling. That's what the Humans call it, right?" His lips curved in an almost-wistful smile. "Spend a little time with him. Enjoy him while you can. That's what Babas do, when they find a man who attracts them. There is no need to make it so complicated. "

Baba sighed. "He's not the type to have a fling, Koshei. And I'm everything he can't stand; chaos to his lawfulness, lies instead of truth. I don't stay in one place, and he never leaves this one. And I'm not sure his heart isn't already given elsewhere." She snuggled against Koshei's reassuring warmth, enjoying the familiar feeling of his rock-hard chest beneath her cheek. "Besides, he knows I'm hiding something. He's the sheriff investigating the children's disappearances, and I'm pretty sure he thinks I'm involved."

A puff of sulfur-scented breath moved her hair restlessly. "Well, that's inconvenient, isn't it?" She could feel his lips move in a sympathetic smile on the top of her head before he tipped her face back so she could see the affection in his deep, pale eyes.

"I do not know this man," Koshei said, his voice a quiet rumble in her ears. "But if he cannot see your value, then he does not deserve to have you." He pulled her into a hug and slid his lips gently across hers. "I, on the other hand, appreciate you very, very much. I shall miss our nights together." He laughed as he released her and headed back toward the closet door.

Baba opened her mouth to protest and then closed it again with a snap. Damn that sheriff. Even when he wasn't around, he was causing her trouble.

BABA LURKED IN the gnarled shadow of an old oak outside the stately blue-and-gray Victorian that housed the East Shoreham Oil and Gas Company's regional office. She'd seen Peter Callahan leave half an hour ago, dapper and well pressed even at the end of a hot summer's day. He'd gotten into a buttercup-yellow Jaguar and driven away, leaving behind him the lingering taint of exhaust fumes and dirty money.

The lights finally switched off behind the louvered windows of the only room that still showed any signs of occupation, and a few minutes later the *tap, tap, tap* of stiletto heels and the snick of a lock heralded the arrival of the woman Baba had been hoping to see. She waited for Maya to put one hand on the door of her sedate rental car before popping up out of the background like a spring-loaded trap.

"My goodness!" the blond woman said, clutching her chest in apparent alarm. "You startled me." Piercing gray eyes hid behind fluttering mascara-laden lashes.

Baba snorted. "Don't be ridiculous. You probably knew I was here as soon as I hit the street." Amber dueled with gray; the result—a draw. For now.

"Well, you're not exactly subtle, are you?" the woman calling herself Maya said, pert button nose wrinkled in distaste. "I've met ogres who were less obvious. You really need to rein in your power a little bit more. Even these idiotic mortals will figure out there is something odd about you sooner or later. And then where will the rest of us be?"

"I don't know about anyone else," Baba said, "but you're going to be gone from this place, so it won't make a bit of difference to you what the locals figure out."

She was five inches taller than the other woman, even with the stiltlike heels Maya had on, but the seemingly delicate form didn't appear to be at all intimidated. Of course, behind her glamour, she could have been a ten-foot-tall, cyclops with fangs, for all Baba could tell.

Maya pouted prettily. "I don't know why you have to be so difficult. I was here first, after all. And I'm not doing anything to you. Why don't you just leave me be and go about your business?"

"Because you're stealing Human children," Baba said. "I have a problem with that. Which means you have a problem with me."

"That's a pity," Maya said, dropping the sweetness from

her voice and letting the venom slide through. At their feet, the weeds poking through the sidewalk withered and died; nearby grass turned brown in sympathy. "You see, I have things in motion here that are too big to stop, and I have no intention of leaving until I have everything I came for." She glared at Baba. "Why don't you just run off and fix those horrible wildfires in Wyoming. Surely they need a Baba Yaga there more than this tiny, insignificant town does."

Baba shrugged. "One of my sisters is already dealing with that. I think I'll just stay here and fix you instead." Her steady look made it clear that she had a permanent solution in mind, if that was what turned out to be necessary. Suppressed power crackled at her fingertips, and even the brash Maya paled briefly as the trees around them swayed.

"Tell me what you've done with the missing children and how to get them back, and I'll allow you to leave this town unscathed," Baba added.

Glee flitted across the little blonde's visage, although it was quickly replaced by a more cautious cunning. "You don't even know where they are, do you?" Maya said, licking her crimson lips. "You probably didn't even know for sure I was involved."

Baba gave a wolfish smile, completely lacking in humor. "But I know now, don't I?" she said softly. "So I suggest you simply hand them over and count yourself lucky that I'm letting you off with a warning."

Maya sneered. "Warn me all you want, Baba Yaga. Those children are far beyond even your reach now, dead and buried and rotting in the ground with the rest of the trash. And you'd better stay out of my way if you know what's good for you. I can make things very difficult for you, otherwise. I've been amassing power and influence in this area for months. You have nothing but a worn-out old dog and that shiny tin can you call a house."

Baba's fingers twitched with the desire to reach out and slap the smugness right off her adversary's pretty little face, but there were people walking by across the street, so she restrained herself. Barely. Nobody insulted her house. Not even in the old days when it was a wooden hut running around on oversized chicken legs.

"I have an ally or two of my own," she said calmly. "I am not without friends."

"Ha," Maya retorted. "I hope you're not depending on that pathetic sheriff to help you. He can't even do his job, and he doesn't want a woman like you. He's a broken man going through the motions, that's all; he's no threat to me or my interests." She tossed her head, glittering chandelier earrings bouncing against her swanlike neck. "He has to do what his bosses tell him, and Peter Callahan owns them all."

An unpleasant smirk held the echo of pointy teeth. "And I own Peter Callahan, even if he hasn't realized it yet. So I advise *you* to leave town while you still can. You may be stronger and tougher than most Humans, but Babas aren't immortal. You might want to keep that in mind."

With that, Maya slid into her car, slammed the door, and peeled out of her spot, not even bothering to look for on-coming cars driven by insignificant mortals.

Baba sighed, watching her leave. *That could have gone better.* On the other hand, at least she knew for certain that Maya was behind the disappearances. And that somewhere, the children were alive and well. Maya may be great at disguising herself and excel at making friends in low places, but thankfully, she was a terrible liar.

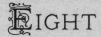IGHT

BABA SPENT THE rest of the evening riding around Clearwater County and checking on the land; now that she was well and truly involved, she thought it was best to get a feel for the essence of the place. Part of a Baba Yaga's gift was the ability to tune in to and manipulate the elements: earth, air, fire, and water. In some places in the Old World, they had even been viewed as goddesses, although the old Baba used to say that it was better to be an herbalist—less responsibility and shorter hours.

Most of the county was lush and lovely, green and verdant in the waning summer sunlight. Waving rows of corn murmured at her as she passed, and cows trotted their calves over to the field's edge to show them off, lowing proudly over black-spotted rumps and twitching tails. Red-tailed hawks soared on thermals above her as they headed for their evening roosts.

But there were places where an encroaching darkness showed to her acute senses as blemishes on the otherwise healthy landscape. Here, a stream where toxic minerals leached in from below, studding the water with pockets of slimy gray algae. There, trees hacked down and fields lying ruined and fallow as the debate over their future raged in meetings like the one she'd attended. Even if the county passed the ban on future fracking, it was too late for some places, where it would take decades for the scarred land to repair itself. The damage made her sick to her stomach, and echoes of bad dreams haunted her like the voices of the damned.

Acid anger boiled in her veins. No matter how long she lived, she could never get used to the callous disregard with which so many humans treated the natural world. Perhaps because their lives were so short, and therefore none would be around to reap the disastrous harvest of their shortsighted choices.

As the dusk slowly hid the countryside from view, she turned her headlights back in the direction of the Airstream, looking forward to a cold beer and an evening spent in an environment that didn't cry out piteously for her to heal it. She slowed her usual precipitous speed as she turned onto the dusty back road. It was long and winding and its gravel surface was pockmarked with ruts and holes. Even she wasn't crazy enough to take *that* road at full bore.

Which was probably all that saved her.

Her only warning was a flash of shimmering antlers as an enormous golden stag raced across her path, kicking up dirt and greenery as it charged directly in front of her, a blur of hide and horn and incredible mass. She yanked the handlebars sharply to one side, veering out of its way, braking and swearing and feeling the bike go down in a sickening nightmare of churning wheels, scraping metal, and the agonizing impact of body against ground.

She lay there for a moment, the breath knocked out of her, heart racing, then reached out one gloved hand to turn the key off and allow the tortured engine to tick slowly over into silence. Of the stag, there was no sign. Cicadas buzzed in the underbrush, the dust from the road tickled her nose. She could feel blood oozing slowly from a scrape along her jaw line, although her helmet had done its job protecting her head.

Slowly, she levered herself up into a sitting position, counting bones and finding them all in place. Her worst injuries seemed to be where her left side had scraped against the gravel as she'd gone down; both elbow and knee were bleeding and bruised, the leather that had covered them torn away by the force of the skid. Still, without the leathers, most of her skin would have been shredded instead, so she had no complaints. It hurt like hell now, of course, the throb of it pulsing in her veins, but by tomorrow she'd be mostly healed, and in a few days there would be no sign she'd been in an accident at all.

Her beloved BMW, however, was another story.

She knelt down by the mangled remains of her motorcycle and patted it gently, as one would a wounded horse. Unshed tears burned against the back of her eyelids. She could use magic to fix her clothes and a few sips of the Water of Life and Death to speed up her own already accelerated healing, but metal was resistant to enchantment. It had been hard enough to convince it to leave its original oversized flying mortar-and-pestle form; once it had taken the shape of a motorcycle, it became vulnerable to the human world, its only magic an ability to travel faster than should have been possible.

The rear wheel still spun lazily, turning in lopsided circles as if to say *let's get out of here*. But the crooked handlebars and crumpled front fender made it clear that her poor, beautiful bike wasn't going anywhere anytime soon. The front tire was already sagging, and the acrid smell of burned rubber assailed the flower-scented summer air and gave her an excuse for her stinging eyes.

"I'm sorry, Old Thing," she said, patting it again before rising as creakily as if she'd suddenly manifested her true age to drag the battered motorcycle the rest of the way off of the road. "I'll come back for you tomorrow at first light and see what I can do."

She limped away down the verge without looking back, cursing Maya Freeman with every aching step and ragged breath. Each time her booted foot hit the ground, cut-glass shards of pain shot through her knee and jarred the elbow she hugged close to her body. The discomfort barely registered, though, drowned out by the fury that beat like a wild bird against the inside of her chest. That stag was no normal animal—it had either been sent by Maya, or possibly, even been Maya herself in another form or wearing another glamour.

The bitch had tried to kill her. This was war.

LIAM DROVE SLOWLY down the long, narrow county highway. Half of his awareness was absorbed by the unpleasant errand that brought him out there, the other half searched the sides of the road for any signs of a lost child, more out of obsessive habit than any conscious intention. His tortoise pace, born of reluctance as much as caution, and that constant, darting sideways glance, were the only reasons he saw the motorcycle at all.

A glint of something foreign and metallic caught in his headlights in the increasing dusk gloom, and he pulled over as much as was possible on a road that barely fit two cars side by side. Wildflowers brushed the passenger side, leaving smeary golden kisses along the neat blue paint. Flashers sending crimson warning signals into the night, he opened the door of the cruiser and walked over to examine his find more closely.

The air whooshed out of his lungs as if he'd been suckerpunched when he recognized the mangled remains of Baba's classic BMW. The lack of an equally damaged body was somewhat reassuring, although he fetched a flashlight from the car and searched for any signs of a wounded woman staggering around, lost and confused. When he didn't find her, he called in to dispatch to find out if the accident had been reported or if Baba had turned up at the local hospital. Two negatives later, he put in a call to Bob at the auto shop, then got back in his squad car to go look for her.

No more than three minutes later, the glow from his headlights picked out a limping figure moving determinedly in the direction of the clearing where the Airstream was parked. This time he didn't even bother to pull over, just eased to a stop and opened the passenger door.

"Good evening," he said cordially.

"The hell it is," Baba retorted, scowling into the dim recesses of the car. "It's a lousy evening, in fact."

Liam smothered a relieved laugh. She sounded too grumpy to be seriously injured. "I know. I saw your bike a little way down the road. Are you hurt? It looked like you took one heck of a spill."

She gave an abortive shrug, stopping the move in midmotion and clutching her elbow. "I'm fine. But my poor motorcycle is a mess." It looked as though even saying the words pained her, although that might have been the elbow. With Baba, it was hard to tell.

"Get in," Liam said. "I'll drive you the rest of the way." When she looked as though she was going to argue, he added, "I needed to talk to you anyway." And at her deepening glower, "I know, I know—I promised you three days. But something's come up. Now get in the damned car before I get out and throw you in."

"You and what army?" the cloud-haired woman muttered. But she slid into the seat, suppressing a wince as she did so.

When they pulled up in front of the trailer a couple of minutes later, she hauled herself out of the squad car and shuffled lopsidedly toward the front door before he could even try to help her. Liam heaved a sigh and followed her in. Chudo-Yudo sauntered over to meet them, sniffing at Baba's ruined pants and whining. She said something in Russian and the dog barked a couple of times. It sounded for all the world like they were having a conversation.

"Hello, Chudo-Yudo," Liam said, not wanting to be left out. Besides, if she wouldn't let him be nice to her, maybe he could get a couple of brownie points being nice to her dog. "How are you tonight?"

Chudo-Yudo sniffed him too, then licked his hand and woofed enthusiastically.

"At least your dog likes me," he said to Baba, trying to check out the damage without being obvious about it. If he had to, he'd haul her to the emergency room, but something told him he'd need the cuffs to do it.

Baba rolled her eyes at him. "Don't bet on it. He just thinks you smell like hamburger."

He'd grabbed fast food on the way out here, but how could—ah. "Very funny. You saw the empty takeout bag in the car. Nice one, though. You almost had me believing you had a talking dog."

"He's not a talking dog," Baba muttered. "He's a talking dragon that looks like a dog. That's much more unusual." She hobbled to the sink and got a glass of water, wincing a little when it touched a cut on her lip.

Liam ignored her silliness. She was clearly trying to distract him. Or maybe she had a concussion. He eyed her intently. "Do you want to tell me what happened?"

She put the empty glass down and turned back around to face him, leaning against the counter to take the weight off her bad leg. "A huge golden stag ran me off the road." She said it like she didn't expect him to believe her.

"A stag?" he said, confused. "Wait, you mean a deer?" Finally, something that made sense. "We have a lot of problems out here with deer-versus-vehicle accidents. Sometimes the deer loses, sometimes the motorists does. And that's when the driver is in a car or a truck. On that bike, you're lucky you weren't killed." His heart clenched at the sudden image of the scene he *could* have come upon, sending out a grateful thought to a god he didn't worship anymore.

"Yes," she said dryly. "Someone is going to be *very* disappointed."

As he tried to figure that one out, she took a shaky yet still somehow threatening step forward. "Not that I don't appreciate the ride back, but why are you here? I thought we had a deal that you were going to leave me alone for three days. It's barely been one."

"I got called in to Peter Callahan's office. His assistant Maya wanted to lodge a harassment complaint against you."

Liam frowned at Baba. "She says you accosted her in the parking lot, made all sorts of crazy accusations. Callahan wanted to have you arrested, but I managed to convince him to settle for a warning and a suggestion that you leave the area." He shook his head, frustrated. "What the hell were you thinking?"

A red flush spread across Baba's high cheekbones and her nostrils flared. "Are you serious? First the woman tries to kill me, and then she sics the law on me?" Her accent grew markedly stronger as her voice rose, and she added a few words in Russian that Liam didn't need a translator to know were probably extremely rude.

Liam stared at her. "Do you know your eyes are glowing?" he asked in a level tone. It must have been a trick of the light, but it was a little freaky. And what was that "tried to kill me" comment all about? They were clearly back to odd, mysterious, and infuriating. Or at the moment, infuriated.

Baba made an obvious effort to calm down, breathing in and out through her nose a few times and clenching and unclenching her hands.

"Sorry. I need to work on my temper."

"You *need* to stay out of these people's way," he said flatly. "They're very powerful around here."

Baba gave him an assessing look, her amber eyes back to their normal piercing stare. It made him feel a little like a bug under a microscope.

"The charming Maya told me that her boss owns the people who run the town—is that true?"

Somehow he thought there was a question there she wasn't asking out loud.

He shrugged. "Maybe. Maybe not. They certainly seem to have a lot of influence these days. I just try to do my job and stay out of the politics. At the moment, I seem to be succeeding." He volleyed the hairy eyeball back in her direction. "By the way, do you realize you're bleeding all over your fancy rug? You should have told me you were seriously hurt. Let me take you to the hospital."

"Pah," she said, curling her lip in a way he found perversely adorable. "It's not that bad. I'm a fast healer."

Liam sighed. He didn't know for sure who Barbara Yager was, but one thing was certain: she was the most stubborn woman he'd ever met.

"Fine. Tell me where you keep your first aid kit and I'll patch you up myself."

She gave him a blank look.

"Right. Of course you don't have a first aid kit. You probably just put herbs on whatever cuts and burns you get." He sighed again. "Why don't you get out of those torn leathers and into a tee shirt and a pair of shorts, and get me a bowl of warm water and a clean cloth. I'll go fetch my kit from the car."

He was almost out the door when she said, "Lavender and aloe for the burns. Maybe honey, depending on the cut. It's antibacterial, you know."

Great. Now he had a mental image of her smeared with honey. He was never going to be able to use the stuff on his toast again.

WHEN HE CAME back in, Baba was sitting on the couch, her bad leg up on the dog's furry back and a bottle of beer in her right hand. The tank top and shorts she wore did a nice job of exposing the extent of the road rash on her left side, and Liam hissed through his teeth in sympathy at the sight.

"That's got to smart," he said, trying not to stare at her long, slim thighs. The bright red blood dripping from her left knee proved to be distracting enough. "Are you *sure* you don't want me to take you to the emergency room?"

Baba shook her head. "Machines instead of medicine; no thank you. I told you—I'm a fast healer. A couple of these," she lifted her beer, "and a good night's sleep, and I'll be fine."

"Right. I don't think so." He found a silver bowl and a linen cloth where she'd placed them on the counter, and winced at putting them to such rough usage. Who kept silver bowls in an RV, anyway? Apparently the woman who was currently oozing blood all over a velvet-covered sofa without a qualm.

He placed the bowl and his first aid kit on the coffee table and got to work, perched next to Baba on the edge of the couch. The scrape along her jaw looked raw and sore, and he had to fight the temptation to kiss it and make it better, settling for a little antibiotic ointment instead. He tried to be as gentle as possible, but the knee and elbow were both full of gravel that had to be cleaned out before he could bandage them. Baba's face was white and set; she looked like some classical European statue of a goddess. If the goddess was covered with bruises and had black tar and grit ground into her skin.

"It's a good thing you wear leathers," Liam said as he picked out a couple of deeply embedded bits of stone with a pair of tweezers that looked tiny in his big hands. "This could have been a lot worse." He blotted away a fresh up-welling of blood and winced. "Not that it isn't bad enough. I'm sorry if I'm hurting you."

Baba shrugged, although he noticed she took a long pull on her beer before saying, "My adoptive mother had a saying about such things." She rattled off a couple of sentences in Russian that sounded like a coffee grinder running in reverse. "It means, roughly, pain is mostly mind over matter: if you don't mind, it doesn't matter."

A chuckle escaped. "My old football coach had pretty much the same saying, only he usually made you do fifty push-ups after he said it."

They both laughed, and Liam could feel a little of the accumulated tension slip away from his shoulders. After patting the knee dry, he dabbed some antibiotic ointment on it and started carefully wrapping a sterile dressing around the joint. Now that the worst part of the job was over, he tried not to look longingly at the beer dangling loosely from Baba's long-fingered hand.

A blunt head nudged his leg and he looked down in

amazement to see Chudo-Yudo sitting at his feet, a beer bottle lightly clenched between alarmingly large white teeth.

"Wow," he said, taking it carefully from his unusual waiter and prying the top off with his Swiss Army knife. "That's a very helpful dog."

Baba just rolled her eyes. "Nice," she said to the huge white animal. "You're two for two. Let's not push our luck, eh?"

As usual, Liam felt like he was missing half the conversation—the half that made sense, at that. So he changed the subject back to the issue that had brought him out here in the first place.

"I hate to bully my patients," he said, tucking in the ends of the bandage and pushing his hair out of his eyes before starting to wrap her elbow. "But would you like to tell me why you thought it was a good idea to hassle Maya Freeman?"

Baba's usual bland expression clouded over with the hint of a frown.

"I was hoping to catch her off guard and get her to admit to something," she confessed. "Not much of a plan, I know. But I thought at least if I said *something*, she'd know that someone was on to her, and no more children would disappear."

Liam said through gritted teeth as he packed up the rest of the first aid supplies, "You do realize that if Maya *is* involved, you have just warned her that you know she is involved, and that will make her much less likely to lead us to the children that have already gone missing." He didn't bother to point out that if Maya were really the culprit, Baba might have even put herself in danger; she'd already had a rough enough evening.

Baba sighed and swung her legs up onto the coffee table, her furry footrest having moved off to nap in front of the refrigerator, as if he was afraid that someone would steal something precious out of it while he slept. A slight snore rattled the cupboards.

"I said it wasn't much of a plan, didn't I?" She let her head droop back onto the crimson velvet cushion behind her, ebony lashes fluttering down to cover those remarkable eyes. "It is remotely possible that I may have acted a tad hastily. It's only that I keep thinking about those children . . ."

Liam swallowed back all the retorts that had been about to zip out of his mouth like angry bees. "Yeah. I get that." He shook his head, forgetting that Baba's eyes were still closed and she couldn't see him. Then he had to push that damned hair out of the way again. Any day now, he was going to find time to get it cut. Like when he was applying for another job because he'd been fired from this one.

"You know, you could have waited," he said, trying not to let his frustration at her lack of faith in him show. After all, they'd just met; how was she to know that he took every lead seriously? Even hers. "I did actually check Ms. Freeman out more thoroughly, and everything looks perfect. No history of trouble with the law, excellent references from her last job—not so much as a parking ticket."

Baba sat up, grimacing a little, and turned to face him. She leaned in closer, until he could feel the heat coming off her body, and locked eyes with him.

"Sheriff," she said, her tone level and matter-of-fact. "If you did the same for me, I assure you, all my information would look perfect too. But almost all of it is a *lie*. Some people have ways of getting around the truth, ways you can't possibly understand. But you can take my word for it: Maya is not at all what she seems."

Liam believed her, although that in itself was almost as disturbing as the fact that she'd just admitted to lying to him. "What, so are you saying that you and Maya are both in the CIA, or the Mafia or something?"

Baba leaned back again, that teasing half smile flitting across her lips. "Oh, no, Sheriff, something much worse than that." For a moment, it almost seemed as though she was going to add something, until the sound of ringing broke the moment and chased the words away.

INE

BABA HAD TO swallow a laugh at the look of stunned amazement on Liam's face. He pulled out his phone and gazed at it as though it had been transmuted into a kaleidoscope, or some other completely unexpected object.

"I don't believe it," he said, still staring at the ringing object in his palm. "I never get service out here."

"Must be magic," Baba said lightly. "Aren't you going to answer that?"

He shook himself and flipped the phone open. She tried without success to follow his half of the conversation, which mostly consisted of variations on, "Yup, uh-huh, that's great." Chudo-Yudo roused himself with a dragonish snort and meandered over to find out what was going on, bringing Baba another beer. This one had a sizable chunk missing from the neck, but she nudged it back into place with a finger flick before Liam could notice.

"It's Bob," Liam said, pulling the phone away from his ear for a moment. "From the auto shop. I had him go out and pick up your bike."

Baba bit back a sharp reply. Nobody touched her

motorcycle but her. Chudo-Yudo growled softly and she gave him an imperceptible shake of the head. The sheriff meant well, and she could reclaim it in the morning when she was back up to full strength. Or in the middle of the night, if she was really feeling twitchy about it.

Liam continued, blissfully unaware of how close he'd come to getting his ass handed to him on a platter. "Bob says the damage isn't as bad as it looks. The frame isn't twisted, and he can mend the front fender, bend the handlebars back into shape, and replace the tire. A decent paint job will take longer, but you should be back on the road in a week or so." He gave her a broad, white smile, clearly proud of himself.

Baba vacillated between irritation that he'd dealt with the issue without her permission and gratitude that the motorcycle wasn't as badly mangled as it had first appeared.

Eventually, gratitude won out and she managed to say, more or less graciously, "Thanks. You can tell Bob to fix the metal bits; I can take care of the paint job myself. I'd rather not be without the bike any longer than I have to." She could feel the space where it was supposed to sit outside the Airstream like an empty socket from a missing tooth. "Tell him I'll pay double if he can put a rush on it."

Liam raised an eyebrow at that but relayed the message. A startled look flitted across his face at Bob's reply, and he gazed at the phone thoughtfully for a moment after he hung up.

"He said you don't have to pay him double, but he'd really appreciate it if you could make him an herbal remedy for his father's gout. They share the garage, and when the gout is acting up, the old man is as grumpy as a hibernating bear." Liam shook his head. "He said someone told him about you when he was in Bertie's this morning and he was going to contact you anyway."

Baba was pleased. It was probably irrational, but she felt better being able to barter for part of the work. When she was growing up, that was the way it was done. The previous Baba was paid in chickens far more often than in coin.

"Excellent," she said, already thinking of which herbs she might use from her current stock and which ones she would need to forage for. "I'll make him up something right away."

Liam patted her leg, carefully avoiding the bruised bits that were already turning vibrant purples and blues, like a garden of pansies sprung up overnight. "Don't worry about the bike," he said, sympathy softening his tone. "Bob is a wizard with anything that has wheels and a motor."

"I don't need a wizard," Baba said, rolling her eyes. Wizards tended to be annoying and smell like sulfur. Too many alchemical formulas and not enough bathing. "I just need a mechanic."

"What?" Liam looked confused for a second, then laughed. "You have the strangest sense of humor." A shadow wiped the smile away, leaving somber lines behind.

Baba braced herself, fingers clenched around the sweating beer bottle. One cold drop ran over a knuckle and hit the floor with a silent plop. In the woven carpet under her feet, a tiny lizard flicked its tongue out to catch the unexpected moisture. Why did she find him so attractive? He did nothing but annoy her. Well, bandage her wounds and annoy her. How was it possible he could make her feel like this?

"Look, we have to talk about this Maya thing," Liam said, reluctance giving his deep voice a sharper than usual edge. "I don't understand why you are so sure she is involved in the disappearance of all these children. Most crimes are motivated by love, money, or revenge—which one do you think this is?" He tilted his head, apparently willing to listen to her reasoning, although clearly not expecting to agree with it.

Baba tried to figure out something that would make sense to him. As an explanation, "She's using magic and I'm pretty sure she tried to kill me with it," wasn't likely to go over well.

"Maya works for Peter Callahan," Baba said slowly, feeling her way. "Big money there. And she told me that he has a lot of influence in this area now. I have a feeling that the kidnappings have something to do with one or both of those."

Liam pondered this for a minute. "Are you suggesting Maya is stealing the children and selling them to raise money for Callahan's drilling project? Or trading them to people who want small children for some kinky reason in exchange for influence in some way?" He looked doubtful, but was apparently giving the idea due consideration, in the manner of a lawman who isn't willing to rule out any possibility, no matter how improbable. "There are a lot of very rich people involved with the oil and gas industry overseas. Do you think they're shipping the kids out of the country? That would explain why there has been no trace of them."

Then he shook his head. "No, no way. It's just too Movie of the Week." At Baba's baffled look, he added, "Too far-fetched. Peter Callahan has a lot invested in pushing this fracking thing through—he stands to make millions if it all goes according to plan—but I can't see him doing anything so drastic."

He tapped one finger against his empty beer bottle before putting it down next to the first aid kit and saying in a low voice, "Peter Callahan might be a son of a bitch, but he has a young son of his own. I can't believe he would be involved in selling children for some kind of twisted business advantage." Baba hoped she was wrong too, but she had less faith in humanity than he did. Still, if that was what was happening, surely they'd be subtler about it.

But the children had to be going somewhere. If Maya wasn't just killing them (and sadly, that was still a possibility), then what was she doing with them? A glimmer of an idea floated to the surface of her brain, like a will-o'-the-wisp in a swamp full of marsh gas; flitting to and fro, impossible to pin down. But something, nonetheless.

"Maybe we're looking at this the wrong way," she said, trying to grasp the errant notion.

Liam grunted and shoved himself to his feet, fatigue showing in the long lines of his body and the shadows that hung under his eyes. "There is no *we* here, Ms. Yager. Let me be perfectly clear about that." He met her glare with a steady gaze.

"I'll give this all some thought, and I'll look into it in any way I can, but you need to stay away from Maya Freeman, Peter Callahan, and anyone else associated with the gas company. There is only so much I can do to protect you."

Baba snorted through her nose, wishing she could breathe flames like Chudo-Yudo. It would serve the sheriff right if she accidentally set him on fire. "I don't need you to protect me, Sheriff. I have been taking care of myself for a very long time."

She gave him a measured look. "On the other hand, I have been told that you are a broken man, and that's why they don't consider you a threat. Is that true?" Maybe it was tactless to ask, but if she was going to have to rely on him for an ally, even a reluctant one, she needed to know for sure that she could depend on him. And she'd never been known for her tact.

A hint of color touched his strong cheekbones. He looked, for a moment, as though he might stalk off without answering. One deep breath brought him back under control with an effort that bespoke of long practice. Baba suddenly found herself reassessing his constant calm, which she sometimes found so provoking, and seeing a vision of an armored wall instead, built brick by brick with bloody fingers.

"No," he said. And the pain in his eyes was so deep, for a moment, she almost forgot the question. "Not broken. Just a little banged up. Kind of like you. And like you, I'll heal. It's just not a rapid process." A sly smile gave her a glimpse into the keen brain hidden under his too-long hair and deceptively mellow exterior. "Besides, in some ways, my troubles work in my favor. The people around here like me. As much as the county board would like to get rid of me, they haven't wanted to look bad by firing a man who survived a major tragedy."

Baba opened her mouth to ask and then shut it again when he shook his head.

"Don't worry about it." A shadow flitted over his face,

like a cloud blowing across the full moon. "I doubt you'll be around long enough for it to matter."

She couldn't argue with that; he was almost certainly right. Babas didn't stay.

"I'll talk to Bob in the morning," he added. "I can call you to let you know when he thinks the bike will be ready."

"I don't have a phone."

"You don't have a phone," Liam repeated in a disbelieving tone. "Then how the hell do people get in touch with you?"

Baba shrugged. "Usually they just show up at the front door."

"That's ridiculous," he said.

"Really?" She raised one eyebrow. "You did."

Before he left, Liam turned around and gave her a hard look that sent a little shiver down her spine. She chose to blame it on the cool night air instead of the chill in his eyes.

"Remember what I said about staying away from Peter Callahan and his assistant. I don't care what you suspect them of—I am the law here and you are a professor who is very far away from home. Make no mistake; I like you, but that won't keep me from tossing your ass into jail if I have to." He turned his back on her and left, slamming the door behind him to emphasize his point.

Baba scowled at the place where he'd been, and fingered the perfectly applied bandage on her elbow. It had been a long time since anyone had bothered to take care of her—she couldn't tell if she liked it or not. She felt oddly off-balance, as if the gravity in the room was no longer what she was used to. The air tasted strange, like strawberries and spring. *He said he liked her.*

"I had a thought," she said slowly to Chudo-Yudo.

"Gods help us," he growled. "The last time that happened, we had to replace all the furnishings."

"That fire was not my fault," Baba said crossly. "And not that kind of thought." She sank down on the couch, feeling every bruise and scrape complain in an unmusical chorus. Now that Liam was gone, she could get herself a tiny glass of the Water of Life and Death. That would speed up her healing and kill the pain at the same time.

"It just occurred to me that right now, Maya and whoever she is working with think Liam is nothing more than an annoyance. What do you suppose will happen if he starts digging deeper into their business and actually finds something that could hurt them?"

Chudo-Yudo hopped up on the sofa next to her, making it creak in protest. He lay his blunt head on top of a red-and-purple tapestry pillow and sighed. "In that case," he said in a mournful tone, "I suspect he dies."

EN

LIAM HAD EVERY intention of following through on his promise to Baba and checking up on Peter Callahan. If nothing else, he was perversely looking forward to his next confrontation with Baba and seeing that strange light flashing in her eyes. He didn't know how she did it, but she was astonishingly beautiful when she was angry.

If she was his, he'd make her angry from time to time, just to watch the fireworks. Not that she would ever be his. Especially not now, when finding three missing children was a lot more important than suddenly, inexplicably discovering he still had an interest in women after all. One woman anyway.

It made no difference, since he hadn't had time to see her in days—or investigate anything to do with Peter Callahan. He'd been way too busy answering call after call from irate citizens who kept him hopping with their bizarre complaints.

He pulled into the parking lot of the sheriff's department, so relieved to be back that the long, narrow building actually looked good to him, faded red bricks, straggling shrubbery, dirty windows, and all. The summer heat radiated up off the concrete sidewalk, and the few weeds that were attempting to work their way through the cracks looked depressed and wilted.

Kind of like he felt after spending over an hour standing in a field of reeking cow patties, trying to convince Stu Philips that his neighbor Henry hadn't deliberately pulled down the fence between their farms so his heifers could eat the crops on the other side. The two men had finally stopped yelling long enough for him to point out that said cows were now halfway down the hill, leaving trampled rows of young corn as evidence of their passage. When he left, both the cows and farmers had been headed for home, none the worse for their adventures. He wished he could say the same for his boots.

The cooler air inside the station was like a melody written in the key of relief. He nodded at a couple of deputies sitting at their desks in the outer room, ignoring the wrinkled noses and grimaces that followed in his wake. He'd come in smelling like worse things than manure; they'd live. The ancient AC units wheezing within the frames of windows with peeling white paint would eventually clear the air.

His secretary, Molly, trailed him into his office, her low heels tapping on the beige linoleum floor. "Nice aftershave, boss," she said, waving a sheaf of colored papers in front of her nose. "Something new you're trying out?" The message memos were color coded in various shades to indicate urgency, and Liam noted an unusual number of oranges and reds in the midst of the usual yellows. It was a hell of a stack too.

"I've only been gone for two hours," he complained. "How many problems could possibly come up during that time that somebody else couldn't handle?"

Molly's normally placid face pinched with worry. "Almost everyone else is already out dealing with other things. Sorry, Sheriff. It's been like a zoo. The phone hasn't stopped ringing since I got here."

Liam gave her an apologetic smile. It wasn't her fault the

sudden summer heat wave was making everyone cranky. "Hey, at least this zoo doesn't come with livestock." He pointed at his boots, which still had manure embedded in every nook and cranny, despite his efforts to wipe them off. "Go ahead, hit me."

Molly looked over the top of her glasses at the first note, held at slightly less than arm's length. She'd turned forty the year before, but was still resisting the bifocals she clearly needed. One strand of brown hair had slipped out of her usually tidy bun, and while she was as calm and pleasant as always, something about the set of her shoulders told Liam she hadn't had an easy morning either.

"Roy Smith called," she said, reading the yellow note written in her precise cursive hand. "He says that something savaged three of his lambs—either a wolf, or some kind of wolf-dog hybrid. He wants you to look into it."

Liam rolled his eyes. "Call him back and tell him I am neither the game warden nor the animal control officer. Next?"

This note was on orange paper. "Clementine Foster called because someone poisoned her well. She helpfully provided a list of suspects, most of them kids she had in last year's math class." Molly tucked that one behind the rest of the batch, and read off the one after it. "Lester Haney wants you to investigate the vandalism on his farm. Says someone is sneaking around at night letting all the air out of the tractor tires, stealing plastic parts off the equipment, and hiding half the tools."

"Just the plastic parts?" Liam thought that sounded odd. "Maybe it's teenagers, doing it on some kind of a dare?" Molly gave that theory a dubious look, which he tended to agree with. "Well, tell him I'll get out there when I can, but in the meanwhile, maybe he should tie his dogs outside at night for a bit." He took a deep breath, bracing himself as he looked at the size of the stack still remaining. "What else ya got?"

She flipped through them rapidly, finishing up with, "Sherwood Latham wants you to find out who is threatening his migrant workers; suddenly they're packing up their families and leaving town in droves. He says if you don't get to the bottom of it, the crops are going to rot in the fields."

Oh, for the love of Pete. "How am I supposed to know why the migrant workers are leaving? Maybe they got a better offer from someplace else. What the heck is going on around here, anyway? Has everyone lost their minds?"

He took off his hat and threw it on the pole in the corner, running his fingers through his hair to try to get some shape back into it. The coatrack was as utilitarian and functional as the rest of the room; the message memos were by far the most colorful thing in it. But even though he'd never admit it, Liam loved this office, with its clunky old wooden desk covered with towering piles of neatly organized files, and the big dusty window that overlooked the town he'd pledged to keep safe. The thought of losing it sent a shockwave of pain through his chest. He wasn't sure he could bear one more loss. But he couldn't think of any way to prevent it, short of a miracle.

"You look like you could use this, Sheriff," Nina said, walking through the door with a grease-dotted takeout container in one hand and a cup of coffee in the other. She plopped them both on the desk blotter, carefully moving an active file out of the way with one well-placed elbow. The aroma of grilled meat and hot coffee filled the room and made Liam's chest loosen so he could breathe again.

"Is that from Bertie's?" he asked. As if Nina would take her lunch break anywhere else.

"You bet your bippy," the older woman said, a smart-assed grin creasing her narrow face. Her chin was pointed and her eyebrows sparse, and even when she was younger she'd been no one's idea of a beauty, but Liam valued her more than any ten runway models for her loyalty and her brains. "Bertie's special bacon cheeseburger with the bacon extra crispy, just the way you like it. I had a feeling you probably didn't remember to stop and eat."

Molly nodded in satisfaction. Nina and Molly had been mothering him since Melissa left. Since before that, really.

Sometimes it got on his nerves, but he knew they meant well. Besides, if it got him a bacon cheeseburger from Bertie's, it was worth it. They both stood there and waited until he'd taken three huge bites, savoring the moist ground beef, the sharp bite of the cheddar cheese, and the smoky richness of the bacon, almost moaning as the juices dripped onto the napkin spread out in front of him.

"Thanks, Nina," he finally said, swallowing the last delicious mouthful. "You may have saved my life."

She sniffed. "Hey, I was there anyway. It's no big deal." It was their unspoken agreement: she pretended not to care, and he pretended to believe her. Nina liked to believe that no one saw through her tough exterior to the warm heart underneath, and everyone at the station played along, just to keep her happy.

Molly put the memos for Liam to deal with down on the desk, their corners neatly aligned. "I'm glad you're back, Nina," she said, a tiny wrinkle appearing between her brows. "Dispatch has been hopping since you went out; I thought Deputy Lewis was going to give himself a muscle spasm trying to keep up."

"Crazy," Liam repeated, shaking his head. He pushed the second half of his lunch away, his appetite suddenly gone. "What the hell is going on around here?"

Nina pursed her thin lips. "You should hear the talk at Bertie's. People are saying their feed supplies rotted overnight, or are infested with rats. Frank Shasta said he had a plague of snakes—just harmless garter snakes, but apparently they were everywhere. His wife Mildred got so freaked out, she went to stay with her mother until he could get rid of them."

"Seriously?" Molly looked amazed. "That must have been a hell of a lot of snakes; Mildred's mother is a crabby old harpy."

Nina nodded in satisfaction. There was nothing she liked better than a good gossip, and lately, it seemed like there was a never-ending supply of weird news, bad news, and just plain oddness.

"Carter Hastings told me that he had a giant sinkhole open up in the middle of one of his fields. Nothing there one day, and the next, a hole big enough to lose a whole herd of cattle in. He said it hardly mattered, though, because all his best dairy cows had gone dry. The vet's got no idea why. Poor Carter's going to have to sell off a quarter of the herd at rock-bottom prices."

"Huh," Molly said. "I've heard of a couple of other farmers who had the same problem. The cows going dry, not the sinkhole. It's like someone cursed the whole county." She gave Liam a halfhearted smile and handed him three matching red message sheets. "And speaking of curses, here's your special one: the mayor wants to see you in his office at two."

A sigh escaped Liam like air from a balloon at the end of a party. "Did he say what he wanted?" Not that it mattered. Whatever it was, it wouldn't be good.

She shrugged. "No. But he's called three times to see if you were back yet, so I'm guessing it's important." She shoved the remains of Liam's cooling burger back toward him. "You'd better eat that. Something tells me you're going to need your strength."

As she and Nina left the room, he muttered to himself, "I think I'd rather be chasing wolves."

BABA SAT AT a small table in Bertie's, drinking coffee and trying to pretend that she belonged there. To her amazement, it seemed to be working. One thing about small towns, she thought, word got around fast. People she'd met nodded to her as she came into the room; people she hadn't met looked at her curiously, seemed to figure out exactly who she was, and went back to their food. It was an odd feeling for someone who was always a stranger everywhere she went. Odder yet, she almost thought she liked it.

"Sorry I'm late," Belinda said, sliding into the seat across from Baba. "We've been going crazy down at the station, trying to keep up with all sorts of weird calls from normally sane people." Dark circles shadowed her eyes as she gazed across the table at Baba. "I don't suppose you've made any progress finding Mary Elizabeth?" Hope and despair warred with each other on her pretty face, the despair winning when Baba shook her head.

"I've got a couple of leads I'm following up on," Baba said. "I'm sorry I don't have anything more concrete to tell you than that. But we *will* get your daughter back, I promise you." She found herself making the promise as much to the universe as to the deputy; she liked this woman, with her brave heart and her unyielding faith in the Baba. Barbara wasn't going to let her down.

"Heya, Belinda," a waitress said as she came up to the table. Lucy, Baba thought, recognizing the pouf of blond hair. "Hey, Miz Yager. I gotta tell ya, that cream you gave me for my bunions worked a treat." She wiggled one wide foot, clad in bright red sneakers with zebra-striped laces. "First time my foot hasn't hurt in two years." She turned her beaming smile on Belinda, patting the deputy on the shoulder with a motherly air. "How ya holdin' up, honey?"

Belinda gave the older woman a shaky smile in return. "I'm doing okay, Lucy. Just a cup of coffee for me, okay? I'm not too hungry."

Lucy scowled. "You're on your lunch break, ain't ya? Then you're havin' lunch. I'll bring ya some of the chicken soup we got on special; nothin' goes down easier than chicken soup. It'll cure just about anything that ails ya." She snorted a laugh. "Of course, whatever it don't cure, Miz Yager here will, ain't that right?" She patted Baba on the shoulder too, and walked jauntily off in the direction of the kitchen.

Baba blinked. "People around here certainly are friendly," she said, not sure if that was a good thing or not. Friendly usually made her twitch. This town must be getting under her skin.

"Well, I think word's getting around about all the good you're doing with your herbal remedies," Belinda said, toying with the little gold stud in one ear. Baba noticed that her nails were chewed down to the quick.

"Huh," Baba said. "It's a good cover story, and I like

working with the plants. Earth is my primary element, I guess you could say. Still, it's not a big deal; I like healing people."

"Just not talking to them, right?" Belinda said with a tiny smile. "I appreciate you meeting me here. I can tell you're not much of a 'let's have lunch' kind of woman."

Baba snorted. "Not hardly." She looked around the room. "But I like this place. And the coffee is damned good. Besides, you asked nicely." She just wished she had more than empty reassurances to give the poor woman. "And maybe now we can discuss that second impossible task."

She smothered a chuckle at the look of alarm that spread over Belinda's face.

"Um, okay," Belinda said, swallowing hard. "What is it?"

Baba gave her a serious look, then gestured at the covered cases that lined the counter. "Help me figure out which kind of pie to get. I'm completely torn between the strawberry rhubarb and the mixed berry with the crumble topping."

Belinda's startled laughter was reward enough for coming. Damn—this place *really* was getting to her.

THE MAYOR'S OFFICE was designed to be imposing. It was situated in one of the oldest buildings in town, a certified historical monument to a more prosperous time, when the railroad still ran and Dunville was a hub of commerce and travel. Outside, the marble steps and ornate columns gave way to massive carved wood doors that opened on to a spacious lobby with high, painted tin ceilings. Unlike the sheriff's department, this building was kept in perfect condition, the white walls shining and the oak trim oiled until it gleamed.

The mayor's office was off a side corridor so the hustle and bustle of the mundane business transacted in the county clerk's office up front wouldn't impinge upon the more weighty matters of running the town. The current mayor was more competent than some Liam had worked with in his years with the sheriff's department, although he tended to waffle on issues rather than risk offending one of his more influential supporters. What he lacked in spine he made up for in charm, so he'd recently been elected to a second term.

The mayor's secretary seemed to have stepped away from her desk in the small outer chamber, so Liam knocked on the door to the inner room. A deep voice said, "Come in," so he did, and was dismayed but not completely surprised to see Clive Matthews standing next to the taller, slimmer form of the town's mayor. Due to the small size of the town and the surrounding area, the sheriff's department had been acting as law enforcement for both since budget cuts had done away with the town police chief's job. Liam reported directly to the mayor, but the country board was technically still in charge of the hiring and firing for the position. He had a feeling Matthews wasn't there to give him a raise.

"Mr. Mayor, you wanted to see me?" Liam nodded at the board president politely, but focused his attention on the man who had called him.

To his credit, Harvey Anderson didn't look any happier than Liam felt. He glanced sideways out of the corner of his eyes, clearly hoping the other man would do the talking. When Matthews just crossed his arms over his chest and stood there looking stern and disappointed, Anderson gave a sigh and said, "Liam, we all know you've had a tough couple of years, but the board—" Matthews cleared his throat meaningfully. "That is, we all have some serious concerns about how you are doing your job."

Matthews's musky cologne wafted across the space between them, making Liam's breath catch and stutter. *The man must bathe in the stuff,* he thought, his mind caught by an inconsequential butterfly fluttering of ideas, so it wouldn't focus on the words coming out of the mayor's mouth. *The air conditioning in here is a lot quieter than ours down at the station. That must be nice.*

"I'm doing my best, Harvey," Liam said in a carefully measured tone, trying not to let his anger percolate to the surface. He was so damned tired of Clive Matthews yanking his chain. "My men are working around the clock, trying to find out who is behind these disappearances. There just aren't any clues."

"Or maybe there are, and you're just not finding them," Matthews put in sourly. "We're in the midst of a major crime wave, with children involved, and you've accomplished *nothing*. It can't go on."

Liam opened his mouth to argue, to say that the state guys hadn't found anything either, despite having better equipment and more men, then closed it again as the mayor said, "I'm sorry, Liam, but Clive is right. Maybe you just don't have what it takes to do this job anymore. The board is giving you until the end of the month to come up with something concrete. If not, we'll have no choice but to replace you. I'm very, very sorry."

Fury bubbled over like a pot on a too-hot fire, despite his best intentions. There was no way some damned mealy-mouthed politicians were going to keep him from doing his job. The people of this town needed him—and his job was all he had left.

"I've been working around the clock," he growled. "*Nobody* wants to find these kids more than I do. The state cops pop their heads in for a few days, then go back to chasing drug dealers and giving out speeding tickets, saying they don't have enough manpower to spare to stick around. I live and breathe this job twenty-four/seven.

"If you take me off this case, who are you going to give it to? Some guy with no experience who will have to start from scratch? You clearly don't have the slightest idea how police work is done, or you wouldn't be wasting my time with this petty crap. Why don't you just get off my back and let me do my damned job?"

Harvey Anderson's mouth dropped open and he started to sputter an apology, but Matthews cut him off before he could get more than a few words out.

"It is just this kind of attitude that makes you unsuitable for such a sensitive position," Matthews said, his chest puffed out like a rooster. "You heard the mayor. You have until the end of the month."

"The end of the month is only two and a half weeks from now," Liam said from between clenched teeth.

Matthews smirked. "I guess you'd better get to work, then." He gestured toward the door, and Liam somehow made it outside without punching Matthews into the next county. That in itself was a minor victory of sorts.

Once outside, he closed the heavy wooden door behind him and took a deep breath. *Two and a half weeks.* To find the answers that had eluded him for almost five months. *Hell.*

"Hello, Sheriff," a warm contralto voice said from the desk next to him. The mayor's secretary, Lynette, had a daughter who used to babysit for one of the missing children. "Is there any news?"

He closed his eyes for a minute and inhaled through his nose and out through his mouth, like the grief counselor had taught them. Then he forced himself to smile at Lynette, despite the churning in his stomach.

"Sorry, no. The mayor and Mr. Matthews just wanted to have a little chat with me about the way I'm doing my job, that's all."

She gave him a sympathetic look, her kind, pretty face colored with concern. "I know; I heard them talking about it earlier." She grimaced. "Mr. Matthews has one of those voices that carries."

Liam chuckled in wry agreement. He'd been in enough meetings with Clive Matthews to know that he always talked louder than anyone else in the room, like a steamroller on steroids.

Lynette dropped her own voice and said quietly, "You should know that they've already set up interviews with possible candidates for your job." Her glance skittered away from his and she looked at the floor. "I'm so sorry, Sheriff."

He sighed. "Me too, Lynette. Me too."

ELEVEN

BABA WALKED OVER to the door. Opened it, looked out, glared at the empty green meadow, then slammed it shut and stomped back over to throw herself down on the couch again. A litter of empty chocolate wrappers crinkled as she sat on them, and she disposed of them with an irritated snap of her fingers.

She'd been in a foul mood since waking up from a hideous nightmare, and waiting around for a client who was clearly not going to show hadn't done anything to sweeten her temper. It didn't help that it had been three days since she'd seen the stubborn yet appealing sheriff. Yes, she'd told him to leave her in peace, but for some reason, she found it incredibly annoying that he'd actually done so.

It had taken two hours to mix up that decoction for a local woman who'd pleaded for something to ease her nerves. If she didn't show soon, Baba was going to drink it herself.

She'd spent the last few days treating the folks who lived nearby for everything from third-degree burns to warts. Apparently Bertie down at the diner had taken it upon herself to spread the word about Baba's herbal remedies, and when Bertie spoke, people listened. Of course, even without Bertie, patients would have found their way to her; they always did. But for some reason, Baba had made a little more effort than usual to be helpful. Bizarrely (for her, anyway), she actually *liked* these people.

Except the woman who was currently standing her up. *She* was going on Baba's list.

The antique silver pocket watch she pulled out of her black jeans said it was after two, and Bob the mechanical wizard had sent her a message yesterday to say the motorcycle would be ready by one. She clicked the cover shut decisively and shoved the timepiece back into her pocket—that was it; she was done waiting. Time to go get her baby back.

"I'm going out for a bit," she said to Chudo-Yudo, who was sprawled on his back in a lemon-meringue splash of sunshine, looking more cat than dragon. "If that lady comes looking for her order, you have my permission to bark at her." Bah. She hated when people didn't do what they said they were going to do.

"Going to hunt down that yummy sheriff?" Chudo-Yudo asked slyly, cocking one eye open to check out her outfit. He seemed to find the jeans, embroidered crimson cotton peasant top, and clunky motorcycle boots acceptable, since it slid closed again a minute later. He yawned, showing off sharp white teeth. "I noticed he hasn't been around lately. You scare him off already?"

Baba bared her own teeth at him, which didn't make much of an impression since he couldn't see it. "Don't be ridiculous. I'm going to get my damned bike back; I'm tired of driving around in the truck. It's like being cooped up inside a big silver tank. I miss feeling the wind against my skin."

Chudo-Yudo snorted, rolling over onto his belly and producing another bone out of nowhere to gnaw on enthusiastically. "You'd think you were some Otherworld creature, sensitive to the touch of cold iron, the way you talk." He glanced around the Airstream. "Of course, you couldn't very well live in this glammed-up tin can if you were, could you?"

She threw a pillow at him, which he incinerated in mid-air. The ashes drifted down like volcanic ash. You'd think she'd learn.

"Do *not* insult my hut, damn it," she said, rummaging through the cupboards to find the stash of hundred-dollar bills she'd hidden someplace clever, long enough ago that she'd now forgotten where. She could magic up some more, of course, but she always worried that the money would crumble into nothingness in typical Otherworld fashion once she was gone, and she didn't want to cheat the man who'd worked so hard to fix her precious motorcycle.

"Aha!" she said, finally unearthing the roll of cash inside an old hand-painted Matryoshka. The set of Russian nesting dolls, each one smaller than the one enclosing it, made a perfect hiding place. If you could remember that's where you put things. The gaily decorated faces of the dolls seemed to mock her, their crooked smiles and rosy red cheeks far too cheerful for her current mood.

Baba grabbed the cash and her keys and headed for the truck, stopping to glare one more time around the empty field and the road that carried neither errant sheriff nor missing client in her direction, and tore off in the direction of town. She'd feel better when she had the bike back. Although, just to be on the safe side, maybe she'd pick up some more chocolate while she was out.

O'SHAUNNESSY AND SON Auto Service was perched on the outward bend of a hairpin curve on the edge of town, where the motley assortment of cars, trucks, and vans in various stages of disrepair couldn't bring down the property values or irritate the neighbors. Other than the collection of vehicles, the place was neat and prosperous looking, with a row of four open bays lined up in a long, dark gray garage and a smaller office tucked away like a forgotten second cousin at the far end.

Baba pulled the big silver truck into the gravel lot and

parked it in front of the office space, where a brick doorstop held the door open for whatever breeze there was. The temperature hovered around the ninety-degree mark, which the locals told her was well above normal, and the air was so humid, it clung to your skin like syrup. She didn't mind, though, and stood for a moment in the hot sunshine drinking in the sounds of hammering and the high-pitched whine of a power tool. The pungent odor of old oil, metal being ground under pressure, and the sharp bite of some kind of solvent drifted out of the nearest bay like a mechanical alchemist's air elemental. The smell made her smile.

As did the sight of her beloved motorcycle, its normally glossy blue paint scratched and scuffed, but upright on two wheels and ready to sail her away down the road at speeds unsafe—and most likely unattainable—on any normal bike. As soon as she paid for it, drove it home in the back of the truck, and did a little quick magic on the paint job. There was no way she was riding it down the road in its current condition. A girl had to have her standards.

Baba walked into the office, which was only a few degrees cooler than the scorching atmosphere outside. Three small fans revolved frantically, trying with futile perpetual motion to cool the space. One of them had a bent blade and clicked irritatingly on every revolution. *Whirr, whirr, click. Whirr, whirr, click.*

The room was dim and empty, other than a countertop that separated the waiting area from two small desks and a doorway that led to the garages, and maybe a bathroom. The only decorations, if you could call them that, were posters of tires, a wilted and dispirited spider plant, and an auto parts calendar featuring an improbably large-breasted woman holding a huge wrench, perched on the roof of a red corvette. But the room itself was clean, and the plastic chairs for customers to sit on all bore colorful paisley cushions.

Baba nodded in satisfaction, perversely reassured that all the money and effort for this business was clearly focused on the cars, and not on the people who owned them. Just as it should be.

A tall man with faded red hair, a spattering of freckles, and a receding hairline came into the room and stopped dead when he saw her standing there. He gave a jerking glance over his shoulder, tugging gray overalls into place with a nervous gesture. The name embroidered over his chest said *Bob*, so she assumed this was the wizard she'd come to see.

"Hi," she said. "You must be Bob. I'm Barbara Yager. I've come to pick up my BMW. Thanks so much for fixing her. I really appreciate it." She remembered something and pulled a small white porcelain jar out of her pocket. "And I brought you the salve you wanted for your father's gout."

Bob glanced furtively behind him again, and reached under the counter to grab her keys and toss them onto the smooth laminated surface. Not meeting her eyes, he shoved the jar back toward her and said in a low voice, "Look, just take the bike and go. You can pay me later. And I don't want the salve. His leg is much better." He looked toward the back of the room again, and an expression of near panic flitted across his face as she stood there, not moving. "Go on, the bike is fine. I didn't bother with the paint job, like you said, but otherwise, she's good as new."

What the hell was going on here? Bob had been perfectly pleasant the one time she'd called from a rare pay phone in town and talked to him about the motorcycle; now he was acting like she had some kind of contagious disease—one with unpleasant social ramifications, at that.

She shook her head and pulled the roll of bills out of the front pocket of her jeans, peeling off five hundred dollars' worth and placing them on the counter next to the little white jar. "How much do I owe you?" she asked.

Bob scrambled for a handwritten invoice, almost dropping it in his hurry to get her out of there. But before he could pick it up, a door slammed in the back and a tornado blew in on a wind of bluster and bellowing. A smaller, shorter version of Bob, with close-cropped white hair and the bearing of an ex-military man, he limped up to the counter, grabbed Baba's money, and threw it at her. It drifted down like autumn leaves to rest by her booted feet.

"Is that her?" the senior O'Shaunnessy demanded of his son. Not waiting for an answer, he turned to Baba and said with a snarl, "Get out of here. We don't want your kind here. Take your damned motorcycle and be grateful we didn't put it into the crusher. And don't come back."

Baba could feel her mouth drop open, and she blinked a couple of times to see if that made the world make any more sense. Nope. No help at all. She looked at Bob for a clue, but he just lowered his gaze, an embarrassed flush spreading across his freckled cheekbones.

"I'm sorry," she said to his father. "Have I offended you somehow?"

Veins pulsed rapidly in the old man's neck as he glared at her. "You are an offense to all good Christian people. I heard about you down at Bertie's. Taking money off of people who can't hardly spare it, and givin' 'em fake medicines that make them sick. That tea you made for Maddie over at the library to fix her allergies made her sneeze so hard she fell off a stepstool and broke her ankle. You should be ashamed of yourself."

Baba's stomach clenched as if he had punched her. Normally, she would have yelled back. Hell, normally, she wouldn't have cared. But she liked this place, with its open meadows and high pine-covered hills. She liked going into the slightly ramshackle old town and having people greet her by name, and smile at her when she passed them in the grocery store aisle. She liked the folks who'd come to her for herbal remedies. What the hell had gone wrong?

"My preparations *do not* make people sick," she said through her teeth. "Try the ointment I brought for you, and you'll see."

The senior O'Shaunnessy picked the little jar up off the counter and threw it into the garbage can at his feet. "Not on a bet, missy. They're saying you're some kind of witch. That maybe all the stuff that has been going wrong around here is your fault. I'm not using nothing you made, no how."

He turned to his son, somehow towering over the younger man, even though Bob was a good six inches taller. "You're an idiot, Bob. Letting her trade some poison voodoo for your hard work. You're like that boy with the cow and the magic beans." He shook his head, looking like a bee-stung bear. "Jee-sus. Get her the hell out of here, will you? Idiot." He limped back out the way he'd come, cursing under his breath the entire way. The door slammed hard behind him, like a death knell in the quiet room.

Bob's freckles stood out in his white face as he bent down to pull the jar out of the trash. The tips of his ears glowed a vivid, embarrassed red. "Sorry," he mumbled, still not meeting her eyes. "His gout is acting up. It makes him a little difficult."

Baba swallowed a dubious snort. She thought it was more likely that the old man was more than a little difficult at the best of times. Still, his reaction to her had been fairly over the top.

She bent to pick up the scattered hundred-dollar bills from the floor by her feet, placing them together in a neat stack on the counter top. "I'm a bit crabby on occasion myself," she said in a neutral tone. "But my medicines *never* make anyone sick, I assure you."

No point in trying to explain that they were two parts herbs and one part magic, especially if someone was trying to pin the name "witch" on her. She was a witch, of course, but no good could come of folks starting to call her one. But there was no way her mixtures could make someone sick— the worst that could happen was that they simply did nothing. And even then, they'd smell like heaven and feel like a caress.

Bob darted a glance over his shoulder and stuffed the money into a small gray cashbox. Finally, he looked her in the face, his eyes a startling blue framed by pale red lashes. "It's true what he said, though. People seem to be having bad reactions to the stuff they bought off of you." He gave her a halfhearted smile as he pushed her keys and the ointment onto her half of the counter. "I'm sure you didn't do it on purpose."

"I didn't do it at all," she growled, more to herself than

to him. "Something is seriously wrong with this scenario." She bit her lip, thinking madly as she jammed the jar back into her pocket. "Look, Bob, I need to find out what the devil is going on here. Can you tell me the names of some of the people who had problems with my medicines and where they live?"

He looked doubtful, and she added quickly, "If the herbs didn't work, I need to collect them to see why. And give everyone their money back, of course."

"Oh," he said. "Well, that would be good. Folks around here don't have much extra. If you gave them their money back, then they could go to the drugstore and buy something else for whatever ails them." He grabbed a pencil and a piece of paper and starting writing down names and addresses. "Are you going to be able to find these places? I know you're not that familiar with the area."

Steely determination caused tiny sparks to arc off the tips of her fingers, singeing the paper slightly as she slid it into her pants with the rejected ointment. "Don't you worry," she said. "I'll find them." The words *and find out what the hell is going on here* were added only inside her own head.

TWELVE

THE FIRST PLACE she stopped was only about a mile down the road from Bob's, on a rough gravel street that dipped into a gulley off the main route that ran through town. The place she was looking for perched precariously on a hillside overlooking a stream that looked like it flooded every spring. The house had faded, peeling white paint, and the roof was patched with mismatched shingles. A few chickens wandered lazily through the front yard, pecking at the dirt and clucking at Baba when she got out of the truck.

"Hello, girls," she said, magically producing a few handfuls of corn to toss in their direction. Baba liked chickens; they were cheerful, useful, and entertaining. If she ever settled down in one place, she was going to get herself some chickens. Of course, if she did, Chudo-Yudo would probably just eat them.

"Are your people home?" she asked the nearest hen, a black and white beauty with fluffy feathers that covered her feet. "I need to talk to them."

The door to the house opened a crack and a skinny man

of around thirty stuck out his head, gazing at her with a pleasant but slightly befuddled expression.

"Are you talking to my chickens?" he asked, opening the door wide enough for her to see two small children peeking out from behind his gangly legs. "I wouldn't bother, if I were you. They're not very bright."

"That one's Esmeralda," the little boy added. "She lays a lot of eggs, so we're not going to cook her for dinner."

Baba glanced down at the hen at her feet. "Do you hear that, Esmeralda? That's good news, isn't it?" Esmeralda squawked loudly and both kids giggled. The boy looked to be around five and his sister maybe a year or two younger.

Baba took a few steps closer to the house and said, "Hi, my name is Barbara Yager, and I'm looking for a woman named Lily. Does she live here?" She aimed a small smile at the children, which made the girl duck her head shyly and stick her thumb into her rosebud pink mouth.

"Lily is my wife," the man said and looked more closely at Baba. "You're that herbalist who sold her the cream for her tendonitis." He shook his head ruefully, catching the boy by the back of his overalls when he tried to make a break for the yard. "I'm not so sure she's going to want to talk to you. Her arm swelled up like a balloon when she put that stuff on it."

"Like a balloon," the boy said in his high-pitched voice, giggling some more and spreading his arms out to show how big the arm had gotten. "Whoosh!"

Baba winced. "That doesn't sound good. I heard from Bob O'Shaunnessy that there was a problem with some of my remedies, and I've never had that happen before. So I came to give Lily her money back and see if I could figure out what went wrong." The knot in her stomach pulled itself tighter, making her suck in her breath.

"Oh," the man said. "Well, we could use the money, although I know she said it wasn't much." The threadbare shirt he wore seemed to prove his point. "If Bob sent you, I'm sure it's okay. He's good people. Fixed my old Toyota for next to nothing." He held the door open wider. "Come on in. I'm Jesse, and these little monkeys are Trudy and Timmy."

Baba thought it wouldn't hurt to have these folks on her side. Besides, she liked Jesse and his little ones. "Actually," she said, "I've got a double-your-money-back guarantee on all my herbal medicines. So you'll be getting back twice what Lily paid me." She looked down at the chicken and added, "Isn't that right, Esmeralda?" which made the children giggle again.

Jesse's smile grew a little wider. "Well, that's pretty fair," he said. "Though I suspect Lily would be happier if her arm didn't look like a giant sausage."

Baba winced again, dismay rattling her bones. Jesse and the kids led her down a short passageway into a small rectangular living room with pale blue walls and homemade denim curtains pulled shut against the afternoon sun. Children's toys were everywhere; three dolls and a stuffed bear sat in mid–tea party, and a pile of colorful plastic interlocking blocks seemed to have exploded over half of the worn wooden planks. An equally worn-looking woman was stretched out on a battered sofa, one arm encased in an ice pack that was slowly dripping onto a few red and yellow blocks on the floor underneath it.

She lifted her head as they all trooped into the room. "What's going on?" she said, then hoisted herself up with a grunt when she saw Baba. "Hey, I was going to come by and see you." She held up the swollen arm. "I think there was something wrong with that stuff you sold me."

Ouch. Baba could feel the dark, prickly aura coming off the arm from half the room away. She didn't know what had caused it, but it wasn't anything she'd made, that was for sure. She handed a twenty to Jesse, who stuffed it into his pocket as if afraid she'd change her mind, and went over to perch on the sofa next to Lily.

"May I take a look?" Baba asked, peeling off the soggy pack and handing it to the little boy. Lily's pale skin was covered with tiny reddish bumps and the arm was so swollen it felt more like a tree limb than a human one. She laid her hands gently on the surface, feeling for the malignant energy that overlay the normal healthy muscle, bone, and skin and pulling it out, bit by bit, until it was gone. For good measure, she mended the original tendonitis, easing the strain and inflammation caused by too much lifting of small wriggling bodies.

It wasn't a good idea to do such a blatant healing—one of the reasons she used herbs instead of magic most of the time. But this woman had trusted her to help, and she couldn't just leave her suffering.

"Wow," Lily said, her voice colored with something like awe. "That's amazing. It feels so much better. What did you do? Reiki or something?"

"Um, yes, Reiki," Baba said. The popular energy healing technique was as good a cover as any. "The salve should have worked without it, but since you seemed to have a bad reaction to something in the mixture, I thought I'd better use the, um, Reiki to fix it."

Lily was so happy to have her arm back to a normal size; she clearly wasn't interested in questioning the logic of the statement. "Gee, well I really appreciate it." She glanced at her husband ruefully. "I guess we should give you your money back, since you cured the tendonitis after all."

"Oh, no," Baba said, waving one hand in negation. "Not after what you went through." She paused, and then added, as if the thought had just come to her, "Although since you're obviously not going to be using it, I'd be glad to have the salve back."

"Sure thing," Jesse said, and ran off to fetch it.

Baba enjoyed a cup of invisible tea with Trudy, Timmy, and the dolls until he got back, and was almost sorry to leave. She had a rare moment of wistfulness, thinking about what it might be like to have a child of her own. Impossible. But still, there were times . . .

"I apologize again for the bad reaction. That never happens," Baba said to Lily on her way out.

Lily shrugged, her tired face still pretty and astonishingly cheerful, under the circumstances. They were clearly people who made the best of what they had. Baba found herself liking them a lot, and wondering if there was some way to help them out. Too bad that geese who lay golden eggs were no longer in fashion. And a surprise oil well in the backyard would only pollute the stream.

"Do you ever play the lottery?" she asked Jesse as he let her out the front door.

"Huh?" He shooed away a couple of chickens with one foot. "Sure, every once in a while, when we have an extra dollar to spare. Never won more than ten bucks, though." Brown eyes gave her a puzzled look. "Why do you ask?"

"Oh, no reason." she said, and waved good-bye to the kids, who waved back enthusiastically as she pulled out of the driveway. Their uncomplicated good will made her smile all the way to the main road, but her pleasant mood vanished as soon as she pulled to the side to check out the container that Jesse had returned to her.

It was hers, all right—a small white, almost translucent jar with a faint gray cursive *BY* etched onto the porcelain. But the contents inside bore only a passing resemblance to the salve she'd so lovingly crafted. Bits of dark green matter flecked what should have been a pure beige cream, and it smelled *wrong*, like rotting wood and curdled milk and the dawn of a sullen day after a night of bad storms.

What the hell?

Lips tight, Baba put the truck back into gear and pulled onto the highway, headed in the direction of the next address Bob had given her. There was something decidedly odd going on here, and she was going to find the explanation if it killed her. Or better yet, whoever was behind what was clearly a plot to discredit her. Somehow, she had a feeling Maya had her dainty hands in there somewhere. If that bitch was ruining Baba's good name, there was going to be hell to pay.

BY THE TIME she got back home, Baba was so angry, she was shaking like an aspen in a hurricane. It was all she could do to roll the BMW down off the ramp she kept in the back of the truck and park it to the side of the trailer until she could find the time to fix the paint job. Right now, she had more important things to do. Like track down whoever was making her clients sick and beat the living crap out of them.

"Feeling better now that you have the bike back?" Chudo-Yudo asked when she came in the door. He was sprawled across the entire length of the couch, one large white paw holding his place in one of Baba's historical romances. He liked to read as much as Baba did, although he preferred fantasy—especially those with dragons in them.

He ducked as one of her boots went flying across the Airstream and bashed into a cupboard on the far end. It was quickly followed by its mate, which hit the exact same spot with a hollow thud. A stream of cursing colored the air inside a light robin's egg blue.

"I take it that's a no, then," Chudo-Yudo said, closing the book with a broad canine sigh. "Didn't the mechanic do a good job?"

Baba stomped over to sit next to him, flexing her toes in the soft fibers of the rug with relief. She hated wearing shoes. And never wore socks.

"Bah," she said. "The bike is fine. At least as fine as it can be, until I can do something about the way it looks. But I ran into a problem."

Chudo-Yudo cocked his head to one side. "How unusual for you," he said in a sarcastic tone.

"This is serious," Baba said, scrubbing her face with both hands, as if she could wash away the last couple of hours. After visiting three more people, and being variously yelled at, cried on, and threatened with a lawsuit, she felt like she was covered with some kind of viscous, malignant sludge. "Someone's been tampering with my herbal remedies," she told the dog.

That got his attention, and he sat up straight, the book sliding unnoticed to the floor, where tiny silk flowers helped to break its fall.

"The hell you say!" His brown eyes went wide. "All of them? How? Why?"

Baba shook her head. "All the ones I could track down

anyway. Bob told me that people had been complaining, and his father—" she took a deep breath at the memory of the old man's nasty accusations—"let's just say that 'witch' is the nicest word being used to describe me. I had one woman whose arm swelled up when she used my cream on it, another who sneezed so hard she fell off a stool and broke her ankle, and a guy who came to me for a hair growth shampoo that made his hair fall out instead." *And hadn't that been fun to try and fix subtly. Great goddess.*

"Holy Mother Russia," Chudo-Yudo said. "That's awful."

"Those aren't the worst, though," she said, heart heavy as she remembered the hysterical mother who swore Baba's cough syrup had made her baby so sick, she'd had to take him to the emergency room.

The woman had been distraught, and wouldn't let Baba into the house, slamming the door in her face when Baba asked to come in. She'd had to do what she could to help the infant from outside, standing in the insubstantial shadows by the bedroom window and praying that no one would drive by and ask what the hell she was up to.

"As to how, I have no earthly idea," she added. Her head felt like it was reverberating with the accusing voices of all those she'd let down; she couldn't think a clear thought past the murk and the misery of it all.

"All the medicines I've been able to get back look like my mixtures in my bottles, but every single one of them has been adulterated with something horribly wrong."

She pulled the vials and jars out of her pockets, which as usual held as much as she wanted them to hold. Chudo-Yudo put his massive head down next to them and sniffed. Then he let out a huge snort, eyes watering and black nose twitching.

"Ugh. That's nasty," he said, rubbing a paw across his muzzle. "Feh."

Baba looked for something else to throw, frustration making her fingers itch to break things. "Tell me about it. And all those people now think *I'm* responsible for making the dreadful concoctions. I *hate* this."

She didn't normally care what anyone thought about her, but this was different. For one thing, she'd found the town, and the people in it, unusually charming. Before this all happened, she'd actually been daydreaming about staying. Just an idle fancy of course, but still. For another, it touched on her honor; that made it matter. And anyone who dared to make a baby sick on purpose and blame it on her? That person was in for a world of pain.

Chudo-Yudo's furry face rumpled in puzzlement. "But how could anyone tamper with all those treatments without someone noticing? It's not like a person could go from house to house messing with the jars in every single place. Someone would have seen something suspicious, wouldn't they?"

Baba sighed. "You'd think so. And if Maya was behind it for some reason, she's not exactly a 'blend in with the locals' kind of gal."

"Maybe she crawled in through their windows?"

Baba snorted at a vision of the neat and polished Maya slithering in past gingham curtains to land in someone's bathroom sink. "Somehow I don't think so, but I suppose anything is possible. For all we know, she's really some creature the size of a cat." She shook her head. "This is getting out of hand. I think it's time to call in the Riders and see if they've learned anything useful. They've been out wandering around all this time, and the only messages I've gotten from them are variations on, "Sorry, nothing yet." Maybe they saw something while they were searching for the missing kids."

She looked down toward where her dragon tattoos curled around her arms and shoulder; as long as the Riders were on a mission for her, each one bore her link in his own symbol. That made the task easier, since while they carried the mark, she could summon them with a thought—albeit a concentrated and directed thought. After all, it wouldn't do to have them show up every time one of them happened to cross her mind.

She closed her eyes, sat up straight, and centered herself,

letting go of the anger and frustration, breathing them out with every exhalation until she was calm and focused. Then she drew a picture in her head of Mikhail Day: his almost too-handsome features that hid a childish love for puns and riddles, and a weakness for damsels in distress, sweet desserts, and showing off. She visualized the white clothes he always wore that never seemed to dare show a smudge, and the long fall of his blond hair when it hung loose in the evening as he carved a wooden figurine by the light of the fire in the old Baba's hut. *Come back,* she sent out silently into the ether. *I need you. Come back.*

Next, she saw Gregori Sun: always serene, with a quiet glow that seemed to emanate from some deep well in his being that no amount of ugliness or violence could touch. His face appeared stern to those who did not know him, but she had seen him nurse a wounded fox back to health, tending it and taming it just enough to heal, and then sending it back into the wild where it belonged. His long slender fingers could snap a man's neck or strum a balalaika with equal ease and skill, and she had never heard him utter a word in anger in all the years she'd known him. Behind her closed eyes, his dark hair and slim figure coalesced into a solid representation of his essence. *Come back. I need you. Come back.*

Last, but certainly not least, she summoned the image of Alexei Knight, so different from the other two, and yet equally valued. Unlike Mikhail's suave bravado and Gregori's calm assassin's grace, Alexei was brute force and animal instincts. He fought at the drop of a hat with a berserker's wild joy for the battle, whether the cause was a mission of mercy or a careless word from a drunk in a tavern. As a child, Baba had once seen him tear an evil man apart with his bare hands, crimson blood bathing the sandy ground at his feet as he roared with laughter.

But he was also the only one of the Riders who took the time to play with the little adopted Baba-in-training, telling her tall tales and tickling her with the ends of her own braids until she giggled helplessly, while the old Baba rolled her

eyes as she tended her cauldron nearby. During their intermittent visits, when the Riders weren't off assisting some
other Baba, it was Alexei who took her for walks in the
woods, pointing out the tiny mushrooms that grew in the
hidden nooks of mossy gnarled tree roots, and teaching her
to punch and kick, so she would have something to defend
herself with until she grew into her magic.

There were not many Babas, but there were only the three
Riders, and she knew them almost as well as she knew herself. *Come back, Alexei. I need you. Come back.*

When she was done, Baba sat back with a sigh. She'd
sent them out with a vague hope that they would see or sense
something helpful. But they were running out of time. And
now that things were going from bad to worse, she needed
them at her side. She'd called—they'd come as soon they
could. Now there was nothing to do but wait.

THIRTEEN

FOUR HOURS LATER, she was still waiting. The long summer's day was sliding slowly into night, a strange purple dusk erupting like a bruise on the horizon. The wind had picked up; it whistled a discordant tune through the trees surrounding the meadow and rattled the metal pieces on the outside of the Airstream until they sounded like a steel drum band.

Baba ran around for a few minutes, tying things down and generally battening down the hatches, and then sat down on the top step leading up into the trailer to peer fretfully into the darkening evening sky. Chudo-Yudo came to stand in the doorway behind her, resting his muzzle companionably on her shoulder.

"I don't like it," she said, finally. The breeze pulled maliciously at her hair, forcing her to put a hand up to hold it out of her face.

"Which don't you like?" Chudo-Yudo asked. "The fact that none of the Riders has reported in yet, or this storm?"

"Both," Baba said, raising her voice a little to be heard above the bellow and shriek of the rising wind. "It never takes the boys this long to come in once I've summoned them, and they shouldn't be that far away." She shook her head, spitting a strand of hair out of her mouth. "And this storm is all wrong. There was no sign of it earlier, and I should have felt it coming; a storm this strong would have been echoing in my bones like a rock slide in a cavern."

A crash of thunder punctuated her words, followed a moment later by a ragged flash of lightning through the clouds overhead. The sky opened up and dropped buckets of rain, coming down in sheets of water too thick to see through. Baba and Chudo-Yudo scrambled back into the Airstream and slammed the door behind them.

Baba uttered a rude word, fists clenched. "This is no natural storm," she said to Chudo-Yudo. "It feels . . . malevolent, somehow." She shivered, disconcerted and unsettled without knowing quite why.

"Do you think Maya—or someone working with her—is trying to keep the Riders from getting back to you?" Chudo-Yudo leaned up against her leg, his warm bulk solid and reassuring.

"Maybe," Baba said, her brow furrowed as she thought it through. "But that would mean Maya, or whoever it is, knows who the Riders are, and could feel me summon them. Back in Russia, that wouldn't have been unheard of, but here? Who would be familiar with the Riders here?"

"Huh," the dog snorted. "And have the power to create a storm of this magnitude. That's even worse."

She nodded in grim agreement. "It could just be a coincidence, I suppose. Maya calling up a magical storm to torment the poor locals—this is going to wreak havoc on their crops—just as I happen to be calling in the Riders."

Chudo-Yudo looked up at her, brown eyes wary. "I don't believe in coincidences."

"No," Baba said softly. "Me neither."

Hail pelted down on the metal roof, sounding like weapon fire. Baba ducked involuntarily, although the Airstream had so much magical protection built into it, it could probably drive through a volcano without incurring any damage greater than a slightly charred aroma. The Riders, out on their motorcycles, would be much more vulnerable.

Another crash of thunder directly overhead made the ground shake, and Baba marched over to the door and flung it open.

"That's it," she said. "I'm putting a stop to this. The elements are *my* sphere of influence; I'll be damned if I let some other witch or magic user mess with the folks under my protection."

Chudo-Yudo cocked his head to one side quizzically, as if asking if she meant simply the Riders (who normally didn't need protecting) or the missing children or everyone in the entire area. Then he gave a shrug and came to stand in the doorway behind her again.

"Go ahead, then. I'll just watch from here. If I get soaked, you'll be complaining about the wet dog smell for a week." He gave her a look of exasperated concern. "Just try not to get struck by lightning, okay? You still haven't gotten around to training your replacement, and I'll be damned if I'm going to do it."

Baba rolled her eyes at him and strode out into the storm, bare feet squelching in the viscous brown mud and wet grass catching at her ankles as if to hold her back. She was instantly soaked to the skin, the cotton shirt and long skirt she wore clinging to her chilled body. Above her, the night was rocked by simultaneous explosions of lightning and the feral roar of thunder, until it seemed like the entire meadow must soon disappear in a flare of smoke and fury, never to be seen again.

Baba ignored it all—churning noise and electric crackle and shuddering ground, the slash of the pelting rain and the biting fingers of the wind. She planted her feet firmly on the dirt, digging her toes in until the rich soil oozed up around her arches. Her arms flew up into the air as she flung her power against the raging energy of the storm.

"By the earth that is my body," she shouted, the words reverberating up from her core, "by the air that is my breath, by the water that is my blood, and by the fire that is my spirit, I command you, elementals of nature, to return to your natural balance. This is my will and my desire, and so mote it be!"

A bolt of lightning struck the ground so close to her, she could feel her hair crackle with static. But then the rain began to ease, dropping back to a drizzle that was soon barely more than a mist in the suddenly quiet evening. Water dripped from the Airstream's roof in musical pitter-pats, and a sliver of moon poked its head out from behind a web-thin cloud. It was over.

She padded soggily back to the doorway, where her faithful dragon-dog sat.

"Nice," he said. "Can I have a cookie? Storms always make me hungry."

ALEXEI WAS THE first to arrive, pounding on the front door and growling like the great black bear he resembled. "Baba, I'm drenched to my skivvies out here, let me in, will you?"

Her heart warmed with relief at the sound of his familiar gruff bellow, and she ran to open the door. In the dim mahogany light outside, his dark bulk blended with the night so he seemed only a shadow of black on black, ominous and foreboding. Forward movement brought his features into focus, a black-and-white photo morphing into color.

Once inside he shook himself, sending droplets of dank water scattering across the room, and making Baba and Chudo-Yudo cry out in protest.

"Alexei! Are you trying to drown us?" Baba snapped her fingers and the moisture disappeared, leaving a dry but still-grumpy man-mountain standing in the middle of her kitchen.

"Came close enough to drowning, myself," he said, scowling down at her. "Might as well share the joy." He stomped off to sit down on the sofa at the near end of the Airstream as another, less forceful, knock came on the door.

"Mikhail!" Baba said, letting him inside and drying him off too. "I was starting to worry about the three of you. Are you okay?"

His bright blue eyes flashed like the lightning. "I am now. I assume you're the one who stopped that benighted storm?" He shook his head, his gorgeous face uncharacteristically dour, and his long hair lank from his drenching. "For a while there, I wasn't sure I was going to make it back at all."

"Me neither," a voice said from behind him, and Baba gasped as Gregori Sun made his way into the trailer, a limp marring his customarily graceful walk. A large gash made a livid path across his forehead, and he held his body as if it hurt to move. "Hello, Baba. Mind if I sit down?"

Baba closed her mouth and led the two Riders to the lounge area at the right of the door. Alexei slid over on the couch to make room for the other men, and Baba grabbed a stool for herself. Chudo-Yudo sat at her feet, black tongue lolling as he stared in fascination at the three battered-looking Riders.

Before she sat down, Baba said, "Can I get you some tea? It will warm you up."

Alexei grimaced. "Tea? We all come in half dead and battered and the best you can do is offer us tea? I don't know about these guys, but I could use a stiff drink. Vodka, preferably." The other two nodded in agreement, even Gregori, who rarely drank.

"Oh, sure," Baba said, and pulled a bottle of Stolichnaya out of the freezer. She poured four large shots, although she didn't touch the one in front of her. Something told her she was going to need to keep her head.

"Confusion to the enemy," Mikhail said, raising his glass.

"Surviving to fight another day," added Gregori, lifting his.

Alexei rolled his eyes. *"Na Zdorovie!"* And muttered under his breath, "Philosophical idiots."

They all drank, and Baba filled their glasses again, fetched a plate of pickles to go with the vodka in traditional Russian fashion, then sat down and looked them over carefully. The Riders looked better already, a combination of their fast healing powers and the anesthetic qualities of the alcohol.

"I was starting to think you hadn't gotten my messages," she said, sipping more circumspectly at her own vodka. "I'm glad you're all okay."

Mikhail snorted. "I got it, all right. But as soon as I headed back in this direction, all kinds of freaky stuff started happening. And then that storm came up and everything *really* went to hell." He upended his second shot and slammed the glass down on the table for emphasis.

"What kind of freaky stuff?" Baba asked, pouring him another and putting the bottle down where they could all get at it.

The Riders all looked at each other.

"I ran into a bank of unnatural fog," Gregori said, fingering his empty glass but not refilling it. "It was endless, and the bike's headlights just got swallowed up in it. I felt like I was riding forever and getting nowhere. Creepy as hell. And there were creatures in that fog that didn't belong here; things with fangs and claws and a foul stench that saturated the mist until I could barely breathe. It was almost a relief when the storm blew up and dropped that damned oak tree on me." He shuddered, and refilled his glass, throwing the contents back with a compulsive swallow.

"I had creatures too," Mikhail said. "But mine were some kind of small chittering thing, like demented squirrels on a bad acid trip. They chased me down back roads until I was completely turned around; there were so many of them, it was as if the ground behind me had fur and teeth." He held up one leg to show them what looked like a series of tiny bite marks in the white leather pants he wore. One white boot had a chunk missing from the sole. "Thank the gods for thick leather, that's all I can say. They disappeared when the storm came up, but then the road washed out in front of me like someone erased it, and I had to backtrack the long way." He crunched a pickle between strong, white molars. "Freaky."

Alexei growled. "That is nothing," he said, tension making his accent so thick it sounded like *Dat iz nuh-tink*. "I was riding along, minding my own business, and a stream tried to swallow me up." Another shot of vodka slid down his throat. Baba had lost track of whether it was number four or five. Of course, he was as big as any two normal men, so he probably didn't even feel them yet.

Chudo-Yudo raised one furry eyebrow, and eyed the nearly empty bottle suspiciously. Clearly, he was wondering how much of the Riders' strange tale was real, and how much was the natural Russian penchant for exaggeration while drinking. Baba was wondering the same thing, and said so.

"I'm not making this up," Alexei said, his long mustache turned down in grim assertion. He reached into one pocket and pulled out a small green frog, who blinked wetly at the assembled company, almost lost in the giant's large out-stretched palm. "I was riding down the road next to a small creek, and the next thing I know, this huge wave of water washes downstream in a rush, overflows the banks, and engulfs the exact spot where I happened to be."

Baba gaped at him. "What did you do?"

He shrugged, making the entire couch shake. Mikhail held his glass out away from him so as not to spill a drop of the precious liquid inside.

"I held my breath, prayed to all the gods I could think of, and kept going. But I can tell you, if I didn't have a magical motorcycle that still thinks it is a horse, I would be lying by the side of the road, lungs filled with water and a pissed-off expression on my cold, dead face." He took a long pull straight off the bottle. "There is something very wrong here, Baba. I swear, that river water had arms in it. I could feel them, cold and hard and clammy, trying to drag me under."

Baba decided to have another sip of her vodka after all. The stories they'd told sent little mice of doom scampering up and down her spine.

"Maya has to be behind all of this. There's no other ex-planation. But I can't believe she's that strong a witch and I didn't feel it." She could kick herself for not just grabbing Maya when she was standing right next to her. It could have prevented all this mayhem. Of course, then they would have had to try to force the location of the missing children out of her, and something told Baba that wouldn't be easy. *Damn it.*

"I don't think so, Baba," Gregori said in his calm voice. "This could not have been the work of just one woman. No matter how powerful she is, she can't have been in three places at once."

"Plus throwing up one hell of a storm," Chudo-Yudo added.

"It's more than that," Mikhail said, looking up from the depths of his glass. "If those creatures I ran into are from around here, I'll wear black for a month. We're clearly dealing with in incursion from the Otherworld."

Alexei nodded in agreement, the braid at the end of his beard nearly sliding into his vodka. "Yeah, I'd say mine was something from the Otherworld too. Some water elemental, maybe."

Baba's jaw dropped open. "That's impossible. There's only one way to get from there to here, and there is no way anything came through it without my knowing!"

Four people and one dog turned to look accusingly at the closet. It looked back, rattling its wonky knob as if to say, "Not me, folks."

"What about another door?" Mikhail asked. "It's not like you have the only one."

"Of course not," Baba scowled. She was very zealous about her job guarding the passageway between the two worlds. "There are a few natural gateways left, but the nearest ones are in Ontario and New York City, and they're watched over twenty-four/seven. There's no way an entire battalion of supernatural creatures could have waltzed right through one of those doorways, swarmed across New York State, and nobody noticed. You boys must be wrong."

"Or Maya found another door," Gregori said quietly.

The silence that followed that simple sentence resembled the hush after an explosion, before the chaos hit and bits of things began raining onto the ground.

"Another door," Mikhail repeated. He shook his head. "Impossible."

" 'When you have eliminated the impossible, whatever remains, *however improbable*, must be the truth,' " Gregori said.

"Huh?" Alexei just stared at him.

"Sherlock Holmes, you moron. Don't you ever open a book?" Mikhail smacked the large man on the shoulder, then shook out his hand. "Damn. I have *got* to remember not to do that."

Baba thought about it for a minute while the boys argued good-naturedly about the merits of Russian versus English literary works. It *should*, in fact, be impossible for a new door to the Otherworld to simply appear. But the existence of one would certainly explain much of the strange activity in the area, if Otherworld creatures were responsible for the damage and mischief the locals were experiencing. And if Maya was from the other plane, a glamour could mask alien features, rather than disguise human ones. Not to mention that would sure as crap explain the huge golden stag that had almost killed her. She *had* sensed something Otherworldly when she first saw Maya at that meeting, but she'd dismissed the feeling. Maybe she'd been too hasty.

"You know," she said, thinking aloud, "there was one time when a huge earthquake somehow accidentally opened a portal that hadn't existed before. Do you remember?"

"Nineteen sixty, Lumaco, Chile," Gregori said. "The South American Baba called us in to help with cleanup. It was a nightmare." He looked thoughtful. "I'd forgotten about that. But there haven't been any earthquakes here lately, have there?"

She shook her head, curling one strand of black hair around her finger and chewing on it absently as she pondered. "Noooo . . . but they've been doing all this drilling deep into the shale. Fracking, they call it. You don't suppose that could have opened up a new doorway, do you?"

"No matter how improbable," Gregori said again. "If there was one, that would explain where all the creatures we sensed came from."

Baba could feel the blood rush out of her face, and she suddenly felt as if the air temperature had dropped twenty degrees. "Oh gods. And why we haven't been able to find any trace of the missing children here. She took them to the Otherworld."

Four sets of eyes looked at her, appalled. "But. But that's against the rules," Chudo-Yudo said, dropping his current bone on the floor with a crunch. "No one is allowed to steal Human children and bring them across anymore. That's punishable by banishment!"

The Riders' faces grew, if possible, even grimmer. Banishment was one of the most feared punishments in the Otherworld. For people who lived almost forever, "never able to go home" was a very long time.

"Maya didn't strike me as the type to care about rules," Baba said. "But if those kids are on the other side . . ."

She didn't have to finish the sentence. They all knew that humans who spent any amount of time in the Otherworld were sometimes changed in ways that were next to impossible to undo.

"We can look for them there," Mikhail said, doubt coloring his voice like gray smoke, "but if someone wants to hide something in the Otherworld, it usually stays hidden."

Baba knew he was right. In a place that constantly changed and shifted according to the needs and desires of those who lived there, there were too many forgotten corners and veiled niches to search before it was too late.

"I asked Koshei to see if he could find anyone who knew Maya on the other side," she said, knowing he would have already reported in if there was any news. "Maybe he'll turn up something that can help."

Gregori cleared his throat and gave Baba a meaningful look.

"What?" she said. "Why are you staring at me like that?"

Mikhail added his own cool blue gaze. "Somebody has to tell the queen and king."

"Oh, no," Baba held up both hands as if warding off a

blow. Or something a lot worse. "Not me. The last time someone gave the queen news that really upset her, she turned six of her handmaidens into swans. For all I know, they're still swimming around in the royal moat. One of you should tell her."

"I'd make a lousy swan," Alexei said with a slightly slurred snort. "Probably sink like a stone. Besides, you're the one who called us in on this; we're just the hired help."

Gregori gave a particularly Russian shrug, one shoulder shifting up and down expressively. "Sorry, Baba, you're going to have to do it. And better sooner than later. You know how the queen feels about people who keep secrets from her. And despite your autonomy in this world, the Babas all report to the queen at the end of the day. She rules over all magic. You do *not* want to piss her off."

Baba sighed, drank the rest of her vodka down in one fiery swallow, and stood up as decisively as her slightly shaky knees allowed. "Fine. I'm going. I'm going." She turned to Chudo-Yudo. "I'm leaving you in charge. Try not to let the boys wreck the place while I'm gone."

The dragon-dog licked her hand. "Try not to get turned into anything nasty. I'd hate to have to eat you."

She'd taken two steps in the direction of the wardrobe, when Mikhail said, "Stop."

FOURTEEN

"WHAT?" BABA ASKED, just a little testy. Maybe he was going to offer to go in her place after all.

"Is that what you're wearing?"

She started to roll her eyes but thought the better of it after glancing down at her bare feet and funky skirt. "Damn. Definitely not a good idea." The queen was a stickler for protocol.

She ran into the back bedroom and changed quickly into her formal court attire, coming back out dressed in a scoop-necked red silk tunic that hugged her curves, and black velvet tights tucked into high leather boots so glossy you could see your reflection in them. A narrow silver sword sat on her right hip, and a small ornate dagger was on the left, both hanging from a jeweled belt. Her usual wild mass of dark hair was caught up sedately in a gossamer net decorated with tiny garnets and rubies that glittered like stars in the gold filigree, and around her neck was a simple necklace in the shape of a dragon with ruby eyes.

"Better?" she asked, twirling around so they could all see. The stiletto heel of one boot dug into the carpet under her feet, and a tiny orange salamander gave a high-pitched squeak and wiggled out of harm's way.

Mikhail waggled his eyebrows at her, leering enthusiastically. "Much! You clean up quite nicely, Baba."

Gregori and Alexei nodded in agreement. Even the dog looked impressed.

"You know, Chudo-Yudo," she said. "Since the boys are here, they could guard the Water of Life and Death for you, and the doorway for me. You could come with me," she said hopefully. "Wouldn't you like a chance to change out of that big furry form and spread your wings again?"

He shook his massive head. "Thanks, but no thanks. I'd rather be a live dog than a dead dragon. No way am I taking bad news to the queen. But be sure to give her my regards."

Baba shrugged. There was no point in more stalling—time to go tell the most powerful woman in the Otherworld that not only was there a breach in her defenses not one of her people had caught, but that someone had been using it to break the rules on both sides of the gateway. That was going to go over well.

She walked over to the closet door and opened it—directly onto the passageway, with no juggling required. It figured that it worked without arguing . . . the one time she wished it wouldn't.

ONCE ON THE other side, however, things didn't go so smoothly. In theory, since she had a specific destination in mind, the door should have opened nearby, and a short walk would have taken her directly to court. Instead, she ended up in a murky back corner she recognized from her youthful misadventures as the home of an antisocial troll and his wife, a carnivorous tree fairy named Lucinda. Not people she wanted to meet up with again, even if she hadn't been in a hurry. Focusing on her goal of seeing the queen and king, Baba took a deep breath and followed the nearest path that led elsewhere.

Thorny blue vines caught at her feet as she almost tumbled headfirst into a ravine filled with giant roses in garish hues of acid pink, electric green, and maroon. Petals larger than her hand rained down on her head as she tried to catch her balance, and the sickly-sweet fragrance caught in her throat. She concentrated harder, fighting her way out of the dell and onto another path.

Iridescent lizards the size of Buicks sunned themselves on desert rocks piled one on top of another until it seemed they would reach the sky. Nothing else lived under the cloudless ochre canopy except spiky cacti and a carpet of low-growing red moss that bled orange as she trod across it in her equally spiky boots. She chose yet another path.

Sticky dirty-white threads crisscrossed the dusty passageway. It seemed to be the inside of some ancient dungeon or basement, although not one Baba recognized. The only light came from a far-off corner, where a strange clicking sound heralded the arrival of a gigantic white spider that let off a malevolent glow as if to attract anything foolish enough to seek solace in the dark. Fangs dripped wetly over a gaping maw as the arachnid raced across the room, setting the web to vibrating like a possessed and weeping harp. Baba turned and sped back in the direction she'd come from.

An endless chartreuse forest held no path at all. Only trees, as far as the eye could see, blocking out the dim pseudosun of the realm, and replacing it with gloomy shadows that colored the air with sadness. There were tall trees whose branches creaked and groaned in an unseen wind, and small trees, struggling to survive in the footsteps of their elders, bent and twisted with the effort. Unhealthy-looking mushrooms sprouted from cracks and crevices, pale yellow gills under gray caps spotted with oozing black spores. As she watched, a bird nibbled on one, and let out a horrible shriek, its last breath bubbling out like lava as it died.

"Okay," Baba said out loud. "That is just about enough of this nonsense." She swiveled on one heel so fast, the air hummed, her sword thrust forward to catch the tail of a pale string bean of a creature, all bulbous eyes and long nose, as it slid behind the cover of a lurking tree. Chameleon-like, the creature's coloring changed to match the bark of the tree trunk it had been endeavoring to hide behind, which explained why it had taken her so long to catch a glimpse of the source of her tortuous, meandering route.

Leaving its tail skewered in place, she used the hand not holding her sword to drag the four-foot-tall being out into the open. Its mouth opened and closed like a fish thrown on dry land, but the only sound that came out was an indignant squawk.

"I hope you have more to say for yourself than that," Baba said grimly, her fingers tightening around the creature's throat. "After you've led me hither and yon for the last hour, I'm not in the mood for excuses. Who are you, and why have you been hiding the path to the palace from me?" She shook him briskly, to further emphasize how *very* out of patience she was.

Eyes wide, the creature said in a hoarse squeak, "Not my fault, Baba Yaga! Not my fault! Rusalka made me hide path from Baba Yaga! Told me to! Told me to!"

Baba scowled down at him. She was pretty sure it was a him anyway, although she wasn't going to look closely enough to find out for sure. "What do you mean, a Rusalka told you to lead me astray?"

The Rusalkas were water nymphs with bad reputations and worse habits. In the Old Country, they'd been known for luring young men to their deaths by disguising themselves as beautiful maidens, then drowning any man foolish enough to follow them back to their streams. Occasionally, they killed children as well, back in the days when wee ones were sent out to gather wood or herbs without someone older to watch over them.

Now that almost all the mythic creatures had been restricted to the Otherworld, Rusalkas were simply beings out of stories told around the fire on cold winter nights. They had no power in the human world, and little enough left here.

"Why would a Rusalka care where I go?" Baba asked the

squirming manikin. "And why would you do what she said? Water nymphs have no right to command the likes of you."

The weedy little skulker whined and moaned, clutching at its tail with one six-fingered hand. Its fingers were long and the undersides were covered with tiny suckers; clearly its natural environment was a far wetter place than this forest. "This one different," it insisted. "This Rusalka strong and powerful. Very angry about what Humans do to water in the mundane lands. Makes water creatures like Rusalka weak and sick on this side. She no like being weak. Has many friends. Drinks their magic like wine. Trades for it. Many, many friends."

"Who?" Baba demanded. "What friends?"

"Don't know!" the creature said in a low voice, bulging eyes glazed with what looked to Baba like genuine fear. "Don't care! Rusalka scary. She say do, I do."

Baba pulled her sword loose with a moist *snick* and held it under the creature's lengthy nose. "*I* am a lot scarier than any Rusalka," she said with quiet threat. "I suggest you stop messing with me and run away to hide until this is over." The creature whimpered and wrapped both narrow hands around its punctured tail.

"Sorry, Baba Yaga," it whispered, and took off into the woods, disappearing as soon as its skin changed color again.

"You might be sorry," Baba muttered as she set off down the path, clearly visible now that the creature's subtle magic no longer disguised it. "But that damned Rusalka is going to be a *lot* sorrier."

THINGS WENT MUCH faster without someone putting stumbling blocks in her way, and five minutes later, Baba emerged from the trees onto a manicured lawn that seemed to stretch for miles. Looming over it all in ethereal splendor was the royal palace, a spun-sugar and stone confection of graceful towers and arched windows, with festive banners flying from its tall spires.

Crafted an eternity ago from magic and moonlight, the

castle gave the illusion of floating over the landscape while still being strong and formidable. Like so much of the Otherworld, it rarely looked the same from year to year, but its essence was always the same—pure enchantment, beauty, and power. Much like its queen, who had ruled the land for as long as anyone could remember.

Overhead, the sky resembled something much like dusk, although days here never really began nor ended, and a true sun never shone. Three moons cast a brilliant white light over the landscape, one a first quarter crescent, another the waning quarter, and in the middle, a glorious fecund round full moon tinged a slightly bloody red.

As Baba neared the palace, she passed courtiers playing croquet in evening dress, the ladies dripping with diamonds and other sparkling precious stones, wide skirts of crimson, or pale blue, or lilac continually threatening to knock over the wickets as they glided in elegant processionals from place to place. The men were almost as dazzling as the women, wearing silk tunics in bright colors over velvet tights, and silver swords much like the one that Baba bore. Many of the court had hair that swept almost to the ground, and ears that rose to delicate points. All of them were strikingly attractive in a way that humans could never hope to attain.

In among the courtiers ran smaller less gaudy creatures, most of them brown or green in tone, with attire to match, usually bearing trays laden with golden goblets or dainty snacks. They were kept scurrying, carrying this and that to the players, and to the clumps of nobles who stood around in threes and fours, watching and gossiping, and otherwise whiling away the tedious hours until the next party started, or a hunt was called.

Many of those she passed called out greetings to Baba, who had been a regular, albeit sporadic, visitor since childhood, but she only nodded at them and walked on in the direction of the castle.

When she drew closer to her goal, she stopped one of the tiny servitors, a brownie by the looks of her, and asked where she might find the queen and king. The brownie bobbed a curtsey, not spilling a drop of the nectar in the glasses she carried, and pointed down the lawn and past the building itself.

"They be in the rose garden by the pond, mistress, at tea with some of the court," the little woman said, and ran off to bring the drinks and a pile of lacy fans to a group of haughty-looking ladies standing under the casually drooping bows of a weeping willow.

Baba strode on, rounding the edge of the castle to see the rulers of the Otherworld, along with a number of ladies-in-waiting, knights of the court, and some attendants, seated at a carved wooden table overlooking an azure blue pond the size of a small lake. The pond was dotted with notch-edged lily pads, their brilliant blossoms a vivid contrast to the crystalline waters.

Small orange frogs croaked in three-part harmony, and majestic white swans floated by decorative statues of scantily clad youths. In the middle of the pond, a fountain shot sprays of water twenty feet into the air, creating a rainbow-filled mist that arced down over the fishtailed maidens who frolicked underneath its perpetual showers.

Baba ignored most of the scenery, although its unearthly loveliness always made her heart soar for just a moment. She approached the group seated by the end of the waterline, and going directly to the queen, dropped to one knee and gave a flourishing bow.

"Your Majesties," she said, nodding at the queen and her consort. Although the king had a title equal to hers, it was the queen who was the true power in the Otherworld. "I greet you, and bring news of the world beyond your walls. May I beg leave to speak with you in private?" Baba thought it might be best to limit the people who knew what was going on. Besides, that would reduce the number of innocent bystanders.

The queen rose from her ornate, thronelike chair and gestured for Baba to rise, embracing her, and kissing her on both cheeks. As always, the queen's long, silvery-white hair was piled in a tower of complicated braids, emphasizing her long neck and high cheekbones. Her pale, almost translucent skin made her look fragile and delicate, an illusion reinforced by her willowy figure and fine, long-fingered hands. A gauzy gown of pale pink silk matched the roses that grew all around, and a tiara of pink diamonds glittered in the light of the moons. She was almost too beautiful to look at, and capable of both remarkable generosity and mind-blowing cruelty.

"My darling Baba!" the queen cried in a voice that sounded like music. "It has been far too long, my dear. Come, you must sit and have tea with us."

Baba put on her best court smile. She got along well with the queen, for the most part; it wasn't so long ago, in the long lives of the royals, that Baba was a small child, visiting with her mentor, playing with dolls underneath the table at the queen's feet, and the queen still had a tendency to think of her as a beloved younger second cousin, very much removed. That didn't mean Baba was foolish enough to think she was safe from reprisal if the queen decided to hold her responsible for the bad news she brought.

"I would love to have tea some other time, Your Majesty, but I'm afraid I have urgent tidings that cannot wait. I beg an audience, if you please." Baba kept her eyes slightly lowered, trying to see the queen's face without staring rudely.

"Pish tosh, my dear," the queen said dismissively. "Any news you have to share can be told in front of the rest of this company. There is nothing you can say that my beloved consort and the most trusted members of our court cannot be witness to." She waved one languid hand at Baba. "So, what is this oh-so-important information that cannot wait until I finish my tea?"

Crap. Well, she'd just have to spill the beans and hope for the best. Presumably the members of the queen's inner circle had gotten good at ducking over the centuries.

"Highness, I have had a number of run-ins with a mysterious woman wearing a glamour and wielding powers unlike those available to most Humans. And then today, the White Rider, the Red Rider, and the Black Rider were all attacked by creatures they swear could only have come from the Otherworld. We assume they were acting under the command of this woman, who calls herself Maya."

There were gasps from the assembled company, although the queen's expression didn't change. The Riders were considered to be utterly dependable and beyond reproach in their service to the Babas, and by extension, the kingdom as well, since Babas guarded both worlds.

"That seems highly unlikely," the queen said, a slight chill in her voice. "How could she have such creatures in the Human lands?"

Baba braced herself and looked directly at the queen. "We believe that she has somehow discovered a new, unauthorized door somewhere in the area. It is the only explanation for the presence of so many magical creatures, many of whom she is using to torment the local citizens, as well as directing them in attacks against the Riders and against my own person."

There were more exclamations from the courtiers around the table, but Baba kept her attention on the only person whose reaction truly mattered.

The queen's regal face grew even sterner, if that was possible. A few of the surrounding people started to edge away from the space.

"That would be an extremely undesirable situation, were it to prove to be true," she said. Frost crept out from underneath her pointed silver shoes and turned the grass below her feet to dust. The closest rosebush faded from a healthy pink to a lackluster gray, its petals dropping one by one to litter the ground. "Are you certain these beings are not crossing through another gateway? Yours, perhaps?" The queen narrowed her eyes at Baba, who tried not to flinch.

"They could not be coming through my trailer . . . er, hut, that is, Your Majesty," Baba said in as firm a tone as she dared use. "Either Chudo-Yudo or I have been there at all times. And the nearest other known doorways are many leagues from the area where the incidents occurred, in the Human places known as Ontario and New York City. It is unlikely in the extreme that the guardians of those doors would have allowed so many to pass from this world into that one without permission, and even if they had done so, how would the creatures have gotten so far without someone noticing?"

The queen pursed her perfectly shaped lips, tapping them lightly with a dainty filigreed fan. "If you are right, dearest Baba, I shall be *quite displeased.* There is a reason why all the passageways in and out of our world are guarded and those who are allowed to pass through them are few. The balance between the Otherworld and the Human lands is precarious enough as it is; such wanton use of an illicit doorway could destroy that balance irrevocably. As a Baba, it is part of your job to make sure that doesn't happen."

Sudden storm clouds appeared overhead, and whitecaps danced on the surface of the pond, which a moment before had been perfectly calm. The king reached out and patted the queen's hand.

"Now darling, I'm sure things aren't as dire as all that," he said in a soothing voice, casting a wary look at the sky. "We'll just send Baba back to find what is no doubt just a tiny little hole in the fabric between the worlds, and then we'll fix it. No harm done." He gave his consort his most charming smile. "Why don't you let me pour you some more tea? Yours seems to have gotten a little cold."

Baba cleared her throat, wishing she were anywhere else but there, with any other words about to come out of her mouth. Despite her height and the three-inch heels she wore, she felt very small. And sincerely hoped she wasn't about to get smaller. Like swan- or frog-sized.

"I'm sorry, Your Majesty, but I'm afraid it is worse than that." She braced herself, and spit out the rest. "There are a number of children who have gone missing from the local area over the last few months, and I now believe that this woman has been stealing the children and bringing them here."

At this, the queen sprang to her feet, her porcelain teacup shattering as it hit the ground. "What?" she shrieked, almost unmusically. "Preposterous! Unacceptable!"

One of the crescent moons exploded, sending a rain of sparks out of the dusky sky to sizzle where they landed. Six lovely naked women suddenly appeared, floundering in the middle of the pond, shedding white feathers as they made their sputtering way to the edge of the water and staggered out to lie panting on the ground. The silver teapot the king had been about to pour from vanished, to be replaced by a multihued parrot that squawked indignantly and flew off to sit in a locust tree.

"Crap," muttered the king.

Baba could feel all the blood drain out of her face. "I am so very sorry to be the bearer of such unpleasant news, Your Majesty. But I thought it was important that you be told as soon as possible."

The queen took a deep breath, perceptibly getting a grip on her temper, two bright spots of color visible on her normally pale cheeks. Two slightly sheepish-looking ladies crawled out from where they'd been hiding underneath the table, their elegant gowns a little worse for the experience.

"Stealing children is what got the Otherworld into so much trouble in the old days," the queen said, a grim expression turning her beautiful visage merely average stunning. "Nobody cared if a goblin stopped up a chimney or a brownie borrowed some milk, but steal their children, and Humans will stop at nothing to hunt us all down." She sank back into her chair. "This is very, very bad news indeed."

The king handed her his teacup and cast a dubious glance at Baba. "Surely you are mistaken. No one would be so foolish. What would she have to gain?"

"On my way here, I ran into a creature who was attempting to keep me from reaching the court. When I confronted him, he told me he was following orders from a Rusalka who had achieved great power and influence somehow." Baba gave the king a rueful smile. "I can't think of any other way a lowly Rusalka could achieve such a thing, frankly, so

I'm guessing that this Rusalka and the woman I have been dealing with are one and the same, although as yet I have no proof to back up my assumption."

The queen tapped her fan on the edge of the table sharply. "Are you suggesting, my dear Baba Yaga, that there are those *in my own court* who are cooperating with this woman in return for the gift of a Human child?" Her scowl made Baba wish she'd stayed at home, which was no doubt the queen's intent.

Baba stood her ground, although her knees trembled slightly. "I'm afraid so, Your Majesty. I gave this some thought on my way here, after the creature told me this Rusalka was gathering power from others. It stands to reason that whoever this woman is, she started out with more cunning than ability. If there are those from the Otherworld who are giving over some of their power to Maya to use in the mundane world, they must be very powerful themselves." She raised an eyebrow, glancing around at the assembled company, which had somehow grown to include most of the court members who had been dallying on the lawn. Otherworld denizens had an unerring instinct for any kind of drama that might entertain them. "Obviously, those with the most magic to spare are within your own inner circle, Highness."

She braced herself for another moon to plummet from the sky, but the queen simply shook her exquisite head in denial. "I refuse to believe such slander. You must be mistaken. Perhaps this woman is a talented witch who has somehow stumbled on the secrets of the gateways between our worlds." The queen narrowed her eyes. "Perhaps it is even a Baba gone wrong. Have you talked to any of your sisters lately?"

Baba gritted her teeth but answered politely. "I have, Your Majesty. The other two American Babas have their hands full with their own issues, far away from the area in which I am staying. And I fail to see how a witch, no matter how mighty, could command scores of Otherworld creatures."

The queen flipped open her fan, as if to waft away the unwelcome argument, and rose with inhuman grace to face those who had gathered to listen avidly to this fascinating conversation.

"We will settle this right now," she said, raising her voice without effort to be heard by all. She addressed her courtiers using her most regal attitude. Around the table, knights snapped to attention instinctively, and the ladies sat up straighter. Baba thought she heard the king let out the tiniest of sighs.

"It has been suggested that some among you might knowingly be assisting a woman, possibly a Rusalka, who is stealing Human children and bringing them to our lands through an illicit and unauthorized doorway," the queen said, looking out over her subjects with glittering amethyst eyes. Her gaze seemed to focus on each one in turn, like a laser scalpel, dissecting their thoughts and uncovering any hidden secrets.

"Should such a thing be true, it would be a violation of our strictest laws, and a direct threat to the well-being of our land," she went on. "If, in fact, any here are involved in such a travesty, speak up now, or be found out later and punished most severely for your crimes against me and this court. I, your queen, so command you."

There was utter and complete silence, although people could be seen subtly checking out those standing nearby, waiting, perhaps, for someone to confess. No one did. In fact, most of the company wore their most haughty, forbidding expressions, as if to imply that even the suggestion was ridiculous. But Baba thought she caught a few guilty looks; a twitch here, a tightened lip there, and made a mental note of them for future reference. Of course, Otherworld faces were different enough from human ones; it was possible she was simply imagining it. But she didn't think so.

"There, you see?" said the queen, as if that settled things. Which in theory, it should have, since it was a very bad idea to lie to the queen. Very Bad.

"No one here is involved." She stared at Baba, twirling her fan between long, slim fingers adorned with jewels that twinkled like the stars this world lacked. "That does not, of course, negate the possibility that this person is bringing children here and hiding them, somehow. Nor does it solve the problem of this door, if in fact it does exist."

The king stroked his neatly pointed beard, as dark as the queen's hair was pale. "There have been a number of odd occurrences lately," he pointed out. "Parts of the land shifting in and out of existence unexpectedly, time fluctuating even more erratically than usual." Concern wrote unaccustomed lines on his handsome face. "Overuse of a newly created door could cause such imbalances, could it not, my dear?"

The queen's face was as calm as ever, but the delicate ivory fan snapped into pieces between her palms. "Indeed it could, my love, indeed it could. And if true, the chaos will only become worse as the miscreant continues to use it." She dropped the remains of the fan on the ground, dusting her hands as if to rid herself of the problem at the same time.

"Baba Yaga," she said decisively.

Baba's stomach felt like it was attempting to join the broken beige shards lying at her feet. "Majesty?"

The queen drew herself up to her full height and spoke in her most imperial and dulcet tone, like exotic flowers shot out of a cannon at full force. "Baba Yaga, I hereby command you to find this woman Maya and discover, by whatever means necessary, the location of the door she is using, so We might close it before it further harms this world. You will also discover the location of any children she has illegally transported to the Otherworld, should this in fact be the case." Her words rang out for all to hear and those surrounding the table nodded in approval and began to wander off, satisfied that the show was over.

In a quieter but no less intimidating voice, she added flatly, "I am depending on you, Baba. Bring me this woman. Find the door. Rescue these children. Or else." The queen looked meaningfully in the direction of the six bewildered women currently shivering under borrowed cloaks. "And don't take too long about it. You do *not* want to try my patience."

FIFTEEN

LIAM HAD INTENDED to drive over and visit Baba as soon as he'd finished his dinner at Bertie's. The chatter there had been unusually malicious and unpleasant, swirling around the restaurant in snippets of suspicion and superstition, most of it aimed in Baba's direction. He'd barely managed to choke down his fried chicken and mashed potatoes in between all the conversations he'd had with people who had *casually* stopped by his table on the way in or out to complain about "what that woman was up to."

He'd done his best to calm everyone down, but his stomach was in knots by the time he left, Bertie's usually tender chicken sitting like a rock right under his heart. The threats and accusations were probably no more than hot air—a way for folks to let out their frustrations—but he didn't like the hysterical quality of some of the allegations, or the way the word "witch" was being bandied about, as if they'd all suddenly slid a couple of centuries back in time.

Liam didn't suppose that Baba would thank him for disturbing her peace by coming by to warn her, and he suspected she was perfectly capable of protecting herself if necessary. If nothing else, the sight of Chudo-Yudo's sharp white teeth and enormous bulk were enough to scare away any sensible person. But none of those things was going to stop him from checking to make sure she was okay. Neither was the mocking little voice in the back of his head quietly suggesting that maybe this was just an excuse to catch a glimpse of the lady's flashing amber eyes and that amazing cloud of dark hair that floated around her shoulders like a tangible aura of magic and mystery.

But circumstances conspired against his good intentions, first with repeated calls from people reporting strange sightings and possible break-ins (none of which turned out to be anything) and then dealing with the violent storm that sprang up out of nowhere, causing intermittent power outages and blocking roads with snarls of fallen limbs. He'd even had to rescue the proverbial kitten up a tree, shinnying halfway up a crooked old oak to fetch down a bedraggled ball of fur with tiny sharp claws and a piercing yowl that far outpaced its diminutive size.

By the time the winds had died down and the rain eased to a gentle drizzle, it was much later than a normal social call would allow. He didn't let that stop him either, although he did bring a little something along to sweeten the rudeness of his late arrival.

He'd been a little concerned that Baba would have already gone to bed, but apparently he'd worried for nothing, since the Airstream was still brightly lit, the glow from its windows sending shafts of light out to fall on damp grass, scruffy shrubbery, her battered blue BMW, and—most unwelcome sight of all—the three additional motorcycles parked out front.

Liam recognized the white Yamaha, red Ducati, and black Harley from the day he'd seen them at the bar. Apparently Baba's friends were still in town. Nobody had mentioned odd-looking strangers with even more Russian accents after that night, so he'd kind of hoped they'd gone away. Not that he was jealous, or anything. They just seemed like disreputable sorts, that's all.

Grabbing a flat box and a plastic-coated to-go bag off the passenger seat, Liam made his way to the front door and knocked briskly. There was a moment of silence as the voices he could hear inside stopped talking abruptly, then the door swung open and a man with long blond hair peered out into the night at him.

"Ah, Sheriff McClellan. What a pleasant surprise." His acerbic tone suggested that Liam's appearance was anything but, although his handsome face was smiling.

"Mikhail Day, wasn't it?" Liam said, transferring the bag to underneath his left arm so he could shake hands with his right. "We met at The Roadhouse the evening you got into town. Nice to see you again." He took a step forward as they shook, forcing the other man to take a step back. Once inside, he let go and shut the door behind him, wiping a spatter of rain off the rim of his hat.

"I've come to see Dr. Yager," he explained, glancing around the room to look for her. Gregori sat at the banquette table, sipping tea, and the huge black-leather clad form of Alexei lounged on the couch, his long legs stretched out in front of him and taking up most of the space. Of Baba, there was no sign. "I need to talk to her. Is she in the back bedroom?"

He started to walk in that direction, and Mikhail stepped into his path. "I'm sorry you came out here for nothing, Sheriff," he said with smooth grace, "But Baba . . . er . . . Barbara isn't here now. She stepped out for a bit of fresh air. No telling when she'll be back, I'm afraid." He put one muscular arm around Liam's shoulder and started to usher him back toward the door.

Liam ducked around him and placed both his packages on the countertop. "Really? She went for a walk at ten o'clock at night. After a big storm? That seems a little strange." An eyebrow emphasized his skepticism.

Gregori lifted one shoulder in a shrug. "You know our Barbara," he said, his lilting accent more noticeable than Mikhail's, who sounded as if he had practiced hard to remove it. "She is rarely predictable."

"I doubt I know her at all," Liam muttered. "But yes, she is that." He faked a bright smile as he looked around at the three men. "Not to worry—I brought pie from Bertie's and a little something for Chudo-Yudo. Is he here, or out walking too?"

Alexei perked up. "What kind of pie?" he asked, sitting up straight. Mikhail scowled at him, but the big man just grinned. "What? I can't help it, I love pie."

"Chocolate pecan pie," Liam said, opening the box and pulling it out so they could see the glistening mound of whipped cream on top. "If it's not the best thing you ever tasted, I'll eat my sheriff's hat." Which he laid on the counter next to the pie, in case they hadn't figured out yet that he wasn't planning to leave anytime soon.

A large head nudged the top of his thigh, and he looked down to see Chudo-Yudo, mouth gaping in what Liam hoped was benign curiosity.

"There you are," he said, pulling his secret weapon out of the bag he'd carried it in. "I told Bertie about you, so she gave me this."

"This" was a huge bone from that night's roast, with large meaty shreds still clinging to it. Chudo-Yudo's eyes widened and he stood up on his hind legs, almost knocking Liam down as he bestowed a wet doggy tongue wipe on the sheriff's face before grabbing the bone and wandering off to sit in a corner, gnawing on it. A rumble almost like a purr emanated from his broad white chest.

Mikhail looked from the dog to Alexei, who was hovering over the pie, sniffing hopefully. One suspiciously finger-shaped section of whipped cream was missing, and the big man was making a noise not unlike that coming from Chudo-Yudo.

The blond man's mouth curved into a reluctant grin. "You seem to have solved the riddle that gets you past the door keepers," he said, shaking his head. "I suppose you might as well stay, although Baba could be gone a long time."

"I'm in no hurry," Liam said cheerfully. He moved over toward the coffeemaker sitting on the counter. "Why don't

I make us some coffee to go with our pie? I'm sure Barbara wouldn't mind."

He reached one hand out toward the container marked Coffee that sat on the counter, but a slim beige hand already rested on it. Liam blinked. He hadn't even seen the other man move, but somehow Gregori had gotten there before him.

"Why don't you allow me to make the coffee," Gregori said easily, edging into Liam's personal space so he was forced to move out of the way. "This coffeemaker is a little . . . temperamental . . . best to let me do it."

"Uh, okay," Liam said. "Point me to the cupboard where she keeps the plates, and I'll slice us each a piece of pie."

He turned around, and Alexei already had a huge chunk lying in the middle of one equally large hand and was eating it with his fingers.

"I'm good, thanks," the big man said around a mouthful of chocolate and nuts. Whipped cream fringed the edges of his mustache like ice on a pond.

Mikhail handed over plates and forks for the rest of them with a dramatic eye roll. "Just ignore our ill-mannered friend," he said. "He was raised by wolves."

Chudo-Yudo raised his head and barked.

"Good point," Mikhail responded. "I didn't mean to insult the wolves. They actually have much better etiquette than Alexei."

Liam looked from the man to the dog and back again. "You know, Barbara does that too. Talks like she is actually carrying on a conversation with the animal."

"Does she?" Mikhail drawled, eyes a deep, guileless blue. "Fancy that."

Liam took his pie and slid into the banquette table, with Mikhail across from him. Gregori brought over a steaming cup of coffee and placed it in front of the sheriff, then stood next to Alexei at the counter to eat his own piece with considerably more dignity.

Liam lifted his mug, a heavy pottery creation decorated in shades of deep purple and carved with symbols he didn't recognize, and took a deep sniff. "Hey, does anyone else smell roses?" he asked.

The other men just looked blank and shook their heads, although Liam could swear that one of them choked back a laugh. He shrugged, figuring it didn't matter, and let the deep sweet bliss of Bertie's pie dissolve on his tongue like a forkful of love with whipped cream on top. His eyes closed in ecstasy for a moment, but then snapped back open at a distinctive creaking sound. Liam gazed in disbelief as the wardrobe at the end of the kitchen swung open and Baba stepped through the door.

"Son of bitch!" she said, as she bumped her head on the doorframe on her way out. "I always forget to duck. Damn, that smarts." Behind her, the clothing that usually hung there seemed to have been replaced by a swirling gray mist filled with iridescent sparkles. Before she slammed the door shut, Liam could have sworn he saw a tiny green and pink hummingbird fly by, vanishing even further into impossible depths.

Alexei and Gregori moved toward each other as if to try and block Liam's view of the closet, probably not realizing it was already too late. So he couldn't see Baba when she asked testily, "What the hell is wrong with you two? Why are you standing there like a couple of mismatched statues in Aphrodite's garden?"

They shifted aside to show Liam sitting at the table, and he was treated to an intriguing slideshow of shock, anger, consternation, and something a little like fear as various expressions came and went on Baba's normally unreadable face. She finally seemed to settle on resignation, and took a hesitant step in his direction.

"Uh, hi," she said, lifting a hand in greeting.

"Hi yourself," Liam said, feeling remarkably calm, under the circumstances. "Did you just walk out of that closet?" He looked her over, taking in her unusual attire, jewels, sword, and all. She looked exotic, stunningly beautiful, and in some intangible way, more herself than he'd ever seen her.

"Nice outfit. Special occasion?" He was fairly certain

she hadn't just come from a costume ball. Unless it was one that involved some kind of giant pumpkin and a fairy godmother.

"There's pie," Alexei mumbled, mouth full, and retreated to sit on the couch, out of the line of fire. "It's really good pie."

Chudo-Yudo made a noise that sounded suspiciously like laughter and covered his eyes with one mammoth paw.

Gregori just sighed and said, "You might as well tell him, Baba. And while you're at it, you can tell all of us what the queen said when you broke the news that Maya had discovered a door into the Otherworld."

He cut a piece of chocolate pecan rapture, put it on a plate, and nudged her into the seat opposite Liam. "Here. You look like you could use this." He handed her a full cup to go with it.

"Did he say 'door to the Otherworld'?" Liam asked incredulously. His coffee mug suddenly weighed about twenty pounds, and he put it down before he dropped it. "What the hell is the Otherworld? And why are you wearing a sword?" He wondered if it would help if he pinched himself, and tried it surreptitiously under the table. *Ow.* Nope. The room was still filled with crazy Russian men and one impossibly gorgeous, frustrating, mysterious woman. Who was wearing a sword.

"I think I'm going to need more coffee," he said. "A *lot* more coffee."

BABA WANTED TO beat her head against the table. Barring that, she'd be willing to settle for someone else's head. There were four names on her short list already. It was bad enough to come back from the court with the queen's threat still ringing in her ears, but to discover that the Riders and Chudo-Yudo had allowed the already curious sheriff in, just in time to watch her walk through a doorway from nothing . . . well, that made her night perfect.

"Try the pie, Baba," Mikhail suggested with a gentle

smile and no visible sympathy at all. "It's practically magical."

She dug her fork in, more for an excuse to avoid looking at Liam than because she had any appetite for dessert, but once the creamy-smooth bittersweet chocolate melted on her tongue, she had to admit, it was pretty amazing pie. "Bertie's?" she asked, finally daring to meet the sheriff's gaze.

He nodded, not taking his eyes off her. "Yep. Now, about that explanation . . ." He tilted his chin up, clearly not going anywhere until she answered him.

"Fine," she said, resigning herself to the inevitable. "But I'm warning you, you're not going to believe me."

Broad shoulders shrugged, and she was distracted again by the sheer male presence of him. The tiny cleft in that stubborn chin, almost covered by the late hour's stubble; the strength in his arms; the powerful line of his shoulders as they moved under his slightly muddy uniform jacket. The back of one calloused hand was curled around her favorite coffee mug, revealing a line of thin new scratches that looked red and sore. She wanted, just for a moment, to reach out and heal them with her touch, wishing she could save him that small amount of pain, if nothing else. It seemed unlikely, at this point, that there was much else she could protect him from.

"Barbara?" Liam's slightly impatient voice called her back to reality. "Or should I call you Baba?"

She sighed. "Sorry, it's been a rough night. I was . . . daydreaming . . . there for a moment. Sorry." She took another bite of pie, chewed, and swallowed past the lump in her throat. "Yes, you might as well call me Baba. My real name is Baba Yaga, although in this world, most know me as Barbara Yager."

He raised a dubious eyebrow. "*This* world?"

"Yes," Baba said. "There is this, what some call the mundane or Human plane, and the Otherworld. The Otherworld is a place where magic exists, and it is home to creatures out of legend, many of which you might recognize and some which are beyond your comprehension." Tired, she rubbed a hand across her face, wishing she could have had this conversation some other time. Sometime when her head was clearer, or her heart less muddled. Or never. *Never* would have worked for her.

Liam's hazel eyes stared at her as though wondering if she was making fun of him, or merely out of her mind.

"And you're dressed like something out of a Renaissance Faire because that's how everyone dresses in this Otherworld of yours?" he asked, pointing at the jewels in the net restraining her usually unruly hair. "It must be a pretty fancy place."

"You have no idea," Mikhail said, pushing Baba out of the way so he could get another piece of pie. "She's actually somewhat underdressed. But she doesn't like to stand out, our Baba."

"I don't know how she could avoid it," Liam muttered, the sideways compliment making her heart skip a beat. But then he shook the stray thought out of his head and added, "So you're trying to tell me that you just went through your closet to visit a magical land, like Alice through the looking glass?"

"More like the kids going through the wardrobe into Narnia," Baba replied, hoping that they'd at least read some of the same books, even if she hadn't seen his *movies*. "But yes, something like that."

Liam was abruptly on his feet, moving past Mikhail and yanking the closet door open. He stared at black leather and red silk, his face an almost comic mix of satisfaction and disappointment, like a kid who finally proves to himself that Santa doesn't exist.

"Uh-huh," he snarled. "Pull the other one." He walked back over to stand in front of Baba, arms crossed over his chest, muscles tight. "How about now you tell me what is *really* going on?"

Baba ran out of reasonable, which was bound to happen eventually. It was never her best thing anyway. "Fine," she snarled back at him. She rose from her seat and said to the others, "Better make room." Three sets of faces looked alarmed and tucked themselves into the corners of the trailer the best they could.

Liam just looked confused. "Make room for what?"

"Chudo-Yudo," she said, and gestured at the dog.

As Liam turned to see what she was talking about, Chudo-Yudo moved into the middle of the lounge area, which was as close to a clear space as the Airstream allowed, and shook himself, as if shedding water. Instead, he was enveloped in a greenish-purple mist that sparked and glowed, letting off an odor like charred meat, cold starlight, and eternity. When the mist cleared, the dog was gone, and instead there was a large dragon with scalloped iridescent black scales and blazing red eyes curling in on himself to take up as little room as possible. Still, his tail rolled out onto the tiled kitchen floor, and one leathery wing poked Alexei in the stomach until the burly biker moved a little to the left with an *oof.*

"Hey, man," the dragon said. "Thanks for the bone."

Despite the seriousness of the situation, Baba had to choke back a laugh at the expression on Liam's rugged face. His jaw had dropped open and his hazel eyes were wide. She was pretty sure he'd forgotten to breathe. He bent down slowly to touch the knobby end of tail that rested on his booted feet.

"Yes, it's real," she said. "Sorry for the shock, but I thought it would save us a lot of useless argument. It's late, and I'm tired. I just didn't have it in me."

"Uh, right." Liam dropped back onto the banquette bench with a thud. "So, your dog is a dragon and you just came back from a visit to a place called the Otherworld. The entrance to which is in your closet." He shook his head ruefully. "Anything else I need to know?"

"Lots, unfortunately," Baba said. A nod at Chudo-Yudo had him changing back into his pit bull form, at which everyone breathed a sigh of relief.

"You know, I always forget how big he is, until he does that," Alexei said, rubbing his stomach.

Liam glanced around the room at the Riders. "You guys aren't all dragons too, are you?" he asked, almost despairingly.

Mikhail chuckled. "Not most of the time, no." Alexei grinned and Gregori's lips edged up into a small, compassionate smile that lightened his stern face.

Baba stiffened as Liam's gaze swung around to her.

"And you? What are you?" he asked in a low voice, as if afraid to hear the answer.

She slid back in across from him and took his large hands in her somewhat smaller ones, running a thumb lightly across the slightly raised and reddened lines left by the kitten.

"I'm a Baba Yaga," she said. "I was born as human as you, but I've lived with magic a long time, and it has changed me. I don't really know what I am anymore."

Where her touch ran, the little scratches healed and disappeared. She hung on for a moment or two longer than was necessary, or probably wise, sending him energy and healing she didn't really have to spare, simply enjoying the temporary pleasure of the warmth of his hands in hers. But the sight of his shoulders loosening imperceptibly and the grooves next to his mouth growing slightly less deep made the sacrifice worth the doing. And it was little enough, considering what they had to look forward to next.

When she let go, he lifted the once damaged hand and pondered it with wonder. She could see in the warmth of his smile the exact moment when he chose to believe.

"Wow," he said. "So you really are a witch."

SIXTEEN

"WHAT?" BABA SAID. Then realized what his words meant, and had to consciously unclench her fists. "Oh, let me guess. That's what they're saying at Bertie's."

Liam nodded, guilt shadowing the movement. "I came out here to warn you, but I guess you already knew."

She shook her head, feeling sadness welling up like blood from a fresh wound. "No, not exactly. But I'd already discovered that someone—one of Maya's little friends, or maybe Maya herself—had been going about town contaminating and changing my herbal medicines so they harmed instead of healed. I've been around long enough to know what happens next."

They all glanced in the direction of the road, as if expecting to see villagers with pitchforks and torches marching toward the Airstream. For the moment, thankfully, there were only a few fireflies, flitting to and fro in the slowly drying summer air.

"Why would Maya do that?" Liam asked. "And how? A few people complained to me about your remedies, but it's not like Maya could have broken into all those folks' houses and done something to your . . ."

"What?" Gregori asked, leaning forward over the counter. "You've thought of something?"

Liam shoved his still-too-long dark-blond hair out of his face. "I keep getting called out to people's houses because they're hearing strange noises, or think their homes have been broken into. But I haven't seen any signs of anything. I'd just been chalking it up to the general tension in the area."

Alexei grimaced. "More accurate, perhaps, to chalk it up to brownies and goblins." He spat on the floor. "Sneaky little things, goblins. Always getting into places they shouldn't." If any of the creatures he mentioned could have seen his face, they would have run back home and hidden under a rock for a century or two.

Baba thought about it. If Maya had a number of small beasties under her control, she could certainly be using them to sneak in through bathroom and kitchen windows to mess with her clients' treatments. If Liam hadn't been sitting across from her, she might have spat on the floor too.

"As to why," she said instead, answering Liam's first question. "Maya is from the Otherworld herself. From what I've discovered, it looks like she is a being called a Rusalka." The Riders all wore startled expressions at the mention of Maya's probable identity, but Baba held up a slim hand to hold off their questions until she could finish explaining to Liam.

"Rusalkas are a kind of water nymph," she said. "In the Old Country, before the supernatural races were sent back to live in the Otherworld, the Rusalkas were known for disguising themselves as beautiful women to lure young men to their deaths by drowning. They don't have much power these days, now that the pollution of the water here has drained the waters of the Otherworld of much of their essence."

"Oho!" Alexei shouted. "I told you I felt hands grabbing me in that weird flood that almost wiped me off the road. A Rusalka, it figures."

That did make sense, Baba thought. "Anyway, I believe that Maya is trying to discredit me with the locals, so they won't trust me to help them. Maybe even convince people that I am somehow responsible for the disappearance of the children, to shift any possible suspicion away from her."

"That's ridiculous," Mikhail said, staunchly loyal as always. "You only just got here, and she's been in the area for months. No one is going to believe you had anything to do with this."

"Folks are pretty irrational when their families are threatened," Liam said, face grim. "That sort of rumor is already being whispered in corners. I heard it myself, although no one came right out and said anything. That's why I came out here to talk to Barbara and try and convince her to leave the area until things cooled down."

"Fat chance of that happening," Chudo-Yudo said from near Liam's feet. His new bone was already half gone, but he happily resumed chewing on what was left, slobbering a little on Liam's boots.

Liam jumped. "Jeez—you can talk!"

Chudo-Yudo rolled his eyes. "Right. So a talking dragon is okay, but a talking dog freaks you out? Dude, you're going to have to adjust to this crap a lot faster than that if you're going to be any help."

Clutching his coffee cup like it was a lifeline to reality, Liam stared beseechingly at Baba. "I promise I'll try to catch up on believing the impossible. But I really think you should consider leaving—or at least lying low for a little while until things calm down."

Baba shook her head hard, causing half the pins that held the gossamer net over her hair to tinkle musically down to land on the table and floor. Annoyed, she tugged the fragile bejeweled web the rest of the way out so the long masses of her hair came tumbling down. Liam's fingers reached out as if against his will, then reluctantly returned to the safety of his mug.

"I can't leave," Baba said. "Or lie low either." She could feel a headache forming behind her skull, as if all her bones were suddenly too tight. "I went through to the Otherworld tonight to tell the queen we were fairly certain Maya had discovered an unguarded door between the two worlds."

"That's bad," she explained to Liam, "because too much use of the doorways, especially to bring things back and forth as Maya seems to be doing, can upset the delicate balance between the Otherworld and here. The effect of that can eventually be devastating, especially on the other side, where the energy flow has been limited since they withdrew from regular contact with the Human world."

She shook her head. "And the pollution of the water and air here leaks through at places where the worlds meet, causing damage to the sensitive Otherworld environment."

"Bringing things back and forth," Liam repeated, his voice dropping to a register that made him suddenly sound like a dangerous man. "Things like these creatures you're talking about. And three missing children." He stared at Baba, as if daring her to deny it.

She didn't bother. "That's what we think. It would explain why you haven't been able to find any trace of them here. And if she's using her glamour to lure them away and cloak them from sight as soon as she's grabbed them, it also explains why the children seemed to vanish in a moment's time."

"But why would she take them at all?" he asked, a question that had clearly been tormenting him since the disappearances started. "Is she . . . are they dead?"

"We don't believe so," Gregori said, laying a comforting hand on the other man's shoulder. He turned to Baba. "Did you get any clue as to what she was doing with them while you were there?"

Baba bit her lip. "Of a sort. If I'm right, she's bartering them to Otherworld folk in exchange for some of their power and magic."

"Which means that whoever has the children on the other side is someone with lots of extra power, which means they are likely to be high up in the court," Mikhail said, his usually pleasant visage set and harsh.

"I don't understand," Liam said. "Why do they need our kids? Don't they have their own?"

Baba shook her head. "Otherworld folks are very

long-lived, but they rarely reproduce. Part of the trade-off, I suppose, but tough on those who want to be parents. Because of their rarity, children are valued beyond almost anything else there."

"So they steal ours," Liam said bitterly. "That's rather ironic."

"I know," Baba said. "If it is any consolation, stealing Human children was outlawed centuries ago, at the same time the worlds separated. Anyone who is involved with Maya's scheme will be severely punished if they are caught."

Liam pushed his hair out of his eyes again. "*If* they are caught. How the hell are we supposed to catch some woman who can use magic, has a veritable army of mythological creatures at her beck and call, and could steal another child right out from underneath our noses at any time?" A muscle pulsed along his jaw.

"I don't honestly know," Baba answered. "But we're going to have to do it. The queen has given me strict orders to find the door, track down the children, and bring Maya to her. Soon. Or else." She drew a hand across her throat in the classic gesture.

"Or else?" Alexei didn't seem overly concerned. Of course, he hadn't been there. "Maybe she didn't mean that kind of or else."

Baba grimaced. "She was so angry, she blew up a moon."

"Oh," Alexei blinked. "Then I guess we'd better find Maya." His face brightened as he had a thought. "Did the queen say we had to bring her in *alive*? Because if not, then I vote for dead. Really, seriously, extremely dead."

LIAM WONDERED IF Bertie had started baking hallucinogenics into her pies. That made a lot more sense than this conversation. But he was nothing if not practical, and he had seen too much to be able to deny the new reality he had to cope with. The missing children didn't have time to spare for him to come to terms with it gradually, protesting all the way. Some things, however, hadn't changed.

"We are *not* killing anyone," he said flatly. "I'm the damned sheriff, for god's sake. It's my job to uphold the law. No matter what she's done, or what she is," he swallowed hard, trying to get that one out without twitching, "Maya Freeman will be arrested and tried, like anyone else guilty of a crime."

Baba had the nerve to roll her striking amber eyes at him. "Good luck finding a jury of her peers, *Sheriff*. Or holding her in a cell, for that matter, even if you could somehow prove she was responsible for the children's disappearances."

Liam opened his mouth to argue, and she put up one slim hand to stop him. "I agree, however, that we can't kill her. She's our best chance to find the children, for one thing. And for another, I think the queen is looking forward to punishing the woman herself. We *do not* want to get in the way of the queen's vengeance."

He watched as Baba shuddered, clearly remembering something that had happened while she was away. Whatever the experience had been, it had etched new lines next to her mouth and cast a shadow over those wondrous eyes. For the first time since Liam had met her, she actually looked tired, and less than iron-tough.

"So what do we do, then?" Mikhail asked in a reasonable voice. "The Otherworld is too big to search, and the children will be well hidden by whoever she's given them to, since they wouldn't want to risk the queen discovering their involvement."

"I still think our best bet is waiting for her to grab the next one, and following her," Alexei rumbled. "She'll have to lead us to the door then."

"I am not purposely allowing her to take another child," Liam said through gritted teeth. "We are not going to put some other poor parent through hell if there is any way to avoid it. All these children are very much loved, and their parents are suffering horribly, waiting around to find out if their babies are even still alive, and envisioning every horrible scenario in the book." He knew that for a fact, since he too had been living out every nightmarish possibility day and night since the first kid vanished.

Gregori got a thoughtful look. "They *are* all valued, aren't they?" he said, tapping one finger against his lips. "So why pick these particular children in the first place? After all, there are always plenty of Human children who are unwanted, and won't be missed. Even in this small place, there must be scores of them." His dark eyes were sad. "There always are."

Liam wished he could disagree, but of course, it was true. Poor folks with more mouths than they could feed, wealthy folks with better things to do than pay attention to their offspring, the unexpected and undesired infant, the neglected children of drug addicts and abusers—there were at least twenty kids he could think of off the top of his head that had parents who would be happier without them, and that wasn't counting the ones already in the foster care system.

"So how is she finding these particular children?" Mikhail asked. "Do they have anything in common? Something to do with their parents, maybe?"

"Not that we've been able to find," Liam answered, bitterness oozing out of his pores like sap from a lightning-struck tree. "But that doesn't mean there isn't a link—just that the incompetent sheriff hasn't been able to uncover it yet."

Baba patted his hand, a butterfly touch that almost undid him. Rudeness he could handle; sympathy might unman him completely.

"There has to be something we're missing," he said, frustrated. "But what?"

A frown creased Baba's forehead. "Maybe we're asking the wrong question," she said. "Instead of 'why these children?' maybe we should be asking why Maya is working for Peter Callahan?"

"What? What the hell does that have to do with anything?" Alexei said, snagging the last piece of pie. Liam thought briefly that if he'd known there would be such a crowd, he would have brought two. Or maybe, considering Alexei's size, three.

"Maybe the job is just part of her cover," Mikhail suggested. "A reason to explain why she is around so much."

"That's my point," Baba said, drumming her fingers on the table in front of her restlessly. "Why is she hanging around at all? She could spend most of her time in the Otherworld, come through this damned doorway none of us can find, snatch the kids, and go back. But instead, she's worked for Peter Callahan for six months, establishing herself in his office, becoming his trusted associate. *Why?*"

"Well, it's not for the pleasure of his company," Liam said in a wry tone. "The man's a slime bucket. A smooth and polished one, maybe, but still a slime bucket."

"Maybe that makes him her type," Alexei suggested with a leer. "Rusalkas aren't known for their kindly personalities."

"It's got to be more than that," Baba said, drumming her fingers louder until Chudo-Yudo gave her leg a gentle—or not so gentle—nip. "What does Callahan have that she would want?"

Liam tried to make his tired brain do something more useful than spin in circles, or babble quietly to itself about Baba's dark hair, floating enticingly across the table from him, just out of reach.

"Well, Callahan has been in the area for the last two years," he said, thinking out loud. "Doing lots of in-depth research on the community to find the best places to drill and the people who might be the most open to selling their land to his company. He's undoubtedly amassed a huge amount of information. Could there be something in there that she's using?"

Baba raised an eyebrow. "Huh. I hadn't thought of that. Maybe, although I'm not sure what or how." The tapping fingers stilled, wrapped themselves around a sword hilt instead. "I guess we're going to have to take a look inside that office."

"Oh, no," Liam protested. Why did all of these people's

suggestions seem to involve committing some kind of crime? "You are not going to break into Peter Callahan's office."

He didn't like the sparkle that had suddenly entered her amber eyes. "Seriously. No. Isn't there some way you can er . . . magically . . . get information out of Callahan's computers, maybe?"

Baba shook her head, a grin materializing out of what had been grim discouragement. "Sorry, not possible. Magic and technology don't mix."

He looked around at the Airstream they were sitting in. "What about all this?" he asked. "There's plenty of technology here."

"Not so much as you'd think," Baba said. "This whole place started out as a wooden hut on chicken legs. It voluntarily changed its form, and the more it is perceived as real, the more real it becomes. But most of what you see is still illusion." She shrugged. "But illusion isn't going to help us now—we need facts. And I suspect we're going to have to get them the old-fashioned way."

Her grin widened, making his pulse beat faster.

"So, Sheriff," she said. "How do you feel about a life of crime?"

SEVENTEEN

THE MOON POKED its head out from behind a cloud and leered at them as they crouched outside a window at the rear of Peter Callahan's office. It was somewhere around two in the morning and the neighborhood was silent, all its law-abiding citizens tucked safely into their beds.

"I don't understand why the Riders aren't doing this," Liam hissed in Baba's ear.

She suppressed an involuntary shudder when his warm breath caressed her neck, and told herself it was just nerves. Except, of course, that she didn't get nerves.

"They're the brawn, not the brains," she whispered back. "They wouldn't know what to look for. And can you see Alexei tiptoeing around inside? We'd be better off sending Chudo-Yudo. Or a parade of elephants in army boots."

She gave the sheriff a sidelong look. He'd changed into civilian clothes; dark jeans and dark long-sleeved tee shirt, which had the unfortunate effect of making him even more attractive than usual. One lock of dark-blond hair had fallen into his eyes again, and she had to resist the impulse to brush it away. *Focus, Baba. Focus.*

"A better question," she added, "might be "why are you here?" I was just kidding when I suggested you take up a life of crime, you know."

"I know," he said shortly, examining the wires he could see lining the windowsill.

"You're the sheriff," she persisted. "You're supposed to uphold the law, not break it. You should have stayed home. Or at least back at the Airstream."

He shrugged minutely, the barest ripple of muscles along his broad back. "I know this area and the people a lot better than you do. There's not much point in breaking in to look at information if you don't have the knowledge to make sense of what you're seeing."

"But still—" It was bad enough that most of the folks she'd befriended in her short time here now thought she was some kind of evil witch. She didn't want to destroy Liam's career too.

Liam swiveled on his heels, turning so he could look her in the eye. For a moment, their faces were so close, she thought he might kiss her.

But instead he said, "Baba, they're going to fire me at the end of the month anyway if I can't find out who's doing this. So I don't have much to lose. Besides, finding those kids is more important than anything else. If this is the only way to accomplish that goal, then I'm in."

Baba's heart skipped a beat. "They what?" For a moment, a red fog obscured the building in front of them, and she wanted to find Clive Matthews and beat him into a pulp for threatening the thing Liam held most dear. She took a deep breath. "They're fools, then." Amber eyes met hazel ones. "Why didn't you tell me?"

Liam raised an eyebrow, barely visible in the diffuse light from the distant streetlamps and the moon overhead. "I didn't think you'd care."

She bit her lip. She didn't care. Of course she didn't care. It had nothing to do with her. She was here to do a job, and then she'd be moving on. "Right," she said.

"Besides," Liam added with a mischievous grin, "if we're

caught, I'm going to say I spied you sneaking in and followed you. Then I'm going to arrest you, and throw you in jail. I'll be a hero."

Baba looked at him, startled. She thought he was kidding . . . but she really wasn't sure. Hopefully, she wouldn't find out the hard way.

LIAM TRIED TO keep a straight face, but it was difficult. Baba had been throwing him off-balance since the day he'd met her; it was something of a treat to be able to return the favor for once. Sooty lashes fluttered over wide eyes as she tried to figure out whether or not to believe him. If it weren't for the serious nature of their task, he would almost say he was having fun.

"Instead of worrying about which one of us is going to jail tonight," he said finally, "maybe we should worry about how on earth we're going to get past this alarm system. It's pretty sophisticated."

Baba snorted through her long nose and waved a slim hand through the air as if drawing a figure eight. "What alarm system?" she asked.

Liam pointed at the windowsill, then dropped his finger in amazement at the sight of melted wires, dripping down the side of the building like tar on a hot summer's day. He was vaguely aware that his mouth hung open as he turned to Baba.

"Did you do that?" he asked, knowing as he did that there was no other explanation. "I thought you said magic and technology don't mix."

She inclined her head in the direction of the wires as she slowly moved the window upward on silent tracks. "I'd say that's a pretty good example of not mixing." She gave a tiny laugh, almost as noiseless as the sliding glass. "Trying to make technology work with magic is hard. Trying to make it *not work*, now that's another story."

He tried not to stare at Baba's perfect butt as she lifted herself up and slithered in over the sill. Her attire was a match for his, with the addition of the black leather jacket she wore, since she'd ridden over on her battered BMW. He couldn't believe she wasn't sweating in the summer evening's heat, but she seemed as icily cool as ever. He, on the other hand, could feel a bead of sweat trickle down his back, sticking his shirt to his skin. Of course, that might be the company as much as the warm weather. Something about this frustrating, mysterious woman just set his blood on fire.

"Are you coming, or are you going to stand out there all night admiring the stars?" Baba hissed from inside the building, startling him out of his reverie.

"Right behind you," Liam growled, and committed his first-ever felony by following her into the building.

They'd at least found the right room. A dim light from Baba's hand shone on a massive walnut desk covered with electronics and neat stacks of paper, and then moved across the space to briefly illuminate walls covered with maps and charts, and rows of filing cabinets. Boring beige curtains hung over off-white shades. A lone plastic plant tried in vain to bring some life to the otherwise sterile room. It failed.

"Be careful not to shine your flashlight near the windows," Liam warned. "We catch thieves that way all the time. Just because we're at the back of the building doesn't mean some insomniac neighbor won't see something suspicious and call the police."

Baba lifted an elegant eyebrow. "I don't have a flashlight," she said, holding up her hand to show him the muted glow coming from the center of her palm. "This shouldn't be visible by anyone other than the two of us."

"More magic," he said, swallowing hard. He was *never* going to get used to this. "Handy."

Baba snorted quietly. "Puns during a break-in. You are a constant source of amazement to me, Sheriff McClellan."

Right back atcha, lady. Squared. Liam eyed the computer on the desk. "Think there is any point in turning this thing on?" he asked, mostly rhetorically. "You don't have some voodoo that can get you his password, do you?"

She shook her head. "Nope, sorry." The light lingered on a section of wall with what looked like a huge map of the county. "But come over here and look at this. I'm guessing it's important, but I'm not sure what the heck it means."

Liam stood behind her, close enough to feel the heat from her body, like magnetic north's tug on a compass needle. The map she was looking at was covered with pushpins, maybe as many as two hundred of them, some crowded close together and others spread well apart. The pins were in four different colors: red, blue, yellow, and green.

"Huh," he said. "That's interesting." He pointed to a three-by-five card with notes in a precise hand, delineating the meaning of each color. The card was taped to the wall under the map. "I love organized people. This says that red stands for 'Yes—lease signed,' blue stands for 'Definite no,' yellow is 'No—but persuadable,' and green means 'No—but vulnerable.' "

"What do those mean?" Baba asked, a wrinkle creasing the skin between her brows. "I understand the lease-signed ones, and the definite no's, but what about the other two? The yellow and green pins?"

Liam took her glowing hand, not without some trepidation, and aimed the light downward toward the file cabinets underneath the map. The drawers were as neatly labeled as the chart above, and he pulled open the one with a large red dot on it first. He got a sinking feeling as he perused the names on the folders within.

"Shit," he whispered, sliding the drawer shut again.

"What's the matter?" Baba asked, glancing around with concern. "Did you hear something?"

He shook his head, then had to push his damned hair out of his face again. "No, nothing like that," he said. "I didn't expect to see that so many of the folks who've signed drilling leases live near me. Truth is, according to these, my property is pretty much surrounded. If the county votes down the drilling moratorium, I'm screwed."

He was a little surprised to realize how much he cared. He never talked about it to anyone. Most days, he even managed not to think about it for whole hours at a time. The house had mostly been just a place to sleep and occasionally eat since the baby died and Melissa left. If you'd asked him yesterday, he would have said it could burn to the ground for all he cared. Apparently, that wasn't quite true. He ground his teeth together, thinking this was a damned inconvenient time for his heart to finally come back to life again.

Baba's slender hand rested gently on his shoulder for a moment. "Sorry," she said. "Hopefully we'll find something to stop them."

Liam nodded wordlessly and opened the next drawer. There weren't quite as many files with blue tags on them, but there were enough to be heartening. His own name was written clearly on a label that sat between Landry, Frank and Meadows, Charles and Felicia. He'd said "no" loud and clear from the first time one of Callahan's flunkies had come knocking on the door. In fact, it was distinctly possible he'd said, "HELL, no."

The yellow-tagged drawer was next, and it was considerably more revealing. Liam cursed under his breath.

"What?" Baba asked. "More people who own property near yours?"

"Worse," he said through clenched teeth. "These are folks who want to say no, but Callahan has found ways that he thinks they can be persuaded." He pointed at a file labeled "Johnson, Clara."

"See this one? Clara is a widow, whose husband died suddenly last year with no life insurance and a pile of debt. It says here that her kids are pressuring her to sell and move into a nursing home." He flicked another file open. "This one is the Mulligans. They're in the middle of an ugly divorce. Callahan has apparently convinced the husband to sign the lease, and is helping him out with an expensive lawyer so he can get an advantage in the court battle."

"Nasty," Baba said, looking more disgusted than shocked. "Are they all like that, the yellow ones?"

Liam riffled through a few more. "Pretty much, although

some are more sneaky than vicious. Here's one where a couple wants to retire to a warmer climate. Callahan apparently paid their real estate agent to convince them that their property will be worth more with a signed drilling lease in place." He shoved the drawer shut, stopping it from slamming at the last minute. "But the files all look like they're full of actions that are at the very least morally repugnant, if not out-and-out illegal."

Baba's eyes got that odd fierce glow, as if they'd been lit from within. Liam tried to tell himself that it was just a reflection from her magical light, and not a sign that she was thinking of ripping certain people apart with her bare hands. Then he tried to convince himself he thought that would be a bad thing. He wasn't notably successful in either case.

Truth be told, he was having a hard time reining in his own temper. The more deeply they delved into Callahan's dirty dealings, the harder it was to remember that he was supposed to uphold the law, no matter what his own personal feelings in the matter. And he had a sinking feeling that the remaining drawer was going to make that even more difficult. The sound of his own harsh breathing echoed in his ears like a dirge as he tugged open the green dotted drawer.

"Huh," he said, a few minutes later. "That's curious." He hadn't known exactly what to expect, but what he'd found hadn't even been on the list.

Baba peered over his shoulder as he knelt in front of the low drawer. "Hey," she said with surprise, "I recognize a few of these names." She pointed one slim finger at a file. "Look, there's Belinda. And isn't that one of the other families whose child went missing?"

Liam could feel his face set into grim lines as his heart clenched. "They're all in there, Barbara. Maybe that's a coincidence, but if so, it's a pretty big one."

"Well, their names could have been added to the 'vulnerable' list after the disappearances," Baba said, voice uncertain. "There's no proof that says otherwise."

"That's true," Liam agreed reluctantly. "On the other hand, I've been inundated lately with calls from folks who've been experiencing weird issues and problems—sabotage of farm equipment, vanishing workers, strange plagues of mice and snakes—and every single one of those people has a file in this drawer. That can't possibly be a fluke."

Baba slitted her eyes, and the light in her palm flickered for a moment from pale white to bloody red before she let out a hissing breath and it returned to what passed as normal for a magical glowing light. "No. No, it isn't. That's Maya's handiwork; I'm sure of it."

"But we still don't have any way to prove it," Liam said, frustration tensing his shoulders and clenching his jaw. "We need more time to look at these files, but I don't dare take them. The last thing we want to do is tip Maya off that we're on to her."

"It's too bad we can't copy them," Baba said, glancing over at the huge printer-copier that sat on Callahan's desk. "But it would take too long. We're already pushing our luck."

Liam agreed, but he suddenly got an idea. "Hang on," he said, pulling his cell phone out of his pocket. "If you shine your light over this drawer, I can at least take a few pictures with my phone. Then we can take a closer look at the names later, when we're someplace safer."

Baba looked impressed. "You can do that with your phone?"

He rolled his eyes and started grouping the files together so he could get a bunch of names into one shot. "You have *got* to move into this century, Baba."

She gave an ironic snort that somehow contained a joke he was pretty sure he wasn't getting. He was about to ask her what was so funny, when Gregori materialized out of the darkness, almost giving Liam a heart attack.

"Jesus!" he said, grabbing onto the metal drawer so hard, the edges cut into his fingers.

"No relation, I'm afraid," the Asian man said dryly. "Although I have been known to walk on water occasionally."

Gregori turned to Baba. "I caught two Otherworld creatures skulking around outside. I took care of them, but there's no telling if there are more on the way. I think it's time for you two to get out of here."

Liam tucked his phone back into his pants and turned around to thank Gregori, but the other man was already gone.

"How the hell does he do that?" Liam muttered under his breath.

Baba just laughed quietly and headed for the window. She gave the room an unreadable look, shrugged, and hopped back over the sill and out into the silent night. Liam followed, slightly less gracefully, then almost tripped over two long-limbed beasts with lizardlike snouts and tails, and claws that dripped with a tarlike viscous substance.

They lay on the ground in a position that suggested their narrow, pointy heads had been knocked together with considerable force. Liam couldn't tell if they were still breathing or not, and he didn't particularly want to get close enough to find out. Something about the way their teeth and claws glistened made him think of rattlesnake venom.

"Don't worry," Baba murmured in his ear, startling him. "Gregori is very neat; he always cleans up after himself." She kicked one of the creatures hard with one heavy boot as she walked past. "Basilisks. I hate those things."

They walked in companionable silence back to where they had left his cruiser and her motorcycle a few blocks away, tucked behind a tiny neighborhood convenience store. As usual, Liam had very little idea what Baba was thinking, and his own thoughts skittered like water bugs on a murky pond, from the possibilities they'd opened up with their illicit explorations to more personal possibilities he didn't dare explore in any depth, lest they root themselves any further in the unfertile soil of his damaged soul.

"I'm going to go home and download these pictures onto my computer," Liam said as they stood next to the BMW. "I want to see if I can compile a list of all the people in the green-coded files. It might tell us something we don't know yet."

Baba cocked her head to the side as she thought, errant

strands of hair escaping from the braid she'd tucked it into for their after-hours foray. "You know, if all the missing kids are from names in that group, maybe we can figure out which families have children that are still at risk. If you eliminate the people without kids, or with kids who are too old, you'll have a short list of which children might be Maya's next target. There can't be that many of them."

Liam's heart beat faster. "If the list is short enough, maybe we can prevent her from taking any more children." A fraction of the two-ton weight he'd been carrying around on his shoulders seemed to lighten and drift off into the dark night.

A wicked smile flitted across Baba's austere face, making her seem for a moment like some wild and dangerous beast out of legend. "Better yet," she said, looking into Liam's eyes, "if we can catch her in the act trying to steal another child, you get to keep your job. I can make her tell me where the doorway is, so I can tell the queen and get to keep my head. And the queen can make Maya give the missing children back. All we have to do is narrow down the list enough to figure out who her next target is, and we solve all our problems at once. *And* protect the child, at the same time."

Liam gazed at her in the moonlight. "You're a genius," he said. And seized by an uncontrollable impulse, he put his hands on the side of her face, leaned in, and kissed her soundly. Pulled back, looked at the stunned expression on her face, and did it again. Her lips tasted like blackberry wine, felt soft like rose petals as they gave under his, and the elusive scent of orange blossoms floated through the air like nature made manifest.

Stepping back, he grinned at her, ridiculously pleased by the mixture of shock and pleasure he could see in her wide amber eyes. He was a little shocked himself by the strength of the longing that surged through his body, and had to fight the impulse to put her up against the closest wall and claim those lips and everything that came with them.

"Try to get some sleep," he said in a rough voice over his shoulder as he walked to his car. "I'll come over tomorrow when I can get away from work, and we'll see if we can come up with some kind of a plan, depending on what information I've been able to gather from the pictures."

In his rearview mirror, he could see Baba standing where he left her, one slim hand touching her mouth as if to hold on to the sensation he'd left there.

EIGHTEEN

THE MEMORY OF the look on Baba's face kept Liam going through the long day that followed. Like the previous days, he waded through stacks of ever-accumulating paperwork whenever he got back into the office, instead of being out chasing after elusive, impossible crimes. But unlike the days before it, this one was occasionally broken up by flashes of memory like lightning that jolted briefly through the mundane annoyances: the feel of Baba's skin beneath his hands, softer than silk; her quick intake of breath when he'd kissed her the first time, the slightest hint of a response from her rose-petal lips when he'd kissed her again. Those magical eyes, which seemed to cast a spell on him even when they were nowhere near.

Nina gave him a funny look when she'd brought his lunch in, asking if he was coming down with something. He'd smiled and said no. But maybe he was. That would explain the strange fever in his blood. Of course, as always, he'd simply blamed it on stress and not enough sleep. That made more sense than anything else he could put into words.

He was finally grabbing a late supper in a nearly deserted

Bertie's, when he got a call telling him he was needed at the emergency room in the West Dunville hospital. Someone reporting an assault, the dispatcher said. Liam pressed for more information, visualizing a crowd of irate locals and a battered and bloody Baba. But the night dispatcher, neither as efficient nor as helpful as Nina, didn't know anything more. Just that Liam had been requested by name.

He waved an urgent hand at his waitress, signaling her to bring him the check, but Bertie herself came out of the kitchen to plop the remains of his turkey, avocado, and bacon sandwich in a to-go box and give him a scowl that was only partially due to the insult to her carefully prepared food.

"Looks like something's up, Sheriff. Not another disappearance, I hope," the older woman said, drying chapped red hands on a sauce-stained apron.

Her short-cropped gray hair bristled as stiff as her manner, but what she lacked in charm she made up for in both her cooking skills and the care with which she fed the people who entered her front door. Barbara might even call it magic, Liam thought, wanting to be gone.

"No," he said shortly. "Nothing like that. There's been a report of an assault victim from the hospital. I have to go check it out."

He handed her a twenty and waved away the change. He knew Bertie probably would have closed up already if he hadn't come in. As it was, the lone remaining waitress was putting the chairs up on the tables as they spoke, weariness dragging at her sneaker-clad feet.

Bertie's plain, mannish face crinkled with concern. "Not anyone we know, I hope." Of course, she knew almost everyone, so that was unlikely. Her eyes widened. "It's not that poor herbalist they're calling a witch, is it? I told that ignorant lout O'Shaunnessy that he was being an ass when he was in here earlier shooting off his mouth. Like folks need any help getting more riled up, what with everything that's been happening."

Liam's stomach pulled itself into intricate knots that

would have made his Boy Scout leader proud. "Thanks, Bertie," he said, grabbing his hat and pushing it down onto his head. "I've got to go. You're the best."

She snorted at him, pushing him toward the door. "You just say that because you don't have anything to compare me to. One of these days, you're gonna have to get yourself another woman."

Right, Liam thought. That was exactly what his life needed right now. He slid into the squad car, flipped on the siren, and raced off toward West Dunville, praying that the one woman who could never be his was not at the other end of his journey.

LIAM FORCED HIMSELF to walk at his usual measured pace as he entered the hospital emergency intake area. He nodded at the clerk sitting there, a woman he knew slightly from around town.

"Hey, Louise," he said. "I got a call that you had an assault victim here who was asking for me. You know anything about that?"

The woman nodded, her professional manner slipping to show disgust for a moment before she regained her poise. "It's a terrible thing when a woman isn't safe to walk the streets at night, Sheriff. I'm glad they called you in. Not everyone does, you know." She shook her head and pointed at the door to the back area, hitting a buzzer to allow him through.

Damn, he thought as he moved in the direction of voices. *I should have made her go home with me last night. Or put her in police custody. Something. This is my fault.* The fact that Baba wouldn't have put up with any of that didn't make him feel any better. There was nothing worse than not being able to keep those you cared for safe. Nothing.

Liam pulled back the curtain over the only occupied bay to be faced by a completely unexpected sight.

The woman in the bed was battered and bruised; one eye almost completely closed, the cheekbone underneath it swollen. Various spots on her bare arms showed a turbulent rainbow of mottled black and blue and green that clashed with the red from her bloody nose. But her hair was an icy fall of platinum blonde, and the untouched eye shone a bright, innocent blue instead of the cloud of black and mysterious amber he had been expecting.

"Ms. Freeman!" he said, shocked and relieved in equal measure. "I was told someone had called me in on an assault case. I'm guessing that would be you." He pulled out his notebook and a pen, feeling vaguely guilty by how grateful he was that the pathetic figure in the bed was Maya, and not Baba. "Are you up to telling me what happened?"

Liam had been so focused on Maya, he'd barely taken in the presence of the other people in the room. But his sense of relief evaporated rapidly as he took in Clive Matthews standing on one side of the bed, and Peter Callahan on the other, sitting in a chair, holding an oversized bouquet of flowers in a pretentious crystal vase.

"Actually," Callahan said, rising and looking around for someplace in the Spartan space of the emergency room bay to put the roses. Finally, he gave up and set them down on the chair he'd vacated. "I'm the one who called you. Miss Freeman was hesitant to bring the law into this matter, but I told her she had no choice. That woman cannot be allowed to stay at large. Not after this."

Liam blinked, gazing from Maya to Callahan and back again, although he was pretty sure he knew exactly which woman she meant. "I'm sorry, I'm confused. What woman?" He turned to Maya. "Are you saying a woman did this to you?"

Maya looked up at him, her eyes brimming with unshed tears she dabbed at with a handkerchief. She practically radiated an aura of virtue and honesty; one which Liam almost bought, even knowing better as he did. The other two men were clearly mesmerized by her fragile, damaged beauty.

"It was Barbara Yager," Maya said in a soft, hesitant voice. "She attacked me as I was getting out of my car in the parking lot behind the apartment I'm renting in town."

One big blue eye focused on Liam accusingly. "I *told* you she was stalking me, but you didn't take me seriously."

"This is on your head," Callahan blustered, big hands clenched in fists at his side as he hovered protectively over Maya's bed. "You were told that Ms. Yager was harassing my assistant, but you did nothing about it. And now look what's happened! I expect that woman to be arrested immediately."

Liam had a momentary vision of Baba, her face suffused with anger at the thought of children being snatched away from their parents and sold to the highest bidder in the place she called the Otherworld. There was no question in his mind that she *could* have done this. She was bigger and stronger than Maya, and he had no doubt she was capable of fighting like a cornered panther if she had to. But attacking Maya had never been a part of their plan. Besides, as furious as Baba might get, he couldn't envision her risking those missing children simply for the chance to hurt someone who had pissed her off.

No, Baba hadn't done this. Which meant that either someone else had and Maya had taken the opportunity to put the blame on Baba, or worse, Maya had somehow staged this in order to get Baba thrown in jail. Maybe Maya had figured out somehow that they'd been in Callahan's office, and had gone on the offensive before they could use the information they'd found there.

Either way, he was in a lousy position now. And from the gleam in the tiny woman's uninjured eye, she knew it. A martyred sigh oozed malice in his direction.

"I'm afraid I am going to have to press charges," Maya said, a sad expression on her bruised face. "Otherwise I would just be living in terror that she would come after me again."

Liam made sure his own expression was neutral and professional before he spoke. "Not that I'm doubting your story, Ms. Freeman, but why would Barbara Yager have attacked you so brutally? Did you do something to provoke her?"

Callahan gritted his teeth. "The woman is crazy. She

didn't need a reason. Everyone in town is talking about how she is selling phony herbal remedies to people in need. She's clearly a con artist."

"Actually, she's a professor," Liam corrected him in a calm, even tone. "And my investigation into the problem with the medicines she sold turned up evidence that a third party had been interfering with the remedies *after* people had taken them home." He purposely didn't look at Maya when he said it.

"I don't care if she's the Queen of Sheba," Callahan shouted, a purple vein pulsing madly in his forehead. "She doesn't get to attack an innocent woman. I want her arrested immediately, or I'll have your job!"

Privately, Liam thought it was a little late for that threat, a supposition that was reinforced a moment later when Clive Matthews stepped in too close and said, chest puffed up like a Bantam rooster's, "Make sure you take a couple of deputies with you. We don't want her to get away."

Then Matthews fixed his beady eyes on Liam's uniform and added with a sneer, "Surely even you can manage to capture one unarmed woman. I trust that I can depend on you to do your job and protect the people of this county from a dangerous criminal. After all, there's a first time for everything."

LIAM PULLED HIS cruiser into the space in front of the Airstream, its silver bullet shape glistening in the light of the tangerine moon overhead. Two deputies in a second car edged in behind him, choking a little on his dust as they got out, the road as dry as a desert from the summer's unusual heat despite the storm earlier in the week. One, a youngster with the whitewall crew cut of a guy who spent his weekends training with the National Guard, let his hand hover over his service weapon until Liam glared at him.

"I don't care what you've heard," Liam said to him, including the older deputy with a sideways glance, "but the woman we've come to question is a respected professional, and I expect you to treat her like one unless I tell you otherwise. Is that clear?"

Stu, the younger of the two, rolled his eyes. Butch, who'd been on the force for over twenty years, just shrugged. As long as he got home to his dinner on time and nobody took a shot at him, he was a happy man.

Liam looked around and spotted both the silver truck and the BMW, which had miraculously been restored to all of its former glory. He made a mental note *not* to ask how she'd managed that. And cursed a little under his breath, since he'd been hoping that Baba would be out when they got there. Somehow he didn't think she was going to take it well when he informed her that he had no choice but to arrest her.

Settling his hat more firmly on his head, he walked up to the door and knocked briskly. Behind him, the two deputies stood like a uniformed wall of menace, as if they were about to confront a band of bank robbers instead of one slightly eccentric traveling herbalist.

The door creaked open slowly, and a tousled white head poked cautiously around the edge.

"Hello?" a querulous voice said. "Can I help you gentlemen with something?"

The woman attached to the voice was so old, she looked like she'd been around when dirt was invented. Her back was bent in a dowager's hump, and her hair was as white and fluffy as a puff of dandelion. Wrinkles slid in layers down her cheeks and neck, disappearing into the lacy blue shawl tied over her drooping bosom. A strong gust of wind might have blown her over, which probably explained the way one age-spotted hand clung to the door. The other was wrapped around a wooden cane as gnarled as the fingers that clutched it, its head in the shape of a roaring dragon.

Liam blinked rapidly, recognizing the little old lady he'd caught a glimpse of that first day in his rearview mirror. Maybe she lived nearby, and he'd somehow never met her. Some of the older folks in the backcountry had an innate distrust of the law and tended to avoid strangers.

"I'm sorry to disturb you," Liam said. "I'm looking for the lady who lives in this Airstream, Ms. Yager. Is she home?"

The ancient crone gazed at him with cloudy eyes that still managed to shoot sparks in his direction. "Miss Yager? You mean *Dr.* Yager, don't you?" She shook her head, wisps of dandelion hair floating around her crumpled face. "You young people. No respect these days." She made a *tsk*ing noise that reminded Liam of a particularly terrifying third-grade teacher. Behind him, he could hear Stu shifting uneasily, and had to stifle a laugh.

"My apologies. Dr. Yager, yes. Is she at home?" This was *not* going at all the way he'd expected it to. Of course, he was dealing with Baba. Why was he surprised? "And can you tell us who you are, please, ma'am?"

His good manners seemed to appease the old woman, and she opened the door a little wider. "I'm a distant relative of Dr. Yager's," she said in her light, high, birdlike voice. "I'm passing through the area and stopped by for a visit. But I'm afraid she's out at the moment, collecting herbs. She says there are a few that work better if they are collected under the light of the moon. Why don't you run along now and come back later when she's home?" She made a shooing gesture and started to close the door, arthritic hand trembling with the effort.

Butch took an assertive step forward, thrusting his gut past where Liam was taking up most of the front step. "I'm sorry, ma'am, but we're under orders. I'm afraid we're going to have to come in and check to make sure Miz—I mean Dr.—Yager isn't in there."

Her lower lip quivered, making Liam feel like a cad. But there was no way the deputies were going to let him just walk away from the trailer without searching it for Baba. They had a warrant, and no doubt, special instructions from Clive Matthews to make sure Liam did his job.

"Don't worry, ma'am," he said in a gentle tone, speaking a little loudly in case she was hard of hearing. "We'll just come in, prove to ourselves she isn't here, and then we'll leave you alone."

Thin lips pressed together, she nodded at him and opened the door the rest of the way. "Very well," she said. "But mind you wipe your feet. I won't abide a lot of mud tracked in on these beautiful carpets."

The three law officers trooped in, dutifully wiping their feet, and Liam watched with amusement as the other two gaped, openmouthed, as they looked around at the luxurious interior with its rich fabrics and glorious blues, and crimsons, and greens. The place looked as neat and tidy as always. There was no sign of Baba.

Chudo-Yudo crawled out from underneath the banquette table, and Stu nearly shot him.

"Jesus Christ! What the hell is that thing?" he asked, his gun suddenly wavering in his hand.

Liam sighed. "That thing is Dr. Yager's dog, and I think she would object to you shooting him. Put your damned gun away; he's not going to hurt you." He made a point of going over to pat Chudo-Yudo on the head.

"Feel free to poke around if you have to," the old woman said, waving one skinny arm toward the back of the Airstream. "Can I make you boys some tea?"

Butch glanced around at all the jars of herbs and muttered, "No way, José," visibly suppressing a shudder.

Liam laughed, turning it into a cough behind one hand. He accepted the purple mug he was handed, although he sniffed at it cautiously before taking a sip.

"No, dear, my name's not José," the crone said. "You can call me Babushka, everyone does."

Stu and Butch ignored her, stomping through the Airstream, peering into the back bedroom, and opening closets. Liam winced when they rattled the wonky handle of the wardrobe that led to the Otherworld, but Babushka tottered over helpfully to open it, revealing only clothes and a wealth of black leather boots with various heel heights.

"Well, it looks like she's not here after all," Liam said with ill-concealed relief. "We're sorry to have bothered you, ma'am."

"No bother at all," Babushka said graciously. "Can I tell her why you came by?"

Stu, still smarting from his overreaction to the dog, said stiffly, "We have a warrant for her arrest. She brutally attacked an innocent woman earlier this evening."

Babushka opened her rheumy eyes wide and put one hand dramatically over her heart. "Oh my. I can't imagine Barbara would do such a thing. She's a prominent professor and a sweet, sweet soul. There must be some mistake." She sat down and covered her face as if overcome with emotion at the news.

Liam choked on his tea, casting a searching glance at the old lady, whose shoulders were shaking. He placed the mug down carefully on the counter and cleared his throat.

"We appreciate your cooperation, ma'am. We'll be leaving now." He stared at the deputies until they started heading for the door, then turned back to meet the remarkably tear-free eyes across from him. One white-lashed orb winked at him so quickly he almost missed it.

"I'd appreciate it if you could give Dr. Yager a message for me," he said. "Tell her it would be best if she turns herself in." He glanced at Stu and Bernie, waiting impatiently at the entrance, and added pointedly, "And it would really be helpful if she happened to have an alibi for six p.m., the time the attack occurred."

Once outside, Butch said, "I can't believe anyone would be out picking herbs in the middle of the damned night. Do you think she's making a run for it?"

"Not at all," Liam answered. He gestured at the Airstream. "She's living in a portable house. If she was going to leave, I'd think she'd take it with her. Besides, all her vehicles are here." He took a couple of steps toward his car. "I'm guessing we'll find that this whole thing is just a big mix-up. In the meanwhile, there's no point in waiting around; she could be gone all night. I'm sure she'll come into the station when she gets the message from er . . . Babushka."

Stu looked over his shoulder at the trailer. "She seems like a nice old lady, but jeez, that's a big dog."

"Yes," said Liam. "But a small dragon."

Stu stared at him. "Sheriff, you get weirder all the time."

Liam smiled. "You have no idea, Stu. You have no damned idea."

NINETEEN

BABA STROLLED INTO the Sheriff's Department at nine the next morning, clad in a tailored black skirt and white sleeveless top, her head held high against the stares and mutters that greeted her. Coming in right behind her, Belinda nodded at her fellow officers, and the Ivanovs lifted their hands in halfhearted hellos to people they knew. Mouths gaped open as they all processed in to the front desk, accompanied by the irregular hum of the overburdened air conditioners.

"Hi there," Baba chirped in a perky voice that would have made the Riders choke on their breakfast beer. "I got a message that Sheriff McClellan was looking for me. Is he in?"

The sergeant at the desk fumbled for the phone and called Liam's secretary. A moment later, the sheriff popped out of his office, a middle-aged woman trailing in his wake and gazing at Baba with ill-concealed curiosity.

"Ah, Dr. Yager," Liam said, his voice cool and professional, "I take it you got my message?" He opened a gate that led to the central office area. "Please come on back."

He guided the group to a large table in the middle of the room. It was probably used for meetings, and from the variety of mustard and ketchup stains marring its wood surface, any meal that wasn't eaten at someone's desk. Baba raised an eyebrow when she realized he was going to question her there instead of in one of the formal detention areas. Clearly, he wanted the largest audience possible. Nice.

"If you'll take a seat, my secretary, Molly, can take notes here. We wouldn't want to drag the Ivanovs into the back of the station." He pulled out a chair for Belinda's mother, then took one for himself next to her, across the table from Baba. Molly clutched her pad and pen as if they were an all-expense paid ticket to the best show in town and sat down next to him.

Baba plastered a serious look on her face. "So, Sheriff, I gather you have some questions for me? Something about a crime I'm supposed to have committed?"

He nodded, then pushed his hair back out of his face. "Can you tell me where you were at approximately five fifty last night?"

Molly's pen hovered over her paper like a bird about ready to take flight.

"Of course," Baba said. "I was at the Ivanovs' house. They very kindly invited me to dinner last night, along with their daughter. I got there around five, and didn't leave until, oh, sometime after nine, I think."

The pen scribbled down the pertinent facts as mouths dropped open around the room.

"Ah," Liam said, a dimple she'd never noticed flitting in and out of view at the corner of his mouth. "So at five fifty, you were with Deputy Shields and her parents?"

"We had a lovely roast chicken with potatoes and beets," Mariska said, beaming. "And then we talked about the Old Country for hours. The professor spent her childhood there you know, before moving to the United States with her adoptive mother." She patted Baba's hand. "It was so nice to be able to chat with someone who had been to Russia, no matter how long ago."

Baba smiled back at her. "It was my pleasure. And that chicken was sublime."

Liam nodded at Belinda. "And you can back this up?"

"Absolutely," she said without missing a beat. "The chicken was definitely sublime."

The front door of the station slammed open with a bang that had half the officers reaching for their weapons before they realized where the noise had come from. One of the air conditioning units wheezed to a stop, belching a puff of gray smoke into the already dense air.

Clive Matthews stormed up to the front desk and gestured for the officer on duty to open the gate, his plump face glistening with sweat. On his heels, Peter Callahan lent a gallant arm to a pale but upright Maya, limping across the floor with her Technicolor bruises standing out in stark contrast to her lacy blouse and upswept hair.

"What the hell is going on here?" Matthews demanded. One pudgy hand pointed at Baba. "Why isn't that woman in cuffs?"

Baba could see Liam's glance dart to the clock on the wall and saw him come to the inevitable conclusion that the only way that Matthews could have gotten there so fast was if someone at the department had called him. A clenched jaw was the only sign of his distress at this act of betrayal, and when he rose to greet the board president, his expression was a picture of artless confusion.

"Did we have a meeting scheduled that I forgot about?" He turned to Maya. "Goodness, Ms. Freeman, should you be out of the hospital? You look terrible." Liam bounded around the table and pulled out a chair for the blond woman, thankfully one that placed the Ivanovs between her and Baba. Baba wasn't sure she could sit next to the little monster without strangling the bitch with her bare hands. As it was, she had to settle for watching Maya wince as Liam politely insulted her.

Maya's face was a study in purple and green and barely concealed displeasure. "Thankfully, there were no internal injuries," she said, wafting gracefully into the seat. "And they tell me that the pain will subside in a few days. Or maybe a week." She batted her eyelashes at Peter Callahan, clearly not realizing that having one eye swollen half shut rendered the gesture more grotesque than appealing.

"See here," Callahan said, recognizing a cue when he saw one. "Why isn't this woman under arrest? Miss Freeman told you that she was attacked by this so-called professor. Shouldn't she be locked up in a cell?"

Liam settled one hip on the edge of the table and crossed his arms. "That's right; Miss Freeman did say that Dr. Yager was the one who injured her, didn't she?" He gazed at Maya thoughtfully. "That is very interesting, considering that we have three witnesses who will swear to the fact that she was with them at the time of the beating."

Clive Matthews sputtered a protest. "That's impossible! The witnesses must be lying. She paid them off. Or put them under a spell. Or something."

Molly made a tiny choking noise and scribbled faster. Around the room, you could have heard a pin drop, even over the laboring sound of the ancient cooling system.

"The witnesses in question include one of my deputies and her elderly parents, who are longtime respected members of this community." Liam raised one eyebrow and gestured around the table before turning back to Matthews. "And personally, I don't believe in spells or any of that mumbo-jumbo. I do, however, believe that Miss Freeman lied to me, which I assure you, will have much worse side effects than any spell."

He swiveled to give Maya the full force of his stern glare. "Now, Miss Freeman, since Dr. Yager is clearly not the culprit in this case, perhaps you'd like to tell us who is. I'm guessing that since you didn't want to name the person who actually attacked you, this was some kind of lover's quarrel—maybe with a married man?" He gazed pointedly at Clive Matthews and Peter Callahan.

Callahan sputtered wordlessly, and Matthews's face got so red, Molly ran to get him a glass of water.

"My goodness, Mr. Matthews," she said. "You should see a doctor about that high blood pressure of yours. I had an uncle who looked like that right before he keeled over and died."

Baba bit her lip so hard, she thought it would bleed.

Liam went on, ignoring the indignant protestations from the two men and focusing his attention on the little blonde, who seemed slightly flustered for the first time since Baba had seen her.

"I . . . I'm afraid I jumped to a conclusion," Maya said, trying the eye-batting at Liam with no noticeable effect. "My attacker wore motorcycle gear and a helmet. I couldn't see the person's face, but since Barbara Yager had already been harassing and threatening me, I assumed it was her." A woeful expression highlighted her battered face. "I am so very sorry for any trouble I might have caused."

From under lowered eyelashes, she shot a virulent glare at Baba. Baba showed her teeth in a not-very-convincing smile and shot one right back.

"No problem at all," Baba said. "I barely noticed the inconvenience."

A sound like a distant wolf growling greeted this blithe statement, and Clive Matthews stopped sputtering long enough to look around for the source of the noise, shivering a little as if the room had suddenly gotten cold.

"Well, that is very kind of you, Dr. Yager," Liam said in his most official tone. "Miss Freeman, I suggest you consider yourself lucky that Dr. Yager doesn't want to press charges against you for making a false accusation. I hope next time you will think twice about making assumptions without any facts to back them up."

He stood up. "Feel free to let me know if you remember anything else about your attacker, Miss Freeman. I wouldn't want Mr. Matthews here to accuse me of not doing my job."

"Oh no," Mariska said sweetly. "I'm sure he would never do that. Would you, Mr. Matthews?"

Matthews and Callahan ushered Maya out, stalking stiff-necked through the crowd of gawking sheriff's department employees. Nina waved at them gaily from her perch at the dispatcher's station. Maya's limp had mysteriously disappeared, and she seemed remarkably healthy as she slammed the door on her way out.

"Goodness," Molly said, tucking her pen into her pad and heading back to her desk. "Wasn't that exciting?"

"Yes," Baba said, one corner of her mouth twitching up. "Wasn't it?"

Liam's face was all stern lines and cool composure; his jaw looked like it had been carved from granite. "A little more excitement than I prefer in my day, I'm afraid. It's a good thing you had an iron-clad alibi, Dr. Yager, or things might have gone quite differently."

Baba stood up and offered a hand to Mariska Ivanov as she struggled out of the hard metal chair. "A very good thing indeed, Sheriff. Lucky for me the Ivanovs invited me to dinner last night."

Belinda helped her father up and said to Liam, "I'm just going to drive my parents and Barbara home, and then I'll be back in to work, if that's okay with you, Sheriff."

Liam nodded at her, and only Baba saw Belinda's tiny wink, like a glittering star in the dark night sky.

BABA STRETCHED HER long legs out in front of her and watched the sun set in vivid colors of red and orange behind the nearby hills like a fireball announcing the coming apocalypse. Crickets chorused gleefully along with the more doleful sounds of a mourning dove's coo, and the evening's first firefly blinked into view and then vanished again.

She and Liam sat on lawn chairs in front of the Airstream with Chudo-Yudo lying between them, roasting hot dogs over a portable copper fire pit and washing them down with, in Liam's case, a beer from the local microbrewery, and in Baba's, a crystal chalice filled with a crisp and fruity Riesling. Chudo-Yudo lapped at a large bowl of Guinness stout; his dragon physiology didn't even notice the alcohol, he just liked the rich bitter taste.

The outside light by the Airstream's door cast its warm glow over the encroaching darkness, making their impromptu cookout seem even cozier than it was. Baba felt as close to relaxed as she ever got; a sensation that, ironically, simply caused her stomach muscles to tense and her shoulders to hunch defensively.

Cozy made her uncomfortable. Cozy with Liam made her even more uncomfortable. Maybe because it felt so good. So right. Like something she could do every night, for the rest of her life. *Absurd.*

"Thanks for the help with the Maya mess," she said finally, stirring the fire with a cast iron poker and tossing on another branch that Chudo-Yudo had fetched earlier in a fit of playful doggieness. Sparks flew up into the night sky like demented fairies.

She and Liam had barely spoken since he'd shown up about twenty minutes ago. She'd fetched him a chair and put his first hot dog on a stick, and he'd pulled a six-pack out of his car, along with a file folder, which he'd plopped on the ground next to him. Other than that, they'd mostly just sat there in companionable silence, chewing and sipping and occasionally reaching down to pet Chudo-Yudo on the top of his massive, shaggy white head.

Like an old married couple, she thought, shoulders edging up a little closer to her ears. She shook it off, purposely stretching her legs out even further, and snuck a glance at Liam out of the corner of her eye.

He was clearly off duty, since he wore jeans and a dark blue tee shirt that clung to his broad shoulders and chest in a way that made her think thoughts she'd be better off ignoring, but otherwise, he hadn't said much about his day.

Liam gave her a bad imitation of an innocent look when she thanked him. "Me? I just got my secretary to take notes. You're the one who conveniently showed up with three impeccable witnesses to prove you couldn't have committed the crime." He stuffed the second half of his third hot dog into his mouth with all the enthusiasm of a man who hadn't eaten all day, and cracked open another beer. The shadows from the flames emphasized the dark circles under his eyes and the deepening lines around his mouth, highlighting the few tiny silver hairs just starting to show in his beard stubble.

Baba thought he looked tired and frazzled and a little bit chewed on, like a favorite old boot that Chudo-Yudo had gotten at when she wasn't looking. Without conscious intent, she reached out and gently moved a strand of dark-blond hair off his face, making him smile.

They both froze for a moment, taken off guard by the power of the connection between them. Liam shook it off first, but she caught a glimpse of something that looked a lot like the attraction she was trying so hard to fight.

"I know," he said, "one of these days I have to take the time to get it cut."

"It's growing on me," Baba said, pulling her hand back awkwardly and stuffing it into her lap, where it would hopefully stay out of trouble. She steered the conversation back to business. Safer that way. "And I meant it when I said thanks. Without your hint to find an alibi, I could be sitting in a jail cell right now, eating bad food, and fighting off some junkie streetwalker who wanted to make me her bitch."

Liam startled, and dropped his hot dog in the fire, suppressing a curse as he watched his meal burn to a cinder. "Oh, for heaven's sake. How do you even know about this stuff if you don't watch TV?" He pulled the last dog out of the package and politely offered it to her before putting it on his now-vacant stick and leaning forward to place it gingerly over the fire.

"The Riders hang out in a lot of bars," she explained, giving him a rare grin. "They tell me things."

Chudo-Yudo snorted with laughter, a little Guinness foam clinging to his black lips and giving him a frothy mustache.

"For your information," Liam said acidly, "Dunville is too small to have streetwalkers. We may have a few women who sleep with men for money, but if they do, they're subtle enough about it that the sheriff's department doesn't have to get involved. And frankly, the food in the jail would have been better than hot dogs." He blew ashes off his slightly charred wiener before plopping it into a bun and squirting copious amounts of ketchup on it. For a moment, Baba saw a stream of blood flowing through the air and shuddered.

"Ha," she said, scooting her chair a little closer to the fire. "I can't believe you came out here, enjoyed my gracious hospitality, and then insulted my gourmet cuisine. I'm going to start thinking you don't like me."

There was a moment of silence from the other chair. "Ha," Liam said, echoing her. But his voice sounded a lot more serious than hers had. "You're odd, mysterious, and infuriating. What's not to like?"

Baba tried to ignore the heat that flushed her face. He probably hadn't meant those things as a compliment, but she rather liked being described that way. At the very least, it was honest.

"Want me to eat him *now*?" Chudo-Yudo asked from his spot at her feet. "I've still got a little room left after those hot dogs."

Liam jumped, still not used to having a talking dog around, and Baba tried to swallow a laugh along with her wine, spattering them both in a flash of droplets that made the fire flare and flash. She hid her smile behind the hand wiping dampness from her lips.

"Don't worry," she said to Liam. "He's probably kidding."

"Right," Liam said, not looking reassured. He put his beer down with a sigh and turned his chair a little so he was facing Baba. "You know, part of me is almost getting used to all this weird stuff. The other part of me still thinks I'm hallucinating, and should seek out medical help and some form of heavy medication."

Baba sighed too, more quietly, so he wouldn't hear. It's not as though she really thought he was going to be okay with witches and dragons and magical doorways. But a girl could dream.

"I'd stick with beer if I were you," she made herself say in a bright tone. "Fewer side effects, and less likely to get you locked up in a room with padded walls." She shrugged. "Besides, the weird stuff is only temporary. We'll solve the Maya problem, get your missing kids back, and I'll hit the road to chase down the next Baba Yaga call. Everything will go back to normal." Liam winced, no doubt in response to her weak attempt at a smile.

"Normal," he said flatly. "I'm not sure I'd even recognize it anymore."

He gazed at her for a moment and asked, in the tones of a man who wasn't sure he really wanted an answer, "So, was that actually you last night? The little old lady who called herself Babushka?"

Chudo-Yudo snorted, spraying beer foam over Liam's shoes. "It's traditional."

"Traditional?"

"The Baba Yaga usually appears as an old crone," Baba explained. "The tales got a little exaggerated over the years, and gave her iron teeth and a long nose that bent down to meet her equally long chin, which curved up." She felt her own nose a little self-consciously; really it wasn't *that* long. Just a bit, um, regal. "I still use the old woman guise on occasion, but it is just a glamour. Illusion."

"An impressive one," Liam said. "You had me fooled for quite a while, and I'm pretty sure that my deputies still think they met someone's not-very-sweet grandmother."

He thought about it for a moment. "So, Maya's dramatic bruises and colorful black eye—was that all a glamour too?"

Baba nodded. "A glamour on top of her already existing illusion of a beautiful Human woman." She grimaced. "If she's really a Rusalka, I assure you, her true form isn't nearly that attractive. Unless you like deathly-pale green skin, stringy hair that looks like seaweed, and long sharp pointy teeth."

Liam made a face. "No thanks, not my type." His eyes strayed to Baba's wild hair for a moment, and she tried to smooth it down before giving up with an annoyed mental shake. As if she cared what his type was, and that she clearly wasn't it. Bah. Humans. Way too complicated.

"I'm sure Maya will lie low for a couple of days, then reappear, miraculously healed except for a few tiny, tasteful bruises to get her sympathy," Baba growled. "And in the meanwhile, people will still be giving me dirty looks, no matter what lengths the Ivanovs and Belinda went to in order to clear my name."

"I think she's definitely lying low," Liam said, looking thoughtful. "Today was remarkably quiet; no irate calls from farmers whose machinery had been sabotaged overnight, or neighbors wanting to blame each other for something crazy. I even managed to get some work done in the office." He reached down and picked up the folder he'd brought.

"Is that the information we got from Peter Callahan's office?" Baba perked up. Finally, something concrete to focus on. Besides the sheriff's flat abs and strong arms, that is. And his own particular masculine scent, which seemed to winnow its way straight to her core. "Were you able to come up with anything helpful?"

Even Chudo-Yudo sat up and paid attention as Liam opened the folder and tilted his notes so he could see them better in the arcing white light from the trailer behind them.

"I think so," Liam said, scooting his chair closer to Baba's, the dragon-dog circling around to sit at their feet. His tail inadvertently hung into the fire for a moment before he twitched it away, but the heat didn't seem to bother him.

"I double-checked the three missing kids against the list of families in the green files, and they're all in there," Liam said.

His hands clenched on the folder until the papers inside crunched like dry bones in an abandoned graveyard.

"Ah," Baba said, resisting the urge to reach out and touch him. The best cure for both of their frustration and anger would be to concentrate on catching Maya and getting the children back. If that was even still possible. She wasn't about to mention that it might be too late.

"Were you able to figure out how many of the people in those files have children who might be at risk?"

He nodded, pushing his hair back impatiently. "There are eight families on the list with children; a total of fifteen kids, since some of the families have more than one child."

"Gah," Baba said, letting out a discouraged noise that startled a nearby bat into flying crooked. It banged into the side of the Airstream and clung to the windowsill, stunned, before taking off again, wobbly-winged, into the encroaching darkness. "That's a lot."

"It's not as bad as it sounds," Liam said, holding up one sheet of paper. "Some of the kids are too old to fall into her pattern, I think. So hopefully they're not vulnerable. But that still leaves us with seven children, which is definitely too many to try to watch. I thought maybe we could talk them over and figure out a way to narrow the list down a little."

"Do you think Peter Callahan knows anything?" Baba asked. "I'd be happy to try to beat the information out of him. I could wear my motorcycle helmet and jacket, and we could blame it on Maya's theoretical assailant." She gave a happy smile at the thought, and Liam flinched.

"I'm never sure if you're joking, or if you're really as bloodthirsty as you make yourself out to be," he said. "But no, I don't think beating up Callahan is going to help us any. I'm not sure if he is a willing participant or if Maya is just using him; the jury is still out on that one. But he must have at least an inkling that all those people in trouble came from his files. How could he not?"

"Willful ignorance is a typical Human failing," Baba said, shrugging. "But you're probably right—trying to coerce him openly would no doubt just set Maya off again. If she's being quiet for the moment, I'd just as soon keep her that way. Maybe we'll come up with a plan in the meanwhile."

Liam ignored the insult, most likely because as a lawman, he'd seen the effects of willful ignorance all too often. "Well, then, we'll just have to figure it out ourselves." He took another sip from his beer. "I know all the families who have lost children, and there is one thing I've noticed: all these kids are particularly well loved, just like Gregori said. Take Mary Elizabeth, for example. She's her mother's and grandparents' treasure. Her father was a drunken idiot, but the rest of her family loves her enough to make up for any three fathers."

He scowled into the dimming light of the fire pit as if the fading orange fire could give him answers to impossible questions. "Would someone really be so cruel as to purposely choose the children who would be missed the most?"

"Maya would," Baba said grimly. "She could have kidnapped any number of kids from homes where they weren't wanted. She's not only picking her victims from the list of people Peter Callahan wants to pressure into signing over drilling rights; she's intentionally taking the ones whose loss will cause the most pain. Maybe as some kind of twisted revenge for the damage Humans are doing to the water that is so precious to her." She sighed. "I take back everything bad I've ever said about human beings. Otherworld creatures can be much, much worse."

"Hmmm. Maybe we can use that," Liam said. He held the list up to the light. "There are two kids out of the remaining seven who stand out as unusually cherished. Davy is the only child of an older couple who tried for years to have kids, and finally succeeded after sinking every penny they had into in vitro fertilization. The other one is the only survivor of a car accident that killed her brother and twin sister; if her parents lost Kimberly, I think it would destroy them."

Baba tapped her fingers on her thigh. "Either one sounds like a perfect target for Maya. Of course, if we're wrong, then we're leaving the other five kids vulnerable for nothing." The crystal stem of the wineglass in her other hand snapped in two. She dropped it on the ground before Liam noticed, sucking on a small cut until it closed. Damn it, she did *not* want Maya to get her grimy supernatural paws on one more child.

"Well, I could have deputies patrol near all the kids' houses, but there's no good way for me to explain why I think those children are at particular risk without admitting we burgled Callahan's office." Liam grimaced. "And if I did that, I'm pretty sure I wouldn't be giving orders to anyone."

"Yeah, there's that," Baba agreed. "So we have the Riders keep an eye on the five we think are less likely to be her next victims, the best they can anyway, and you and I each watch one of the two kids we think she's most likely to grab next. She'll probably make a move soon; I'm guessing her attempt to get me locked up was because she's worried that I'll discover the location of her secret doorway. She must be feeling the pressure even more now that we've thwarted her again." She straightened. "Which kid do you want me to take?"

There was a palpable lack of response from Liam's direction, and when she looked over at him, his eyes slid away from hers.

"What?" she demanded. Then the other shoe dropped.

She stood up, one booted foot crunching pitilessly on what had been priceless crystal. "I get it," she said. "After all this, you still don't trust me enough to have me watch one of the children. In fact, you don't trust me at all, do you?"

The drowsy coals flashed into sudden wakefulness, flames shooting upward as if to meet the stars halfway. Baba's heart roared with matching fury and pain, its intensity catching her by surprise. One rare tear fell onto the fire and evaporated, like a stillborn dream of happiness.

"Barbara—" Liam stood up too, his face a conflicted arena of guilt and some emotion too intangible to name. "Baba. It's not that I don't trust you, exactly. It's just—"

"I know," she said, bitterness seeping out of her like poison gas into the clean night air. "I'm odd, mysterious, and infuriating. And you can't put the lives of those you are sworn to protect into the hands of someone like that."

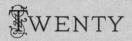WENTY

LIAM FELT LIKE the world's biggest heel as he watched Baba wipe her face of all emotion, returning it to its usual cool, unreadable mask. They'd been having such a pleasant time, despite the grim subject, and he had to go and stick his foot in it and hurt her feelings. Until that very moment, he hadn't even been certain she had any to hurt. He should have known better.

The problem was—he really *didn't* trust her. Yes, he believed that she was trying to help the children. But her methods were . . . unpredictable at best. And they clearly had some very different ideas on what constituted acceptable ways of arriving at a solution to the problem.

Still, none of that was the real issue.

"It's not that I don't trust your intentions," he said, standing there helplessly, trying to figure out how to explain himself without making the situation worse. "It's that I don't understand you. I don't know who you are—what you are—how you can do the things you do."

He pointed at the shattered crystal goblet, its brilliant shards currently reflecting prisms of red light while poking out from under Baba's black leather boots. "For instance, you can actually fix that, can't you? With your, um, magic, I mean." Hell, he could hardly bring himself to say the word; how was he supposed to work with someone who actually *used* it?

Baba shrugged, shooting him a cool glance from underneath inky lashes. "Sure. If I wanted to expend the energy it would take to collect all those little pieces and meld them back together again. But I'm a practical kind of witch. I'm much more likely to just go inside and get another damned glass." She turned her back on him and stalked inside, heels clomping on the metal steps with teeth-rattling force.

Chudo-Yudo sighed. "Now you've done it. Benighted Human idiot. I have to live with the woman, you know." He picked up the half-empty wine bottle gingerly between large, sharp teeth and followed her into the trailer.

Liam debated his options for about a half second: turn tail and go home, or try to explain what he meant and fix the damage he'd done. Then he picked up the rest of his beer and walked into the Airstream, hoping he wasn't going to get struck by lightning or turned into something slimy and unpleasant. Either way, he felt a lot more comfortable having this conversation with Baba in the bright lights of the Airstream's interior than having it outside in the darkness.

"You still here?" Baba asked without looking around as he closed the door behind him. She pulled a plain, slightly tarnished copper tankard out of a cupboard, clearly not in the mood to risk a more delicate piece. "I thought we were done."

Liam's heart, which he'd been sure no longer functioned, skipped a beat at the thought of ever being done with Baba. *No, not bloody likely. Not yet anyway.*

He sat down on the couch and spoke in a reasonable tone. "I didn't say that. What I said, in my usual clumsy fashion, was that I'm a simple country sheriff. I've seen some unusual things in my career, but nothing that prepared me for the kinds of stuff I've come up against since I met you. I've never known anyone who could masquerade as a little old lady without using a disguise, or who lived with a talking dog that was really a dragon. How am I supposed to adjust to that?" That last sentence may have come out with more anger and frustration than he'd intended it to.

But at least Baba took pity on him and sat down by his side, the greenish-orange mug cupped between her fingers. Chudo-Yudo relinquished the wine bottle, rolled his eyes, and plopped down on the floor, his huge head pillowed on his massive paws; a big, furry referee. Or maybe just waiting to be entertained.

"I guess it was unreasonable of me to expect you to," she said, a little wistfully. "But I don't have a magic wand I can wave that will make you think I'm any less strange."

Liam could feel the corners of his lips curve up. "You're mostly strange in some pretty wonderful ways," he said. *That veil of ebony hair, for instance, or those amazing amber eyes. Or the way you kick ass when it really matters.* "It's just, well, you have all these secrets you can't or won't share, and abilities I don't understand."

Baba took a sip of wine, a thoughtful expression on her grave face. "Maybe I can explain some of it, but I'm warning you, it is kind of a long story. And it's . . . complicated."

Liam put his arm out along the back of the couch, resisting the urge to run his fingers through the glossy raven strands just inches away. "I've got all night," he said, raising his beer at her. "And I love a good story."

"I'm not sure it's all that good," she said soberly. "But it's mine." She sat in silence for a minute, clearly trying to pick the right place to start.

"Baba Yaga is more of a job title than anything else," she said finally. "It's a time-honored position that originated in Russia and the surrounding Slavic countries, and has spread slowly over time to most of the occupied world. There aren't very many of us, though, and the job requires a certain single-minded dedication, as well as an aptitude for magic, so it can be hard for any individual Baba Yaga to find a replacement to train who will eventually take her place."

"Also," Chudo-Yudo put in, "the Babas tend to be a

seriously antisocial lot, and most of them don't want a small child underfoot, getting in the way and making messes." It sounded like a direct quote from someone. "So some of them put it off *way* longer than they're supposed to."

"A small child?"

"Most Babas feel that it is better to start the training early, when the mind and spirit are still malleable," Baba explained. "My Baba found me in an orphanage when I was about five. I was abandoned, so nobody really knew my age for sure. But the Baba must have sensed something special in me, some potential for the talent to wield the kind of power the job requires, and she brought me home to live with her."

Liam was appalled, although he tried to keep from showing it. Who takes a five-year-old child to live in the woods and trains her to be a witch?

Apparently he wasn't as successful as he'd hoped, because Baba gave him a crooked smile. "You have to understand, Liam. Russian orphanages at that time were brutal institutions, where cruelty and neglect were the standard fare. Children were clothed, housed, and fed a subsistence diet, but otherwise, they got little in the way of care. It was a long time ago, but I still remember shivering in the cold, with nothing but a ratty gray blanket to keep me warm, and an empty belly that kept me awake when the chill didn't."

The smile slid away like a shadow in a storm. "The Baba at least fed me well, and made sure I was warm and dry. Unless we were out tramping through the woods and fields in the rain or snow, which was often." She shrugged, and a stray lock of night-colored hair fell over his hand, feeling like silk.

"Was she at least kind to you?" Liam asked, caught up in a vision of a tiny, solitary child trudging stoically after a crone like the one he'd met the day before, struggling to carry a basket almost as big as she was filled with dirt-encrusted herbs and odd-colored mushrooms.

Baba shrugged again. "Kind, cruel. I doubt she knew the difference. Babas live a long time, and mine had waited until near the end of her life to take on an apprentice. By then, she wasn't very good at Human emotions anymore, either expressing them or understanding them. She taught me well, and kept me from harm; affection never really entered into the equation. And having spent the beginning of my life in the orphanage, I didn't know enough to expect it."

A sip of wine covered some spasm of emotion she doubtless hoped he wouldn't see—regret, maybe, or sorrow.

"I grew up without some of the essential foundations that make a human being Human," she said softly. "I know I'm not very good with people, or making connections. We moved around a lot, in the Baba's hut on chicken legs, going to wherever she was called, or was in the mood to be."

Liam reached out, caressed her cheek for a brief moment. She leaned into him for a moment before pulling away. "You seem plenty human to me, Baba. And folks around here liked you just fine before Maya started her campaign to discredit you. Belinda and the Ivanovs still do. And just yesterday Bertie actually kicked someone out of her diner for daring to call you a witch within her hearing."

Baba looked at him, blinking rapidly. "She did?"

He nodded, dropping his hand back down as if he'd accidentally touched the sun. "Didn't you get lonely as a child?"

"Not really," she said, sitting up straighter and jerking off her boots. Chudo-Yudo ducked as one went sailing over his head. "Ah, that's better."

Liam smiled. He got a kick out of the fact that she hated to wear shoes, although he couldn't have said why. Just part of who she was.

"I had the Riders as friends, when they came to visit my Baba, and Koshei." A slight flush turned her tanned cheeks rosy for a brief moment, then vanished. "And Chudo-Yudo, of course."

Liam raised an eyebrow. "Every girl should have a dog. Even if he is part dragon."

Chudo-Yudo coughed a tiny spurt of flame, singeing Liam's shoe. "Dude—I'm *all* dragon. I just look like a damned dog. Try and keep this stuff straight, will ya?"

"I'm trying," Liam said, "Really, I'm trying." He looked

at Baba. "So the old Baba raised you, and taught you about herbs, and uh, all that other stuff?"

"Magic, yes." She bit her lip, trying not to laugh at him. "It's not as bizarre as you think. More like a type of science you simply haven't learned enough about to comprehend."

That actually made a kind of twisted sense to him. "You mean like physics? I never could wrap my mind around physics."

Her smile finally reached her mysterious eyes, washing away some of the sadness there. "I wouldn't worry about it. Most of what people believe about physics isn't true anyway." She pointed at Chudo-Yudo. "That whole 'conservation of mass' thing? How on earth could a dragon with a ten-foot wingspan become an only-slightly-larger-than-normal pit bull?" She snorted. "Physics. Bah."

Liam pushed his hair back out of his eyes again. He wasn't sure if it was good or bad that Baba was starting to make sense to him.

"Is there anything else you need to know?" she asked. "I don't want us to have any more secrets between us. I want you to be able to trust me to help."

Secrets. He looked down at his shoes, one of which now bore a large charred spot, and thought about the things he hadn't told her about. Melissa, in particular. The truth was, he didn't think he could ever trust another woman after what he'd been through with Melissa. Not even one he had to fight the urge to kiss every time he got within two feet of her. He opened his mouth to say something; to reward her story, which had clearly taken courage for her to tell, with his own.

What came out instead was, "I don't suppose you have any pie?"

BABA SUPPRESSED A surge of irritation. She tells him her life story, and his only response is to ask for pie? Seriously?

"Pie?" she said, sparks flickering dangerously at the tips of her fingers. "You want pie *now*?"

The man had the nerve to grin at her, that elusive dimple flashing at the corner of his lips. "Well," he said in a practical tone, as if he wasn't ten seconds away from being set on fire, "we'll need to keep our strength up if we're going to be out tomorrow and who knows how many other days, watching the two kids we think Maya is most likely to target next."

Oh. "Does that mean you've decided to trust me after all?" she asked, the sparks dying away harmlessly.

Liam sighed. "It means I realized I've trusted you all along. I've just been letting my discomfort with the idea of magic and the Otherworld and all that comes with it get in the way of my common sense and my instincts." After all, it was a simple thing to trust her to help, really. Just so long as he didn't have to trust her with his heart.

He looked for someplace to put his empty beer bottle down, and Baba made it disappear with a snap of her fingers. Liam jerked. "See—like that! I will never get used to that." But he smiled as he said it. "Now how about that pie? Or I'll settle for cookies or some ice cream, if you don't have pie. Man can't live on hot dogs alone, you know."

"Dogs can't either," Chudo-Yudo said, endeavoring to look pitiful. A pretty difficult look for a two-hundred-pound pit to pull off, no matter how cute he was.

"Fine, I'll check," Baba said, and got up to look in the refrigerator. "Well, there's pie," she said, not terribly surprised. "But I hope you didn't want milk to go with that, because apparently we're all out."

Liam wandered over to have a look, and burst out laughing at the sight of what must have been dozens of pies, all stacked on top of each other.

Chudo-Yudo made a disgusted noise. "They're all cherry. I hate cherry pie."

"Sorry, baby," Baba said, patting him on the head and nudging a couple of pies out of the way to make sure that the bottle with the Water of Life and Death was still in there. She eyed it speculatively for a minute, giving Liam a look that made him ask with alarm, "What?"

"Nothing, nothing." She couldn't exactly tell him that she was thinking that the magical water could extend his life, so he could live it out with her. As if. Baba grabbed one of the pies and plopped it on the counter, pulling out some Limoges plates and silver forks to go with it. It was too soon to even consider such a thing. She must be losing her mind. It was just that when he stood that close to her, it made it nearly impossible to think at all.

"Well, if all there is is cherry," Chudo-Yudo said, growling menacingly at the stainless steel fridge, which responded by showing his reflection with a pink tutu and fairy wings, "I'm going to go outside and pee on things." He stalked over to the front door, making hideous faces at it until it opened with a reluctant squeal and then slammed shut behind him.

Baba ignored all the drama out of long habit, although Liam's face held a slightly shell-shocked look. She hid a smile behind masses of dark hair.

"I hope *you* like cherry," she said, cutting them each a precisely equal slice and sliding them onto plates. "Apparently that was what the Airstream was in the mood for."

They went back over to the couch and sat down next to each other, knees almost touching. Liam forked up a bite and made a blissful noise deep in his throat that sent shivers down Baba's spine. She didn't even taste the bite she ate, distracted by the way his eyes closed slightly as he savored the sweet-sour tang of the fruit.

"You know," he said, when he'd devoured most of it, "I envy you a little."

Baba blinked, confused. "You want a magic refrigerator?" She swallowed a tiny mouthful of glistening red paradise, licking the juice off one finger where it had fallen.

Liam laughed. "Hell no. I'm happy enough with regular appliances like my simple, everyday toaster. You put bread in, you get toast out; that's magic enough for me."

She narrowed her eyes at the toaster sitting on her counter, which sometimes popped out a piece of toast (although not always of the type you put in), but was just as likely to toss out a bagel, a buttered croissant, or on one memorable occasion, spaghetti Alfredo. Man, and hadn't that been a nightmare to clean up.

"I see your point. Then what do you envy?"

Liam gestured around the Airstream. "All this. You travel around the country; no roots, no ties, having all sorts of adventures and meeting new people. It must be nice not to constantly have folks tugging at you, expecting you to solve all their problems for them, knowing everything about you down to whether you wear boxers or briefs."

Baba raised an eyebrow, and he flushed a little.

"Briefs. But that's not my point."

She smiled. "But that's what you like about this place, isn't it? It's home. And solving people's problems is your job. I thought you liked that too." She would *not* think about Liam, naked except for a skimpy pair of briefs. She stuffed some more pie into her mouth as a distraction.

"I do, mostly." He sighed. "When I don't have Clive Matthews and the county board breathing down my neck, and children disappearing right and left." Outside the open window, an owl hooted, and the shadow of a wing seemed to glide across his face.

"But I've lived here all my life," he continued, stealing a forkful of Baba's pie, now that all of his was gone. "Except for a short stint in the military when I was young. Everyone knows me and my business, and thinks they know how I should live my life. There's a certain freedom in anonymity; maybe I envy you that."

A sliver of something caught in Baba's throat; maybe a tiny fragment of a cherry pit. Or a glimmer of irrational hope. Fracture lines appeared in the wall she'd built around her heart, as if an earthquake rocked the world all unseen.

"Have you ever thought about just picking up and leaving?" she asked casually. "If they're going to fire you in a couple of weeks anyway, there's nothing to stop you, is there?"

"There was a time, a few years ago, when I seriously considered moving out of town," he admitted.

Surprise made her blurt out, "Really? What on earth

happened?" Despite their current conversation, she couldn't imagine Liam without Dunville. Or for that matter, Dunville without him.

He hesitated, looking down at his hands as if the calluses there held some kind of map to guide him through the mine-field of his memories. "I had a baby," he said slowly, voice low. "A little girl. She died. SIDS—you know, Sudden Infant Death Syndrome. It was . . . terrible. One day she was alive, smiling and kicking out with tiny feet and grabbing onto my finger with her strong little hands. The next she was gone. Dead in her crib. I wasn't even home when it happened; out on a late-night call trying to keep some drunken asshole from breaking up a bar."

His face was so sad, Baba's chest contracted with sympathetic pain.

"It destroyed my marriage. Just about destroyed me, to be honest. The pity was the worst. Everyone knows, and everyone is sorry, so sorry. For a while, around then, I thought about leaving." He shrugged. "But the job was the one thing that kept me sane, and people needed me, which gave me a reason to get up in the morning. So I stayed."

Baba realized that at some point during his agonizing recitation, she'd taken his hands, or he'd taken hers. The plates and forks were nowhere to be seen, although she didn't remember removing them.

"That's awful," she said. "I can't imagine losing a child. No wonder it bothers you so much that other people are losing theirs." He grimaced, and she squeezed his hands a little tighter. They felt good under her fingers; strong and capable, large without being clumsy. She could envision them mending a fence or cradling a rescued kitten. Or doing other things, preferably to her.

"Time passes. You adjust," he said, straightening up and pulling his hands back so that he could run them through his too-long hair, moving it off his face in what was clearly becoming a habitual movement. She tucked hers under her arms, suddenly cold, moving away from him to curl her legs up underneath her.

"Still, I could see why you would want to get away, to someplace where there were no memories. Start over again." She stared at the wall across the room, as if a pattern on the wallpaper there had somehow become more fascinating than usual, its subtle cream silk moiré holding all the secrets of the universe if only you looked long enough in the right light. "You could come with us, you know. Travel the country with me and Chudo-Yudo for a bit."

Liam made a slight choking sound; surprise or pleasure or alarm, she couldn't tell.

"Like you said that first day, almost every piece of furniture in the Airstream folds out to be a sleeping space." She waved a hand around with an airiness she didn't quite feel. "If you were going to be around long enough, I could even have it create an extra room for you. I'm sure Chudo-Yudo would like to have someone else to talk to besides me." She shrugged. "It might be fun."

Liam brushed one large hand gently across her cheek again, smoothing back her cloud of raven hair with a gesture that was surprisingly erotic in its simplicity. For a moment, she thought he was going to kiss her.

"It does sound like fun," he said, with something that sounded like regret. But maybe that was only what she wanted to hear. "Very tempting. But I can't go anywhere until those children are back home where they belong, whether or not I'm dealing with the case in an official capacity or not. And as much as the town sometimes drives me crazy, I suppose this is where I belong."

Baba mustered up a smile. "I guess I knew that. It was just a silly notion. I've lived alone for such a long time, I doubt I could stand to have anyone else around on a day-to-day basis anyway."

"Anyone who didn't shed white fur or breathe fire, you mean." Liam smiled back.

"Right."

He gazed into her eyes for a minute, and then asked hesitantly, "Do Babas ever settle down in one place? Stop traveling and set down roots?"

She snorted. "Not exactly. Back in the Old Country, when there were more of us in a smaller area, each Baba tended to have her own territory she watched over. Her hut would travel around within a certain boundary, but never strayed all that far, so people could find her if they wanted to badly enough."

"Here, though," she circled her arm to indicate the whole country, and not just the trailer they sat in, "there are so few of us, we tend to travel wherever we are needed."

"Doesn't that make it difficult to teach your classes?" Liam asked. "Or are they just part of the illusion?"

"Ha. They're mostly a cover, although I do teach a class every once in a while when I get a chance. I actually like doing it. But I'm almost always officially off on sabbatical; traveling, researching, collecting samples." She gestured at the many jars and bottles and leafy green things tucked into corners and in some cases hanging off cast iron hooks on the walls.

"There are only three of us Babas in the entire United States, so we just go where we are called. That's how I ended up here."

"Good grief," Liam said, taken aback. "Wouldn't it be more efficient to divide the country up into thirds, with one of you taking the eastern part of the country, one the middle, and one the west?"

"I suppose so," Baba said, brow wrinkled. "No one has ever suggested it before. And at the moment, two of us are actually based out of California, so I'm not sure how we'd decide who got which territory." She shifted one shoulder carelessly. "Besides, why bother? Things are working well enough the way they are."

"Oh, I don't know," Liam said in an echo of the casual tone she'd used earlier. "I just thought maybe you'd want to settle down someday. Don't Babas *ever* do that?"

"Some do," she said, thinking about it. "Usually when they are training the next Baba in line. It's too hard on a young child, moving around constantly like that. Then the other Babas tend to cover the calls that come from too far away. Honestly, I've never really thought about it much. It never seemed like the right time."

His hazel eyes gazed into hers for one long minute. "Is there anything that might make you think about it?"

Somehow her hands had found their way back into his again. Her heart beat against the inside of her chest like a caged bird trying to escape. The colors of his irises changed from blue to green to gray like the ocean, promising adventures completely different from any she'd experienced in her long, wandering life.

Then he leaned in and kissed her, placing one strong hand on either side of her face with surprising gentleness and sliding his lips slowly over hers. Heat roared up from her belly as if she'd walked into a volcano, the molten lava of lust and wanting rising up inside of her like a force of nature.

She kissed him back with enthusiasm, almost growling from the joy of finally having him in her arms, and she could feel the curve of his smile under her lips.

"God, I want you," he said, pulling back and gazing at her with darkened eyes. "I think I've wanted you since the first day I saw you, standing next to that motorcycle in all that leather with this amazing hair floating down around your shoulders." He ran his hands through her dark tresses as if they were some precious silk from far-off lands.

His desire just inflamed her own, and she pulled her shirt off over her head, loving the stunned and admiring look on his face when he realized she was naked underneath. Then there was only the glorious chaos of ardent kisses, fevered caresses, and low-voiced moans as they explored each other's secret places, discovering the tender and the hard, the sweet and the salty, reveling in each new find.

At one point they rolled off the couch onto the floor, and it was there that she finally took him into her, drowning in the wonder of it all, surging on the tide of furious passion that swept them both away, leaving them finally storm-tossed and spent, lying in each other's arms.

Afterward, they were both a little off-balance, awkward with the unexpected intimacy. Clothes rearranged, they sat next to each other, trying to catch their breath and figure out what to say. Liam opened his mouth to speak.

Then the door burst open, and Chudo-Yudo came bounding in, shaking water all over everything, including the two of them. Liam jumped, moving away from her on the couch.

"It's raining again," the dog announced.

Baba rolled her eyes at him. "We can see that," she said acerbically. "You seem to have brought half of it in with you."

Chudo-Yudo eyed them with hopeful curiosity. "I hope I'm interrupting something." He waggled furry brows.

"Don't be ridiculous," Baba said, standing up. "We were just talking. About the case. And stuff."

Liam rose too. "It's late," he said, wiping a splash of moisture off of one arm. "I should go. Talk to the Riders about keeping an eye on those five kids, will you?" He handed her the file, which had somehow gotten knocked onto the floor. "Why don't you take Kimberly, and I'll check on Davy as often as I can without neglecting the rest of my job. Hopefully it will stay quiet for a few days."

Baba shook her head. "I doubt that Maya will wait long to make her move. Not after everything that's happened." She could feel the pressure of intuition behind her skull, like the shifting air from an impending storm. "If I had to guess, I'd say she'll move sometime in the next day or two." She made a face. "And probably try to find a way to lay the blame on me in the process."

Liam nodded in grim agreement. "We'll have to be on our guard," he said, brushing his hair back one more time. "Especially if we want to catch her off hers."

Their eyes met, and he gave her a broad smile, making bright blue butterflies materialize outside the window, unseen as they flew off into the rainy night sky.

"Thanks for the pie," he said. "And everything. I'll check in tomorrow."

And then he was gone.

Baba watched out the open front door as his taillights vanished into the darkness. For a moment, her mind followed him, imagining a fantasy world where she drove off to deal with a Baba Yaga call, coming home to a little house with welcoming lit windows and someone to talk to who didn't occasionally breathe fire by accident. In this illusionary dreamworld, a child's laughter echoed in the distance, chasing a ball with a giant white dog.

Chudo-Yudo tugged on her pant leg and said irritably, "You're letting all the rain in. And I've been talking to you for five minutes. Where is your head at?"

She closed the door regretfully on her foolish fancy and went over to plop down on the couch. "I was just thinking about how we were going to capture Maya," she lied.

"Uh-huh." Chudo-Yudo plopped down beside her, his head leaning against one thigh. "You were thinking about the hunky sheriff. I don't blame you. If I weren't a dragon, and a male one at that, I'd be drooling over him myself." He lifted his muzzle to look at her. "So what are you going to do about him?"

Baba sighed. "Probably something truly unwise."

"Excellent," Chudo-Yudo said. "About time. No one should be wise all the time. Not even a Baba."

TWENTY-ONE

BABA SWUNG HER leg over the BMW's shiny black leather seat and started into the town's only grocery store. The Airstream's refrigerator was still filled with beautiful, glistening red cherry pies—all very good, but not what she wanted for breakfast. So she figured she'd make a quick run into Dunville to stock up before setting out on her mission to watch over little Kimberly.

She brushed against an older woman with tightly curled, improbably orange hair as they passed each other, and started to apologize. The woman's face suffused with anger as she recognized Baba, and she shoved past with a snarl and a muttered, "Some people." Baba tried not to react, but she could feel her jaw tighten.

Walking around with her basket over one arm, head held high, and shoulders braced, she watched as a man she'd successfully treated for a nasty personal infection ducked around a corner to avoid her. It would have been nice to believe it was out of embarrassment, and not a fear of being seen in her company, but she wasn't that good at deluding herself.

The only friendly face she saw belonged to Jesse, who waved at her from the cereal aisle before being pulled back into a debate between little Trudy and Timmy over the virtues of Cocoa Puffs instead of homemade granola. Otherwise she was either ignored or scowled at.

Soft background music followed her, and the air was scented with the aroma of fresh bread and pungent local cheeses. She'd loved this tiny mom-and-pop store when she'd first gotten to town, finding excuses to come in even when her refrigerator wasn't playing games. Todd, the proprietor, had gone out of his way to welcome her, and his plump maternal wife June had insisted Baba try a homemade cookie from the bakery counter she manned with the enthusiasm of a woman who lives to feed others.

But once Baba reached the front counter and placed her purchases down by the cash register for the clerk to ring up, Todd came bustling hurriedly out of the back room, his normally friendly face closed and resentful.

"You're not welcome here," he said, pushing the teenaged clerk rudely out of the way and scooping Baba's groceries off of the counter and into the garbage can underneath, as if she had contaminated them beyond saving by her very touch. "You should be ashamed of yourself, coming into a place like this where decent people shop." His scowl made him look like the monster he obviously thought Baba was. "Children come in here, for god's sake. Get out. Get out right now and never come back. And if you know what's good for you, you'll get out of town too. Your type isn't welcome here."

Baba could feel her face freeze into a mask of calm indifference. "As you wish," she said. "I'll just take my business elsewhere."

A purplish-red flush spread from collar to bald pate, following the trail of his righteous anger. "No one in this town will serve you," he hissed. "Everyone knows what you are. *Witch*." He hissed the word. "You tricked people into buying your fake sideshow medicines, and then poisoned them with the stuff. And nobody thinks it is a coincidence that all these freaky things have been happening since you got to town. The Franklins who live down the road from me, their cows dried up for no reason. If they can't sell milk, they'll lose their house, their land, everything."

"I didn't do that," Baba said softly, knowing he wouldn't listen. "I wouldn't do that."

The once kind man pulled a baseball bat from behind the register, obviously kept there in case of would-be troublemakers. He brandished it in her direction with shaking hands. "Get out of my store!" he shrieked.

Baba walked away and didn't look back. She'd lost her appetite anyway.

BACK AT THE Airstream, there was still pie. Lots and lots of pie.

"Remind me to *never* ask this damned refrigerator for anything specific again," she said to Chudo-Yudo. "I'm really not looking forward to spending the whole day watching a kid play with nothing more than a slice of pie in my stomach."

"That's the least of your worries," Chudo-Yudo said, swinging his big head ponderously toward the back of the trailer. "You've got a guest."

Her heart skipped a beat as she moved quickly toward the tiny but sumptuous bedroom. Maybe Liam had . . . but no, it was Koshei who waited for her, looking as handsome and relaxed as ever as he sprawled comfortably on her bed, tasseled pillows propped up behind him in vivid crimson and azure silk. Only someone who knew him as well as she did would have been able to detect the tension in his muscles and the shadows that lurked at the back of his bright blue eyes. Something told her this wasn't just a social call.

He put down the leather-bound herbal book he'd been thumbing through and said, "About time you got back. The queen is asking for you." He swung his long legs over the side of the bed and got up, giving her a quick hug before tugging her relentlessly in the direction of the wardrobe that led to the Otherworld.

"I can't go like this!" Baba protested, gesturing at the simple tee shirt and black leather pants she wore.

Koshei shook his head, looking grim. He did give her a minute to change, turning his back although he'd never done so before.

"The queen isn't going to care what you're wearing," he said when she was ready, glaring at the handle to the closet so it squeaked in protest and opened promptly onto the foggy path to the other side. "The Otherworld is starting to warp. We lost one whole section of the enchanted forest this morning. It was there, then it wasn't. No one knows what happened to the creatures that were inside at the time."

He suddenly looked very much like the warrior he was as he added, "The queen wants answers, and she wants them now. This woman Maya is throwing the entire Otherworld out of balance with her mischief and it is starting to show." He gave Baba a hard look. "If you're going to find this unauthorized doorway, you'd better do it soon. The Otherworld is running out of time."

WHEN LIAM GOT to the sheriff's department, hoping to find a way to set up the deputies' patrols so he would be free to keep an eye on Davy's parents' house, he found a summons to an emergency meeting of the county board instead.

Hat literally in hand, he stood in front of a dozen hostile faces and forced himself to stay cool as he listened to Clive Matthews rant on about how Liam had been seen consorting with a known criminal, when he should have been out searching for innocent missing children.

"There has been no evidence Dr. Yager has committed any crimes," Liam pointed out. "Her record prior to arriving in Dunville is spotless, and she was cleared of any involvement in Maya Freeman's beating. All you have is rumor and innuendo, and the last time I checked, those things did not a criminal make."

"There's no smoke without fire," a businessman named Harry Williams muttered. "You can't tell me that so many people would be talking about her if there wasn't *something* going on."

"That's *exactly* what I'm telling you," Liam explained as patiently as possible, despite the rage that bubbled just below the surface. The rim of his sheriff's hat crumpled under the pressure from his clenched fingers, and he forced himself to take a deep breath and loosen his grip.

"These rumors are just that: rumors. Maybe they are being spread by someone with a grudge against Dr. Yager. Possibly they are just the result of a town that has been dealing with months of stress and grief and fear, and is looking for a scapegoat. She's a stranger in town and she's different from the folks around here, and that makes her an easy target. But it doesn't mean she has actually committed a crime."

Matthews shook one stubby finger dangerously close to Liam's nose. "Listen to me, Sheriff," he spat. "Your job is already hanging by a thread; don't make things worse by associating with a woman who is obviously trouble. I'm warning you for your own good. Some people are considering suing her for making them sick with her phony herbal cures. And the county will be revoking her permit to park in Miller's Meadow."

"As soon as we can find the damned paperwork," someone else grumbled.

"Yes, yes," Matthews agreed. "As soon as we can find the paperwork. And when I figure out who gave her permission in the first place, heads are going to roll."

"Never mind all that," one of the mayor's cronies said. "I think we should have the sheriff kick her out of town, permits or no permits. The woman is a menace." He glared at Liam as if the sheriff were somehow responsible for the missing paperwork, his morning indigestion, and possibly the high price of gas.

"She hasn't done anything illegal," Liam repeated, hanging on to what was left of his patience the way he was hanging on to what was left of his job—by his teeth, and barely. "I can't just go around telling people to leave town because a few folks have decided they don't like 'em."

"I don't see why not," Harry Williams growled under his breath.

"Because you hired me to uphold the law," Liam said through his teeth, "not to make it up as I go along."

"Well, as far as I can see, you're not doing much of a job at either," Matthews said, his double chin quivering indignantly. "I suggest you remedy that while you still have one."

LATER THAT AFTERNOON, Baba returned to the Airstream after a long, fruitless, frustrating day spent skulking around Kimberly Chamberlain's house, her day care, and then back to the house.

After being ranted at by the queen and half her court earlier in the day for her failure to find and close the mystery doorway, Baba had *really* been hoping to run into Maya. Preferably with a truck.

But everything had been quiet. Baba had been reassured to see that the girl's parents seemed to be taking every possible precaution; she hadn't seen the child left alone for a second.

On the other hand, since they were being hypervigilant, Baba had been forced to use all of her wiles not to be seen, at one point actually spending two very uncomfortable hours pressed against a tree, projecting oaky thoughts with all her might. She was afraid to look too closely in the mirror for fear she'd see green leaves growing out of her dark hair.

Liam had stopped by briefly on his way in to work to give her a cell phone so they could reach each other should one or the other of them manage to spot Maya. Baba had just snorted down her long nose, holding the little plastic gizmo by the tips of two fingers as though it might suddenly start to ooze some mysterious green slime.

"What am I supposed to do with this thing?" she'd asked. "Give it wings and send it flying to you? Bah." Instead, she'd given him a medallion to hang around his neck, tucked under his shirt so no one would see. An enchanted coin, broken into two halves, which would allow either of them to summon the other. He'd rolled his eyes at her, but had finally given up and slid the talisman over his head.

Now she pulled her half out from under the green tee shirt she wore (had it been black before she left the trailer . . . or maybe blue? she couldn't remember) and glared at it. The medallion remained stubbornly silent, unimpressed by her hard amber stare.

Fine, she thought, climbing the steps to the Airstream and feeling a rush of relief as she eased through its door, like an animal returning to its lair. She'd find something to eat, put her feet up, and relax for an hour before going back out to watch some more. The Riders had assured her they could keep an eye on the five children who were less likely targets, especially since three of them lived fairly close to each other in an area near the town's small park.

Chudo-Yudo sniffed at her as she came in, and gave her the lick on the hand that was as close as he got to a hug.

"Tough day?" he asked, scratching behind an ear with one enormous back paw.

"Useless day," she said. "At least so far. Anything happen here?"

"I ate two squirrels and a skunk."

"Nice. That explains the breath." She wiped surreptitiously at the place where he'd licked her hand. Although, having missed both breakfast and lunch, she was half inclined to send him out to catch something a little less disgusting for her to eat.

A quick prayer to the gods in charge of independent-minded refrigerators seemed to pay off, though, and when she opened the door, a whole roasted chicken greeted her with a showy display of crisp brown skin and plump legs, like a Vegas showgirl after a day by the pool. Inviting mounds of ivory mashed potatoes sat in a dish next to the chicken, and the wild carrots she'd picked during her wanderings had miraculously reappeared. Creamy fresh butter in a crystal bowl seemed to chat conversationally with the

Water of Life and Death behind it, an occasional soft note added in by a leftover piece of pie.

"That's more like it!" Baba exclaimed, putting her hand out to start pulling things out of the fridge. Her stomach grumbled in raucous agreement.

"I'm not sure this is a good time to start making dinner," Chudo-Yudo warned from behind her. He was up on his hind legs, peering out the window and down the road. "It looks like we have company. And I don't think they're coming for a neighborly potluck."

Baba closed the refrigerator reluctantly, patting its stainless steel surface as if to reassure it of her speedy return. A glance over Chudo-Yudo's furry white shoulder made it clear that it was likely to end up an empty promise.

A long procession wound its slow dusty way up the narrow, pitted road, led by an oversized red truck on a jacked-up chassis with monstrous tires and a Union Jack painted slightly off-kilter on the side. A dozen more reasonably sized trucks in various colors followed it up the gravel highway, interspersed with a few SUVs and even one VW Bug, which bobbled along between two large vehicles like a comma in a run-on sentence. To Baba's unhappy eyes, it looked like a rainbow of iron and steel and plastic, fueled by fury instead of refracted prisms of light.

"Oh yay," she said with a glower. "It looks like we're having a party. And me without my party frock on."

"I'm thinking your battle armor might be more useful," Chudo-Yudo remarked with his usual accuracy. "Do you want me to get you a sword?"

Baba was seriously tempted. She'd love to see the faces of these yokels if she barreled out of the Airstream, clad in gleaming silver armor and waving a huge scimitar over her head. One ululating battle cry and they'd all be peeing their pants as they ran screaming back down the road.

Unfortunately, since she was still trying to find a way to live here, at least until the children were found, scaring the locals even further probably wasn't her best approach.

Too bad. She loved a good battle yell.

Instead, she brushed an errant twig out of her long hair, pushed it back over her shoulders, and walked out to face her uninvited guests. A tee shirt and black leather would have to do. At least she was wearing her shit-kicking boots.

TWENTY-TWO

A MOTLEY ASSORTMENT of men assembled on her erst-while front lawn. A few faces she recognized, more that she didn't. What she did recognize, though, was the madness in the mob-fever that gripped them all, and the weapons they'd brought along to back it up. She saw at least three shotguns, as well as a number of baseball bats and even a few pitch-forks. How traditional. All they lacked were the flaming torches; with those, it would be just like home in the tiny superstitious rural villages of Mother Russia.

As she stepped outside, with Chudo-Yudo in the doorway at her back, a roar like a wounded bear rose up to greet her. Wild and feral, mindless with fear and rage, it flowed over her with bestial power, one of the most frightening sounds in the universe.

The mob raised their arms, flailing their weapons at her, although as yet, they weren't aimed with purpose. Individual voices rose above the crowd, yelling incoherent threats, and ugly obscenities. The high-pitched tones of the few women in the group assaulted her ears with shrill hysteria, like angry crows trying to drive a hawk away from their nests.

One man, larger and angrier than the rest, stepped forward. He was clearly the owner of the mammoth truck, wearing a tee shirt that matched the logo on his Chevy and tattoos over much of the visible parts of his body. The weak late-afternoon sun arced off of his shaved head, and a length of gleaming chain hung loosely from a hand the size of a catcher's mitt.

"Witch!" he yelled at her, the sound of his voice reducing the others to the background murmur of waves beating on a rocky shore. "This here is your unwelcomin' committee. We've had enough of your mischief around these parts, and we aim to get your ass in that fancy trailer of yours and headed down the road to anywhere but here!" The others howled in agreement, and a fist-sized rock came whizzing by her head and crashed into the Airstream behind her.

"You know," Baba said in a conversational tone, "it's really not polite to throw things. Especially not at my house. It tends to get quite peeved."

The big man blinked at her, thrown off his stride by her calm demeanor. "Look, you whore," he said loudly. "We'll do whatever it takes for you to get the message. You're not wanted around here. Everybody knows you've been messing with people's animals and their crops, doin' some kind of voodoo and making folks sick with that crap you've been sellin'." He lifted the chain he held threateningly. "So are you goin' to get out on your own, or are we goin' to have to help you along? Because one way or the other, you're leavin'."

Baba sighed. Despite their numbers, their weapons, and their leader's size, she wasn't really worried about her own safety. She figured that she and Chudo-Yudo between them could take care of a mob three times this size, even without calling in the Riders, which she could do quite easily. But she didn't want to have to hurt anyone here. Underneath the belligerence and nasty words, they were just people who had been manipulated and misled, and she'd just as soon not have to punish them for allowing their fear to be turned into anger and directed at her.

On the other hand, she wasn't going to let them scare her away either. And the sooner they figured that out, the better.

Centering her mind, she concentrated on sending calming vibes out into the assembled mass of churning emotion. While she waited to see if that would have any effect, she tried talking some sense into the people confronting her.

"Gentlemen, ladies, I haven't done any of those things, honest," she said, trying to project earnest innocence. Not her best look, really, but it was worth a try. "A few folks did get sick after using my herbal remedies, but the sheriff was able to figure out that someone was altering the medicines. And if you ask the people who bought them, you'll find out that I gave everyone their money back, *and* gave them new medicines that worked just fine."

A few muttering voices agreed that yes, that was true, they'd heard that down at Bertie's.

"But that don't change the fact that you've been castin' hexes on people's property and their livestock," the leader shouted.

Another rock went sailing by, thudding against a window that somehow not only didn't break, but caused the rock to go ricocheting back along the exact same trajectory from which it had originated. Someone in the crowd let out a howl of pain and Baba bit her lip so she wouldn't laugh. A glance out over the group erased any temptation toward merriment, though, when she saw that they were still too riled up for her efforts at mental soothing to work. *Shit.*

"Are you really trying to tell me you believe in all that stuff?" Baba asked, raising her voice. Behind her, Chudo-Yudo growled, looking menacing in the way only a huge, jagged-toothed pit bull can. One man in the front of the group started edging his way subtly toward the back.

"Witchcraft?" Voodoo? Hexes?" She lifted her hands, sending out tiny impulses to the clouds above while trying to appear as harmless as possible. "Come on, really? You can't honestly think that stuff exists, can you? This is real life, not some fairy tale." Of course, her real life kind of *was* a walking fairy tale, but this was no time to try and explain that. Hell, there never would be a time. Not with these people.

For a moment, she thought her rational argument might sway them. A few of the saner types lowered their weapons, doubt starting to slide over their features like the clouds that had temporarily covered the sun.

But a voice from the back of the crowd shouted, "Someone is doing all this crazy stuff! You're the only stranger around these parts right now, and everybody says you're a witch! I say it's true and I want you gone, away from my family!" A small flurry of stones accompanied the high-pitched rant, whistling through the air too close to her head for comfort, and as one, the mob took a few steps closer to Baba, raising their varied impromptu tools of destruction with renewed purpose.

Right, Baba thought to herself. *No more Mrs. Nice Guy. I've had a long day and I want my damned dinner.* She took a deep breath and pulled her hands down with a drooping motion that might have looked to the crowd like surrender but actually tugged on the suggestion she'd planted in the atmosphere up above.

The misty purple heavens opened up and dropped icy-fingered rain in torrents on men, women, trucks, and base-ball bats alike. Thunder crashed and roared across the sky, accompanied by jagged flashes of lightning that turned the suddenly darkened afternoon intermittently bright as mid-day. Hail pelted exposed skin like BB's, stinging and pelting the mob as they stood openmouthed, the sudden unexpected storm cooling their fury in a way that Baba's kinder methods had failed to do.

The big man who'd led the mob tried to urge his followers on, screaming above the sound of the ice and rain that pinged and sang as it hit the Airstream. "See! See! She's a witch! Get her!"

But he spoke to an emptying field as his friends all raced through the downpour to reach the shelter of their trucks and SUVs. The owner of the VW Bug struggled for a mo-ment to raise the convertible top she had lowered in the earlier warmth, then gave up and hopped into a nearby vehicle, leaving the small car abandoned amid the mud, slowly filling with water and pea-sized hailstones.

Baba and her accuser faced each other across a two-foot space, water coming down so hard she could barely make out his contorted, reddened face. Slowly, he let the hand holding the chain drop, but he stood there for another minute, glaring through the wet, before raising one finger in an obscene salute and stalking off to his outsized truck.

Huge wheels spun futilely, flinging great gouts of mud up to cover the side of the truck and much of the surrounding area until Baba, deciding she'd had enough fun for one day, twitched the tip of a fingernail and boosted it out. Two deep ruts filled with the blue smoke from the truck's exhaust as it lumbered off in pursuit of its fellows.

Annoyed and disgusted, and not inclined to repeat the entire incident again in an hour, Baba decided to let it keep storming. The rain and thunder suited her mood. Maybe she'd get lucky and the whole county would wash away. The only things left standing would be that damned doorway to the Otherworld and the water-loving Rusalka. She could deal with them both and be done with this place, once and for all.

THE RAIN HAD driven Liam into the dubious shelter of a rickety kids' fort cobbled together from old planks and some bright blue tarps in a corner of Davy's backyard. Before that, he'd watched, perched up in the oak tree overlooking the yard, as Davy, his mom, and a tiny, hyperactive, brown dachshund had picnicked and played for hours behind the safety of a high wooden fence. When the rain came, driving the family inside, Liam got ready to leave. But as he began to slide down from his lofty roost, he was hit by that visceral feeling that longtime lawmen learn not to ignore, a little voice that said, *Don't go; something bad is coming.*

So he waited for them to settle inside, and then he crept down an overhanging branch until he could get close enough to the ground to drop down safely. Which made him think grimly: if he could do it, so could someone else. So he tucked himself into the furthest recesses of the tiny fort and watched through the window as Davy's mom prepared their dinner amid the warmth and light of a cozy kitchen, and hoped that no one would find him skulking in a child's playhouse and ask him to explain what the hell he was doing there.

The rain pelted the top of the less-than-waterproof structure, dripping on Liam's hat and occasionally finding a stealthy path to the back of his neck and down over his shirt collar. The damp seemed to work its way into his bones and his stomach complained bitterly as Mrs. Turner stirred something on the stove that sent tantalizing aromas drifting out the open window, hinting at tomato sauce and onions simmering in butter.

Liam had almost convinced himself that his instincts had steered him wrong when the back door opened again to reveal five-year-old Davy and his dog, whose wiggling body hesitated briefly before heading out into the rain to pee against the nearest tree. Once done, however, the already drenched animal was in no hurry to return back inside.

"Trevor, come back here," Davy called softly, patting his leg and making what were probably supposed to be whistling sounds, but come out more as whooshing puffs of air. "Come on, boy! It's almost dinnertime!"

The tiny dog yipped in excited defiance, chasing some smell more interesting than the dry indoors and ignoring his pint-sized master with an attitude that bespoke of common practice.

"Trevor! Trevor!" Davy hissed at the dog, then looked furtively over his shoulder toward his mother, who was rummaging through a cupboard on the far side of the room. Even through the window, Liam could see that she was focused on finding something deep in the cupboard's recesses that had so far eluded her.

Davy gave one more backward glance and then came sprinting across the yard, intent on recapturing his pet and getting him back inside before his mother discovered them missing, and they both got in trouble. He skidded across soggy leaves and pounced, coming up with the squirming dachshund clasped firmly in his pudgy little arms.

Liam started to pull his too-large body even farther into the too-small fort, worried that the child might spot him, when something *wrong* tugged at his senses. A foggy gray shadow solidified into a beautiful blond woman, standing almost on top of the boy, who glanced up in surprise, blue eyes wide and mouth opening to call for his mother.

But Maya held out something that looked like a spinning, glowing ball of sunlight, its brightness only slightly defused by the foggy mist that surrounded her. The child's eyes fogged too, turning to empty marbles the color of the sky at dawn, and then closing altogether. The dog slid unnoticed from his limp grasp to run under the fort, shivering and whimpering.

Liam put his right hand on his gun, and then hesitated. She was so close to the boy, standing right over him. It was too dangerous, even though less than two feet separated him from the creature as she stooped to pick up her latest victim. Liam stepped out of the lean-to, taking a giant step in her direction.

"Step away from the child," he said in a low, authoritative voice. "Step away now."

Maya lifted her head, startled by his sudden appearance, then let loose a silvery laugh that sent cold fingers down his spine. "I don't think so, Sheriff," she said, reforming the ball of light that had mesmerized the boy. "I think I'll take this one too, and leave you lying here in the rain, looking even more incompetent than ever."

She closed the distance between them, holding the whirring light up in front of his face. For a moment, he felt the world as a distant echo, far away and as illusory as a fireside tale, then a burning sensation from the medallion hanging over his chest snapped the spell like a spinner's broken thread, unraveling it back to its source.

Maya faltered for a precious second, stunned by the unexpected failure of her magic, and Liam pulled out the Taser he'd been holding behind his back and shot her with 50,000 volts. She fell to the ground with a satisfying thud and lay there spasming uncontrollably.

By the time Davy's mother had flown out of the house with a shriek, Maya's hands were firmly handcuffed behind her, the cold steel holding her in place in more ways than the obvious. Davy sat up, looking dazed and confused, and Trevor the dog barked loudly as if taking credit for his enemy's capture.

Mrs. Turner clasped the boy to her so tightly she threatened to cut off his oxygen, tears streaming down her cheeks. "Oh my god, oh my god," she kept saying. "My baby, oh my god."

Liam patted her on the shoulder, and then heaved a glowering Maya to her feet. "Don't worry, Mrs. Turner. It's all over now."

But of course, it wasn't.

TWENTY-THREE

LIAM PULLED HIS cruiser into the sheriff's department parking lot and cursed fluently under his breath. Someone had clearly been listening to a police scanner, because it looked like half the town was already there.

He got out of the car and fetched Maya from the backseat, her hands still cuffed. Her lovely blond hair was disheveled, and there was a brown smear of mud on her once pristine white blouse. She looked like she'd been ridden hard and put up wet. Somehow, despite this, she managed to appear cool and professional. Liam, in contrast, felt rumpled and disreputable after an afternoon spent lurking in a tree. It hardly seemed fair.

On the other hand, he wasn't the one wearing the cuffs. There was a certain satisfaction in that.

Mrs. Turner and her husband (who'd returned home from work just in time to be greeted by a hysterical wife, a crying son, a sullen Maya, and Liam) followed the sheriff and his prisoner in through the front door and into a cacophony of chaos. Mrs. Turner hadn't let go of Davy since she'd reclaimed him in the backyard, and he seemed happy to cling to her hand as they walked into the midst of dozens of competing voices raised in demand of answers that no one there had.

Molly was frantically trying to contain a crowd made up of most of the board members (including Clive Matthews, of course, who had apparently been dragged away from the dinner table by the news, if the napkin tucked into his top pocket was any indication), the families whose children had been taken, and every deputy who wasn't officially out on patrol. Liam's eyes scanned the room for Baba, since he'd made sure to send her a message via the medallion—which apparently had more uses than he'd been told. But there was no sign of a tall fierce-looking woman with a cloud of black hair and piercing amber eyes.

His secretary, on the other hand, greeted him with a cry of gladness. "Sheriff! Thank goodness you're back." Her gaze darted to the handcuffed Maya briefly, but by force of will dragged her attention back to the issue at hand. "Everyone heard that you caught someone trying to kidnap another child. Is it true?" Her normally sweet face hardened into granite as she looked at his prisoner. "Is that her? Did she take all those poor children?"

Liam nodded. "So it would appear." He motioned to the Turners. "Can you get the Turners seated in my office please, and get them some coffee or tea, or whatever they need? I'm going to process Ms. Freeman, and then I need to get an official report from them."

Before Molly could even take a step, Clive Matthews and Peter Callahan shoved their way out of the crowd, like a mismatched suit-wearing Tweedle Dee and Tweedle Dum.

"What is the meaning of this?" Callahan bellowed. "Take those cuffs off my assistant immediately!"

"I'm sorry, I can't do that," Liam said mildly, but with a certain justifiable satisfaction. "I caught Ms. Freeman in the commission of a crime, trying to take Davy Turner right out of his own backyard. She's going into a cell and that's where she's staying. If you want to be helpful, you might try to convince her to tell us what she's done with the other three children she's stolen."

The parents in the throng swarmed forward en masse and started yelling at Maya, Liam, and the Turners, more or less indiscriminately: "Where is my child?" "What did you do with my son?" A few threats floated out of the sea of faces like angry hornets.

Liam handed Maya over to the closest deputy, stood on a chair, and said loudly, "Everyone shut the hell up!"

As Clive Matthews's mouth gaped open amid the suddenly quiet room, Liam added, "Please. We have a traumatized child and his parents here, and the last thing they need to deal with is all this shouting and confusion." He dismounted and nodded at the Turners.

"Okay, folks, here's what we know so far," he said, addressing the entire room. He clearly wasn't going to be able to finish booking Maya or talking to the Turners until he gave everyone there some kind of basic rundown.

"I caught Maya Freeman a little while ago, grabbing little Davy while he was outside chasing his dog. She hasn't admitted to anything yet or told me where we can find the other children, but I assure you, those are only a few of the many questions she will be asked over the next couple of hours."

He looked at the distraught parents, huddled together with each other for moral support, like bean plants wrapped around corn stalks in a field. "As soon as I have any information on your children, I promise you I'll let you know. For now, there is nothing useful you can do here, so I need you to go home, please, and let me do my job."

Out of the corner of his eye, he caught a glimpse of black leather walking in the door and breathed a silent sigh of relief. He wasn't sure how Baba being here would make any difference; he just knew he felt better now that she was.

"This is an outrage!" Callahan stuttered. "I'm calling my attorney right this minute."

For a change, Clive Matthews seemed to be on Liam's side. "Peter, if the sheriff caught her in the act, well, you know, the children did start disappearing right after she arrived . . . maybe she really is guilty." He winced as one of his biggest campaign contributors shot him a dirty look and backpedaled rapidly. "Although, naturally, a lawyer is a good idea, no matter what."

Maya wrenched herself away from the deputy who'd been holding on to her arm—not very tightly, since she appeared so slight and harmless—and threw herself down at Callahan's feet in a theatrical move guaranteed to draw all eyes.

"Please, Peter, you can't believe him! I'm innocent! I was passing by the Turners' house and saw the sheriff's car hidden halfway up a vacant driveway. When I spotted him hiding up in a tree, I went in closer to see what he was doing, and then," she paused dramatically, "I looked through the fence and saw him climb down into the yard and grab poor little Davy!"

There was a unified gasp from the gathered crowd, although Molly, and Nina behind her, just rolled their eyes and most of the deputies seemed unimpressed by her story.

Callahan helped Maya up from the floor. "What happened then?"

She fluttered her lashes, blinking back tears that only served to magnify the beauty of her stormy gray eyes. "I didn't even think of my own safety, I just ran back there to try and stop him. I was going to yell for help, but he Tasered me, and threw me down into the mud! If Mrs. Turner hadn't come out and seen us, I just don't know what would have happened to me."

"That's ridiculous," Liam said. He turned to Davy, getting down on one knee so he was the same height as the child, and speaking gently. "Honey, can you tell these people what happened to you? It's okay, you're safe now."

The little boy peered shyly out from behind his mother's leg and shook his head. "I don't 'member," he whispered. "Trevor was being a bad dog and I had to go outside in the rain and get him, so Mommy wouldn't yell." His mother squeezed him even tighter, sobbing quietly. "I saw a shiny light in a puddle. And then Mommy was holding me and crying. I don't 'member anything else."

Liam wasn't surprised, although the boy's lack of

recollection might complicate things. Even a few seconds under the influence of whatever that ball of light was had scrambled his brains. He couldn't imagine what it would do to a small boy at full force.

"That's okay, Davy," he said. "It doesn't matter. You did just fine."

He turned to Callahan, and said, "You are welcome to call Ms. Freeman a lawyer, but in the meanwhile, she's going to sit in a cell where she belongs, and she *is* going to tell us what she did with those other children."

Baba's grim face stared at Maya from a few feet away, making it clear that a cell was the safest place for her. Her arms were crossed over her chest as if to keep them from involuntarily reaching out and strangling the other woman.

As Liam put out a hand to take Maya, lifting her up off the floor, she said plaintively, "It wasn't me, I swear! It was him all along. He's been stealing children and killing them, and now he's using me as a scapegoat to take the blame. As sheriff, he's got the perfect cover—pretending to search for the children he's already murdered and looking for new victims along the way. No one would ever suspect him." She paused, took a deep breath, and added, "What's more, he killed his own child three years ago, and I can prove it!"

LIAM FELT AS though someone had slapped him, the blood draining from his face like water from a breached dike. His fingers tightened involuntarily around Maya's wrist and she let out a gasp of pain that was only partly feigned.

"That's enough," he said in a voice like sandpaper. "More than enough." Out of long habit, he schooled his features into a mask that hid the anguish ripping through his heart, and marched her over to the nearest intake desk. With an efficient twist, he unlocked the manacle from one slender wrist and reattached it to the circle imbedded there for the purpose, placing her firmly in the seat facing the desk.

"Watch her," he said through gritted teeth to the deputy who had allowed her to slip away earlier. "As if your life depended on it. I will be right back. You can start on her fingerprints while you wait for me."

He turned back to talk to Peter Callahan, only to see the tall businessman disappearing out the door. On his way to go get a fancy lawyer, no doubt. Fine. Whatever.

Clive Matthews was busy reassuring the parents of the missing children and his fellow board members that every measure would be taken to discover the location of the other victims. His smug and self-congratulatory air made it seem as though he personally had been responsible for the apprehension of the culprit, while at the same time snidely insinuating that if Liam had been a little more on the ball, they would have caught her long before this. It all made Liam sick.

He swallowed bile as Baba came up and laid a gentle hand on his arm. Her touch seemed to send waves of comfort straight to his battered heart.

"No one believed her," Baba said. "They could see she was just trying to shift the blame to you. She's a desperate woman, and desperate people will say anything to try to talk their way out of trouble." Her amber eyes gazed at him with concern.

He shrugged, as if Maya's words—and the momentary doubt on the faces all around them—hadn't stung like aftershave on a fresh cut. "I know. And at least we've got her. She won't steal any more children, and that's what matters. That, and getting her to tell us where she stashed the first three." Across the room, he could see Belinda Shields and her parents, standing together by Belinda's desk and glaring at Maya.

Baba shook her head, long dark hair swinging. "She's never going to tell you, Liam. And you can't use the kind of tools it would take to get the information out of her. You have to let me take her to the Otherworld. Ten minutes with the queen, and Maya will be singing like a canary." She gave a laugh without humor. "Hell, she might *be* a canary."

"No."

"What do you mean, no?" Baba asked, taking a step back. "We agreed; when we caught Maya, I would take her back to the Otherworld. Otherwise the queen is going to have my head!"

Even though they were already speaking in a relatively quiet tone, Liam lowered his voice even further. All he needed was for Clive Matthews to overhear him talking about some kind of fairyland. At the moment, he might have saved his job, but that would certainly lose it for him, arrest or no arrest.

"I'll let you talk to her in private, after these people have all gone home and things are calmer," Liam said, thinking he was being perfectly reasonable. "I'll even let you work whatever voodoo you want to get information, as long as there are no physical signs of it when you are done. But I can't just allow you to take her out of here. Not only would I get fired as soon as it was discovered that she'd escaped, but people would start to wonder about her accusations. I could even end up facing an official inquiry. I'm sorry, Barbara, but she has to stay here."

Baba's face became a frozen lake of cool disdain. "I see," she said. "So your career is more important than the fact that the Otherworld is falling to pieces because that bitch you currently have chained to one of your desks has been overusing magical power through the door I haven't been able to find," she said, scorn dripping like acid. "And if I can't find that door without removing her from this station, that's just too bad?"

Liam's chest hurt, as if he couldn't get enough air. "Barbara, I just can't—"

Before he could finish the sentence, there was a stir in the group nearest the door. Liam heard Molly said, "*Oh my god*!" and saw Nina's face turn so white, she might have seen a ghost.

Fearing that something had happened to Davy, Liam pushed his way through to the front, only to see a sight so unexpected, it made the room spin in dizzying circles for one insanely long moment as his brain tried to process the impossible. His pulse pounded in his ears and his heart raced, skipping a beat erratically in the process.

Peter Callahan stood in the doorway, a triumphant sneer on his patrician face. Next to him, an ethereally lovely, very pale, rail-thin redhead in a demure white sundress looked at the neighbors she hadn't seen in over two years. Her pointed chin was held high and delicate wisps of hair escaped her tidy bun to curl coyly around the heart-shaped face he used to love.

"What's the matter, Sheriff?" Callahan asked archly. "I thought for sure you'd be happy to see your wife."

TWENTY-FOUR

LIAM WAS A lot of things, but happy didn't enter into it.

After they'd buried Hannah's tiny body in an obscenely small casket, nothing had been the same. Melissa blamed herself for the baby's death, and in some irrational twist of a sorrowing brain, also blamed Liam for not being there. That he could understand, since he blamed himself.

But what he couldn't understand was how his once beautiful, caring wife had turned cold and remote, slicing him to the bone with every slantwise accusatory glance, shying away from his touch as though it burned like acid.

He'd tried to comfort her—tried to have them comfort each other. But she'd found her comfort first in alcohol, then in drugs, and then in the arms of every man in town who would have her. There were many. So many, he eventually lost count. She'd wander the hills for hours, coming home late at night with twigs in her hair and empty wine bottles rattling around in the backseat of her car. People turned their heads away when they passed him on the street, not wanting him to see the pity in their eyes.

He saw it anyway.

And then, about a year after little Hannah's death, Melissa simply disappeared. He awoke to an empty bed, and waited all the next day for her to stumble in, stoned or high or drunk, reeking of tawdry sex and some other man's cologne. But she never came home. Not that night, nor any after.

No one ever saw her again. A small circus had been in town that week; two shows a day in a tattered big top, with a few acrobats and a depressed-looking elephant. People started to say she'd run away with the circus, a clichéd joke that only a vicious few actually found amusing.

But Liam figured it was probably true. She'd been saying for months that she couldn't stand to be there, living in the haunting shadow of their once beloved daughter, mocked by the memories of happier days. Grief and drug use ate away at her soul and her body until only a thin wraith with dry, cracked lips and unwashed red hair remained in the place where beauty had once captured his attention from across a crowded high school lunchroom.

After Melissa disappeared, Liam looked for her for six months straight, calling in favors with law enforcement across the state, checking on every report of an OD or a Jane Doe's body that showed up in a hospital or morgue. He'd finally broken down and hired a private detective, but the man couldn't turn up a trace—not even any evidence that she'd ever been seen with the circus after its last night in Dunville.

Eventually, Liam had given up the search, almost relieved when he didn't find her, and tortured by guilt because he was relieved. Life had become all about work and doing his best to save everyone else, because he couldn't save the two people he had loved the most. Until lately, when it suddenly seemed like he couldn't save anyone at all.

He'd never expected to see Melissa again; he sure as hell hadn't expected to see her under these circumstances, looking pale and almost as unhealthy as the day she'd left, although considerably cleaner and better put together, her fragile beauty shining through like the sun behind misty morning fog.

And how the *hell* did she get involved with Maya and Peter Callahan?

BABA'S BODY WENT rigid with shock as she heard Callahan refer to the delicate redhead as Liam's wife. She knew she should be paying attention to Maya, but all she could focus on was the word *wife* echoing in her ears. Liam had a wife. Not an ex-wife. A wife.

It was little compensation that Liam seemed to be as stunned to see the woman as Baba was. His face was the color of the faintly green institutional walls behind him, and his large hands were balled up into fists. She could see the tension in the ropy muscles in his neck and shoulders, like the supple human flesh had been replaced by badly carved marble.

Part of her wanted to go up and stand behind him, supporting him with a discreet touch. The other part of her wanted to kill him on the spot and bury his dead, dismembered body where no one would ever find it. Unsure of which impulse would win if she moved, she stood where she was and simply watched as his world fell apart.

Liam's mouth opened and closed, as if he was struggling to find the right words to say and discarding all the available options. In the end, he simply asked flatly, "What are you doing here, Melissa?"

The redhead's shoulders were tense too, and a flush darkened her pale cheeks. Whatever was going on here, this was no joyful reunion. The knowledge made Baba feel not one iota better. Her stomach clenched in anticipatory dread, shards of jagged glass churning at her core.

"I heard about what happened," Melissa said in a low voice that still managed to carry across the room. "I had to come."

The silence was deafening as everyone there turned to watch the unexpected drama. From where she stood, Baba could see Maya, seated at the deputy's desk, leaning back with her shapely legs crossed and a faint satisfied smile on her face, as if she were watching a play from the comfort of a cushioned throne. Alarm bells went off in Baba's head, but she felt helpless to do anything but watch with the others and see what happened. Whatever it was, if Maya was smiling her crocodile smile, Baba could be quite certain she wasn't going to like it.

"Heard about what?" Liam was asking, two parallel lines appearing between his brows. "And how? Where the hell have you been all this time, Melissa?" Frustration warred with concern in his voice. Like Baba, he could clearly sense a sizable and devastating shoe about to drop. Plus, of course, he was confronting his long-lost *wife*.

Melissa shook her head sadly. "I didn't go that far away; just far enough to be safe, and to deal with my problems. And I've always kept tabs on what was going on here in Clearwater County." She looked around the room at all the people she used to know, giving them each a private little smile, as if to say, I *missed you the most*.

Nina could be heard to mutter an indelicate word under her breath, but others smiled back hesitantly, responding to the woman they'd known and liked before tragedy had changed her into a wild and pitiable stranger.

"So why come back now?" Liam asked in a harsh voice. "Why now instead of anytime in the last two years?"

"Because you gave me no choice," Melissa said, wiping a tear away with one white, trembling hand. "I had to come forward, no matter how frightened I was, because I couldn't live with myself if someone else was going to take the blame for what you'd done."

She smiled tremulously up at Peter Callahan, who put one arm protectively around her shoulders. Next to the tall man, Melissa looked tiny, vulnerable, and delicate, as if she might blow away with the smallest breeze.

"I contacted Mr. Callahan because, as someone new to the area, he had no preexisting loyalties to you, Liam. And I thought he would be powerful enough to protect me."

Liam scowled and crossed his arms. "What on earth are you talking about, Melissa? Protect you from what? Are you still on drugs? Because if you are, we can get you to a treatment facility, but right now I'm in the middle of something that just can't wait."

She blinked big green eyes at him, as if amazed he was pretending not to understand her. "Liam, I know what you've done. I kept telling myself it wasn't you; that if it was, you'd stop on your own. I admit it—I was too big a coward to come forward before."

Melissa turned to Clive Matthews and those gathered around him, including a number of deputies in her glance. "Liam murdered our baby three years ago," she said, spelling it out plainly. "And he said it was Sudden Infant Death Syndrome. I was afraid, so I covered for him, but the loss of my poor little Hannah, and the knowledge that the man I'd married had done such a thing, well, I'm ashamed to say it made me turn to alcohol and drugs."

Baba felt the whole room sway in stunned distress. Or maybe that was just her, and the others were simply standing still as her world shook around her.

"I'm clean and sober now, and I've found God. I know I need to tell the truth, and get this whole horrible thing out into the open." The petite redhead gazed beseechingly at Liam, tiny streaks of salt water glistening on her perfect cheekbones. "I'm still your wife, no matter what you've done, but I can't let this go on. You're sick, Liam. You need help. When you killed our baby, shaking her to get her to stop crying, it was an accident. Killing all these other children won't bring our baby back. You have to confess and clear your soul. And you have to stop blaming that poor innocent woman for the crimes *you* committed."

LIAM COMPRESSED HIS lips together into a thin line and said, "Melissa, you know that's not true."

He felt like he'd been run over by a truck, blindsided by lies that sounded like truth, spoken by the last person he'd expected to see, least of all in this context. He didn't understand why she was saying what she was saying. Or how on earth she was involved with this whole mess. Words swarmed around his ears like gnats, senseless and annoying, until one sentence finally stood out enough to get his attention.

"I'm *what*?" he said to Clive Matthews.

Matthews had crossed the floor to stand in front of Liam, backed up by his cronies on the board.

"You're suspended," Matthews repeated. "Pending an investigation of these very serious allegations." His round face was pink and greasy with sweat in the inadequately air-conditioned old station. "I've been suspicious all along about your lack of progress on this case, and we are going to take a very serious look into both your current dealings and your child's death three years ago."

The board president wiped his forehead with the napkin that had been tucked into his jacket pocket and added portentously, "You should probably call a lawyer."

Cold ran down Liam's back and pooled at the base of his spine. Even his mouth felt numb and stiff. "I don't need a lawyer," he said, forming syllables out of blocks of ice and dropping them into the unfriendly atmosphere. "I haven't done anything wrong."

Nina and Molly came to stand by his side, both of them glaring at the board like lionesses defending their cub.

Molly said doubtfully, "Sheriff, are you sure? Just because you're not guilty doesn't mean you shouldn't get an attorney. You need to defend yourself against these ridiculous charges." She narrowed her eyes at Melissa, as if daring her to say one more negative thing.

Liam didn't care. The damage was already done. He looked around the room at the faces full of doubt, uncertainty and distrust radiating from the very group who should have known him best. He refused to defend himself. He shouldn't have to. His character and his actions all these years should speak for the kind of man he was. And if these people didn't know that already, nothing he could say would make any difference.

Besides, maybe this was some twisted kind of justice—

the universe's way of punishing him for failing his baby, and later, his wife. He wasn't guilty of the things she'd said, but he was guilty nonetheless. And he was so very, very tired. Too tired to fight this unexpected enemy.

"No," he said to Molly, "I'll be fine. No lawyer. Let them investigate. There's nothing to find, and you know it."

"Well *of course* I do," she said caustically, hands on her hips. "But there are a thousand innocent men sitting in jail cells who probably said the same thing."

Liam shrugged, too numb with shock to think beyond getting through this utterly insane moment. He'd deal with everything else later, when he'd had a chance to remember how to take a deep breath.

"We caught Maya, and she can't steal any more children," he said. "That's all that matters right now."

"Under the circumstances," Peter Callahan said, stepping forward smoothly, "I don't believe it would be fair to hold Ms. Freeman." He turned to Clive Matthews. "I'd like to ask that she be released on my recognizance; I promise that she won't leave the county, and will make herself available for any questioning required by whomever you appoint as acting sheriff."

"Absolutely not!" Liam snapped, jolted out of his stunned inertia at last. "I caught her in the act of trying to kidnap a little boy!"

"So you say," Callahan pointed out acidly. "But your word isn't very good right now, is it?"

Liam swiveled back to face Matthews, only to see the man shaking his head in officious agreement.

"I do see your point," Matthews said, snapping his fingers at the deputy sitting with Maya. "After all, Mrs. Turner says she didn't see anything, and little Davy can't seem to remember what happened, poor boy. So all we have against Ms. Freeman is Sheriff McClellan's word, and that isn't exactly proof, is it?"

The deputy brought Maya over, not meeting Liam's eyes, and delivered her to her boss. She shot a triumphant look at Liam from under downturned lashes before smiling gratefully at the other men. Melissa stared at the ground, as if the dusty, scuffed linoleum had suddenly grown more interesting than the drama being acted out right in front of her.

Liam couldn't believe this was happening. He'd finally caught the kidnapper, brought her in, and not only was he still out of a job, he might even end up going to jail for the crimes she'd committed. It was as if the entire world had gone mad. Or maybe he had.

He turned on his heel and walked outside, before Matthews could think to ask for his gun and his badge. The soft click of the door closing behind him sounded like a death knell.

Suspended. He was suspended.

He put both hands out and braced himself against the hood of the cruiser for a minute, trying to make some kind of sense out of the last half an hour and failing miserably. The clicking of Baba's high-heeled boots gave her away before she spoke.

"Well," she said in a low, discouraged tone he'd never heard from her before. "That didn't exactly go the way we thought it would, did it?"

Liam turned around, knowing he'd let down the woman he'd come to care for; knowing she had every right to condemn him for allowing Maya to be on the loose again.

"I guess I should have handed Maya over to you when you asked me to," he said softly, shuffling the toe of one boot against the gravel. "I should have known she'd have some kind of a plan in place in case she got caught, although I never in million years would have seen this coming."

Baba narrowed her eyes and said grimly, "I know exactly what you mean."

He had a sinking feeling they weren't talking about the same thing.

"Baba—"

She just shook her head, that cloud of hair moving through the air like silk flowing through water. "And you accused *me* of having secrets," she said bitterly. "When were you going to tell me you were still married?"

TWENTY-FIVE

BABA SLAMMED THE door of the Airstream behind her and threw her boots one at a time against the far wall as hard as she could. Maybe if she broke something, she wouldn't feel so much like crying. Not that she would cry. She never cried. But by golly, she was going to have to break a *lot* of stuff.

"Oh-oh," Chudo-Yudo said, his head appearing from around the counter. "I know that look. What the hell happened?" He ambled over and head-butted Baba in the stomach affectionately, almost knocking her over and yet still perversely making her feel better.

"Do you want the long version or the short version?" she asked, tossing a small brown-and-red antique porcelain vase up and down in one hand as she tried to decide if it would make a large enough crash to be at all satisfying.

Chudo-Yudo eyed the motion dubiously. "Uh, better give me the short one. I kind of like that vase. It goes with my eyes."

Baba snorted, but put the piece back down more or less gently. She walked over and plopped onto the couch, putting her head into her hands for a minute as she tried to figure out the best way to sum up the disastrous last couple of hours.

"Okay," she said, finally. "Liam caught Maya in the act, trying to kidnap a little boy. He arrested her, brought her to the sheriff's department, and summoned me using the amulet I gave him. By the time I got there, so had a bunch of other people. Including Liam's *wife*, who accused him of murdering their baby three years ago, as well as all the children who have gone missing around here in the last six months. The board put Liam on suspension, and let Maya go. End of story." She decided there was no point in mentioning that Liam had also refused to allow her to take Maya back to the Otherworld. The tale already sucked enough without that little tidbit.

Chudo-Yudo's tongue lolled out of his mouth as he gazed at her in amazement. Eventually he curled it back up, shook his whole body from nose to tail and said, "That's one hell of a story, all right. I think it's time to call back the Riders, don't you?"

"HE HAS A *wife*?" Alexei repeated. "Son of a bitch." His massive arms flexed. "Do you want me to pound him into dust for you? It would be my pleasure."

"Don't bother," Chudo-Yudo said with disgust. "I already offered to eat him, and she won't let me do that either."

"Let's focus on the real issue here, shall we, boys?" Baba said, trying to ignore the gnawing in her gut that showed up every time anyone said that word. *Wife. Gah.*

"Maya is back on the loose and we have no idea where, or what she'll do next. That's a lot more important than the fact that our friend the sheriff has a wife whom he didn't happen to mention. A wife, who after being out of the picture for two years, apparently, shows up and tells a huge lie that allowed Maya to go free."

Grim doubt shadowed Gregori's already serious expression. "Are you sure it *is* a lie, Baba?" he asked.

She swallowed hard. "Um, call it eighty percent sure that

Maya and Melissa are both lying and Liam is innocent." So, almost sure anyway. "I suppose it's possible that Maya is using the doorway and causing havoc in the Otherworld but isn't also involved in the children's disappearances. After all, I clearly don't know the sheriff as well as I thought I did. Hell, I didn't even know he had a wife." *There's that word again. Double gah.*

The men exchanged glances, silently electing Mikhail to ask the tough question. "Could he have been fooling you all along? Fooling us all, I mean? I really liked the guy." His handsome face was unusually somber.

She sighed. "Anything is possible. But you should have seen his face when Melissa accused him of murdering his own child. I'm not the best at reading Humans, but I'd be willing to swear that what I saw was hurt and shock, not guilt."

Alexei shrugged mountain-sized shoulders. "That's good enough for me, I suppose. So what do we do now? Do you want us to keep watching the other children?"

Baba didn't know what she wanted. Or how on earth they could keep Maya from taking any more kids now that they didn't even have a sheriff on their side. If they ever had one.

"Do any of them seem like liable targets, assuming she doesn't just cut her losses and run back to the Otherworld? Or find someplace else to start again on this side of the doorway?" she asked.

Gregori said, "Two of them, no, but the others are possibilities. If she strikes again, she might go after one of them."

"Assuming that Liam was telling the truth about any of this, and that all our theories weren't based on the lies of a murderous madman," Baba said, blinking furiously. One of Chudo-Yudo's hairs must have gotten into her eye. Suddenly she couldn't take another minute of this conversation. Lying, not lying. Married, not married. What did any of it matter anyway?

"But, Baba, you just said—" Alexei's bearded face creased in bafflement.

"Do what you want," Baba said, getting up from the table. "I'm going for a walk. I need to clear my head." Just when she had been thinking crazy thoughts about maybe not being alone for the rest of her life . . . now she felt more alone than ever. Who knew that could hurt so much?

She started toward the wardrobe door, and got as far as putting her hand on the wonky latch before she remembered with a spearing ache that the Otherworld was no longer her refuge. It took all the self-control she had not to just bang her head against the door. Repeatedly.

Instead, she grabbed her boots from where they'd landed when she'd hurled them, scooped up her helmet, and slammed out the door. A minute later, the sound of a motorcycle roaring down the road filtered in through the open window of the Airstream, which still vibrated from her violent exit.

All three riders sat, speechless, staring after her. Eventually, Mikhail said to Chudo-Yudo, "What the hell was that all about?"

The dragon-dog gave his coughing laugh and sank down, furry white head resting on his paws. "I think our Baba has finally fallen in love."

"Ah," said Gregori. He pondered for a moment and then added, "I don't think it is going well."

Chudo-Yudo rolled his eyes under furry brows. "That, old friend, is the understatement of the century." After a minute, he perked up and added, "On the bright side, I'm pretty sure that eventually I'm going to get to eat *someone*."

"I FOUND YOU wandering lost in this land when you slipped through the door in a drug-addled stupor," Maya said to Melissa in disgust, once they were back on the other side of the doorway, far from pesky sheriffs and overly solicitous bosses. "You were a broken woman, and I took you in. I gave you a new child to replace the one you lost. Fed you and cared for you. All I asked in return was the location of the doorway, and a little unimportant information about the place you came from and the people who lived there. And this one other small thing—to accuse your husband, a man you had already betrayed in a million ways. Why are you whining at me now?"

Melissa was crying, the glowing red light of the biggest moon shining on her tears like blood. "I did what you asked," she said, speaking so softly her words barely disturbed the shimmering air. "But I didn't know it would be so hard to see him again. To see his face when I said he killed our baby."

She cried even harder, making Maya's fingers twitch. She couldn't wring the silly bitch's neck; she might still need her. And it wasn't as though the red-haired woman hadn't played her part to perfection. But all this silly sniveling was going to drive her mad. Humans. Irritating creatures at the best of times. And this was *not* the best of times.

"I can't go back again. I can't. I can't." Melissa made her hands into claws and ripped at her skin, tearing her face until it bled, pulling at her long red hair, crying and screaming and laughing all at the same time.

Maya sighed and slapped her. Melissa just cried harder.

Maya sighed again. "Well, that's the end of that, then," she said with resignation. "Damned Human. You're clearly too unstable to be depended on. It looks like time has run out on my little plan." She'd already come to that conclusion anyway. "But first, one last child before I go. And I know just the perfect one."

Melissa hid her head in her hands, rocking back and forth as Maya's silvery laughter filled the eerie Otherworld sky.

TWENTY-SIX

THE MUSICAL RUMBLE of the motorcycle's engine eventually soothed Baba's churning stomach and frazzled nerves, and she slowed down somewhat from the bone-jarring speed she'd been traveling at to a more reasonable pace that allowed her to check the surrounding scenery to get some idea of where she was.

Tall trees lined either side of a country lane, with the occasional white farmhouse and red barn dotting either side. Black-and-white cows lifted their heads to peer at Baba as she rode by, then returned to their munching, unimpressed by this strange noisy animal. A red-tailed hawk circled lazily overhead, as if leading her on, and it was with more resignation than surprise that she spotted Liam's cruiser parked just inside the gate of what looked to be a small, ancient cemetery.

Apparently even when she didn't want to see him, the handsome sheriff was so strongly rooted in her spirit it was as though some invisible cord tied them together. Given free rein by her mindless driving, her treacherous subconscious had led her straight to him. She was going to have to have a little chat with it, as soon as she had more time.

For now, she coasted to a stop by the pair of weathered stone posts that marked the entrance to the nameless graveyard, flipped down the BMW's kickstand, and parked her motorcycle next to the car. Under the gloomy late-afternoon sky, Liam's figure stood alone in front of a tiny granite headstone, head bowed, a ragged bouquet of yellow-white daisies and pink and purple wildflowers crushed and forgotten in his large hands.

Baba hesitated for a moment, not sure if she would be intruding, but eventually she trudged past leaning moss-covered stones and a scattering of better tended, more modern monuments in the shape of angels, crosses, and in one case, a towering black marble obelisk, until she arrived at Liam's side.

There she stood, gazing mutely at the simple tombstone, carved with the name Hannah Marie McClellan, and dates for a birth and death that fell far too close together. Underneath the dates, there was a single word: Beloved.

Hannah hadn't even lived to see her fourth month. Baba closed her eyes in sympathetic pain and silent respect. When she reopened them, it was to see Liam gazing at her stoically, one eyebrow raised in unspoken question. The wind blew his too-long hair into his eyes. He ignored it, untouched for now by mere human annoyances.

"Hi," Baba said, her voice soft, as seemed fitting for their surroundings. Despite the sadness all around them, there was also a kind of restful beauty in the quiet, out-of-the-way place. A single crow cawed as it flew overhead on its way to somewhere cheerier.

"Hi," he said. "What are you doing here?" He looked at the road and back at her. "For that matter, how did you find me? More magic?"

She shrugged, the leather jacket she wore making a low rasping noise as it slid across her shoulders. "Magic of the heart, maybe. Nothing I did on purpose." An ironic smile tweaked at the edges of her lips. "To be honest, it was just as much a surprise to me as it was to you when I wound up here."

The eyebrow lifted even higher, but he didn't say anything. They stood there for another few minutes in companionable silence, looking down on the place that marked all that remained of his daughter except bittersweet memory.

"It's a nice cemetery," Baba offered, finally. "Calm. Peaceful."

"Yeah." Liam bent and put the slightly mangled flowers down on top of his daughter's stone. "Melissa and I had our first big argument about this place. She wanted Hannah laid to rest in town, where she could stop by and see her every day on her way to work. But my whole family is buried out here; going back to the days when this area was first settled by a bunch of people with more hope than sense."

He gave a wry smile, as if to include himself in their ranks. "After that, it seemed like we argued about everything: Whether or not to give away Hannah's clothes and toys, or turn the nursery into some other kind of room. Whether or not to try and have another baby right away. Or ever.

"And then she began drinking and doing whatever drugs she could get her hands on, so long as they numbed the pain. By the time she started in on the indiscriminate sexual encounters, I'd given up fighting." His hazel eyes were shadowed by guilt and remembered anguish. "So maybe part of this new thing is my fault; her just trying to get back at me for giving up on her."

"Sounds more like she gave up on herself," Baba said practically. "I suspect you kept trying long after most men would have given up and written her off entirely."

She was rewarded with a wan half smile. "Maybe," he said. "But it still wasn't enough." He gazed down at the pitifully small grave. "I never cried, you know."

Baba looked up, startled. "What?"

"The night Hannah died. All those long weeks and months afterward. Even the day we buried her." His hands clenched at his sides. "I never cried. I was trying so hard to be strong for Melissa, for the people who depended on me, I never cried for my own child. What kind of father does that make me?" His voice cracked at the end, although his expression never changed, as bleak and empty as when she'd first walked over to stand by his side.

Baba finally gave in and pushed the hair out of his face, but the wind promptly blew it back. She kissed him lightly on the lips instead.

"The kind of father who locks his heart up in a shell and does his job, I guess," she said softly, one arm winding around his waist of its own volition.

Liam snorted. "Gee, remind you of anyone else you know?"

Well, there was that. "Yeah, just a little," Baba said. "We're a pathetic pair, aren't we?"

He picked up his head and gazed at her steadily, locking his eyes on hers until she was forced to stare back. "Are we?" he asked, in a voice that tried to make it sound as though the question were more casual than it was. "A pair, I mean."

Baba's heart jumped, giving its own automatic answer, but all she said was, "I don't know. Sometimes it seems like the entire universe is designed to keep us apart. I don't know if we can work past all of that."

She remembered their passionate encounter, when for a few golden moments, everything had seemed possible. Even now, she wanted him with a longing that shook her to the soles of her boots. But there was no way they could resolve anything until the current situation was dealt with.

She touched her lips softly to his and said, "One thing I do know—we're going to work together to bring Maya down, once and for all."

Hope leaped into Liam's face as if the sun had come out, although the sky above was still as gray as ever. "Does that mean you believe me? And not Melissa, with her horrible lies?"

Baba tightened her grip into something that was almost a hug before letting go. "Yes. Yes, I do." She wasn't even sure when she'd decided to believe, she just knew she did. "The old Baba used to tell me that the heart is as important to magic as power—and my heart says you're innocent." A tiny smile twitched up one corner of her mouth. "What it's saying beyond that, frankly, is still a mystery."

Liam gave her a brief hug back, releasing her almost before she'd realized his arms were around her. She missed them as soon as they were gone.

"I'll settle for that, for now," Liam said. He knelt down to pat the top of the tombstone one last time, a solitary drop of moisture sliding unnoticed down his sun-browned cheek.

"Don't you worry, baby girl," he said. "Daddy is going to take care of everything. But I'll be back. And I'll cry for you then."

MAYA LET HERSELF into Peter Callahan's palatial rented house and let the door click shut behind her. She'd been there before, of course, so the luxurious furnishings in shades of white and taupe didn't surprise her, nor the smooth marble floors resounding coldly under the *click, click, click* of her stiletto heels. *What kind of person rents an all-white house when they have a four-year-old child?* Not that there was any sign of the usual youthful disarray; everything was pristine and in its proper place.

A sneer distorted her unnaturally lovely face. She'd despised the ambitious businessman since the day she'd met him, applying for a job he'd had no chance of denying her. In truth, she'd been looking forward to this moment for every hour of every miserable day of the six months she'd spent putting up with his smug superiority, greedy ambition, and the twice-a-week unimaginative coupling on the top of the walnut desk in his office. What was coming next would be infinitely more pleasurable.

At least for her. She suspected he wouldn't share her sentiments at all.

Drawn by the sound of her laughter echoing through the house, Peter appeared at the top of the stairs. An alarmed look wiped away the self-satisfaction that usually sat so comfortably on his aristocratic face.

"What the hell are you doing here?" he asked, glancing

down at the fancy diamond-studded wristwatch he always wore. "My wife and son will be home any minute now."

"Good," Maya said, teeth gleaming, "I was hoping to see them before I left town."

Peter stomped down the stairs, meeting her in the foyer that opened up into the showy living room and open-plan granite-countered kitchen. "You can't leave town," he said, indignation spilling out like smoke. "I promised you'd stay here and testify against the sheriff."

Maya laughed at him, rolling her eyes at this display of naiveté from someone who prided himself on being such a canny businessman. "Don't be absurd," she said calmly. "You know perfectly well I was behind the whole thing. Why else do you think the children who went missing just happened to belong to families who were on your special list?" Her fingers made air quotes around the word *special*. "Don't tell me you thought that was a coincidence. Even you couldn't be *that* stupid."

Indignation and fear warred on Callahan's visage. "I did start to wonder, after a bit," he said. "That's why I was so relieved when it turned out to be Sheriff McClellan after all. And I am anything but stupid. How dare you speak to me that way? I can fire you, young lady." The longer he talked, the more his usual confidence came flooding back, as if the familiar pattern of his words could build a palisade to protect him from the unpleasant realities the peasants had to deal with.

Maya was going to enjoy ripping it away once and for all.

"You can't fire me, you moron," she said, tapping one Louboutin-clad shoe. "I'm already leaving. And don't try blaming me for everything that's happened; you caused it all, creating a magical doorway to my world with your destruction of the earth and the water." She gave a bloodcurdling smile that turned his face ashen. "But before I leave, I've come for one last payment for the desecration of the element I hold sacred—I'll be taking your son."

TWENTY-SEVEN

PETER CALLAHAN'S JAW dropped open. "What? Have you lost your mind?" He shook one finger at her, apparently not noticing that it was trembling slightly.

"If you've done this horrible thing, that's not my fault!" he protested. "And I am certainly not going to allow you to take my son. I've been building all this for him!" Callahan waved his hand through the air, as if his empire would somehow appear into view as concrete evidence of how hard he'd worked.

Maya sneered, crimson lips curling in disdain. "Oh, please. You've been building it for yourself. I'll bet you haven't spent more than twenty minutes with the boy on any day since I've been here." She put her hands on her hips, facing down her erstwhile boss.

"You'll give me the boy," she said succinctly, each word dropping into the air like a biting fragment of hail, "or I will bring your world crashing down around your ears. I'll tell your wife we've been screwing since my first interview. I'll tell everyone in town that you helped me to choose which children to steal and that you're behind all the mischief that's happened to the people who haven't wanted to let you drill on their land."

"That was you too?" Callahan looked so stunned, Maya wanted to laugh. "But—but if you were helping me before, why do this now?"

"I helped you get what you wanted because it suited me to do so at the time," she said with a shrug. "And now it suits me to take it away. Just as you Humans took away my power and drained my spirit by destroying the pure waters that link my kind to this benighted world. Be practical, my darling Peter. You can make another son, but can you build another powerful career if I destroy your reputation and implicate you in my crimes?" She rolled her eyes at his deer-in-the-headlights look. "Consider your son the price for all my help. At that, you're getting quite the bargain."

Callahan glanced around desperately, as if some miraculous answer would materialize from behind the overstuffed white couch with its hand-embroidered golden pillows or slide out from behind the bland, expensive artwork hung on the walls.

"He's out with my wife," he said. "You'll have to leave town without him." Callahan pulled his wallet out of a back pocket, the tooled leather gleaming under the lights of the tasteful crystal chandelier that hung from the high ceiling overhead. "Look, I can give you money. My charge cards. I'll write you a blank check."

"I don't need your money," Maya said. She tilted her head as if listening. "Ah, how convenient. I believe I hear your wife pulling in now. I'll just take what I came for and go; you can get on with your empire building in peace."

"But—what will I tell my wife?" Callahan bleated, all his usual polish wiped away. "I can't tell her I simply handed over our son!"

Maya smiled evilly. "Tell her you were wrong about me after all; just another poor victim of the horrible woman who stole away everyone's children. Maybe you'll even get enough sympathy from those foolish locals to sway a few more people to your side."

Tired of arguing, she drew on her borrowed magic and bound his will to hers. The spell hadn't worked as well as she'd hoped on that silly Melissa, protected as she was by her own insanity. But Peter had no such protection, and Maya relished the moment when he realized he no longer controlled his own actions. Only his eyes, darting frantically back and forth, revealed the mind that no longer ruled his body.

She turned her back on him and walked outside, knowing he'd have no choice but to follow. At the top arc of the circular gravel driveway, Callahan's wife Penelope was helping a small boy out of his car seat, a pile of shopping bags on the ground near her feet. She looked up in surprise when she saw Maya.

"Why, Ms. Freeman, I didn't expect to see you here." Penelope gave Maya a cautious look, suspicion edging her voice. "I heard in town that you'd accused Sheriff McClellan of being involved in the kidnappings somehow. I just can't believe it's true. You must have made a mistake."

"Not to worry," Maya said brightly. "It will all become clear soon enough. In the meanwhile, I'm afraid there's been a little problem in your basement. It seems like one of the pipes there sprang a leak, and the water is rising fast." She tapped her toe again, speeding up the flow of the underground spring she'd called on earlier to break through the floor and flood the cellar. Sometimes having control of water was a handy thing.

"Your husband asked me to come take little Peter Junior out for ice cream while the two of you deal with the plumber and all that mess," she continued, moving to take the boy's hand before his mother could react, and walking him rapidly in the direction of her rental car. She would be *so* relieved never to have to use these stupid human metal torture devices again. Even with all her increased strength, it was agony to ride in the things.

"And I was happy to do it. You just take all the time you need. Peter Jr. and I will be just fine, won't we?" She smiled happily down at the child, who craned his neck around to look at his mother uncertainly.

"Oh, no," Penelope said. "I don't think that's a good idea. You don't even have a car seat. Besides, we've been out all afternoon and Petey is tired. And it's almost dinnertime." She gazed as her husband, obviously expecting him to do something.

"Peter. Peter! Tell her she can't take our son!"

Callahan just hung his head and said nothing, holding Penelope back by force when she would have stopped Maya, who plopped their son into the passenger seat of her car, buckled the seatbelt around his tiny waist, and drove off in a spray of gravel and impending sorrow.

LIAM WAS WALKING out of the cemetery with Baba when he heard the crackle and squawk of the two-way radio in the squad car. Technically, he shouldn't even be driving it now, but he hadn't gone home yet to exchange it for his personal truck. Besides, as long as he still wore his uniform and could sit behind the wheel of the cruiser, he could almost pretend he still had an office and a job to go with them.

"Sheriff? Sheriff McClellan, are you there?" Nina's voice spilled out of the radio in a muffled whisper, as if she was trying to talk without being overheard. "Liam? Pick up the damned radio!"

"I'm here, Nina," Liam said as he stuck his head into the car and thumbed on the two-way. "Why didn't you just call me on my cell phone? You're going to get in trouble if someone catches you talking to me over official channels now that I'm suspended."

The dispatcher's exasperated sigh came clearly down the line between crackles. "Because you're someplace out in the middle of nowhere, and your cell has no reception. I've been trying you on it for the last ten minutes."

Liam glanced at the rural countryside surrounding him and grimaced. "Fine. But what's so important you had to reach me right away? If it's a fight at The Roadhouse, somebody else will have to deal with it this time."

Nina lowered her voice even more, and Liam had to bend

down closer to the speaker to hear her, the top of his body twisted awkwardly half in and half out of the open cruiser window.

"Peter Callahan's wife called in, completely hysterical. She insisted on talking to you, no one else."

"Nina," Liam said in his most patient tone, "I'm not the sheriff right now. She's just going to have to talk to someone else."

"You don't understand," Nina said urgently. "She says that Maya took her son."

Behind him, Liam could hear Baba let out a quiet gasp.

"What? When?" he asked, already fumbling for his car keys.

"She wouldn't tell me anything else," Nina said, clearly put out by not being in the loop. "Just insisted on talking to you. Said you were the only one she trusted. She wants you to meet her at the crossroads where Country Route Twenty and Blue Barn Road meet, as soon as you can get there." Nina paused. "You don't think it's some kind of trick, do you?"

Liam had been wondering that himself. "You talked to her; what did you think?"

Nina pondered the question for a second. "I think she sounded like a desperate woman in a world of trouble. Do you want me to send someone else?"

Liam and Baba exchanged glances over the roof of the cruiser. "That won't be necessary," he said. "I've got this one."

AT THE BLUE-PAINTED barn, a long-abandoned landmark that gave the road its name, Baba and Liam found Penelope Callahan waiting impatiently, pacing by her boxy green Volvo and wringing her hands. A large red and purple bruise decorated most of one side of her otherwise attractive face, and she limped slightly as she paced. The Volvo's right headlight was bashed in, its injuries seeming to match her own.

She rushed over to meet them as soon as the cruiser pulled into the lot, ignoring Baba and addressing Liam with barely restrained hysteria. Her carefully coiffed hair stuck out at the sides, as if she'd been running her fingers through it repeatedly.

"Sheriff McClellan, thank god you're here!" Penelope gasped. "Nina said you couldn't come, because they'd suspended you, but I knew you wouldn't let me down." One trembling hand dashed away tears impatiently. "You have to help me get my son back!"

Liam put one arm around her shaking shoulders briefly before stepping back to take a closer look at her face. "What happened, Mrs. Callahan? Did Maya do this to you?" Baba could see the muscles in his jaw tense as he clenched his teeth.

Penelope shook her head, wincing a little. "No, no," she said. "Maya was there when I got home from doing the shopping with Petey. She said we'd had a major flood in the basement and Peter had asked her to take Petey out of the way while we dealt with it." She looked indignant, as if insulted by the suggestion that she couldn't cope with a household emergency and a four-year-old at the same time.

"I said no, of course," she went on, speaking in the rapid breathy tones of the truly frantic. "But she just took him anyway, and Peter didn't do a thing. She didn't even have a car seat!" Panic rose up in her eyes and Liam took one of her hands in his.

"I'm sure that Maya is a very safe driver," he said soothingly. "Now, you said Maya didn't give you those bruises. Can you tell us who did?"

Tears sprang into Penelope's blue eyes, but to Baba, they looked more like tears of anger than the fearful ones she'd been shedding a minute ago.

"I confronted Peter when he tried to stop me from going after Maya. Hell, I knew that she was lying when she said all those horrid things about you, so that meant she had to be involved somehow. But Peter just stared at me like a zombie."

Penelope pulled herself up straight. "When I told him I was going after Maya by myself, he hit me." She touched one trembling hand lightly to the side of her face. "So I knocked him over with the car and followed Maya anyway." She glanced at Liam. "I didn't really hurt him; he was already getting up as I drove away."

Baba let out a choked laugh and looked at the prim and proper Mrs. Callahan with newfound respect. "You ran him over with the car? That's fabulous!"

Penelope sniffed back tears and gave Baba a tiny nod and a lopsided smile, wincing when the action pulled at the bruise. "I know, isn't it? I should have done it years ago." She sobered quickly. "If I had, my son wouldn't be in the hands of that woman now."

She looked from Baba to Liam. "I didn't know what to do. I followed her to a cave, and when she dragged Petey in there, I wanted to follow, but something kept me from going in. I know it sounds crazy, but I tried and tried, and I just couldn't get through!" The last bit was said in a rising wail.

Magic, Baba thought. And could see from Liam's face that he'd realized it too.

Liam patted Penelope's hand again. "It's probably just as well," he said. "That woman is more dangerous than you can imagine. But she's not going to harm Petey. I'm not going to let her."

Penelope nodded damply, and Baba said, "Can you lead us to where you saw her last?" Her heart raced at the thought of finally getting her hands on the woman who had caused her so much trouble. Visions of cracking bones and freely flowing blood filled her mind for one gleeful moment before she pulled herself back to the situation at hand. *I am finally going to get to kick someone's ass. About freaking time!*

Liam and Baba followed Penelope's car about a mile down a back road that led to a barely visible path into thick woods filled with pine and oak and a few spindly birches. The trail was too narrow for vehicles, so they left the cruiser and the Volvo by the side of the road. Birds chirped merrily as they passed by Maya's car, already parked on the practically nonexistent verge. They glanced inside as they passed; the keys still dangled from the ignition, as clear a sign as any that Maya had no intention of coming back.

Baba spotted something long and shining on the driver's seat and crowed with glee, sticking her hand inside the open window to pick it up. "How careless," she said, giving Liam a grin that clearly baffled him. "This should come in handy."

"It's a hair," he said. "It's not even evidence of anything."

She tucked her find carefully into one pants pocket and followed the others down the dusty trail. "You'll see."

Penelope led Liam and Baba to the dark, shadowy entrance of a cave so well hidden by prickly shrubs and spindly young saplings, it would have been almost impossible to spot if you didn't already know of its existence. The opening seemed to shiver and twitch, radiating *wrongness* like a misplucked violin string.

Penelope nodded at the entrance, which was little more than a slit in the hillside, and said in a tremulous voice, arms wrapped around herself for comfort, "There. She took my son in there."

TWENTY-EIGHT

BABA AND LIAM looked at the mouth of the cave, and then at each other. Baba felt a frisson of excitement—clearly, the door she'd been seeking lay within that cavern. Somewhere. But first they had to figure out a way to keep Penelope from insisting on accompanying them when they went in after her son. They couldn't risk her following them into the Otherworld. Baba was going to be in enough trouble with the queen for bringing Liam through. And there was no telling what Otherworld creatures Maya might have lined up as a greeting committee on the other side.

"You should wait by the cars, Mrs. Callahan," Liam said, echoing her thought. "That way, if there is a problem, you can radio for help."

"Hmmm," Baba said. "And I have some friends I can call in. They might come in handy if we run into trouble."

"Friends?" Penelope said doubtfully. "Are you sure you can trust them? Peter always said he had half the town in his pocket."

Baba snorted. "Not these guys. They're not from around here. Besides, they're not the 'in someone's pocket' type."

She gave the woman what was supposed to be a reassuring smile, although from Penelope's reaction, it might have shown a few too many teeth. "They may look a little rough around the edges, but they're really . . . oh, hell, they're rough around the edges. But they're on our side; you can trust them."

Penelope's eyes opened wide. "You're not talking about those three strange men who showed up recently, are you? Someone at Bertie's told me they'd been seen all over town; one of them started a huge fight at The Roadhouse, and I heard that another one swept that shy Lindy Cornwall off her feet and had her walking around smiling like the cat that ate the canary. They're friends of yours?"

Baba ducked her head, hiding a smile. "I'm afraid so. But don't worry; they're even better at cleaning up messes than they are at making them."

Liam added, "I know you want to come with us, but it could be dangerous—you need to stay safe for your son's sake. Please go back to the car and wait for us. If we're not back in two hours, you can contact Nina and tell her where we went."

"Well, okay," Penelope said, casting a reluctant look at the entrance of the cave. "I trust you, Sheriff McClellan." She turned to Liam and gave him a tearful hug. "Bring my son back to me, please." She walked back down the path, head held high.

"That's one tough lady," Baba said with respect in her voice. "She's holding it together under some pretty terrifying circumstances. And she ran Peter Callahan over with her car. You've got to like her for that, all by itself." She grinned at Liam.

He shook his head. "You're a scary woman, you know that?"

She gave him her *who me?* look, which earned her a dubious headshake in return.

"So, do you have another magical medallion you can use to summon your friends Day, Sun, and Knight?" He stopped for a second, listening to the sound of their names spoken all together. "Hey—"

"It's tradition," Baba said. "I'll explain when we have more time. In the meanwhile, I've got something better than a medallion. And a lot more dependable than your silly cell phones." She pulled off her leather jacket and whipped her tee shirt off over her head, handing them both to a stunned Liam. "Here, hold these, will you?"

She bit back a laugh at Liam's startled expression.

"You're getting undressed *now*?" Liam said. "Not that I'm complaining, mind you. I'm not usually a fan of tattoos, but those are damned sexy on you."

Baba flushed a little at Liam's comment. *He thought she was sexy.* But she just said, a touch more acerbically than usual, "Don't be silly—they're magic."

She rubbed each tattoo in turn, reciting the Russian phrase that would summon the Rider attached to it. "There. Each Rider has his own symbol, and each Baba has a matching one she can use to summon them when they're needed."

Liam looked intrigued as he tried not to stare. "So all the other Babas have tattoos like yours?"

"Oh, no," Baba said. "Beka has hers set into a necklace and a pair of earrings, and others use much smaller markings or even sets of decorated rocks. I just happen to like tattoos. And dragons, of course."

"Ah," Liam said, trying to hand her back her tee shirt. "Do we have to wait for the guys to show up? I'm assuming you can get us through whatever barrier stopped Penelope. Maya already has a serious head start on us. If this cavern is anything like the others in the area, it's riddled with twists and turns and dead ends. We could have a tough time finding which way she went; we need to hurry if we're going to have any chance of catching up with her."

Baba shook her head, backing away from him. "The Riders will be here soon. Besides, I know there's no time to waste, but I can't go into the Otherworld unarmed and dressed like this."

She snapped her fingers, and her formal court attire appeared, along with the silver sword and bejeweled knife she usually carried. There was no way she was going to face

Maya without some kind of weapon. And if, heaven fore-fend, they couldn't find her, there was no way she was going to face the queen and tell her so wearing a pair of dusty black leather pants.

"Okay," Baba said to Liam. "You want to turn around so I can change my clothes?" Liam raised his eyebrows ques-tioningly, but obliged. Despite all they'd been through, she suddenly felt self-conscious about having him watch her disrobe. It was disconcerting, the strange way she felt around him, as though the once solid land had turned to quicksand. Lust and longing she understood—this odd push and pull of emotion just confused her. But there was no time to worry about it now.

She shimmied out of her everyday clothes and into her Otherworld garb, then slid her boots up over her calves and fastened the belt around her waist, muttering under her breath as she struggled to tuck her long hair up and pin it into place.

"You can turn around now." She loved the way his eyes widened with admiration when he saw her all dressed up. There was something about the way he looked at her that made her feel all odd and shivery, like she'd swallowed a rainbow sideways. "I'm ready," she said, trying to ignore the bizarre sensation in her gut. What a time to discover that perhaps she knew what love was after all.

Liam took a step closer, dropping her jacket and shirt onto the ground so he could put one hand on either side of her face. He was so close, she could see the tiny flecks of green in among the brown and hazel lights of his irises.

"I'm not," Liam said. "If we're walking into the un-known, there's something I need to do first."

He leaned in and kissed her soundly, his calloused hands gentle on her skin, the sweet taste of his lips the most in-toxicating nectar she'd ever had in this world or any other. Around her, the air trembled with joy; underneath her feet, the ground shook. When he finally stopped, it took a second before Baba could remember how to breathe.

"What was that for?" she asked, her voice a little ragged.

"Luck," Liam said, and kissed her one more time.

"Well, we're going to need plenty of that," Baba said. And thought to herself: *And if we make it back, I'm going to need plenty more of those kisses. Who knew something so simple could be so entrancing?* It made the magic she did seem like nothing.

The sound of laughter heralded the arrival of the Riders, and she tried to wipe the giddy smile off her face before she turned around to greet them and say, "Ready to kick some ass, boys?" A wave of her hand easily dissipated the enchanted barrier Maya had used to block off the entrance, and they were on their way.

THE INSIDE OF the cave was as black as the bottom of a well; a miniscule slice of light trailed them inside from the slit they'd passed through sideways and contorted. Liam sucked on a gashed knuckle as he peered around in the Stygian darkness.

"Shit," he said, voice echoing off the walls he couldn't see. "I'm an idiot."

Next to him, Baba let out a snort down that long nose he found so entrancing. "Not news to me," she said. "Any reason in particular you mention it now?"

"I left my flashlight in the cruiser," he said glumly. "I'd better go back and get it."

A silvery laugh prompted rustling sounds from the direction of the ceiling as bats chased the arcing notes into unseen spaces. Light sprang into existence, emanating in an eerie glow from the center of Baba's outstretched palm.

"Oh, right," Liam said, mentally kicking himself. "I forgot about that."

"Don't worry," Alexei said, patting him on the shoulder so hard it almost knocked him over. "You get used to the magic after a while. If it doesn't kill you first, of course. I can't wait to see what the queen has to say about Baba letting you in on all our secrets." His deep chuckle made Liam's bones vibrate.

As they entered the main passageway, the shimmer of light revealed low, uneven ceilings and cold, dank walls that dripped with slimy water, creating an obstacle course of murky puddles underfoot. Mold spotted the walls, and shards of jagged stones marked old rock falls, hinting at treacherous possibility.

Occasional squeaks and rustling noises made it clear that the place had its own inhabitants, although none of them came out to greet the intruders to their underground home.

"Um, Barbara?" he said after they'd been walking for a few minutes. "What did Alexei mean about the queen? I thought you worked in the human world; she's not your boss or anything, is she?"

Baba ducked under a stalactite. "Not technically," she said.

Mikhail rolled his eyes, the gesture barely visible in the darkness. "As if the queen cares about technicalities." He eeled gracefully around an outcropping that nearly took off Liam's arm. "The Babas' power is primarily tied to the mundane world, and that is where most of their responsibilities lie. They aren't even allowed to use magic in the Otherworld, since that would throw off the balance between the planes as much as Maya's use of magic on your side has. But their power and longevity is aided by the use of the Water of Life and Death, which is a gift from the queen."

"And the queen never gives gifts without expecting something in return," Gregori added in his usual calm tone. "In this case, the expectation is that while on the other side, the Baba Yagas will follow the queen's laws, and when the Otherworld needs to call on a Baba for help with a Human problem, that Baba will do whatever is necessary."

"Or else," Baba grumbled. "It's always fucking 'or else.'"

Liam shut up and kept walking.

Eventually, the main passage widened out into a small circular antechamber where Liam could straighten up. His neck and back ached from walking crouched over, and his knees protested the uneven ground. Baba, although almost his height, seemed completely unaffected, although a few cobwebs hung from the jeweled net that temporarily restrained her floating cloud of hair. The Riders all looked a little battered, especially the very large Alexei.

They stood there for a moment, catching their breath and staring at two identical tunnels that meandered off in opposite directions. There was nothing to indicate which one Maya had taken. Liam scanned the ground, hoping for a handy clue, like a tiny sneaker or maybe a pointing arrow marked "this way." There was nothing.

"Well, crap," he muttered. "Now what? Do we split up?"

Baba moved from one opening to the other, then pointed decisively down the tunnel that veered off to the left. "This one," she said.

Liam made a face. "More magic?" he asked.

She shook her head, the corner of her mouth twitching up in her trademark almost smile. She rooted herself in front of the opening on the right. "Come here and tell me what you smell."

Baffled, he followed her instructions, thinking she'd spent too much time living with a dog. Dragon. Whatever.

"It smells like cave," he said, wrinkling up his nose in distaste. "Wet, dirt, bat guano."

"Fine." Baba moved to the other opening. "And this one?"

Liam sniffed. "Wet, dirt . . . spring." His eyes widened as he caught a whiff of what smelled like flowers and sun and growing things.

"Exactly," Baba nodded. "That's the Otherworld. The door must be close. Come on." She hurried down the passage, leaving Liam and the others racing to catch up before the light vanished.

A few minutes later, musty dirt walls gave way to an archway that shimmered and shivered, filled with a mist that looked like moonlight swirled with a foggy morning's first rays of sunlight. It made his skin crawl and called to his psyche at the same time, in siren tones that would have made him long to walk into it even if Maya hadn't waited on the other side.

"Gotcha," Baba whispered, and took hold of his hand so

they walked through together, coming out the other side into an impossible land where everything looked the same, and yet indescribably different.

For starters, the sky was wrong. Three moons hung overhead, one of them slightly crooked as though it had fallen down and been put back up in a hurry. A light too dim to be sunlight but the wrong shade for night illuminated a stunning landscape of blue and purple trees; crimson grasses waving in a nonexistent breeze and dotted with flowers in colors he didn't even have names for. Unusually shaped birds flung themselves through the tinted sky, eerie and beautiful, as if carving dusk out of day.

"Welcome to the Otherworld," Baba said, letting go of his hand so she could pull her sword out of its scabbard. The long silvery length of it glittered dangerously in the moons' cold radiance, and Baba herself suddenly looked like something out of a fairy tale; both more beautiful and more deadly than she had ever seemed on the other side.

Perversely, Liam only found her more attractive—magic of its own kind, since he wouldn't have said that was possible.

"Wow," he said, for lack of a better word.

Baba sparked a rare grin, becoming just Barbara again. "Pretty, isn't it? I imagine it takes a bit of getting used to, when you've never been here before. Sadly, we don't have time to let you adjust slowly. We need to find Maya before she does any more damage."

Liam glanced around at the empty field and the trees that lay beyond it. There was no sign that anyone had ever walked here before them, not so much as a bent blade of grass or a hint of a path. "How?" he asked.

Grin widening, Baba pulled a long golden strand out of the velvet pouch hanging at her waist. It dangled from her fingers like something a poor miller's daughter had spun out of straw. "Remember this?"

He peered at it, more confused than ever. "That's the hair you took from Maya's car, right?"

"This," Baba stated triumphantly, "is one of Maya's

hairs." She laid it out carefully on the flat of her sword, where it adhered like, well, magic. "Since it is a part of her, it will be drawn back to where it came from—and lead us straight to Maya, no matter where she's hiding."

Alexei guffawed, although Liam still didn't understand, until Baba slowly swiveled in a semicircle, the sword held out straight in front of her like the divining rod Liam had once watched a gnarled old man use to locate a hidden spring. As it came even with a line of trees on either side of a shadowy lane, the strand of hair began to glow, dimming as the tip of the sword moved past, then brightening as she swung it back again.

"Handy," Liam exclaimed, as they started off down a gentle slope toward the trees. "They never taught us that one in the police academy."

A shrill cry broke through the quiet scene, and half a dozen centaurs charged out of the forest's edge, razor-edged silver swords slicing the air before them. At their backs, a motley array of sharp-toothed, long-clawed nasties ran or crawled or flew toward the new arrivals. None of them looked friendly, and all of them looked quite capable of inflicting serious damage.

Liam swallowed hard and reached for his gun, trying to figure out the best place to aim on a part man, part horse. "Since I don't have a sword, I hope my gun still works here."

Baba nodded, her eyes focused on the enemy ahead. "In some ways, it will work better here than it does at home, since most Otherworld creatures can't tolerate lead any more than they can cold iron."

He blew out a breath, marginally relieved to know he still had a functioning weapon. He hadn't been sure how the strange rules here might have affected something so strongly human in origin.

"Of course," she added in a matter-of-fact tone, "most of the beings here have never been to your land, so they don't even know what a gun is. They undoubtedly won't be afraid of it until you actually shoot one of them."

"Oh," Liam said. "In that case, let's hope it doesn't come

to that." But that didn't keep him from taking the weapon out and holding it in a firm grip. It might not scare the locals, but it sure as hell made him feel better.

Gregori nodded grimly at Baba, a wickedly bright silver scimitar in his hands. "You two go on and find the boy. We'll take care of this lot." He and the other two Riders started down the hill toward the oncoming horde, Alexei's eyes bright with berserker glee.

Liam looked at Baba uncertainly. "Shouldn't we help them? Three against dozens . . . it hardly seems fair." Blood-curdling cries rang out as the wave of creatures surged up around their three companions.

Baba just smiled her secretive little smile, as if she knew something he—and the enemy—didn't. "It really isn't fair. Even on a bad day, the Riders could wipe the floor with that bunch without even breaking a sweat. Besides, I think you mean four against dozens." She pointed up at the sky, where a brilliant red dragon was swooping down from the shadow of the largest moon, causing a ruby-hued eclipse.

"What the hell is that?" Liam asked, as they pelted down the hillside past the gory battle being waged on their behalf. Fur and blood flew through the air, green and blue and crimson.

Baba's eyes twinkled. "That," she said, "is Koshei. Glorious, isn't he?"

And then they just ran, following the glowing light on the edge of Baba's sword, onward toward a small boy who was depending on them to find him and bring him home.

TWENTY-NINE

THE SHINING HAIR on the silver sword led them through treelined paths of emerald green and past barren shores where crusted eddies of salt were the only evidence of long-vanished seas. Even the weird and uncanny areas had their own eerie beauty, with the exception of some spots where the fabric of the land seemed warped and distorted, crumpled in on itself in sickly shades of olive gray and mottled brown mixed with a twisted licorice black.

As they sidled past a section where rocks had melted into hissing puddles of molten lava that ate away at everything in its path, Liam asked Baba, "Is this normal? I mean, as much as you can use a word like that in a land like this?"

She shook her head, dislodging a lingering cobweb, and glanced around them with a sigh. "No. Not at all. What you're seeing is the effect of Maya's overuse of a doorway that wasn't supposed to exist in the first place. There is a reason that such things are closely monitored and controlled. Magic has its own rules, and when you break them, well . . . bad things happen."

She gestured at the grim destruction around them. "This

is why the queen was so adamant about finding Maya and the doorway and putting a stop to the imbalance. If it goes on long enough, it could destroy the entire Otherworld, or turn it into something even more unpredictable than it already is."

An odd rustling noise in the underbrush made Liam jump. He glanced over his shoulder, but didn't see anything besides straggly brown bushes that dangled with dayglow orange berries, as if someone had glued the contents of a package of Cheetos to a shrubbery. He shuddered, feeling the hairs go up on the back of his neck.

"I think something may be following us," he said to Baba in a low voice. "Or a bunch of somethings."

Her full lips compressed into a thin line. "Yep, they've been out there for a while. I don't know if they work for Maya, or are just some curious locals trying to figure out if we're edible." At Liam's startled glance, she waved her sword menacingly. "Don't worry, they're not likely to bother us. For some reason, the creatures of the Otherworld find me a bit threatening." An evil smirk lit her eyes from within.

"Huh," Liam said, not feeling at all reassured. He tightened his grip on his gun, just in case.

THE TRAIL LED them to a huge, crooked house like a great mansion built of enormous white boulders and roughly hewn trees, lopsided and misshapen, yet still impressive in its own way. Baba swung the sword to and fro, but it stubbornly insisted on pointing toward the shambling wreck of a dwelling.

"Well, *shit*," Baba said with feeling. *This was not good. Not good at all.*

Liam turned to her, startled. "What's the matter, did we lose her? Did the hair stop working?"

"Sadly, no," Baba said, plucking the hair from the sword and tucking it back in her pouch. "Maya is definitely in there. But I know whose house this is, and she's not going to be happy to see us." She sheathed her sword, and gestured for Liam to put his gun back in its holster.

"Are you sure?" he asked. "The place looks pretty creepy."

"You have no idea," Baba said. "But I assure you, if I can't talk our way out of this, weapons probably won't do us any good."

She led the way up to the massive front door, considered knocking, then shrugged and just walked in, Liam on her heels. Once inside, the entire house revealed itself to be one sprawling, filthy room, lit mainly by the reddish glow of a fire laid in a hearth big enough to roast an entire ox with space to spare. Faint additional light slipped apologetically through smudged windows, as if it knew it had no business being there.

Liam smothered a gasp as his eyes adjusted to the murky dimness, and Baba put out a reassuring hand. Not that she felt all that reassured herself.

Maya was there, all right, along with a frightened, crying boy wearing a blue Yankees cap, a yellow shirt, and denim shorts, now torn and dirty, as if he'd been dragged through mud and brambles. Behind the two of them stood a gigantic woman with one filmy eye in the middle of her forehead and a necklace of bones around her neck. The bones looked alarmingly human.

"No wonder the poor kid is crying," Liam whispered in Baba's ear. "I'm a little tempted to do it myself. What the hell is that?"

"Not what," Baba whispered back. "Who. Don't be rude." She bowed politely to the giantess and said in a loud voice, "Good day, Mistress Zorica. I am very sorry to intrude upon your home, but this woman has something that does not belong to her and we are here to take it back."

Maya sneered at Baba. "Pretty words from one who has already lost the battle. I have given the lovely Zorica this child as a gift. You are too late."

The giantess peered nearsightedly at Baba and Liam. "Baba Yaga, is that you? Why is this any concern of yours?" She pouted, her pendulous lower lip thrust out and sausage-shaped arms crossed over an immense sagging bosom. The ragged dress she wore looked as though it had started life as a circus tent. Twenty or thirty years ago. "I have already given up most of my power in exchange for this child to light up my lonely days. I am not inclined to give him back, to you or anyone else. Go away and leave me be."

At this, poor Petey cried even harder, and Baba had to hold Liam's wrist in an iron grip to keep him from going to the boy.

"I am sorry to be the bearer of bad news, Mistress Zorica, but the queen has sworn to punish this woman, Maya, and anyone who aids her. She has caused great injury to the fabric of the Otherworld, and the queen is sorely vexed with her."

The giantess blanched and covered her single eye with one meaty paw. "I only wanted a little company, Baba Yaga. It is lonely here all by myself. Tell the queen I meant no harm. Perhaps she'll let me keep the child, yes?"

"No," Baba said firmly. "You know quite well that no Otherworld denizen may keep a Human child against his will. This boy was stolen from a loving mother. He must be returned to her."

Her voice softened. "I know your heart was set on keeping him, but perhaps we can find you a nice giant cat instead." *Or maybe something sturdier, like a small pachyderm.* "Come with us to court and explain to the queen how Maya tricked you into giving up your power to her, and perhaps Her Majesty will be lenient, and forgive your crime. But it would be better for you to tell her yourself. We're taking Maya there now; will you come with us and plead your case?"

The giantess wavered and Maya spat on the packed-dirt floor. "Oh for heaven's sake, Zorica, you are four times her size. You can snap Baba Yaga like a twig, and have her pet Human for dessert. The queen need never know you have the child." She put on a wheedling smile. "You know you want to keep him. Just kill Baba Yaga for me, and you won't have to grow old all alone, pitiful and scorned in this ugly tumbledown hovel."

Zorica scowled, her face as terrible as a summer storm. "What did you say about my house? Humph. You want Baba Yaga dead, kill her yourself."

"See?" Baba whispered to Liam, whose hand still hovered hesitantly over his gun. "Rude. Not a good idea." To Zorica, she said, "The queen has declared this woman's life forfeit to the crown for her crimes. I am taking her in to court. It would be best for you not to interfere." She bowed again, even deeper.

"I'm not going anywhere with you," Maya said, pulling out a sword of her own that glowed a sickly poisonous green in the dim light of Zorica's huge room. "I'll kill the boy before I let you take him back. And then I will happily kill you too." Rage distorted her exquisite face and turned her as ugly as the giantess standing above her.

Terrified, Petey started to wail in earnest, and Maya reached out the hand not holding the sword and delivered a vicious slap across his tear-stained face that sent his small body tumbling to the floor. "*Shut up*, you stupid little troll. Your noise hurts my ears."

Baba felt a surge of fury rush up from the toes of her black leather boots and straight to her jewel-netted head. Flashes of lightning seemed to reverberate through the room as she leaped the space between her and the Rusalka, her silver sword in her hand without any conscious intention of drawing it. Since she couldn't use magic here, and Maya could, Baba knew her only chance was to strike first and end this fight before the other woman could use her advantage.

Luckily, that would be a distinct pleasure.

"You. Do. Not. Hit. Children." Each word came out with a slashing strike from her sword as she backed the other woman toward the rear of the cavernous house. "Never, ever, again."

Maya fought back viciously, parrying thrust after thrust,

but she was clearly less practiced than Baba, who had spent her formative years sparring in the forest with Alexei until she could fight in her sleep. Finally, a twisting flick of the wrist sent Maya's sword flying across the room and into the back of a chair, where it hung, quivering for a moment, before the wooden chair started to sizzle and char.

Maya's crimson-tipped fingers curved into claws, and she barred teeth that suddenly looked sharper than they had a moment before. "You will never take me, bitch!" she shrilled. "Come, fight me with your bare hands and I will show you which of us is stronger!" A shimmering ball of magic began to form in the air above her head.

Liam made a protesting noise as Baba placed her sword gently on the floor. But she'd been waiting for this moment for a long time. Besides, it would be rude to turn down such an invitation, and it never paid to be rude in a giantess's home.

Maya had a moment to gloat before Baba hauled back her arm and punched the Rusalka in the face with every ounce of energy she had. She channeled all her anger over stolen children, tormented farmers, her own ruined reputation, a disintegrating Otherworld, and most of all, every single lie that Maya had told about good, honest, wonderful Liam into one glorious, long-overdue blow. Maya slid to the floor with a whimper and lay still.

"And I think you meant to say 'witch,'" Baba said to the unconscious form at her feet.

The sound of applause brought her back down to earth, and she turned around to see Liam clapping his hands, a huge grin on his handsome face. Little Petey launched himself across the room and into the arms of the only person in the room who hadn't terrified him, holding on for dear life, and Liam's applause turned into a hug as the boy threatened to strangle him with his limpet grip.

"Don't worry, Petey. You're safe now," he said reassuringly, trying to move the boy's arms from around his neck. "This nice lady and I are going to take you back to your mama."

Baba looked down at Maya's limp body. "Just as soon as we run one little errand." She heaved Maya over her shoulder with a grunt and headed out the door, followed by Liam and Petey, and trailed by a dolorous giantess in a large flowered tent.

"So, Petey," Baba said. "How do you feel about meeting a real live queen and giving her a present?"

THIRTY

CLOSER TO THE palace, the Otherworld had managed to hold on to its enchanting beauty, although every once in a while Baba spotted a wilting flower or a jagged thorn on a rose that should have had none. As their strange parade neared the throne room, armed guards carrying curved silver rapiers stepped forward to stop them. But one look at Baba and her burden and they just shrugged and stepped aside. The giantess didn't merit a second glance. This was the Otherworld, after all.

They stepped through a pair of twelve-foot-tall black onyx doors carved with fantastical animals into a magnificent room with a vaulted ceiling so high, even Zorica was dwarfed by it. Baba heard Liam's gasp of wonder as he took in the pure white birch trees that grew in measured splendor along a grass-carpeted floor to form a path that led to the throne. A fountain chortled merrily in the middle of the room, throwing rainbows over the crystal chairs scattered nearby. Colorful birds with long, elegant tails flew in and out of its sparkling droplets.

Nobles lounged around the fountain or leaned decoratively

against the ivory walls, most of them tall and stunningly beautiful to human eyes. Pointed ears poked through the long golden hair of some, while others had bodies that you had to look at twice to notice appendages that no normal mortal bore. Curious glances followed them as the courtiers cleared a path for Baba and her party as they made their way across the grass until it was replaced by tiles of green malachite and blue lapis, sparkling with gold-inlaid patterns that told tales of days gone by.

The queen and her consort sat on thrones carved from trees that still lived beneath them, sending out roots and buds and leaves like a tapestry around their feet. The queen raised one perfect eyebrow at the sight of her unexpected guests, and let slip a chilly smile.

"Welcome, Baba Yaga," she said, not bothering to rise. "About time you got here. What on earth have you been up to?"

Baba dropped Maya's flaccid body to the floor, not particularly gently, and gave a deep bow. Next to her, Zorica did the same, and Liam managed to copy them with reasonable grace, despite the small boy hiding behind him and clinging to one leg.

"Just doing as you asked, Your Majesty," she said, gesturing toward the unconscious woman. "This is the person responsible for the current imbalance that troubles the Otherworld. She is a Rusalka, and calls herself Maya, at least in the Human world."

The queen looked down her patrician nose at Baba's gift. "A Rusalka? Impossible. They are weak creatures, only capable of killing and minor mayhem. We discussed this."

"I'm afraid this one has been trading Human children to some of your most powerful subjects in exchange for a portion of their power, Your Highness," Baba explained. "And using it in the Human world to exact revenge for the Human destruction of the water system, which has begun to affect even these lands. I cannot tell you if that was her main goal, or if it was primarily the power she gained from stealing innocent children and bringing them here through the doorway she found. Either way, the result has been dire, as you well know."

"Indeed I do," the queen said, the tiniest hint of a wrinkle creasing her high pale forehead. A diamond-covered crown sat on the top of her pale, silvery hair. She ignored the comment about her court. "So, you have found this door for me, as I commanded?"

"Yes, Majesty. And reclaimed her latest victim, as you can see." Baba indicated Petey, who hung on to to Liam's leg as he gazed around the room with openmouthed wonder.

The queen actually smiled when she saw the child looking at her, although the expression faded like falling leaves in autumn as her glance moved to the one-eyed giantess standing behind them.

"And you, Zorica, what do you have to do with this mess?"

The giantess threw herself down in front of the throne, making the tiles underfoot quiver and shake until her weight settled. "I was a fool, Your Majesty! This creature came to me and offered me a child in exchange for a portion of my magic. I was so lonely. It was selfish, I know, but I had no idea it would cause so much harm." She began to cry, huge globules of viscous tears that stained her ragged dress a pallid blue-gray.

The queen aimed a steely glance at the large woman, and then sent it out to encompass the surrounding courtiers, who had all gathered to see what the fuss was about.

"You are *not* excused from your part in this, Zorica. You knew perfectly well that stealing Human children has been forbidden here for centuries." The queen's scowl caused nearby flowers to droop and leaves to fall off the trees. A few nobles looked as though they might follow suit.

"You may not have been aware that this Maya intended to use her ill-gotten magical powers outside these realms, but all who abide here know that such actions could throw the entire Otherworld out of balance, as has clearly happened." She took her consort's hand, as if to gather strength from him in the face of such betrayal. "I assure you, we *shall* be getting to the bottom of this."

The queen raised an eyebrow again, this time looking from Baba to Liam.

"My apologies, Highness," Baba said, quickly taking Liam's arm and leading him forward one step. "This is Liam McClellan, a Human who has aided our cause at great risk to himself and to his position back in the mortal plane. He is what they call a sheriff; it is his job to enforce the laws there." She gave Liam a mischievous smile. "He only arrested me once, so I think I can safely say he has been very kind."

The queen inclined her head gracefully in Liam's direction. "She is quite trying at times, our Baba. You clearly used great restraint." Courtiers at either side of the throne snickered, but she quelled their mirth with a glance.

Baba held her breath as she waited to see if the queen was angry about her bringing Liam along. Technically, it was against the rules, but he *had* helped Baba to fulfill the task the queen had given her. Hopefully that would excuse them both.

"So, what do you think of our world, Sir Sheriff?"

Liam looked around him at the amazing glory of the Otherworld. "You have a very beautiful land, er . . . Your Majesty. As remarkable as its queen. Can the damage be fixed?"

The queen nodded benignly, and Baba started breathing again. "Indeed it can. Once I take back all the extra power Maya has been hoarding, and close the door she has been using to travel back and forth between the worlds, the balance will slowly begin to restore itself. Another millennia or two and you will never be able to see the difference." She seemed to run out of patience for chitchat and snapped her fingers at a nearby impish-looking creature, clearly some kind of servant.

"Wake her," the queen commanded.

The bat-eared manikin fetched a bucket, filled it from the fountain, and threw it on Maya's prone form. The Rusalka woke with a sputter and jumped to her feet, looking around with wide eyes when she found herself in the throne room. But she regained her poise rapidly and curtsied low to the queen, casting a vicious sideways glance in Baba's direction.

Baba just smiled sweetly and lifted one finger. Liam choked back a laugh.

"Your Majesty! Your Highness!" Maya bowed again at the queen and her consort, who stroked his pointed black beard and gazed back dispassionately. "Whatever this horrible witch has told you, you can't believe her. She has been stealing children with the help of her Human lover, and bringing them here to sell them." As usual, her musical voice was charming and persuasive, and she clearly expected it to have its usual result. "I was trying to get back here to warn you when she ambushed me. You have to believe me!"

The queen curled her perfect lips in a haughty sneer. "Save your breath. I am no foolish mortal to be taken in by your lies. Besides, this giantess has confirmed the Baba's version of the tale, and admitted to conniving with you. No doubt others have done the same, despite my wish to believe otherwise."

She rose and descended from the throne, walking down the polished arc of stairs to stand in front of Maya. The queen's height and dignity made the other woman seem even more petite than usual.

"How *dare* you trifle with my kingdom, you selfish Rusalka?" The queen said, ice dripping from every word. "How dare you?"

Incredibly, Maya stared the queen in the eye, not backing down from her sovereign's rage. "I am no mere Rusalka now," she said. "I have amassed great power. I will fight you if I have to."

The queen threw back her head and laughed; melodious peals of effervescent sound like bubbles in the sparkling air. "Idiot," she said, almost fondly. "I am the queen. I can tap into the power of every being within the Otherworld. What you have accumulated is but a trickle in the floodwaters of my magic, and I can take it from you with a snap of my fingers."

Maya opened her mouth again—to argue perhaps or to plead for mercy—but the queen just said, "Enough. I'm done with this." As she'd promised, her long slim fingers snapped once, twice, three times, and a golden mist lifted from Maya and floated serenely into the stately monarch standing in front of her.

For a moment, Maya remained shrouded in a luminous fog, but when it lifted, what remained bore little resemblance to the beautiful blonde who'd been the bane of Baba's recent existence. In her place, there was only a pale, scrawny water creature with straggly seaweed-colored hair and a fierce expression accented by pointy teeth in a too-long jaw.

Liam took an involuntary step back. "Holy crap," he said in a low voice. "Is that what she really looks like?" Petey hid his face against Liam's leg.

Baba just smiled. "Yes indeed. Not so pretty now, is she?" The Rusalka hissed at her, dripping murky water onto the floor. "It takes energy to maintain a glamour as sophisticated as the one she wore, and she no longer has that power, thanks to the queen."

The queen drifted over to stand in front of Baba and Liam, her movements so graceful she seemed not to touch the ground.

"It is I who should thank you, Baba Yaga," the queen said regally. "I, my beloved consort, and all who live in this magical land. You have done Us a great service on this day, and We are truly grateful." The royal *We* was quite clear in her tone.

"Is there any gift We might give you in return? Jewels, perhaps, or a chest of gold?" She glanced around the throne room in the manner of one who had mislaid her car keys. "I do believe We had one of those around here somewhere." Courtiers started looking around, one going so far as to peek behind the king's throne.

Baba inclined her head. "I have no need for jewels nor gold, Majesty, although I appreciate the generous offer. In truth, there is but one favor I require in return for finding the door and the troublesome creature who abused it."

"Indeed? And what would that be, pray tell?" The queen's haughty demeanor made it clear that Baba was walking a fine line between asking for too much, and not asking for enough.

It didn't matter, though; there was only one thing Baba needed, and she didn't intend to leave until she had it.

"The children," Baba said, and Liam straightened up beside her, Petey still gripping his leg with both tiny arms. "I ask you to help me reclaim the other children Maya stole, so I might return them to their sorrowing parents, in the world where they belong."

"Indeed, the children," the queen said. She mounted the steps to her throne and sat, leaning in close to confer with her strikingly attractive consort. For all his glory, the king was not quite as reserved as his mate, and his warm emerald eyes held just a hint of a twinkle as he glanced down at Baba and her motley group.

The giantess edged away as subtly as an overweight twelve-foot-tall woman can, obviously not at all convinced that the royals would take the request well.

After more muttered discussion, the queen sat up and directed her incandescent purple stare at Baba. "I am more than willing to grant this very reasonable boon, especially since the kidnapping of children is against our strictest laws," the queen said slowly. "But there is one problem. I do not know where this creature"—she sneered at a sullen and adamantly silent Maya, dripping wetly on the malachite and lapis tiles—"has hidden the small Humans.

"I am, of course, quite willing to torture her until she tells me," the queen continued blithely. "But that might take some time, and by then, it may be too late to return the children." She scowled impressively. "And, of course, there is always the chance that I might accidentally kill her in the process. Torture is such an imperfect science."

She looked around the room, her chiseled amethyst gaze swinging from one elegant, well-dressed aristocrat to another. "If what the Baba Yaga has said is true, and some of my own courtiers are involved in this heinous crime, it would be best if the guilty parties stepped forward and returned the children at once before I am forced to take such drastic measures."

Silence greeted this announcement. No one moved. Empty stares and blank faces were the only response.

Liam stirred restlessly, but Baba patted his arm to reassure him. Most of her dealings with the wily Maya had been spur-of-the-moment improvisation, but Baba had been laying tentative plans for this part of the process since her first visit to court.

"I believe I may have the solution to that problem, Your Majesty," Baba said, smiling benignly around the assembled company. "In fact, your own great gifts should lead us to those who have been dealing in secret with Maya, trading their power for the children they now refuse to give up."

"Is that so?" the queen said, the tiniest suggestion of confusion shadowing her hawklike imperial glare. "In what way, exactly?"

Baba did her best to project absolute confidence; right now, attitude was everything. "When you reclaimed the power that the Rusalka had taken from her misguided partners, presumably you sent it back to its original owners in order to begin to correct the imbalance in the land. Am I right?"

The queen nodded. "Of course." Unspoken was the word, *So?*

"As Your Majesty so clearly explained earlier, you are connected to the energy of everything in your kingdom," Baba went on. "This means you have the ability to scan everyone in the room and see who has suddenly received a major influx of power, say, in the last few minutes. Those people, obviously, will be the ones who gave their power to Maya, and therefore, the ones who have the children."

She held her breath and stared at the queen, willing her to understand. Around them, there were uneasy rustlings and whispers behind gilded bone fans. Feet shuffled restlessly. A slow smile crept like a glacier across the queen's face, and one shimmering eyelid slid half closed in a nearly invisible wink as she figured out Baba's ploy.

"Ah, yes," the queen drawled. "Very clever, Baba Yaga." She stood up at the top of the steps and scanned the crowd, one delicate hand moving from one edge of the circle that surrounded them to the other.

Baba gave an imperceptible nod, and the queen's finger reached out to point. By the time the second person had been speared by that finger, the rest stepped forward on their own, a couple of the women weeping openly, their mates white-lipped and shaken.

Baba breathed a sigh of relief, not caring if anyone saw, and sent out a silent but heartfelt *thank you* to Alexei, who had taught her the fine art of bluffing at the same time he'd taught her to fight.

"That was amazing," Liam said, grabbing her hand without seeming to realize it. "I had no idea the queen could do that."

"Neither did she," Baba said, "I just made it up."

Liam blinked. "You what?"

Baba shrugged, too tense to gloat. She'd gambled and won. It could just as easily have gone the other way, and the children been lost forever.

"I suggested that the queen had the ability to sense where the energy returned to, even though I was fairly certain that she would only have felt the energy go—not where it went. Her Majesty is incredibly smart; I hoped that she'd catch on, and we'd be able to trick those who worked with Maya into giving themselves away."

"But—but, she pointed right at them," Liam stuttered.

"Like I said, she's a quick study. You don't get to rule an empire for thousands of years by being stupid." Baba watched with a certain detachment as the queen dispatched a dozen heavily armed guards to escort the three unhappy couples to fetch the children.

"When I was here before and mentioned in court that I thought Maya was giving the children to powerful members of the kingdom, I noticed a few suspiciously guilty looks and twitchy eyes. Since I had no way to prove that any of those people were involved, I didn't say anything at the time.

But I signaled to the queen about the couple I was most sure of, and the rest assumed she would be able to pick them out next, and simply gave themselves away." She squeezed his hand. "Thank goodness, since I didn't have a Plan B. Unless you count 'knocking heads together until someone confesses' a plan."

Liam gazed at her in amazement and something that looked frighteningly like awe. "Remind me never to play poker with you," he said. And kissed her lightly on the lips, despite the glowering looks they were getting from most of the remaining members of the court.

Baba's chuckle was interrupted by a flurry of movement and twittering voices as the guards returned, herding Maya's partners in crime and three small children. The oldest, a girl of about seven, carried the youngest, a boy who couldn't have been much more than two. The youngsters looked dazed and confused, except one small pig-tailed girl with brown hair, brown eyes, and a stubborn chin.

"Sheriff Mac!" she yelled, as she caught a glimpse of Liam, and ran across the floor to be scooped up into his arms.

"Mary Elizabeth!" Liam said. "Boy, is your mama going to be happy to see you!" Baba thought she saw tears shimmering in his eyes.

Baba seemed to be having some kind of problem with her eyes as well. Some kind of exotic dander from one of the queen's menagerie, no doubt. But the soon-to-be-ex-parents were in much worse shape. One slender, fantastically beautiful woman with long pink hair and a flowing dress made up of gauzy sky-blue silks and twinkling star-studded organdy was on her knees in front of the royal couple, begging pitifully to be allowed to keep the child she'd been hiding in a secret underground lair filled with toys and candy.

The child in question huddled with the other kids near Liam and Baba, too stunned and confused to do more than stand in silent unity with those they recognized as humans.

The queen shook her head, a hint of pity amid the frigid

harshness of her gaze. "I cannot reward behavior that could have destroyed the entire Otherworld. The rule against stealing Human children exists for a reason. It was that act which caused us to be hunted and reviled in the mundane world, forcing us to leave behind all our sacred spaces there and retreat to the safety of this realm, only to return now and then on those days, like the summer solstice and All Hallows Eve, when our power is strong."

"But the Humans no longer even believe we exist," another man protested. "They will not hunt what they do not acknowledge as real!"

"Will they not?" the king interjected, gesturing at Liam and Baba. "Will they not move mountains to track down and retrieve that which belongs to them? I say that evidence to the contrary stands before you now. The queen is right. There can be no condoning an action that puts us all at risk. And certainly no rewarding it."

The pink-haired woman staggered to her feet, holding on to her mate as she swung around to search out the child that had been so briefly hers. "But, Majesty, everyone knows that Humans do not value their children as we do ours. And they have so many, and we have so few. How can it be wrong to take one or two for our own?"

Liam took a halting step forward, hampered by Petey's limpet grip on one leg, still holding Mary Elizabeth in his arms. Baba's heart swelled with pride as he stood in front of the court and spoke out in a strong voice.

"You're not completely wrong," he said. "There are some humans who treat their children badly. But most of them love their children more than life itself, and would do anything for them." He pointed his chin at Mary Elizabeth, since both his hands were full. "This little girl's mother went so far as to seek out the Baba Yaga for help, no matter what the cost. All these children have parents at home who have been suffering agonies of sorrow, fear, and loss since they were stolen. They are not prizes to be argued over. They are loved and treasured, and Baba and I are taking them home where they belong."

The queen nodded sadly. "Well said, mortal. And so it will be. The rule will be obeyed and all those who are fool-hardy enough to break it shall be punished most severely."

She reached out one pale, long-fingered hand to stroke Mary Elizabeth's hair. "It is a pity, though. They are so lovely, and they bring such youthful joy to this ancient world."

Liam looked around at all the gloomy despondent faces, the weeping women and stony-faced men. Baba saw the moment when a spark of an idea kindled behind those kind hazel eyes.

"What are you thinking?" she whispered, a little con-cerned. They were about to walk out of here with all the children *and* their skins intact, something she'd had very little hope would happen. Liam didn't know the Otherworld like she did; a single ill-spoken word could still get them turned into swans. And she'd make a terrible swan.

But he just handed Mary Elizabeth to her, and pried Petey's arms off of his leg, attaching them around Baba's instead. Then he swept a deep bow to the queen and said, "Your Majesty, if you'll allow me, I may have a suggestion."

One perfect eyebrow raised, the queen gathered her skirts and seated herself back on her throne. "I'm listening," she said.

Baba held her breath and seriously considered taking up prayer for the first time in her long life.

"As Baba explained," Liam said with a grave expression, "I am a sheriff. It is my job to enforce the laws of my com-munity, much as you enforce yours."

The queen nodded.

"It is true, as one of your subjects pointed out, that not all children are as lucky as these ones. Some are unwanted, even abused." There was a disapproving rumble from the surrounding crowd, but Liam ignored them, speaking only to the queen and her consort.

"In my years as sheriff, I have sometimes come across children who were terribly mistreated; damaged in ways that scarred them mentally and physically, leaving them broken in ways that no one can fix. These children will likely never be adopted, or be able to create happy, normal lives for themselves as adults."

"That is a terrible disgrace," the queen said. "You should be ashamed to be part of a race that would do such things."

Liam sighed. "Sometimes I am, Your Majesty, sometimes I am. But the point is this: if I understand Baba correctly, the children who are brought from our world into this one eventually forget everything about where they came from, and who they were. Is that right?"

The queen lifted her head, her long neck straightening as the meaning of his words sunk in. "Are you saying you would voluntarily bring us such children to raise as our own?" Around the circle that surrounded them, glimmers of hope began to appear, as beautiful and uplifting as the phoenixes that soared overhead.

He nodded. "There would not be many, god willing, but there will always be an unfortunate few for whom forgetting would be a mercy. They would undoubtedly be difficult, in the beginning, until their memories start to fade. But if you can assure me that such children would be treated well, and cared for tenderly while they healed, I would be willing to do so, yes." It was clear to Baba that he had at least one particular child in mind, perhaps one he'd been unable to help through conventional means. Children were Liam's soft spot, just as they were hers.

Baba hugged Mary Elizabeth to her chest, her heart so full she could barely contain it. She would never have thought of such a thing, but it was a perfect solution, both for the children and those who would finally be able to have a child to call their own. No one would lose a child they loved, and perhaps some good could come from the evil humans sometimes visited upon their innocent and defenseless young. As a Baba Yaga, she wished she'd thought of it herself, years ago.

"We would have to work out a way to communicate," Liam added. "And it might be tricky to explain the disappearance of even those who are not truly wanted by anyone."

The king smiled benignly. "That part is easy. In the old days, we would create a changeling—an exact facsimile of the child we'd taken, made out of wood and animated through magic. The problem then was that most parents could detect the difference, since changelings cannot truly mimic Human emotions and actions. But since, as you say, these particular children are damaged and unwanted, it is likely that no one would notice, or else be simply relieved that the younglings were now more docile and well behaved. And the amount of magic needed for such a thing is minute; it should not affect the balance between our worlds."

Liam nodded, and Baba exhaled a sigh of relief. It was settled, the queen was happy, and now they could go home.

Unfortunately, this blissful thought was interrupted by a high-pitched, caterwauling shriek that rang out across the room like fingernails on a chalkboard.

THIRTY-ONE

LIAM'S HEART SHATTERED into a million pieces at the sight of Melissa, writhing between two burly guards, each of whom had a firm grip on one skinny arm. Her face was a mess of torn skin, pink and blotchy from crying, and her red hair was ragged and dirty, hanging in long stringy clumps. She was barely recognizable as the sweet, attractive woman he'd once called his wife. In front of the trio, another guard walked next to a small girl with asymmetrical pixie-cut dark hair, a snub nose, and a solemn demeanor. She looked to be about six years old, too young to be so self-possessed. Melissa's wails cut across the room like a scythe, making all heads turn in her direction and scattering the birds overhead to safer perches far up in the rafters.

He took an involuntary step in her direction, stomach churning and hands clenched, but Baba stopped him.

"Wait," she said quietly. "I know this is hard to witness, but wait." She patted his back lightly, three quick taps that were like a bear hug coming from anyone else. So he waited, although he felt as though his soul was being flayed and shredded.

"What is this?" the queen asked, disgust flitting across her normally impassive countenance. She narrowed her eyes at the lead guard. "Who are these people?"

"You ordered us to search Maya's residence, Majesty, once Zorica told us how to find it," the warrior said, nodding in the giantess's direction. She huddled in one corner of the throne room, trying to make herself seem smaller and failing miserably. "We found these two Humans there and assumed that the child was one of those who had been taken. So we brought them both to you."

Next to Liam, Baba wrinkled her long nose. "I thought you said there were only three children missing," she whispered. "Do you know who that child is?"

He peered more closely at the dark-eyed sprite, who gazed coolly back in his direction, but he didn't recognize her. "There were only three. Maya must have stolen this one from somewhere else."

"Is this one of yours?" the queen asked Liam.

He shook his head. "No, Your Majesty."

"Explain this," the queen demanded of Maya. "Who are these Humans and what are they doing in my realm?"

The Rusalka let out a dramatic puffed-air sigh that reminded Liam of the teenagers he occasionally arrested for shoplifting or spray-painting graffiti on historical landmarks. But she'd apparently decided that she had nothing to lose by complying with the queen's demands, now that she had lost her last playing piece in the game.

Or perhaps she simply wanted an opportunity to brag about her own cleverness, despite the end results.

"I found this woman a couple of years ago," Maya said, pointy chin held proudly in the air. "She had accidentally wandered through a newly opened portal—caused by the disruption of the earth the Humans call hydrofracking— dazed from abusing her body with alcohol and who knows what else. Her mind was so far gone, she barely even noticed she was in a different world." She rolled her murky sea glass eyes at the frailty of mortals.

"I took her home with me and cleaned her up, fed her,

and, once I had convinced her to show me the location of the door, procured an infant to replace the one whose death had caused her to fall so far into despair and madness."

Liam's rage warred with his sorrow like rival boxers in a grudge match at hearing this depressing tale. Poor Melissa—not run away with the circus after all, but lost down a rabbit hole to a fantastical world, then falling into the clutches of a selfish, ambitious creature who used a shattered and despairing woman to further her own demented plans. He suddenly felt as bloodthirsty as Baba, wishing he had torn Maya apart with his bare hands when he'd had the chance.

Baba heard the little growl at the back of his throat and gave him a tiny crooked smile in sympathy. "Wait," she said again. "We need to hear this." *Pat. Pat. Pat.*

"And where, pray tell, did you get the infant?" the king interjected, nodding at the small child. "I assume this is she?"

Maya shrugged, seaweed hair flopping around her shoulders. "Once I had access to the door, I began to explore the world beyond. Not far from where the portal opened, there was an isolated farmstead. I killed the parents, took the child, and burned the place to the ground. It was quite simple." A regretful look flitted over her pallid face.

"Alas, even the dim-witted Humans would have suspected something if I used the same trick twice, so once the woman had been calmed enough by her new baby to be able to give me useful information, I started simply stealing the children away. The added fear and misery this caused was even more fun than watching that building burn to smoking ashes." A horrible sharp-toothed smile accompanied the agreeable memory.

"I remember that fire," Liam said, shocked. "We assumed the baby had perished with her parents. But that was only eight months ago." He pointed at the little girl. "The baby wasn't even a year old. This child must be at least five or six."

The queen shrugged. "Time flows strangely here in the Otherworld, and differently for different Humans. Do your tales not tell of those who ventured here for a day or a month, only to discover that many years had passed when they returned home, and all those they'd loved were dead and they themselves forgotten?"

The blood rushed from his face, but Baba said reassuringly, "Don't worry; the Baba Yagas are immune to this effect, so we can come and go as needed between the worlds. And since you've been with me, you should be fine. No more time will have passed back home than we have perceived here."

He drew in a shaky breath. "Oh. Good."

But then she added, "Obviously for Melissa, though, it has been years, and for all that time she had been raising this child as if it were her own." And his heart plummeted to the tiled floor again, lying there in smoking ruins like the farmhouse Maya had burned.

"Melissa?" The queen's sharp ears had been following their conversation. "You know this Human woman?"

Liam gave another shallow bow, although his spirit wasn't in it. "Her name is Melissa McClellan, Your Majesty. And she is—was—my wife. She disappeared two years ago. I had no idea she was here." He swallowed hard. "When she disappeared, I assumed she'd run away."

The queen's expression softened slightly. "Then the baby she lost was yours?" She inclined her head. "We are sorry for your loss. It is a dreadful thing, to lose a child."

Then the queen glanced from him, standing upright in his uniform, to the wreck that was Melissa, her gaze fixed on the dark-haired child as she alternated crooning at the girl and screaming obscenities at the guards who held them apart.

"You seem to have borne up better under the hardship," the queen said in a wry understatement. "It's a pity."

Liam lowered his eyes to the ground, seeing a distant, happy past rather than gemstone tiles and fanciful designs. He sighed. "Yes, Your Majesty. It is."

"And what do you propose to do with this unexpected child, Baba Yaga?" the king asked. "You were told that you might take all the children back to their homes as your reward for aiding this kingdom. I am sure my beloved consort would agree that this child falls under that agreement."

Baba turned to Liam, her expression bemused. "Huh. What do you think, Liam? Does she have anyone waiting for her at home?"

He pondered the question as he looked across the expanse of floor at the self-contained yet somehow impish-looking girl. "I don't recall the family having any close relatives. And even if there were some, frankly, I'm not sure how I'd explain a baby that was now a six-year-old, even though less than a year has passed. Thank goodness that hadn't happened yet with any of the other children." He shook his head. "But I can't see leaving her here either. Especially with Melissa." The idea was appalling.

"That's a point." Baba stared at the child, looking thoughtful. She tapped one slim finger against her lips. "I might have a solution. Do you mind if I try something?"

Hell, it wasn't as though he had any better ideas. "Go right ahead." *This should be interesting.*

Even the queen looked intrigued as Baba walked over to where the child stood, taking in the exotic court scene with wide dark brown eyes.

"Hello," Baba said, kneeling down so she was at the same height as the little girl. "My name is Baba Yaga. Do you have a name?"

The little girl blinked, throwing a glance over her shoulder at where Melissa stood, still now, her head hanging down. "The Mother calls me Hannah," she said, with a tone that implied she wasn't all that thrilled with the woman she called "the Mother" or the name, or both.

Liam winced when he heard the name. But of course Melissa had used their dead child's name; she probably no longer had any idea they weren't one and the same.

"Huh," Baba said again. "I see." She looked the girl in the eyes as steadfastly as if she was talking to another adult. "Tell me, do you know that there are two worlds—this one, the Otherworld, and the mundane plane, where the Humans live?"

Hannah nodded. "The Mother told me stories about that other place. She didn't like it."

"Mmm," Baba shrugged. "Well, she had kind of a tough time there. It makes sense that she wouldn't. But believe me, it can be a very nice place. Did she also tell you that you are a Human, and that you come from that world, not this one?"

Hannah shook her head, spiky hair swinging around her ears. "The other one told me that. She used to call me 'Human child,' like it was a bad thing." The little girl narrowed her eyes at Maya, who was dripping dourly in front of the throne. "But I didn't care. I don't like her."

"Who does?" Baba muttered under her breath.

Liam could see her brace herself, as if something as yet unknown to him, but important to her, was riding on the answers to her next questions. He had no earthly idea where she was going with all this. Or unearthly idea, for that matter. But somehow, despite everything, he'd come to trust her. Whatever it was, he had no doubt it would be in the best interests of the child.

"You get to make a choice," Baba said. "Do you want to stay here, with her?" She pointed at Melissa, who seemed only marginally interested in the conversation, her attention captivated by an enormous blue butterfly fluttering amidst some yellow orchids.

The little girl shook her head fiercely. "No. She's *wrong*."

Baba raised an eyebrow. "I see. And how do you know that?"

"I just know."

"And me?" Baba asked. "Am I wrong?"

A dark head tilted sideways to survey her, eyes like bottomless pools examining her closely. "No," Hannah said finally. "You're *good*."

Baba smiled. "Well, there might be some who disagreed with you, but I'm glad you think so." She straightened up and walked to a silver candelabrum nearby, a huge silver monstrosity covered with glowing beeswax candles. She blew one out, plucked it from its base, and brought it back over to the little girl.

"Can you light this?" Baba asked, holding out the tall white taper.

Hannah looked around. One courtier held out what looked to Liam like flint and steel, but Baba waved it away.

"How?" the girl asked. "I don't have anything to light it with."

"Just think it lit," Baba suggested. "*Want* it to be lit."

Long dark lashes blinked. The whole room seemed to be holding its breath, although Liam wasn't sure why. Suddenly, the candle whooshed into flame. Baba smiled.

"Nicely done," she said, and put the candle back. Then she held out her hand to the girl and walked with her to where Liam stood with the other children gathered around him at the foot of the throne. Baba addressed the queen and her consort.

"With your permission, Majesties, I will take this child back with me to the mundane world." Baba said. "I believe we might suit each other well."

Liam blinked. *What the hell?* Was Baba saying what he thought she was saying?

The queen gave a regal nod. "Ah," she said, figuring it out before Liam did. "It is about time you found a child to train as a new Baba. An elegant solution indeed. We approve."

"You're going to make that little girl into a Baba Yaga?" Liam said, not sure if he should protest or applaud. "After everything she's been through?"

Baba shrugged, looking down at the child with her usual restrained half smile. "She doesn't really fit in either world, nobody else wants her, and she has a gift for magic. That's kind of the definition of a Baba."

The child gazed up at Liam with her held tilted sideways, her dark steady gaze reminding him of the intelligent mockery of the crows in the cornfields back home.

"Besides," Baba added. "Can you think of anything else to do with her?"

Liam opened his mouth, but another loud shriek rang out instead. For a moment, he thought he'd somehow made the horrible discordant sound himself, but then he realized that Melissa had finally tuned in to the conversation.

"Noooooo," she screamed, face contorted with frenzied madness. "Not my baby! No! You can't take my baby! Not again! It's not fair! Liam! Liam! Please!" Her tearstained countenance turned blindly toward him, as a sunflower turns to the sun. "*Please*, Liam, don't let them take my baby!"

A giant hand squeezed his heart so hard, he was sure it must burst out of his chest. All the horror of that first night came rushing back: the frantic call from the dispatcher, the twirling red lights on the ambulance parked sideways across the end of his driveway; inside the house, a distraught and incoherent Melissa, begging him to make the undeniable dreadful truth somehow magically be untrue.

He couldn't do it for her then. He didn't know how to do it for her now.

A hard, stony burn of anguish began to bubble up into his throat, and it erupted as a single, pleading word. "Barbara?" he whispered.

This time she did hug him; a quick peck on the cheek accompanying the unexpected gesture. She gave him one of her most wicked smiles and a wink, and said, "I've got this, Liam." Then took a step forward to bow low to the throne.

"Your Majesties," she said loudly, to be heard over the desolate keening, "I have had an idea."

The queen raised an eyebrow. "If it will bring peace to my throne room, I will consider almost anything. Come, tell Us."

Baba walked up the stairs and spoke in quiet tones to the queen and her consort, whose shrewd face first showed surprise, then a kind of sharp-edged glee as he sat stroking his dark beard. The queen's stern visage was harder to read, but she glanced from Melissa to Maya to the little girl and back to Melissa again, nodding her head sagely.

"I like it," the queen said finally, gesturing at the guards to bring Maya closer to the throne. "It is fitting."

Baba fetched the child, quieting Liam's involuntary

protest with a quick headshake and a mouthed *trust me.* A devious grin peeked out at him from a sideways glance, then disappeared beneath a more serious facade.

"If you will assist me?" the queen requested her consort, and the two of them descended gracefully to where Maya and the girl waited, exchanging silent expressions of mutual dislike. The queen and king each put a hand out to touch the chest of one that stood in front of them, and when they clasped their own hands together, a sparkling curtain of mist enveloped them all in a translucent rainbow of magic. When the energy cleared, two little dark-haired children stood where there had previously only been one. Of the Rusalka there was no sign, just a wet spot on the floor and a fierce scowl on the face of the second Hannah.

"Aw, shit," the pseudochild said. "You have got to be kidding me."

The queen's steely glance silenced any further complaints. "Considering that the penalty for your actions is normally either death or banishment," she pointed out, "you should consider yourself lucky that you are only being required to serve out a sentence so benign. If you are kind to this poor Human and behave yourself, perhaps in a few hundred years when the mortal is gone, I will consider returning you to your original form. Perhaps. And rest assured; I will be watching you."

Sullenly, the former Rusalka marched across the swirling inlaid tiles to stand next to Melissa. Immediately, the woman's face brightened and she stopped crying, ignoring Liam and everyone else to put her arms around the girl she believed was hers. In her radiant smile, he could almost catch a glimpse of the old Melissa, before life and her own fragile spirit had so cruelly betrayed her.

"Fear not," the queen reassured Liam. "We shall take most good care of your former lady, and make sure she has all that she requires." She raised a questioning brow. "Unless you would prefer to take her back to your world, of course. Although, if so, the 'child' could not go with her."

Liam couldn't think of anything more hurtful than to

deprive Melissa of her daughter one more time. And experience had proven that mortal medicine was unable to help her fight her demons. Perhaps the magic of this world could do better, now that she was no longer under the Rusalka's control. He merely shook his head. "Thank you, no, Your Majesty. I am content to leave her in your tender care."

Baba stepped forward once more, causing the queen to let slip the tiniest breath of a sigh. "Was there something else, Baba Yaga?" she asked. "I tire of this, and wish to move on to lighter, more amusing pursuits."

Liam couldn't blame her. He was ready to be done with this whole thing himself. Of course, being done here still meant facing the music back at home. He bit back his own sigh, suddenly feeling as tired as if they truly had been lost in the Otherworld for half a lifetime. Only the discipline of years on the force kept his shoulders straight and his back firm.

"There is one more small boon I would ask of you, Majesty, but not for myself." Baba gestured from Melissa to Liam. "When the Rusalka forced Melissa to return to the mundane world and accuse Liam of the crimes Maya herself had committed, she did great damage to his reputation. This was the intent, of course, but now, the damage is done."

The king leaned forward, obviously intrigued. "As a keeper of the law, that is most undesirable. And all men value their reputations. But the woman is clearly too damaged to trust with the task of undoing her ill words. What is the boon you seek?"

Liam's whole body tensed, not knowing what Baba could possibly have up her sleeve this time, barely daring to hope.

Baba waved a languid hand around the circle of courtiers that surrounded them. "Any of these, your faithful subjects, could easily don a glamour that would make them look and sound like Melissa. If you could send someone back with us to recant her earlier accusations, that would be most helpful, and both Liam and I would consider your debt to us in this matter repaid completely."

"Ah," the queen said, bestowing a wintery smile on them both. "Easily done, and most clever." A satisfied look revealed that she felt she'd gotten the better of the deal. Baba had told him that those of the Otherworld hated being in debt to anyone, the queen most of all. Liam suspected Baba could have asked for a great deal more, but he was too relieved to protest. While the fake Melissa was in town, he could also have her sign the divorce papers he'd had sitting in his desk for the last two years. It would finally be over.

As the queen picked a noble to accompany them back wearing Melissa's face, and chose a few trusted guards to escort them to the doorway they had entered through, and then close it once and for all behind them, Liam gathered the children together. The more time they spent in his company, the less muddled they seemed, although Baba said that eventually the time they'd spent in the Otherworld would soon fade to a distant dream.

Baba looked down at the dark-haired girl and said, "I'd like to have you come and live with me. Would that be okay? I have a lot of things to teach you. The land where I live is very different from here, but I think you'll like it. And we can come back here and visit if you'd like."

Preternaturally calm eyes stared back up at her. "I'd get to live with you?" Hannah asked. "In the sunlight place?"

Baba nodded. "Yes. And there are stars there too. You'll like stars."

"All right," the girl said, as solemn and reserved as a judge. With her big round eyes and wise-beyond-her-years expression, she reminded Liam of an owl. They shared the same unblinking, somewhat disconcerting gaze. Liam hoped that Baba would remember to teach her how to laugh while she was at it.

"Oh, there is one thing," Baba said with a hint of concern.

Hannah waited patiently. She'd undoubtedly learned the hard way that people were full of surprises, and had lots of practice bracing herself for the unpleasant.

"I live with a *really* large dog. Who is occasionally a dragon. Do you think that would scare you?" Baba seemed to hold her breath. Liam knew he was holding his.

The little girl glanced around at all the various monstrous shapes and sizes of creatures that made up the queen's court. A tiny sliver of a smile snuck onto her rosebud lips. "I don't think so," she said quietly. She put her hand in Baba's.

"Good," Baba said, blinking back something that looked suspiciously like tears. "Then let's go home."

THIRTY-TWO

BABA FELT A little bit like the Pied Piper when she and Liam walked out of the cave entrance, followed by Hannah, Mary Elizabeth, the other missing children, and Petey, with Fake Melissa bringing up the rear. The bright light outside made her steps falter; she was temporarily blinded after her time under the muted Otherworld skies and the murky darkness of the caverns. Beside her, she heard Hannah give a tiny muffled squeak as she saw the sun for the first time since she was an infant.

Penelope Callahan was sitting on a rock, talking to the three Riders. They made an unlikely picture; the well-tailored society wife with her pearls and designer clothing and the motley and exotic bikers in their white, red, and black leather. But they all shared identical expressions of joy as they took in the sight of Baba and her company, and she breathed a sigh of relief to see them all safe and sound. Koshei was nowhere in sight, which was undoubtedly for the best.

"Mama!" Petey broke away from the rest of the children, who still seemed somewhat dazed and lost, bolting across the stony ground to be enveloped in his mother's frantic grasp.

"Thank god, oh, thank god," Penelope said, over and over, tears running down her face. "Oh, my baby. Thank god, thank god."

Baba thought it might be a bit more appropriate to thank her and Liam, but under the circumstances, she didn't really mind.

"Hello, boys," she said cheerfully. "Did you miss me?"

Alexei shrugged shoulders like small mountains. "What, you went someplace? We didn't even notice." But a big grin split his craggy face. "I see you found what you were looking for. Run into any trouble?"

Baba and Liam exchanged glances. "Piece of cake," she said.

"Yeah," Liam agreed. "Piece of cake."

Mikhail snorted. "Why don't I believe you? On the other hand, you're here, you got the children, and neither one of you is quacking or saying *ribbit*, so I'm guessing it all worked out okay in the end."

Baba thought about poor, broken Melissa, trying not to think about how seeing her like that had affected Liam. He'd barely said a word since they left court, carrying the smallest child out in silence.

"Depends on your definition of okay, I guess," she said somberly. "But mostly, yeah."

Alexei had been quietly counting heads. "Hey," he said. "Don't you have an extra kid here?" He bent down to look at them all.

Hannah stared at him coolly, clearly unimpressed by his huge size. The boy broke away from the older girl holding his hand and ran up to Alexei to tug on his braided beard, making everyone laugh. Alexei just sighed and swung the boy up onto his shoulders.

"It's a long story," Baba said, one hand resting on the little girl's shoulders. They couldn't keep calling her Hannah; it must pierce Liam to the heart every time he heard it. "This is . . . um . . ."

"Babs," Hannah said, in her soft tenor voice, like water running over mossy rocks. "Like Baba Yaga. Only shorter, because I'm shorter."

Baba felt something twang and strum inside her own heart; some unidentifiable magic she couldn't put a name to nearly as easily as the girl had named herself. It was as if a piece she hadn't even known she was missing had suddenly settled into place. She gave a brief, affectionate tug at the girl's pixie hair.

"You'll grow," she said. "Now how about you help me get all these other kids back to their parents?"

IT WASN'T QUITE that simple, naturally. Once they'd walked back to the road, Liam had to figure out the logistics of three adults and five children. The Riders would stick to their bikes, of course, but the children couldn't ride with them. In the end, Penelope took Petey in his car seat, as well as the older girl. Baba drove Maya's car—since she obviously wouldn't be needing it again—along with the newly re-named Babs and the little boy. Mary Elizabeth was proudly awarded the shotgun seat in the cruiser.

Before they set off, Baba stuck her head in the cruiser's window and suggested to Liam that he use the radio to call Nina, and ask her to have all the children's parents assemble at the sheriff's department.

"Are you sure?" Liam asked her. "Don't you remember the zoo that we walked into the last time?"

The wicked grin put in another appearance, making his pulse quicken as it always did. "I do," she said. "And I'm thinking we might as well have as big an audience as possible for your triumphant return. We wouldn't want anyone important to miss it now, would we?"

THEY DROVE SLOWLY down the back roads, in deference to the kids who didn't have car seats, and to give Baba's predicted welcoming committee plenty of time to arrive.

Sure enough, when their bizarre convoy of three motorcycles, two cars, and a sheriff's cruiser pulled up to the front of the building, the parking lot was full. Stepping inside the entrance, Liam felt the noise and commotion hit him like a tidal wave, threatening to knock him over with its hectic force. But he strode in with his head held high, waving casually at Nina sitting in her dispatcher's booth.

"McClellan!" Clive Matthews rushed to cut him off before he could get any further into the room, where clots of anxious parents milled around restlessly. "You have a lot of nerve calling all these people in here. You have no authority! In case you've forgotten, you've been suspended!" His pigeon chest thrust out indignantly as he squawked at Liam.

Oh, this is going to feel wonderful. Liam and Baba stepped apart, revealing the children who'd marched in behind them, hidden by the bulk of the Riders, Penelope, and Fake Melissa, who faded back to stand against a bile-green wall.

"I thought it would be best to get these kids back to their parents as soon as possible," Liam said calmly.

Matthews's jaw dropped, and for what might have been the first time in his life, the board president was actually speechless. The room erupted in pandemonium, with parents racing forward to embrace their lost angels, deputies and board members beaming and clapping each other and Liam on the back with hearty abandon. In the background, Liam could hear Nina on the radio, broadcasting the news of the children's return to anyone with a police scanner.

Eventually, things returned to something vaguely resembling order, and everyone clambered for an explanation of how Liam had rescued the children. He'd been thinking about this in the car on the drive there, and remembered one of the theories they'd tossed around before discovering that Maya was behind the entire thing.

"It turns out Peter Callahan was collecting the children to sell to a group of foreign pedophiles; powerful men in the Middle East who would pay him huge amounts of money and make useful connections for his drilling business," Liam said with a straight face. "Thankfully, he hadn't completed the deals yet, so the children were still waiting to be shipped out. It looks like his assistant Maya was helping him the entire time; it may even have been her idea, since it turns out that her entire life's history was a lie."

Hell—it was pretty farfetched, and he knew it. But compared to the truth, it was downright believable. Besides, there was no way for anyone to prove it *wasn't* true.

Clive Matthews's chins quivered indignantly. "How dare you accuse Mr. Callahan of involvement in this atrocity? He's been a fine upstanding member of our community, and he has worked hard to bring new jobs and prosperity into this area." He looked around, as if expecting Peter to appear over his shoulder in his usual spot, but the businessman was conspicuously missing.

"Actually, he is a greedy bastard and a child stealer," a new voice said clearly, ringing out over the hum and buzz of the crowded room. Penelope Callahan stepped forward, her hands resting protectively on Petey's small shoulders. The purpling bruise on her cheekbone made a livid contrast to her otherwise neat appearance.

"When he knew his plans had been discovered," she told her avid listeners, "he took our own son to sell too. And when I tried to stop him, he beat me up." She pointed at the undeniable evidence. "The man is a criminal, and I want him arrested for assault, if nothing else."

Liam held his breath, waiting to hear someone say that Callahan was in the hospital, accusing his wife of running him down with the family car, but apparently, he hadn't been seriously hurt. Too bad.

"Oh, ah, oh dear," Matthews stuttered. Molly walked up and handed Penelope some paperwork to fill out, and turned to the board president, saying artlessly, "I assume this means you'll be reinstating Sheriff McClellan immediately, and giving him some kind of award, right? He's the town hero now."

Liam thought Matthews was going to choke on his own tongue, but the man managed to nod, his complexion an alarming ripe-tomato red, and say, "Yes, yes of course." Then Matthews pulled himself together and added, "That is, if the matter of the very serious charges against him are cleared up. There's still that, you know."

But his relief was short-lived as Fake Melissa stepped forward and confessed to making up the entire thing after Maya blackmailed her. She apologized so abjectly, it made it easy for Liam to insist that he wouldn't be pressing charges. Once that was dealt with, he had Molly take Fake Melissa back to his office to wait for him. A few signatures on a stack of papers, and he would be free. Although free for what, he wasn't sure.

Belinda and her parents came over to talk to him and Baba, Mary Elizabeth holding tight to her mother's hand. The girl still seemed a bit foggy, and remembered only hazy nightmarish images between the time Maya had snatched her from her backyard until she had seen the sheriff across a strange room, but Liam thought that was just as well. Children were resilient, and Mary Elizabeth had the best medicine of all to heal her, the loving arms of her family. Mariska and Ivan beamed from ear to ear, their smiles so wide it was as though the sun had come out after months of only clouds and rain.

He watched Belinda hug Baba, who seemed taken aback for a moment, but also warily pleased. But then, he reminded himself, her life probably hadn't included many hugs up until now.

"Thank you so much for everything you've done," Belinda said, tears of joy sliding down her cheeks. She looked down, noticing the quiet little girl standing by Baba's side, drinking in all the unaccustomed chaos and humanity with wide brown eyes. "Well, hello! Who's this?"

Belinda looked at Liam, baffled. "Was there another missing child we didn't know about?" She glanced around the room, as if looking for another set of exultant parents.

Baba nodded. "Yes and no. This is my daughter, Babs.

Maya stole her before she came to this area. I followed Maya here trying to find out what she'd done with Babs, and that's how I got involved with this whole thing."

Belinda's mouth formed a stunned "Oh, my." She struggled to keep a straight face. "How interesting."

"And once she realized I was here, Maya kept trying to get me in trouble, tampering with my herbs and spreading nasty rumors about me, to keep me from discovering where she was keeping Babs and all the other children. She must have seen Peter Callahan and his connections as a way to make an even bigger profit on the children she stole."

Mariska shook her white head, smiling indulgently. "So that's your story and you're sticking with it, eh?" Belinda grinned, obviously pleased with the neat fairy-tale ending.

"Well, we're very glad you came to town, no matter what brought you here," Ivan said, patting Baba's arm fondly, and beaming down at the little dark-haired girl.

Belinda suddenly looked alarmed. "Oh, dear. I never did the last impossible task! Is that going to cause a problem?"

Liam raised an eyebrow at Baba. She hadn't mentioned anything about impossible tasks to him. Of course, getting information out of her was something of an impossible task in and of itself. He was still trying to get a straight answer on whether or not there was something between them. Well, clearly there was *something*. But what, he still didn't know.

Baba looked around her at the joyful crowd, at Liam restored to his rightful place, and then down at the small child holding resolutely on to her hand. She winked at Belinda and said, "I think between us we've managed to achieve even more than three impossible things. I suspect that tradition has been more than satisfied."

Seeing the Ivanovs and Belinda so happy, and Mary Elizabeth safely home where she belonged, Liam could feel his own face breaking into what was no doubt the first genuine smile he'd let out in days.

Then Ivan said in a calm tone, dropping the words into the conversation like tiny, Russian-accented bombs, "I suppose now that you've gotten your daughter back, and all the children have been returned to their parents, you'll be leaving us."

And Liam felt the smile slide away, to the place where things go when dreams die.

THIRTY-THREE

THAT EVENING, LIAM and Baba sat together on the couch in the Airstream, careful not to look at each other. Baba stared out the window at the plume of dust that floated through the calm summer air, barely visible in the vanishing red taillights of three motorcycles on their way to somewhere else. She supposed she'd soon be on her way too. For the first time in her long life, that thought lacked its usual appeal. Perhaps because something else appealed to her more.

What the hell was she going to do now?

She stole a glance at Liam. Like her, his eyes followed the sight of the Riders disappearing down the road. Unlike her, he was clearly pleased to see them go. Not that they hadn't all gotten on well enough, she thought—just too many alpha males in one room for anyone's comfort. It was like having a cage full of lions . . . and only one steak.

Even Chudo-Yudo had finally said he was going to take a walk and not to expect him back until morning. She had a sneaking suspicion that he was going to pay a visit to a female German shepherd that lived up the road. She didn't begrudge him a little fun after the last couple of weeks, and she could easily watch the Water of Life and Death for him. It wasn't as though she was going anywhere. Yet.

Little Babs had gone home with Mary Elizabeth for the night, because Belinda had suggested quietly to Baba that the best way for the child to adjust back to human life was to spend some time with another little girl. Belinda had an evening of Disney movies and popcorn planned, and Babs had begged to go. She'd never seen a movie either. Baba couldn't say no.

So now she and Liam were alone together. No Riders. No dragons. No Otherworldly threats to fight or battles to win. Just one ridiculously attractive sheriff with broad shoulders, dimples, and shaggy hair, and her. She could feel her heart beating like a caged bird, its wings fluttering against her ribcage like jungle drums in the night. Fear and desire danced a tango in the pit of her stomach, and she took another sip of wine to try to quiet their tapping feet.

A gentle hand pried the goblet out of her fingers and placed it on the table with a quiet but decisive click, then lifted to stroke her cheek.

"Barbara," he said. Then corrected himself. "Baba. Don't be sad."

Baba blinked, surprised. "I'm not sad," she said. "What would I be sad about? Everything worked out perfectly."

Liam raised an eyebrow. "You seem upset. I thought maybe you were sad to see the Riders go. I know they're old friends."

A smile tugged at the corner of her lips. "I love the boys, but they are always a little intense. Not to mention rough on the furnishings. I'm fine with them leaving."

He slid a little closer, dropping his hand to her shoulder to knead muscles she hadn't even realized were clenched. She tried to ignore the feelings that rose in her like heat from a summer road, but his nearness made it hard to think.

"If it's not the Riders, are you worried about trying to raise Babs? I think you'll be a great mentor." He turned her slightly so her back was toward him and he could rub both shoulders at once. His breath tickled the back of her neck, sending shivers down her spine. "She's lucky to have you."

Baba shrugged under his strong fingers, fighting the impulse to shift even closer. Fighting thoughts of a future she couldn't possibly have, with a man she shouldn't want nearly as much as she did. But her pulse raced anyway, and longing rose up in her like the tide, irresistible and overwhelming. The scent of him—masculine and woodsy and something purely Liam—snared her senses. His very essence seemed to have entangled itself around her soul when she wasn't looking. How had that happened? And what was she supposed to do about it? Babas didn't stay. Did they?

"I hope you're right," she said. "I'm not all that good at being Human myself; I'm not sure I'll be able to teach her everything she needs to know. But she's a tough kid; I suspect we'll find our way." She sighed, feeling herself relax despite herself. His hands felt wonderful on her, and she had a momentary fantasy of what else they could do before she pulled herself together.

"Baba," Liam scolded, moving even closer. "Stop tensing up. We won. Everything is fine. You should be celebrating." He slid his hands down her arms, then slowly turned her back around to face him. "Tell me—what's wrong?"

He was so close; she could see the flecks of brown in his hazel eyes, the thick lashes casting burnt-umber shadows as he gazed at her with a look she couldn't quite decipher. But why should she be able to decode what he was feeling when she could barely make sense of the emotions surging up like a wildfire inside her own chest?

"Liam." His name was like a prayer, a spell, an invocation—as if uttering it could make magic happen, no matter how impossible that might seem. After all, who knew more about magic than a Baba? And what was more magical than this strange thing that had happened between them, despite all the odds against it? "You asked me, once, if we were a pair. Do you remember?"

He nodded, his expression solemn yet hopeful, watching her as if he was afraid she would vanish. "I remember. You never answered me." The hint of a smile played around the edges of his lips. "Are you going to answer me now?"

Baba felt as though she was teetering on the edge of a precipice; for one last moment she clung to the safety of the old and familiar, then with a joyous abandon she barely comprehended, flung herself over the cliff into the strange abyss she'd been avoiding for days.

"Yes," she whispered, leaning in to kiss him, feeling the curve of his smile blossoming into fruition. "The answer is yes."

Then his strong arms were around her, holding her tight against the rock-hard muscles of his chest, all warmth and shelter and unconditional acceptance. No more witch and sheriff, only Baba and Liam, and the passion they'd both been holding in for far too long.

He kissed her back, his lips firm and soft against hers. "It's about damned time," he said in a husky voice. "If I had to wait five more minutes to kiss you, I think I probably would have turned into a dragon myself."

And then his lips came down on hers again, and there was no more talking, only the sweet taste of his mouth on hers, his tongue slipping inside to savor her, his hands sliding through her hair, then down to her body, which waited so eagerly for his touch.

Heat burned through her from the tips of her toes to the top of her head, and too impatient to wait for him to finish unbuttoning her shirt, Baba made their clothes vanish with a gesture. Liam looked startled for a moment, then laughed out loud, pressing his naked skin against hers with a restrained strength that made Baba even hotter.

"That's a useful trick," he muttered as he nibbled his way down from her ear to her neck and then set about exploring her as if he could solve all the mysteries she'd hidden from him for so long. She stifled a groan, feeling warmth spreading out from her center in a turbulent aura of need and wanting and emotion.

Laughter bubbled up, joy like bubbles in a glass of champagne, and she started to do some exploring herself, tasting and teasing and running her hands over the warmth and wonder that was the man she'd waited so long for. The scent of their mingled arousal was intoxicating, and the unmistakable desire that darkened his eyes as he gazed into hers was a magic more powerful than any she had ever found in storm or earth or fire.

And then he was inside her, the two of them moving together as one at last, coming together and pulling apart, only to come together yet again, until Baba could barely tell where he left off and she began.

Higher and higher she spiraled, like a roaring bonfire sending its sparks out to light up the darkness, until with a muted cry she burst into flame, a fiery phoenix reborn out of the embers of love. Above her, Liam shuddered and moaned, echoing her joy. They collapsed together in a heap on the couch, all tangled limbs and stuttering breath and murmured endearments.

Outside the window, the full moon glowed, but its light was only a dim reflection of the look in Liam's eyes as he gazed at her.

"I love you," he said, holding her close and running his fingers through her tangled hair as if he couldn't believe she was still in his arms. "I think you've cast a spell on me, wicked witch that you are."

Baba thought that if this is what it meant to be wicked, she was all for it. "Anything is possible," she said with an evil smile. And then slid her hand down the length of his body to prove it.

A COUPLE OF weeks later, Liam sat in Bertie's, morosely drinking a cup of coffee and pretending to read the newspaper so no one would come over and try to talk to him. He'd spent the time since his return from the Otherworld tying up loose ends, taking statements, and filling out endless stacks of paperwork. Every time he reached the bottom of one pile, Molly magically produced another out of thin air.

He should be happy that things were finally getting back to normal. But ever since the day after he and Baba had made love, when he drove out to Miller's Meadow and found it empty, his life had seemed empty too.

Katie, the waitress working his section, stopped by to refill his cup and plop a piece of apple pie with homemade caramel ice cream down in front of him. "Here," she said. "You look like you could use this." She peered at him more closely. "You seem different, somehow. Did you get your hair cut?"

He had, finally, but that wasn't what was different about him. He'd discovered the existence of an entire magical world, and in the process, rediscovered his own heart. His entire reality had been turned upside down and inside out by a beautiful cloud-haired woman who'd disappeared as suddenly as she'd shown up. Little wonder Katie thought he seemed different.

"Yup, I got a hair cut," he said, giving her a wry smile. "That must be it."

He ignored the pie, doodling a few notes on the margins of the crossword puzzle, and trying to decide which stack of folders to tackle when he got back to the station.

Until the bell over the door jingled cheerfully and someone pulled out the chair across from him, saying, "You know, Sheriff, it should be against the law to waste a piece of Bertie's pie. If you're not going to eat that, I will."

He looked up, heart skipping a beat painfully, and there was Baba, forking up a bite of pie with a mischievous look in her clear amber eyes.

Liam straightened, staring at her as if she were an apparition who might vanish if he started to breathe again. "I thought you were gone for good," he said, forcing his voice to sound as relaxed and casual as hers.

"Without saying good-bye? Never. That would be rude." She ate another bite of pie. "Didn't you get my note?"

"Note?" he asked. "What note?"

Baba shook her head, the curly mass of dark hair floating around her like an undeserved halo. "Damned carrier pigeons. They're so unreliable."

With great effort, Liam restrained himself from banging his head on the table. "Baba, you have got to get a phone, damn it."

"Sorry," she said, still calmly eating his pie. "I had some things I had to take care of. I didn't mean to worry you." She glanced around the room, waving at a few people she knew. Once word spread that Maya had been behind all the trouble, the people in town had felt terrible about how they'd treated her. They would have apologized, if she'd been around.

"So," she said brightly, trying the ice cream. "What's been happening while I've been gone?"

"Well, to start out with, Peter Callahan disappeared, along with every cent in the company bank accounts," Liam said, glad for a neutral topic of conversation. "And since Maya went missing at the same time, everyone is assuming they ran off together."

"Huh. Is that good or bad?"

"Mostly good," Liam said. "I'm not happy he isn't going to pay for his crimes, but let's face it, Maya was really behind most of it, and we'll never know how much he was involved. Not to mention that his actions have made it next to impossible for his company to push forward with their drilling, which is a huge relief to everyone who was against the fracking."

"I wouldn't be so sure he isn't being punished," Baba said thoughtfully, licking a dab of whipped cream off the tip of one finger. "He wanted the power and the influence a lot more than he wanted the money, and he's lost his wife and son. I guarantee you, wherever he is, he's not a happy man."

Liam snagged a tiny piece of crust, suddenly feeling his appetite return. "The kids are all doing great, although none of them remembers their time in the Otherworld. So how is little Babs adapting to her new life? It must be quite a change for her."

A shy new smile lit Baba's face, making her even more luminous than usual. "Remarkably well, all things considered. She's a very clever child, and amazingly tough."

"Now who does that remind me of?" he said with a laugh.

She wrinkled her long nose at him, but otherwise ignored the comment. "Still, I didn't think it would be a good idea to make her move around the country when there are so many things she has to get used to. So I took your suggestion and went to talk to the other two United States Baba Yagas about splitting up our territories."

The crumb of delicate pastry suddenly turned to dust in his mouth. He knew what was coming next.

"We've got it all worked out. Bella Young is going to take the middle states, and Beka Yancy is going to take the West Coast."

It took him a minute to realize what she'd said. "Wait—aren't you going to take the West Coast? After all, you teach out of Davis in California."

"That was one of the things I was taking care of," Baba said. "Picking up the few belongings I cared about from my apartment out there and putting in my resignation at the school. There's a nice little community college not too far from Dunville that I can teach at part-time if I still feel the need for some kind of respectable job. And I thought maybe I'd teach folks like Michael and Lily how to grow herbs and harvest the ones that grow wild around here. There's quite good money in that, you know. Could be a boost to the farmers in the area, if they want to get on board."

Liam was dumbfounded. "Here? You're staying here?"

"Where else am I going to find pie this good? Besides, I've grown quite fond of this town, and there are some good people here. If I'm going to settle down somewhere while Babs is growing up, I can't think of a better place to do it."

Liam was still trying to wrap his mind around the concept. "So you're going to raise her in the Airstream?"

"No. It's really too small for a growing child. Besides, I'd kind of like to have a regular refrigerator for a while," Baba said with an infinitesimal twitch. "I bought a house out on the South River Road, the old yellow farmhouse with the gray shutters and the red metal roof."

"I know that one," he said. "It's a great house, but people say it's haunted. It's been empty for years."

Baba laughed. "I'm not worried about a few ghosts. I get along fine with the dead. The house is perfect; not too far from the town and school, but quiet and private enough that no one will notice if things get a little strange from time to time. I'll just park the Airstream out back, so it is handy on the occasions when I have to hit the road to deal with something, and it will still be close enough to keep an eye on the doorway to the Otherworld."

"Oh," Liam said. "Will you take Babs out with you when you travel?"

"Sometimes; she has to learn about being a Baba. Although I just hope I'll do a better job of teaching her to be a human being than my Baba did with me." She sighed.

"You're a terrific human being," Liam protested.

"Oh please, even Alexei says I have the social skills of a cranky mountain lion, and he's been known to start bar fights just because someone didn't pass the peanuts fast enough. I'm not sure I'm a great role model for a little girl." She twisted one strand of inky black hair between slender fingers, as close to nervous as Liam had ever seen her. Apparently trying to raise a child was a lot more intimidating than facing off with monsters or trying to save the world.

"You're smart and tough and dedicated to helping those who need you; she couldn't ask for better," he said. Baba's checks turned slightly pink. "Of course, you're also odd, mysterious, and infuriating . . . but that part actually grows on a person after a while."

"I'm glad you think so, because I was wondering if you might be willing to help out with little Babs; you know, teach her some of the things about being Human that I never really got the hang of. Maybe show her which movies to watch. Take care of her when I had to leave town."

"You want me to babysit?"

"Actually, I was thinking that the house on South River Road was pretty big for just the two of us and one large dog who is sometimes a small dragon. I was wondering if maybe you were tired of living in an old house filled with bad memories, and might be interested in making some new, better ones with us. Maybe help me learn to be a better Human too."

There was a moment of silence as what she'd said sank in. "Barbara Yager—are you proposing to me?"

Her high cheekbones turned even pinker and she looked down at the table, not meeting his eyes. "Yes. Yes, I am. I realize it is a crazy idea, but what do you say?"

There was silence again, and Baba started to get up, fumbling with her chair.

Until Liam said, "Not as crazy as it would be to try to live without you. I haven't been able to take a deep breath since I got to that meadow and found the Airstream gone. I missed you every minute of every day since then. In fact, it was so hard being without you, I went out and bought this, in case by some miracle you actually came back."

He pulled out a black box, and opened it up to show her a ring—a round circle in the shape of a golden dragon, with a sparkling diamond held in its mouth.

A huge grin spread over Baba's face. "You got that for me?" She slid back into her seat as though her legs had forgotten how to hold her upright.

"Well, it would look pretty funny on Chudo-Yudo," Liam said. He slipped it onto her finger and leaned across the table to kiss her deeply, barely noticing the thunderous applause from everyone in the diner.

EPILOGUE

My Dearest Barbara,

I hope this finds you well. Thank you for sending me the picture from your wedding. You all look so happy and attractive (especially that sheriff of yours . . . I don't suppose he has a brother). Your dress was lovely, although I'm not sure about the choice of the spiked leather boots to go with it.

I'm sorry I wasn't able to attend as planned, but I seem to have a small problem brewing out here by the coastal waters. Okay, maybe not so small; it's a little too soon to tell. I called in the Riders for help, but only Sun and Knight showed up. Do you by any chance know where Day is? He appears to have gone missing.

I'm sure it is nothing.

Congratulations again on your new life.

Much affection,
Your sister Baba,
Beka

TURN THE PAGE FOR A SNEAK PEEK
AT THE NEXT BABA YAGA NOVEL

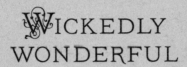

WICKEDLY
WONDERFUL

MARCUS DERMOTT WATCHED the sunrise from the wind-swept deck of his father's fishing boat and wondered if the sea had changed, or if it was him. When he was a boy, growing up on this very boat, the sight of the water being painted with light could make his heart sing, no matter how troubled the rest of his life was. But all he felt now was numb. Numb, and a little bit cranky. The ocean might be beautiful, but it was the last place he wanted to be.

He'd planned to spend his life in the Marines, far away from the restless sea and the memories that came with it. He'd sure as hell never planned to come back to this damned boat. Or to his father. *Especially* to his father. But as the Master Sergeant who'd trained him liked to say, "Life is what happens while you are making other plans."

Turns out that twelve years in the Corps was all he had in him. Three tours in Afghanistan had sucked him as dry as the desert sands, and as much as he missed the action, and the close bond with the other men in his unit, his head just wasn't in the game anymore. He'd been around long enough to know that if you didn't get out when that happened, you were dangerous to yourself and to everyone around you.

So he'd finished out his time, packed his kit bag, and headed home. One of the guys who'd gotten out a year before him had invited Marcus to come help out with the extreme adventure vacation company he'd started, and that seemed like as good an idea as any in the post-exit blur Marcus had been in. But life had had other plans there too, apparently.

"Are you going to stand there daydreaming all day, boy?" a low-pitched voice snarled in his ear. Even the musical Irish lilt couldn't make his father sound like anything other than a bear with a sore paw. "We finally start catchin' some fish after pullin' up empty nets day after day, and you can't bestir yourself to lend a hand? I thought you came back here to help me, not to stare at the sea like you've never seen it before. It's the same ocean it always was—waves and salt and finally, dammit, some fish. So move your ass and check the lines, will ya?"

Marcus sighed. He and his father had never gotten along, and twelve years apart hadn't helped that in the least. When he got the call telling him his father had cancer, Marcus had hoped that maybe if he went home to help, they could move past their differences. But the past had its barbs in them too deep, and the present was as cold and gray as the ocean. He didn't see either one of those things changing any time soon.

THE RED-GOLD GLOW of the rising sun turned the sea into a fire of molten lava that belied the cold Pacific waters of Monterey Bay. Beka Yancy didn't mind, though; her wetsuit kept her warm, and it was worth braving the morning chill to have the waves mostly to herself.

Soon enough there would be plenty of people around, but for now, she reveled in her solitary enjoyment of the frothy white lace overlaying blue-green depths, accompanied only by the sound of the wind and the hooting laughter of a nearby pod of dolphins. She gave a chortling greeting in dolphin-speak as she went by.

Beka paddled her surfboard out until the pull of the ocean overruled the calm of the shore, feeling herself settle into that peaceful space she only found when there was endless water below her and infinite sky above. On land, there were human beings and all their attendant noise and commotion; here, there was only the challenge that came from pitting herself against the crushing power of the rolling waves.

The fresh scent of the sea filled her nostrils and a light breeze tugged playfully on a strand of her long blond hair as she steered in the direction of a promising incoming swell. But before she could angle herself toward it, her board jerked underneath her as if it had suddenly come to life, and she had to grab on tightly with both hands as it accelerated through the water at impossible speeds, cutting through the whitecaps as if they weren't even there.

What the hell? Beka held on tighter, ducking her head against the biting teeth of the icy spray that washed over her. Through squinted eyes, she could barely make out what looked like a pale green hand grasping the end of her surfboard, gossamer webbing pressed against the bright red surface of the board. A powerful tail with iridescent feathery ends undulated just beneath the water, only occasionally breaking through the surface as it stroked forcefully through the ocean.

Mermaid! Beka thought to herself. But the identification of her mysterious hijacker raised more questions than it solved. She doubted the water creature meant her any harm; they normally stayed far away from human civilization, preferring to hide in their own territory concealed by ancient magic within a two-mile-deep underwater trench. And Beka was friendly with most of the local non-Human residents, on the rare occasions that she saw them.

Still, she was glad of the small knife she wore in a waterproof sheath strapped to her calf, carefully disguised from sight with a tiny glamour that kept the other surfers from noticing it. Not that she really expected to need it, as she had other defenses much more powerful than cold steel, but she'd discovered long ago that it paid to be prepared for the unexpected. It came with the territory, when you were a Baba Yaga.

Most people had never heard of Baba Yaga. Those who recognized the name were usually only familiar with the legendary witch from Russian fairy tales; a curved-chin, beaky-nosed crone with iron teeth who lived in a hut that ran around the forest on giant chicken legs, flew through the air in an enchanted mortar and pestle, and ate small children when they misbehaved.

Some of that had even been true, once upon a time. Certainly, the Baba Yagas were powerful witches, gifted with the ability to manipulate the elemental forces of nature. Even the tales about the huts and the odd form of transportation had been true, back when the Babas had been found only in Russia and its Slavic neighbors. Things were done a little differently these days, though.

Beka might have been the youngest and most inexperienced of the three Babas who lived in the United States, but she was still more than a match for a single mermaid. So it was with more curiosity than trepidation that she sat straight up on her board when they finally reached their destination.

A swift glance around showed her that the mermaid had brought her quite some distance from the shore, only barely visible as an ochre-colored smudge on the horizon behind her. Two or three miles out at least then, a guess reinforced by the sight of a commercial fishing boat moving ponderously through the steely blue sea, dragging its gnarly mesh of nets behind it like a stout wooden bride with a too-long train. Red and blue buoys bobbed on the surface, giving the nets a festive look. Up on the bow of the boat, two men argued about something she was too far away to overhear; luckily, they were looking at each other, and not at her.

Beka jumped as the mermaid surfaced without a sound; her auburn hair turned almost black by the wetness that slicked it back from her face, green eyes bright with fear as she started speaking almost before her lips reached the open air. The now-risen sun glittered off shimmering scales and glinted on sharply pointed teeth.

"Baba Yaga, you have to help me!" The merwoman's head swiveled anxiously between the boat and Beka. Beka was about to reply; something about it being good manners to ask first before dragging someone out into the middle of the ocean, when a large cerulean tear rolled down the woman's sharp cheekbone and she added, "My baby—my baby is caught in the net!"

Damn it to Dazhdbog, Beka thought. That was bad. Not just for the poor defenseless mer baby, who was much too young to be able to change shape or breathe outside of its natural watery environment. But also for the water peoples—the mer and the selkies—who had successfully hidden their existence from humans since the rest of the paranormal races had retreated to live in the Otherworld; this situation could be catastrophic for that closely held secret.

And since the Baba Yagas, while acting independently, ultimately reported to the powerful and volatile High Queen of the Otherworld . . . a failure on Beka's part could be catastrophic to her, as well. The queen had once turned a half dozen handmaidens into swans during a fit of pique; Beka had no desire to discover if she looked good in feathers.

"What was your baby doing out here in the open waters?" Beka hissed, trying not to panic. It wasn't that she wasn't sympathetic, but she'd been trying her best to avoid any major issues since her mentor Brenna, the Baba Yaga who'd raised and taught her, had retired a few years ago and left her to handle things on her own. After years of being told by the elder Baba that she wasn't "quite ready yet," a tiny inner voice seemed to have taken up residence inside Beka's head, constantly whispering the same thing.

"Why aren't you in the trench with the rest of your people?" Beka slid into the cold water, barely noticing the chill as she tried to figure out how she was going to rescue the merbaby without being seen by the men on—she peered up at the clean white side of the boat—the *Wily Serpent.*

The sea creature tightened her grip on Beka's surfboard, gazing at the nets with terror in her wide-set eyes. "Didn't you know?" Her head bobbed up and down with the waves as she waved her long elegant tail in agitation. "There is a problem with our home; all the life there is being poisoned by something our healers have been unable to detect. The plants, the fish, even some of the people have become sickened by it. All the mer and selkies must move to a new place closer to land to escape the contamination, and my little one got away from me in the confusion."

She let go of the board to grasp Beka's arm. "Please, Baba Yaga, I know I should have watched him more closely, but please don't let him die."

Not a chance, Beka thought grimly. Then gritted her teeth as she realized the boat had stopped its lazy forward motion and come to a halt. The mechanical screech of a winch disturbed the quiet sea air as the nets slowly started being drawn in toward the boat's hull. Pain accompanied the sound as the merwoman realized what was happening and unconsciously tightened her grasp, webbed fingers turning into claws.

"Oh, no," she said, seaweed-tinted tears flowing faster now. "It's too late."

Beka shook her head. "Not yet, it isn't," she said, and set off swimming with strong purposeful strokes toward the slowly rising mesh of ropes. "Stay here," she ordered, tossing the words over her shoulder. Then she swam as if a life depended on it.

As she drew closer to the boat, she could see that it wasn't as pristine as she'd thought; a blue-black crust of barnacles marred the deep green bottom half where it met the water, and the white paint on top was dull and peeling. For all that, though, the boat itself seemed solid and well constructed—as, alas, did the net that was slowly but relentlessly being pulled in toward its home.

Beka took a deep breath and dove under the water. Thankfully, since she spent so much time in the ocean, she had long ago done magical work that enabled her to keep her eyes open even without protective goggles. Through the gaps between the ropes, she could see the merbaby clearly, swimming in desperate circles round and round the ever-shrinking space. His tiny pale green face was splotched with crying, although any sound he made was lost in the metallic grinding of the winch as it pulled the purse seine in tighter and tighter. As he spotted her, he shot over to her side of the net, making soft eeping noises like a distressed dolphin.

Beka swam up to the choppy surface to gulp another breath, then down again; the trip was noticeably shorter on the way back and she knew she was running out of time. It was tempting to use magic to blast through the net, but she was afraid that she might accidentally hurt the child, and magic often didn't work well underwater, so in the end, she simply pulled out her knife and sawed away frantically at the tough fibers.

Twice more she had to dart above to take a breath, but after the last time, her efforts paid off; she had a ragged hole not much more than two feet long, but large enough for the small merbaby to exit. The fish within were already bolting toward freedom, brushing her with their tickling fins as they flashed past.

She gestured for the merbaby to come closer, only to realize that while she had been fighting with the robustly woven strands, the child's tail had become entangled in a section of net, and he was trapped, unable to get loose from the seine's unrelenting grasp.

Cursing soundlessly, Beka raced to get one more deep lungful of air, then threw herself toward the hole and eeled her way through the impossibly small opening. Frantically, she fought the sinuously twining ropes until the little one was free, and she could shove him through to the other side. Only to find herself trapped in the ever-shrinking net and rapidly running out of time and oxygen.

There's just something about Clare.
Apart from the ghosts…

FROM AWARD-WINNING AUTHOR
ROBIN D. OWENS

GHOST
SEER

A GHOST SEER NOVEL

In Denver, a young woman learns she can see ghosts. And
when the ghost of a Wild West gunman needs her help, she
finds herself getting close to a sexy private investigator.

PRAISE FOR THE NOVELS OF ROBIN D. OWENS

"Engaging…sizzling…almost impossible to put down."
—*The Romance Reader*

"With every book [Owens] amazes and surprises me!"
—*The Best Reviews*

robindowens.com
facebook.com/ProjectParanormalBooks
penguin.com

M1471T0414

FROM *USA TODAY* BESTSELLING AUTHOR

THEA HARRISON

KINKED

A Novel of the Elder Races

═══◆═══

While working on a reconnaissance mission, Sentinels Aryal and Quentin must deal with their escalating antagonism—but their passionate fighting soon builds to an explosively sexual confrontation. And when their mission reveals real danger, Aryal and Quentin must resolve their differences in ways beyond the physical.

"A dark, compelling world. I'm hooked!"
—J. R. Ward, #1 *New York Times* bestselling author

"Thea Harrison is a master storyteller."
—Christine Feehan,
#1 *New York Times* bestselling author

TheaHarrison.com
facebook.com/TheaHarrison
facebook.com/ProjectParanormalBooks
penguin.com